DUNE
THE DUKE OF CALADAN

THE DUNE SERIES

BY FRANK HERBERT

Dune
Dune Messiah
Children of Dune
God Emperor of Dune
Heretics of Dune
Chapterhouse: Dune

BY FRANK HERBERT, BRIAN HERBERT,
AND KEVIN J. ANDERSON

The Road to Dune (includes the original short novel *Spice Planet*)

BY BRIAN HERBERT AND KEVIN J. ANDERSON

Dune: House Atreides
Dune: House Harkonnen
Dune: House Corrino
Dune: The Butlerian Jihad
Dune: The Machine Crusade
Dune: The Battle of Corrin
Hunters of Dune
Sandworms of Dune
Paul of Dune
The Winds of Dune
Sisterhood of Dune
Mentats of Dune
Navigators of Dune
Tales of Dune

BY BRIAN HERBERT

Dreamer of Dune
(biography of Frank Herbert)

DUNE

THE DUKE OF CALADAN

Brian Herbert

and

Kevin J. Anderson

A TOM DOHERTY ASSOCIATES BOOK

NEW YORK

DUNE: THE DUKE OF CALADAN

Copyright © 2020 by Herbert Properties LLC

All rights reserved.

A Tor Book
Published by Tom Doherty Associates
120 Broadway
New York, NY 10271

www.tor-forge.com

Tor® is a registered trademark of Macmillan Publishing Group, LLC.

The Library of Congress Cataloging-in-Publication Data is available upon request.

ISBN 978-1-250-76474-4 (hardcover)
ISBN 978-1-250-76475-1 (ebook)

Our books may be purchased in bulk for promotional, educational, or business use.
Please contact your local bookseller or the Macmillan Corporate and
Premium Sales Department at 1-800-221-7945, extension 5442,
or by email at MacmillanSpecialMarkets@macmillan.com.

First Edition: October 2020

Printed in the United States of America

0 9 8 7 6 5 4 3 2 1

This book, like all our writing, owes a tremendous debt of gratitude
to our brilliant wives, Jan Herbert and Rebecca Moesta.
We would also like to dedicate this novel to
two loved ones who passed away much too young,
Bruce Herbert and Jonathan Cowan.

DUNE

THE DUKE
OF CALADAN

The person with the fewest accomplishments often boasts the loudest.
—CHOAM Analysis of Public Imperial Histories

He was far from home and did not want to be here, but when the Padishah Emperor invited all members of the Landsraad, Leto Atreides had to attend. He was the head of a House Major, the Duke of beautiful Caladan, and Shaddam's distant cousin. His absence would have been noticed.

Fortunately, this trip did not require him to go to the gaudy, noisy capital world of Kaitain. The heart of the Imperium simply did not have room for the extravagant new memorial that the Emperor envisioned, so Shaddam had chosen a planet no one had ever heard of. He needed a place where his accomplishments could truly stand out, and Otorio served that purpose.

As the Guild Heighliner arrived over the new museum planet, Leto sat restlessly in the Atreides space yacht, which was carried aboard the gigantic Guild ship. A pilot and a few retainers accompanied him on the trip, but the Duke kept to himself inside his private stateroom. He had long, dark hair, piercing gray eyes, and an aquiline nose. His demeanor showed a confidence that would not be overshadowed by the spectacle of the new museum complex.

While the Heighliner orbited, smaller ships lined up to descend from the cavernous hold in an orderly fashion. Otorio was a formerly insignificant world that had fallen through the cracks, forgotten for centuries by travelers, businessmen, colonists, and Imperial auditors. Rustic, unsullied, and serene, it had been an isolated tide pool in the ocean of Imperial politics.

Now, though, the planet was home to a gigantic new complex celebrating ten millennia of House Corrino rule. The fact that Otorio held so little else of note meant that Shaddam's congratulatory museum would stand out more prominently than anything on the entire world. Leto knew how the Emperor thought.

Many nobles would strive to catch the Emperor's attention, to build on their wealth, to increase their influence or bring down rivals. Leto had no such agenda. He had his own significant holdings, a stable rule, and had already drawn the attention of Shaddam IV, good and bad, in prior encounters. Duke Leto had nothing to prove, but he would do his duty by attending.

So many nobles had made the Otorio pilgrimage to curry favor with the Emperor, it would take hours for all ships to disembark one at a time, and the Atreides yacht was by no means near the head of the line.

Since leaving Caladan, the Duke had tried to distract himself by working in his stateroom, studying records of the moonfish harvest, accounts of private boats lost in a recent typhoon, a glowing summary of his son Paul's physical and mental training. The Heighliner had traveled from system to system, rounding up passengers from various planets, because there was no direct Spacing Guild route to an insignificant world like Otorio. Shaddam intended to change that.

While waiting, Leto activated the wallscreen to view the planet below. Veils of clouds daubed the atmosphere above oceans and green-and-brown landmasses. Shaddam's massive new complex would have caused fundamental changes to the quiet world. Construction crews had swarmed Otorio, completely reworking the only large population center. Countless square kilometers were paved over. Monuments and statues sprang up like an algae bloom during a red tide: government complexes, civic centers, interactive displays, coliseums, and auditoriums. Expansive new performance stages could seat a hundred thousand people at a time on a world that, according to the census report Leto had read, previously had fewer than a million inhabitants.

His personal pilot buzzed across the yacht's comm. "Our ship is now fourth in the queue, my Duke. We will be departing soon." The man's voice held a rural Caladan accent. Leto had chosen him along with a few local workers, who considered the assignment an adventure, and that warmed Leto's heart. With few opportunities to travel off their homeworld, this was the trip of a lifetime for them.

"Thank you, Arko," Leto said, making a point to use the man's name. He switched off the comm and settled back against the supple leather of the seat.

Looking out the windowport, he mused that he should have brought Paul with him. Although Lady Jessica had no fondness for space travel, nor for court politics, their fourteen-year-old son was curious and intelligent, the pride of Leto's heart. But the Duke decided not to involve his family in what would surely be a tedious, self-aggrandizing event for the Emperor.

He wouldn't be able to keep Paul out of Imperial politics much longer, though. Leto was popular in the Landsraad, and House Atreides had substantial influence, even if the Duke ruled only one planet. Many Landsraad families might welcome a marriage alliance with House Atreides, and at fourteen, Paul was reaching the right age. . . .

Leto watched two vessels ahead of him disengage and drop down through the great open doors of the Heighliner hold. Some ships were nondescript, perhaps even leased for the occasion by poorer families or Minor Houses, while other vessels proudly displayed the colors and crests of House Mutelli, House Ecaz, House Bonner, House Ouard, and others.

After one more ship descended into the fine clouds, the Atreides yacht disengaged from its docking clamp. The suspensor engines thrummed. Leto gripped his seat as the yacht dropped, passing through orbital lanes down toward the upper atmosphere.

Arko transmitted, "It might get bumpy, my Lord. Several obstacles in high orbit across our path, leftover dump boxes and delivery haulers from the construction. Otorio control is diverting us."

Leto peered out the windowport to see clunky drifting wrecks circling Otorio in blind, endless orbits. "I'm surprised Shaddam didn't clear them away."

"Construction was behind schedule, sir. Those are heavy equipment and supply haulers—empty, I'd suppose. Probably wasn't financially feasible for the Emperor to move them all away in time for the celebration."

Leto remarked to himself, "And Shaddam would never postpone the event for a more sensible date." He added into the comm, "I trust your piloting."

"Thank you, my Lord." The ducal yacht diverted around the slowly tumbling objects that cluttered the orbital lanes.

More ships descended from the Heighliner bay, each one carrying representatives who would applaud the Emperor's new complex. Leto would pay his respects and acknowledge the lengthy history of Corrino accomplishments. He would let himself be seen and fulfill his duty as a loyal subject.

"Just give us a soft landing, Arko," Leto said into the comm, "and keep the yacht ready to depart. I'd like to go home as soon as I can reasonably make my excuses." His heart, and his priorities, were with his people on Caladan.

The pilot sounded disappointed. "Will I have time to buy a gift for my sweetheart, my Lord? And souvenirs for my nephews?"

Leto smiled, indulging the man. He was sure the other retainers felt the same. "Of course. I doubt any part of this event will be speedy."

As the craft glided smoothly toward the surface, he could see the geometric complex of Shaddam's new Imperial museum, comprising many square kilometers of towering buildings, wide boulevards, plazas, and monuments—as if a swath of Kaitain's metropolis had been uprooted and transplanted across the galaxy.

Arko brought the yacht down on the priority landing field adjacent to the new Imperial Monolith. The extraordinary spire was shaped like a narrow wedge, wider at the top and delicately balanced on a fulcrum in the central plaza below. From a distance, some claimed the structure looked like a huge spike driven through the heart of Otorio.

Leto's pilot and crew were awestruck by the grandeur and would no doubt talk about this experience in Cala City taverns for the rest of their lives. With a quiet smile, Leto gave them a discretionary bonus of funds so they could buy commemorative trinkets, and turned them loose to explore. They went off with delighted gratitude, while he turned to his own official duties.

As Leto emerged from the yacht, he faced a cacophony of sensory impressions. Visiting nobles bedecked with gloriously colored robes and flashing jewels put on quite a show with excessive entourages, trying to look important. Pursuing their goal of being noticed, these ambitious nobles preened and strutted, and few gave him a second glance in his formal but unremarkable clothes. Content with the reputation of House Atreides, Leto ignored the snub. He didn't need to prove his importance or wealth.

Even though he was the Duke of Caladan, he let himself vanish into the crowd. He often did the same at home, enjoying a few hours as a nondescript person so he could walk unnoticed among his own people. Now he strolled by himself into the vast network of fountains, statues, obelisks, and museum exhibits.

Imperial security forces patrolled the streets dressed in Corrino scarlet and gold, accompanied by fearsome Imperial Sardaukar, the Emperor's private terror troops. Leto found their presence here interesting. Sardaukar were used for only the most elite missions; the fact that Shaddam assigned them here emphasized the importance of the gala. While Kaitain had innumerable centuries of established security routines, this planet was a clean slate. The show of force was not surprising.

Confident, Leto strode along the broad boulevards, where multi-terraced fountains gushed water and jets of steam; glass prisms split sunlight into rainbows. Towering statues of past Corrino Emperors made every ruler look handsome and brave. A polished biographical tablet on each plinth summarized that Emperor's accomplishments.

Since the end of the Butlerian Jihad ten thousand years ago, the Corrinos—who took their name after the Battle of Corrin—had ruled as the dominant dynasty. There had been interregnums, coup d'états, and interim administrations by other noble houses, but some vestige of House Corrino always returned to power, marrying into the ruling families, taking control through bloody civil war or administrative fiat. With this celebratory city, Shaddam IV would make certain everyone remembered him and his ancestors.

Leto looked up at a three-meter-high metal colossus of Shaddam's father, the "wise and benevolent" Elrood IX. He frowned at the glowing description on the plaque, knowing that old Elrood had been a petulant and vindictive man, and Shaddam himself had despised him. Leto's father, Duke Paulus Atreides, had fought in the Ecazi Revolt to support Elrood, but the leader's dishonorable dealings had greatly troubled the Old Duke.

Leto walked through the endless complex, his eyes oversaturated, his ears deafened by the clamor of celebration. The crowd was composed entirely of nobles or high-ranking functionaries who had received coveted invitations to this grand gala. He could imagine how Paul would have reveled in all these new experiences.

After an hour, already weary of the spectacle, he began to look for a quiet respite before he would go to see the Emperor himself. He circled around the largest statue near the base of the Imperial Monolith—the beautiful Madonna-like figure of Serena Butler cradling her baby, the martyred infant that had triggered the terrible war against the thinking machines. Her statue towered over a robust but gnarled olive tree that sprang up from the flagstones. A plaque noted that the tree was the last remnant of an extensive olive grove that had covered the lands here until recently. Now it had all been paved over.

Behind the Serena statue, Leto noted a back entrance to one of the large museum buildings. The enormous monument hid what appeared to be a warren of back alleys and service entrances. Confident that no one would pay any attention to him, he slipped under the sheltered overhangs, where bright sunshine dwindled into shadows. The plaza's artificial mists and perfumes faded to more conventional smells, warm generator exhaust, a hint of garbage, the sweat of workers.

Leto ducked into a sheltered doorway under an overhang, and found the delivery entrance locked. He was alone. Shadows and silence breathed around him like a relieved sigh. Leaning against the alcove wall, he reached into his pocket and removed a tight shigawire spool and a pocket-sized crystal player. He smiled as he activated the recording.

The image shimmered before snapping into focus. Leto was glad to see the beautiful Lady Jessica, his bound concubine, his lover, the mother of his son. She wore a blue gown, a necklace of reefpearls from the Caladan coast. Her long, bronze hair was bound up in pins and carved seashell combs that highlighted her green eyes.

Her voice flowed like music, especially after the noise of the museum complex. "Leto, you said you would not view this until you reached Otorio. Have you been true to your promise?" Her voice held a teasing lilt.

"Yes, I have, my love," he said aloud, in private.

Her generous lips curved upward, and she touched one of her ornate combs. She knew him well.

One reason she had not accompanied him to the celebration was that she remained his mere concubine, not his wife, and that was how it must stay, for political reasons. Although he remained technically available for a marriage alliance, he accepted that it would never happen. Not after . . .

He winced as he thought about the bloody disaster of his near wedding to Ilesa Ecaz. So much blood . . . so much hatred. As a Landsraad noble, he had to keep his options open, technically, but he had made up his mind not to accept any more offers of a marriage alliance. He needed to keep Jessica safe. Not that she couldn't protect herself, with all of her Bene Gesserit training. . . .

On the holoprojection, Jessica continued talking, but her voice was itself the message, and that was all he needed to hear. His deep love for her was a weakness he could not allow anyone to see. "Come home to me safely," she said. "Caladan will be here for you, as will I, my Duke."

"My Lady." He smiled as the message ended and the shimmering image faded away. He drew energy from her that he would need for the political obligations and maneuverings he must face now.

Before Leto stepped out of the sheltered doorway, another man darted into the narrow service passageways. He wore a charcoal-gray worker's jumpsuit with tools at his belt, a loose pack over his shoulder. Knowing he was out of place, Leto prepared to make excuses if anyone asked why he was here, although a worker would not likely challenge a noble.

But the stranger did not notice him as he pressed into a sheltered corner and unslung his pack, glancing from side to side. With instinctive wariness, Leto remained in the shadows. Something didn't feel right. This man's manner was not that of a weary worker going about a tedious daily assignment; his movements seemed furtive.

Leto thumbed off the power to the crystal player so Jessica's message would not replay.

The worker dug into his pack and removed a thin crystal filmscreen, to which he attached a transmitting device. Leto couldn't see exactly what the man was doing, only that he called up images on the screen, orbital charts, curves, and bright pinpoints that burned red and green. The worker hunched over and spoke into the transmitter pickup. Leto could discern only "activate . . . systems . . . wait."

The furtive man touched a corner of the ethereal screen, and from a distance, Leto saw images of the discarded dump boxes and cargo containers in orbit. Lights suddenly winked on in the great dark hulks.

The stranger snapped the screen shut and stuffed it back into his pack. Concerned, Leto drew himself up and emerged from his alcove. "You there! Hold!"

The worker bolted, and Leto sprang after him. The man turned a sharp corner into a side passage, slipped between stacked shipment cases, ducked low under an overhang. One corner, then another, a maze of access alleys. Leto ran after him, dodging debris and calling out, trying not to lose him in the clutter, until he burst out into the full, noisy city again.

A fanfare of brassy music played from loudspeakers, and Otorio's sunlight dazzled him. Crowds and diversions drowned out Leto's shout. He thought he saw the suspicious worker turn left, darting away.

Leto sprinted after the man, shouting, knowing there were countless security forces around the complex, not to mention Sardaukar, if only he could get their attention. He raised a hand, looking for the ubiquitous patrols, but saw only colorfully clad celebrants.

The city guard force found him as he called out again. Dressed in red and gold, the Imperial troops escorted a pompous-looking official who strode up to him. "Duke Leto Atreides of Caladan," he said in a booming voice that somehow cut through the cacophony of the great plaza.

Leto spun. "Yes. I need to report—"

The official cut him off with a well-practiced smile, holding up a bejeweled message cylinder. "We have been searching for you since your yacht landed." With great reverence, he extended the cylinder. "You may keep this personal invitation as a memento, perhaps display it on Caladan for future generations."

The man cleared his throat and recited, "His Excellency, the Padishah Emperor Shaddam IV awaits you at a special reception in the Imperial Monolith. Come with me." The official seemed surprised that Leto wasn't swooning with delight. "Now."

History is a tool to be used, a weapon to be wielded. The past must conform to the needs of the Imperium, otherwise an Emperor has failed utterly in his duty.

—EMPEROR FONDIL III, THE HUNTER, "Private Guidance on the Expansion of Imperial Archives on Kaitain"

From the top floor of the Monolith, Shaddam IV placed his hands behind his back and drank in the glorious Corrino complex as if it were a fine vintage. He turned to the vulpine-faced man beside him with a satisfied smile. "The people look so small from up here, Hasimir."

Count Hasimir Fenring raised his expressive eyebrows as he joined Shaddam in surveying the spectacular plazas and monuments. "So you like to look down on people, hmmm-mmm?" He had a nasal voice, and his sentences often ended with some annoying vocal mannerism.

The plaz window was as transparent as air. The gleaming slivers of many noble spacecraft rested on the nearby field adjacent to the central plaza. "I like to observe my subjects from an objective distance. This vantage gives me a unique perspective."

Shaddam marveled at the towering statues of his Corrino forebears. They looked like titans arrayed in the city. Once word spread, Otorio would become a destination for countless travelers. Armies of tourists would stream here to pay their respects and pour money into the planetary treasury—and hence, into the Corrino coffers. Soon, the Spacing Guild might even offer direct Heighliner routes from Kaitain.

"We brought civilization to this unremarkable place," the Emperor said. Lightheaded with satisfaction, he hummed deep in his throat, then stopped himself as he realized it was the same annoying noise that Fenring often made. "We did a great thing here."

Small-statured but with deceptive strength and considerable acumen, Fenring was the Emperor's boyhood friend and still his most respected adviser on complex and confidential matters. Fenring held one of the most influential positions in Shaddam's government, Imperial Spice Observer on Arrakis. An unattractive man with exaggerated facial features, the Count styled himself in expensive garments: an overlarge frilled collar, cuffs buttoned up with thick blue jewels. His fingers were nimble and fidgety, adorned with gold and platinum rings.

"Yes, hmmm, I am glad I rediscovered this planet, Sire, though I still have questions about why it remained a cipher for so long." Fenring's nostrils narrowed as he sniffed. "I am still investigating. My guess is that Otorio was not accidentally misplaced in the records. The local inhabitants were, ahh, reticent to provide information. They're either ignorant about Otorio's previous rulers, or they are complicit."

Shaddam didn't care. "It is irrelevant now. Otorio will forever be known as the site of the Grand Corrino Museum."

By happy coincidence, an eccentric Mentat—actually, the failed Mentat Grix Dardik—had stumbled upon a misfiled mention of the planet Otorio in old Imperial records. The inhabitants of the unnoticed planet did not have so much as a House Minor lord to represent them in the Landsraad. They had no contact with the wider politics of the Imperium, had not participated in any census, nor had they paid Imperial taxes for generations. Dardik had reported the discovery to Count Fenring, the only person who had the patience to keep him around, and Fenring had in turn shown it to Shaddam. With the stroke of his ornate Imperial pen, the Emperor had annexed Otorio and chosen it as the site for his fabulous museum.

With a swirl of diamondweave skirts, a damask corset, and a blouse embroidered with bloodfibers, the new Empress Aricatha approached the two men, slipping between them at the broad viewing window. "Shaddam, my Lord." She gave him a sweet, sincere smile.

Aricatha was his sixth and newest wife—very new after the death of the disappointing, drab Firenza Thorvald, who had been a mediocre political match and a very poor spouse. The lovely Aricatha still had the shine of a fresh marriage, and Shaddam accepted her conjugal company more often than he visited his concubines.

Her full lips were painted a deep maroon, and her teeth were perfect and even, like fine pearls. "You are being a poor host, my dear. Come away from the window. These people have traveled here at your command specifically to see you."

"They came here to *be seen* by me." He glanced at the crowds milling in the penthouse reception chamber. "I can observe them just as well from here."

Fenring let out a snicker. "Shaddam has a point, my lovely Empress, but so do you, mmmm-ahh? Sire, we can scheme and plot any time. Perhaps we should let you be respected and adored today. It doesn't happen often, hmmm?"

Shaddam's brow wrinkled. "You insult me at your peril, Hasimir."

"It is good for a man to hear the truth, if only occasionally. I offer frankness, but only when no one else is in earshot."

"But I could hear you, Count Fenring," the Empress said with a musical chuckle. "Don't worry, I will tell no one. We are all united in doing what is best for the Imperium."

Fenring and Shaddam were both surprised by Aricatha's bold statement. She was indeed a stunning woman with blue-black hair that drank in the light, smooth skin the color of caramels, and large eyes like jet and obsidian. She provided charming company when Shaddam wanted it and was wise enough to avoid him when he wished to be left alone. Fenring watched her carefully and had cautioned Shaddam that she might be manipulating him in many ways. He once remarked, "She plays you not like a musical instrument, Sire, but like an entire orchestra."

Shaddam put little stock in the concerns, believing himself above any manipulation. Considering the pleasurable sensations Aricatha evoked when she played her fingers across his skin, he had no complaint.

Now at the gala, the Empress slipped her arm through his, and Shaddam escorted her across the expansive reception area, which filled the entire top floor of the Imperial Monolith. She led him to the center of the room, as if she meant to put him on display.

The metal doors of the accelerated lift opened to spill out a flock of noble guests in colorful finery with prominent Landsraad crests. Only those invited to this special reception were allowed to ride the elevator that shot them in seconds to the top of the Monolith.

Since Fenring did not much care for public appearances, Shaddam was not surprised to watch the Count melt away into the hubbub as the nobles around him chattered on.

The guests stared at the impressive exhibits and display cases, while servants wandered about with trays of drinks and exotic delicacies. Upon spotting the Emperor, the nobles lit up, having practiced their awe and respect for hours before meeting him in person. They came forward in a rush, but Aricatha intercepted the guests in order to introduce them one by one, somehow remembering their names and Houses. Shaddam flashed his wife a thankful glance, impressed by her social skill. The nobles beamed, pleased to be recognized by the beautiful new Empress, if not by the Padishah Emperor himself.

A crisply uniformed Sardaukar officer stepped up, exuding strength and competence. Shaddam gave the man his attention, grateful for the distraction. "Something to report, Colonel Bashar Kolona?"

The officer spoke in a calm, efficient whisper. "Every guest has been vetted to the fullest of our ability, Sire. Enjoy the reception in comfort. You are safe."

With so much security around him, so many Imperial troops in the city, it had never occurred to Shaddam that he wasn't safe. He dismissed the officer, then turned to the next person who had come to pay his respects.

Shaddam recognized him even without an introduction from the Empress. "Archduke Armand Ecaz." He extended a hand, then awkwardly let it drop at the sight of the Archduke's empty sleeve pinned across his chest, a reminder that the man's arm had been cut off in the bloody assassination attempt at his daughter's ill-fated wedding with Duke Leto Atreides. "You have had a peaceful and productive year? Is that how long it's been since . . . ?" The Emperor could not take his eyes from the empty sleeve.

"One year, one month, and an odd number of days, Sire," said the Archduke, who looked as if he had aged much more than a year since Shaddam last saw him in person.

The Emperor cleared his throat and tried to sound reassuring. "It was indeed a terrible crime, but all the troubles with Grumman are now over. Not even the most distant relative of House Moritani has been invited here."

"There is no more House Moritani, Sire. That has been taken care of," the Archduke said. "I thank you and the Imperium for granting me their planet as an Ecazi holding, though that world has little to offer except maintenance."

Shaddam clucked his tongue. "Any planet added to House Ecaz increases your standing in the Landsraad, does it not?"

"It does, Sire," the Archduke admitted, but he did not sound entirely pleased. "You have my gratitude."

Shaddam saw other nobles standing a few steps away, impatiently waiting to bask in his Imperial presence. He needed to move on. "We shall see about finding some other underutilized planet to add to your control. My Imperium has a million worlds, and many of them have gone unnoticed." He spread his hands. "Like Otorio, for instance. The people here had no ruling noble house for centuries. If there are similar planets, a nobleman like yourself could put them to good use for the benefit of the Imperium."

Ecaz bowed, but did not smile. "As the code says, the first responsibility of a noble is to the Landsraad and to the Imperium." He drifted away, and Shaddam felt disappointed by the interaction. Most nobles would have been overjoyed at the offer of another planetary holding. Perhaps he should find someone more appreciative.

Noble after noble approached, and Shaddam endured as the afternoon waned into the rich colors of sunset. The accelerated elevator delivered another batch of guests, then another.

Returning, Count Fenring insinuated himself into the clustered nobles as if he had been greased. Catching Shaddam's eye, he made one of the special hand signs they had developed as boyhood friends. This one told the Emperor he had something important to convey.

"Excuse me," Shaddam said to a waiting noble. "I'll be right back. A matter of governance has come to my attention." He slipped over to the Count, and they found a place where they could talk in a bubble of privacy.

"After studying the list of arrivals, I am perplexed by a pattern of missing guests," Fenring said in a low tone. "CHOAM President Frankos Aru publicly accepted your invitation, but as far as we can tell, he remains at the Silver Needle on Kaitain." His pale brow wrinkled. "His mother, Ur-Director Malina Aru, did not respond at all. For an event of such significance, we expected her to make one of her rare public appearances—to benefit CHOAM, if nothing else."

The Combine Honnete Ober Advancer Mercantiles, or the CHOAM Company, was a gigantic monopoly encompassing all forms of commerce across the Imperium. Their widespread business dealings were secretive and subtle, and most people in the Imperium never noticed the extent of their influence.

Shaddam brushed aside Fenring's observation. "This sort of historical spectacle is not in CHOAM's usual repertoire. Everyone here wants to be seen and noticed, and you know that CHOAM prefers to remain in the shadows."

Fenring grudgingly nodded. He tapped his chin with a long finger. "After rediscovering Otorio, I dug deeper and uncovered further strings tied to strings tied to a whole intricate web. It is my suspicion, hmmm-ahh, that this particular world was intentionally kept off the books to hide it from you and many Emperors before you. Perhaps by someone connected to CHOAM."

Shaddam felt his face flush. "Everything is connected to CHOAM. Otorio is mine now, and if someone wishes to state an objection, they are welcome to do so. I will speak to the Urdir myself if she is brave enough to show her face."

The Emperor saw that some impatient nobles were attempting to eavesdrop.

Shaddam nudged the Count and watched the Empress valiantly try to distract the guests. "For now, let me enjoy my moment, Hasimir. We will deal with complications and political unpleasantries later." He turned to the crowd, opened his arms expansively, and muttered, "I must meet these sycophants and give them what they need."

Fenring kept his voice low. "Do not consider them all sycophants, Sire. Some are worth noting . . . as enemies or potential allies."

The engraved metal doors of the accelerated lift opened. The first noble to step out was dressed in a green-and-black cape with a hawk insignia on his chest. His gray eyes met the Emperor's, and he gave a nod of acknowledgment. Shaddam knew this man well.

Duke Leto Atreides.

The ability to survive is the ability to face and overcome unexpected dangers.

—Bene Gesserit axiom

Baron Vladimir Harkonnen had never considered himself fat, though others had called him that—at great personal risk, if he ever found out. He was a large man, a *very* large man, and sheer size implied power.

Because of his demeanor and reputation, people could not avoid being intimidated by the Baron. When he moved through a chamber or corridor, buoyed up by suspensors, everyone moved out of his path, even the high officials of other noble houses. Perhaps one day, given the proper circumstances, a Harkonnen might even occupy the Golden Lion Throne. Someday.

That person would not be his crude and unpolished nephew Glossu Rabban. No, that was inconceivable. Rabban's younger brother, however . . . Feyd-Rautha, such a lovely boy. He was a definite possibility to wear Imperial robes.

The Baron kept this at the front of his mind as he prepared to depart Arrakis for Shaddam's gala celebration on some backwater world. It was good to be seen in the Imperial presence.

Wearing his suspensor belt, the Baron glided with ungainly grace through a dusty tunnel beneath the city of Carthag on his secret way to the spaceport. His departure would not be announced, and he expected no one to stop him. Before receiving the ostentatious invitation, the Baron had never even heard of the planet Otorio.

Khaki-uniformed guards jogged ahead, with personal attendants beside and behind him. Members of his entourage moved large trunks of the Baron's clothing for the expedition offworld. He had left the Harkonnen mansion in the fortified core of his capital, and would catch a shuttle to a waiting Guild Heighliner.

The Baron wore a long, black overcoat with a blue griffin on the lapel, the symbol of House Harkonnen. He felt the gentle airflow of cooling fans within his voluminous garment. He wiped perspiration and grit from his fleshy face, looking forward to when he could be comfortable again aboard the shuttle.

This desert world was called "Dune" by the natives, a weak nickname, although they uttered the word as if it had spiritual or mystical meaning. He preferred the Imperial name of Arrakis, which sounded more crisp and proper, a thing that could be known and controlled. Arrakis was an unpleasant place, though, dirty and dusty, unlike the sweet, civilized odors of his home-world, Giedi Prime. But as the sole source of the vital spice melange, Arrakis was an extremely profitable fief, and the Baron could tolerate the discomforts by remembering how many solaris it earned for the Harkonnen treasury.

A diligent attendant sprayed mist in front of him as he moved down the illuminated tunnel. He inhaled the moist air, motioned for the attendant to add more. Refreshed, the Baron proceeded, and attendants alternated mists to help him breathe. The secret tunnel seemed to go on for miles, but at least it kept him unseen.

Finally, the tunnel sloped upward to where it ended at a set of double doors. The Spacing Guild set its own rigid schedules, and he did not want the Heighliner to depart without him.

Before emerging into the open air, the Baron took a welcome sip from the moisture tube beside his mouth. His entourage hurried him across a short distance of furnace-hot hardpan and aboard the waiting shuttle. Once inside the posh private compartment, attendants removed his outer clothing, and the Baron relaxed in the coolness at last.

Rabban filled the doorway, thick-boned and fleshy. "We are ready to take off, my lord Baron. I am your pilot today." His nephew was overly proud of his ability.

"Get on with it. The Padishah Emperor awaits."

The burly man whirled to cover his flushed expression and left.

WHEN HE REACHED the piloting deck, Rabban waved at a scanner to enter the cockpit. The panel flashed orange, refusing to grant him access, and the door remained locked.

To his shock, he felt the deck vibrate as the engines activated—without him! The shuttle was preparing to take off! He pounded on the door with his beefy hands and threw his entire body weight against the barrier. The metal shuddered, but the door did not open.

Hearing the commotion, two Harkonnen guards rushed to help as the shuttle lifted off from the Carthag spaceport. The big men, all armed with blades and shield belts, slammed into the door together, finally breaching the seal. The barricade gave inward with a great crashing noise.

Inside the piloting compartment, Rabban was shocked to discover several desert people in dusty tan cloaks, outnumbering the Harkonnens. A lean woman had commandeered the shuttle controls, guiding the ship in its liftoff.

She slashed a glance at Rabban, shouted a command to her companions in their gibberish language. These were far different from the downtrodden city people in Carthag. They had a fire in their blue-tinted eyes, a hardness that came from the deep desert. Local spice workers? Maybe even the mysterious Fremen?

A swarthy man lunged at Rabban with a curved knife. He stabbed but missed when Rabban slipped out of the way and activated his personal shield in a single gesture. Other desert fighters rushed toward him, each with a deadly blade in one hand and a primitive Maula pistol in the other. His Harkonnen guards drew their own weapons, ready to fight in the close quarters.

One of the rebels fired his spring-wound pistol, but the projectile struck harmlessly against the shield. Four desert men fell as they fought for control of the captured craft, but both of Rabban's Harkonnen guards collapsed, each with a poison dart in his throat, slow-darts able to pass through the field. The piloting compartment was crowded with bodies. Rabban narrowly escaped the same fate, ducking as a dart ricocheted from the bulkhead, close to his neck.

Before the attackers could fire again, he lurched back out of the compartment, shoving the damaged door back in place. The shuttle rose higher from the landing zone, lurching and rattling.

Rabban bellowed for more guards, but none appeared. He glanced out the windowport to see that the shuttle had turned, accelerating overland toward the open desert rather than heading up to orbit.

From the plushly appointed passenger compartment, he heard his uncle bellowing, demanding answers. Rabban could not bother with him now.

Suddenly, the shuttle made a hairpin turn and sped in the opposite direction, now straight back toward the city. A knot formed in his gut as he realized what the desert rebels had in mind. They would crash the vessel somewhere in Carthag, maybe even into the Harkonnen headquarters. And Harkonnen ground security would not dare open fire on the shuttle with the Baron on board.

The wallscreen flickered, and his uncle's image appeared, showing blood streaming down into his dark eyes. The Baron gripped one of his wrists, which hung at an odd angle, obviously broken. "What is happening? I need medical help!"

Five more guards charged down the corridor to help Rabban, seeing the damaged door to the control deck. Together, they lunged forward and slammed back into the piloting compartment. Now that he had reinforcements, Rabban pushed past them. He had to regain control of the craft. As they all pushed into the compartment, blades drawn, Rabban hacked at one rebel, then the next. The desert people fell hard.

Three of the rebels remained alive, dodging behind consoles. They fired their clumsy Maula pistols, aiming wildly, damaging some of the controls even when the projectiles could not penetrate the shields. His guards attacked, while the female pilot continued to drive the shuttle straight toward the tall buildings of the city. When their Maula and dart pistols were expended, the desert rebels fought with knives.

Rabban moved quickly, stepping over bodies, dodging while keeping the Harkonnen guards in front of him. A dagger flew past Rabban's head. Two more of his men dropped.

The rebels seemed to have an endless supply of knives, which they produced from their desert cloaks, but Rabban and his remaining guards had greater strength, and body shields, and soon enough, the rest of the desert rabble lay dead, strewn about the deck near damaged consoles.

The pilot slumped over the controls, thick, dark blood oozing from her mouth. She was still alive, and her intense blue eyes were wild as she reached for the controls to slam the shuttle into a death dive.

Rabban fired one shot from his projectile weapon, splashing her blood all over the front windowport. The sound of the shuttle engines took on a deeper roar as the ship decelerated and plunged toward the city buildings.

Rabban stepped over corpses, smearing blood under the soles of his boots as he lurched to the piloting console. He fought them, trying to get the shuttle to respond. One of the grids sparked and hissed. Many of the systems had been ruined by the projectile fire. Though he struggled mightily, the ship fought back. They were dropping fast, and the central structures of Carthag looked very tall.

Time . . . would he have enough time? He shouted at the controls, swiped a hand sideways to clear a long pool of blood from the rebel pilot. He activated auxiliary systems, striving for thrust to push them higher. Finally, with a strong burst from attitude jets, he altered course and arced away from the city center. He managed to bring the shuttle out of its death dive only a few meters above the ground, then roared back toward the spaceport.

The shuttle was by no means under his complete control, but he did push them back toward an open hardpan apron beyond the designated landing zones. He needed to get the Baron to safety.

A gust of wind hit the shuttle, and he had to struggle to set it down on the hardpan. The shuttle skidded, plowing up a spray of dust and sand. It slewed and finally came to rest. Rabban could only hear a roar of adrenaline and his own pounding heartbeat.

Furious, the Baron floated through the damaged bulkhead hatch into the piloting compartment. Blood continued to stream down his face from a scalp wound, and he grimaced in pain from his swelling left wrist.

Guards flooded in behind him, weapons drawn, but by now, the rebels were all dead.

"I am in control, Uncle," Rabban said.

The Baron glowered at all the bodies on the deck. One man twitched, and the Baron leaned over, partially weightless on his suspensor belt, and slashed the man's throat with a dagger in his good hand.

Rabban completed the shutdown sequence and silenced the still-flashing engine alarms, then turned to grin at the Baron. "I did well, Uncle. Did I not?"

The big man was loath to give compliments. "I am injured. Many of my guards are dead, and my shuttle is ruined. Now how will I make it to orbit before the Heighliner departs?"

Disappointed at the lack of praise, Rabban stepped up to the dead pilot and gave her body a hard kick in the gut. She rolled against a bulkhead, and he felt marginally better.

The guard captain holstered his sidearm, adjusted his personal knife in its sheath. He was shaking and sweating, clearly intimidated by the Baron. In a sudden move, the Baron lashed out and plunged the dagger into the captain's throat. He fell like a broken rag doll, and the remaining guards stood stiffly, afraid to look at the Baron.

"You are fortunate that I have decided to execute someone else, nephew." The grudging sound in his voice was the only acknowledgment that Rabban had redeemed himself, at least fractionally.

The Baron touched his sticky red forehead and shouted to the remaining guards. "Out! All of you! Get me transport back to headquarters!"

They ran to do his bidding.

The Baron rolled his eyes in pain, though his suspensor belt would not allow him to fall. "Now I cannot attend Shaddam's gala celebration on Otorio."

Rabban remained at rigid attention. "Shall I send a note to the Emperor?"

"You shall *not*! I will have someone write it in a polished way. We don't need to tell him that I was nearly killed by a group of dirty desert rats." Rabban could tell that his uncle would continue to vent. "You should have made certain the shuttle was safe before I boarded. For that failing, you are at fault, Rabban."

"But I saved you. I saved both of us."

Baron Harkonnen grudgingly sighed. "You can indeed fight and kill, and you do have a certain crude mastery of applying brute force, but that was only viable in this instance because you were cornered. You must learn to plan several moves ahead and be consistent. Learn to play a strategy game, instead of wielding a cudgel." The Baron's blood-smeared face took on a calculating expression. "Do you even know how to play pyramid chess?"

Rabban shook his head.

"It is a game of many complex moves, and life is just such a game. In both, you must learn to think ahead, to consider the consequences of your actions and avoid pitfalls."

"I will learn, Uncle. I promise." Rabban began to realize how much was on the line, here and now.

With an odd mood shift, the Baron put his good hand on his nephew's arm. "I don't know if that sort of wisdom can be taught to someone like you."

Rabban tried to be earnest and forced himself to accept the insult. "I will get smarter. I promise."

As if speaking through a wall of boulders, the Baron rumbled, "For now, I want you to crack down on the desert rabble. That is in your particular skill set." He paused. "And get me a doctor!"

Some say that contentment with one's station leads to a lack of ambition.
On the other hand, I have observed that ambition can become a cancer
that eats a person from within. A true leader must find the proper balance.

—DUKE LETO ATREIDES, private notes to his son, Paul

Upon entering the Emperor's crowded reception, Leto felt like a combat animal turned loose in an arena, and this was not his sort of battle.

His mother, Helena, had taught him how to be successful at court, since her own ambitions were lofty. Now, he paused to absorb the whirlwind of colors, sounds, and smells from the guests, the fine foods, and the items on display. His father had thrived on public spectacles, hosting fêtes on Caladan, especially spectacular bullfights, one of which had killed him in the end. That tragedy had given Leto the ducal title when he was not much older than Paul was now. . . .

Shaddam caught his gaze and Leto stepped ahead of the other nobles who emerged from the lift, jockeying for position. They wanted to be first, but sensed something about this Duke.

Leto gave Shaddam a formal bow, and the Emperor acknowledged him. "Duke Leto Atreides, cher cousin. It means a great deal for me to see you here. Sometimes it is difficult to pry you from Caladan."

"I devote my attention to my world and my people, Sire . . . all in the name of the Imperium. I am proud to represent House Atreides." He couched his words in a more complimentary tone. "Your new museum complex is the most impressive presentation I have ever seen. One could not possibly absorb everything in a single visit."

"Then you must return to Otorio and spend more time," Shaddam said. "Then you can fully appreciate the legacy of House Corrino."

Against his instincts, Leto found himself playing the game, while also making it clear that he was not merely a sycophant. "Thank you for all you have done for me, Sire. House Atreides is much stronger because of your generosity."

Shaddam pretended to brush the gratitude aside. "It has been years since that business of attacking a Tleilaxu ship inside a Heighliner, and the Trial of Forfeiture."

"A trial I won."

"You were exonerated, that is true. Honestly, I never believed the accusations for a moment. Such treachery is not the way of House Atreides. Since then, I am pleased you have ruled in a reasonable and undramatic fashion."

Count Fenring stepped up and gave the Duke a cool nod of respect. He and Leto also had a history. "You've kept a low profile since those incidents, hmmm? Except for that recent messiness in the War of Assassins between Ecaz and Grumman. Hmmm-ahh. Such troubles may have diminished your standing in the Landsraad." He sounded critical. "You do have so much potential, Duke Leto. I, ahhhhh, have had my eye on you."

Though other nobles were waiting, Leto felt he had to mention the suspicious man with the transmitter he had seen in the alley. He turned to the Emperor. "Sire, I observed something troubling. It may or may not be important."

Shaddam was already looking toward the gaggle of impatient visitors, and Fenring smoothly extracted Leto from the Imperial presence. "If you have a boon to request of the Emperor, now is not the time. I can advise you in—"

Leto shook his head. "It is not a favor I wish to ask, simply a matter of concern. You and I have both faced treachery and assassination attempts, Count Fenring. One cannot be too careful." He described what he had seen.

Fenring snapped his fingers at a Sardaukar officer who stood stock-still nearby. "Colonel Bashar, hear what Duke Atreides has to say. It may warrant investigation."

The officer's gaze was as intense as if he were peeling away Leto's skin, layer by layer, while he listened. The Sardaukar paused, pondered. "You would have no reason to lie or issue a false alarm, Duke Leto Atreides. I will investigate." With a curt nod, he marched off.

Satisfied that the Sardaukar would be thorough, Leto relaxed and surveyed the crowded gathering. The penthouse reception room was an obstacle course of solido-hologram exhibits in which soft-voiced docents described each historic item on display: a robe worn by Hassik II, a braided whip used by Ilnod during his two-week reign, a jeweled tiara from Shaddam's first wife, Lady Anirul. Leto had known Anirul all too well, as the woman who had summoned Jessica to Kaitain during the last months of her pregnancy with Paul.

Jessica had received so much artful Sisterhood training that Leto couldn't begin to guess all the skills she possessed. He just knew he loved her, and he believed she loved him as well. They had been together for almost twenty years, and she understood her own role as bound concubine rather than wife. It was not Leto's choice but the Imperium's.

"She was a Bene Gesserit, and she served the order well," said a woman's voice next to him. "Lady Anirul, I mean."

He turned to see an old woman in nondescript black robes. Leto frowned. "I see the Emperor brought his Truthsayer with him."

"At an event like this, the air is thick enough with lies to suffocate anyone." Reverend Mother Mohiam gave him a strange look, as if her bright eyes walled off a library of secret knowledge about him.

Leto had little fondness for the old witch. He remembered when she had presented young Jessica to him, insisting that the Duke accept her as his concubine. He resented Mohiam for that, although Jessica had indeed melted his heart. He did not trust the Bene Gesserit and their schemes.

"And how is Jessica?" she pressed, as if reading his mind. The old Bene Gesserit crone could infer thoughts from the slightest flickers of expression on his face, a skill that Jessica shared.

"She is well and content on Caladan."

"Of course she did not wish to come to Otorio. A concubine knows her place, and a Sister understands these things. We chose well when we assigned her to you." Mohiam sniffed, her thoughts quickly shifting. "And your son?" Her voice oozed venom, which put Leto on guard.

"My son." He paused, and then emphasized, "My *heir* is excelling in every way. Soon, I will introduce him to important Imperial functions."

"Such as this one," Mohiam said.

"Such as this one. The Emperor invited me to come back. Perhaps I will bring Paul to review the museum's contents."

Her eyes bored into him. "He will soon be of marriageable age. The Sisterhood can be of service."

He stiffened and spoke cautiously. "I do not need to involve the Bene Gesserit in my family matters."

Her thin smile was as warm as a polar ice cap. "But for a noble house, all family matters are relevant to the Imperium."

Leto gave her a hard look, as the background noise of the reception swirled around him. "My father taught me that the first responsibility of a Duke is the safety of his people. I am first and foremost the Duke of Caladan."

Spotting the familiar face of Archduke Ecaz in the crowd, he seized a reason to leave the rigid Reverend Mother. He made his excuses and walked toward the Archduke, annoyed by Mohiam's meddling in his affairs.

Armand Ecaz stood with four other nobles, deep in conversation around a vitrine that displayed a gold-handled Imperial knife, purported to be a blade carried by Faykan Butler at the Battle of Corrin. The provenance of the object was highly suspect, but Shaddam made it the centerpiece of the exhibit, nevertheless.

Leto paused when he heard the low voices of the huddled guests.

". . . Noble Commonwealth."

A bearlike man with a thick mustache scoffed. "People have talked about breaking up the Imperium for centuries. It will never happen."

"Why, Atikk? You don't think your holdings would thrive better under independent rule? Or do you like having tithes and taxes siphoned off for ridiculous expenditures like this grand museum?" The guests leaned closer to one another.

Armand Ecaz said, "This museum shows off what the Corrinos have accomplished in ten thousand years." He glanced at the various displays. "Not much."

The first man, Lord Atikk, muttered, "No one can break up the Imperium. It is just an idea to keep bored gossips talking."

One of the cautious nobles spotted Leto, and the others immediately ceased their conversation. Armand's expression lit up. "Leto Atreides! Old friend!"

The Archduke introduced Leto to his companions, who appeared uncomfortable and awkward. Leto kept his expression unreadable as he processed what he had overheard. Rumors about the Noble Commonwealth movement seemed unlikely, especially here in a gigantic museum that showcased ten millennia of the Imperium.

Leto said without a smile, "I'm here to bask in the glory of the Padishah Emperor."

Atikk grunted, as if sizing him up. "Oh? Not to widen the black market for your Caladan drug?"

One of the other nobles gasped in surprise. Leto frowned. "Caladan drug?" Atikk flushed and turned away.

Interrupting him, Armand Ecaz embraced Leto with his one arm, genuinely overwhelmed to see his friend. "You bring back terrible memories, but we share a pain others cannot understand. I hope you are well."

Leto winced as he thought of Ilesa Ecaz in her wedding dress, slashed to pieces, dead on the floor at the wedding ceremony. He responded to the embrace, ignoring the other nobles. "I am well." Leto carefully avoided mentioning Jessica, though he added, "My son, Paul, is fourteen now. I could not be more proud of him. He will be an excellent ruler."

"Fourteen?" said one of the other nobles, Count Dinovo. "If your son is fourteen, you should start looking for a marriage alliance. It is not too soon. My own daughter is the same age . . ." He smiled at Leto, let the end of the sentence hang in the air.

Already put off by Mohiam's mention of the same subject, Leto responded quickly, "For a father, it is always too soon." He looked around the gathered nobles, not just in his immediate circle but also in the large display room. Was the entire Landsraad looking at his son like predators considering a fresh piece of meat?

Lord Atikk snorted. "Better cast a wide net, Atreides. Caladan is just one planet. Many other noble families would prefer their daughters marry into a House with greater holdings, one that is more . . . prestigious."

Leto bristled at the comment. "A daughter with such shallow ambitions would not be appropriate for my son."

Armand stepped closer to Leto, protective. "When my daughter was alive, I considered House Atreides to be more than acceptable for a marriage alliance." That stopped further conversation. They all knew what his empty sleeve meant.

Leto extricated himself from the uncomfortable conversation, realizing that this glittering reception was full of political traps.

Do not hunger overmuch for attention. Subtle influence is a more potent key to power than a conspicuous display of wealth or bravado. Patience is a coin of great value.

—MALINA ARU, Ur-Director of CHOAM,
sealed letter to her children

Though she could feel faint seismic tremors, the planet was solid beneath her feet. A gray haze of smoke hovered in the air, and distant rivers of open lava illuminated the sky with a scarlet glow.

Tupile had been the secret operational heart of CHOAM for generations, although the hidden world appeared neither on Imperial charts nor in Spacing Guild records. Several planets bore the same code name, equally secret sanctuaries, and Ur-Director Malina Aru found that this only increased the effectiveness of the camouflage.

Her son Jaxson, though, did not care about safety or subtlety. During the restless months he had lived with Malina on Tupile, he had worked himself into an irrational turmoil over the desecration of their family holdings on remote Otorio. Jaxson would leave this sanctuary soon, despite her best advice to the contrary.

Malina had great things in mind for her youngest child, using the influence and resources of CHOAM, if only Jaxson would let her bring her well-developed plan to fruition. Alas, she doubted that would happen. The young man had intensity and drive but lacked patience.

She stood by herself on the open veranda. The smoke from distant eruptions irritated her rich brown eyes, leaving them red-rimmed. She kept her short, dark hair attractively styled, but businesslike, without frivolous ornamentation. Her slacks, made of soft and supple schlag leather, clung to her slender legs like lotion. The planet's single moon loomed huge overhead, as if poised to crash down through the atmosphere.

Tupile's seismic unrest always made Malina feel vibrant, reminding her of the power she controlled. The Imperium had a visible hold on all the worlds of humanity, but the showpiece of the Emperor and the extended politics of the Landsraad were, like the wave of a magician's hand, a distraction for the audience.

Through its web of commerce and alliances, the CHOAM Company was the real framework of civilization. Jaxson, like so many other firebrands, harangued that the bloated Imperium needed to be dismantled. In principle, Malina embraced the same cause, but only under careful and controlled conditions. Her son didn't have the fortitude for that.

Tupile's roots as a hidden sanctuary world extended throughout Imperial history. During the riots following the release of the Orange Catholic Bible, members of the Council of Ecumenical Translators had fled for their lives, vanishing into the mystery of Tupile. Through centuries of careful and patient data purges, the Tupile worlds had been removed from star charts and records. Although no official Spacing Guild routes existed for Tupile, due to a long-standing secret agreement, the most senior Directors of CHOAM received confidential transport.

The planet was distant from its dim, red sun and far outside what should have been the life zone, but gravitational flexing from the large moon heated the landmasses to the point of habitability. Wealthy recluses had built private reinforced structures that could withstand the seismic upheavals.

Hearing a click of nails and padded feet, Malina turned to see her two muscular spinehounds following Jaxson out onto the open veranda. It had been only hours since her most recent argument with him. She hoped the calm would last a little longer, but she could see her volatile son was ready to debate again.

He spent a great deal of time with the two pets, though they were bonded to Malina. The spinehounds consisted of coiled fur, muscle, and fangs, their pelts made of silvery spines too thick to be soft hair. Sharp horns protruded from behind their pointed ears. The rumbling growl they made in their broad chests struck terror into their victims, but Malina heard it as a purr.

Choosing not to acknowledge Jaxson yet, she crouched, smiling, and spread out her hands. The spinehounds bounded toward her, leaving Jaxson behind. "Yes, my dear Har and Kar." She wrapped her arms around them, scratching their muzzles, and accidentally pricked her forefinger on one of the spines. She ignored it. She had many tiny scars from her pets. The spinehounds sat at her feet, doting on her.

Finally, Malina rose and turned to her son, taking charge. "We agree more than we disagree, you know."

"If we agree, Mother, then why haven't we destroyed House Corrino for what they did? You could pull the right strings and eviscerate Shaddam with a single memo."

"Because we are CHOAM, and Shaddam is the Imperium, and we cannot treat this like an undignified schoolyard brawl. The Emperor doesn't even know what he's done to us."

"That does not excuse it! Otorio was our ancestral sanctuary. The damage can never be undone."

"Therefore, there is no hurry," Malina said. "Would you take a brash, impetuous revenge right now, or would you rather properly dismantle the Imperium for all time?"

Jaxson bunched his fists. His short, curly hair was tight to his skull, looking like black smoke. His brows were thick over brown eyes as dangerous as unexploded grenades.

Before he answered, she said, "I admire your energy, son. All your life I have strived to channel that energy to the benefit of CHOAM and our family."

"You want me to be a puppet like my brother and sister!"

Malina let out a burst of laughter at the thought, and the two spinehounds growled in response. One trotted over to Jaxson to be petted, then returned to her. "Frankos and Jalma fill their roles exactly as planned. I wish you would trust that I have great plans for you, too."

"Father always said you were just putting me off, getting me out of the way."

With an effort, Malina maintained an unreadable expression. "Your father said altogether too much, and there are reasons why he was quietly retired to Otorio before he died. I regret that you spent so much time with him. I should have taken more direct control."

Again, Jaxson was quick to take offense, and she held up a calming hand to forestall further comment. Jaxson had always been a challenging young man, but Malina knew how to handle him. She had trained her notoriously vicious spinehounds, and she could tame Jaxson as well. She just needed to use a different sort of disciplinary collar on him.

Reaching into her trim jacket, she removed the gilded sheet of fine-weave paper stamped with the golden Corrino lion. "This is the invitation for us to attend his ridiculous reception. He did not send it as a provocation or an insult. Shaddam is simply oblivious. He has no idea what he has done to our heritage."

She tore the invitation to shreds and lifted her hands to let the scraps flutter beyond the veranda, blowing on the smoky breezes. "I will not attend. Your brother, the President of CHOAM, will not attend. No CHOAM Company representative of any kind will be there, because I instructed them to make excuses. You see, we are on the same side."

"Will anyone even notice?" he asked bitterly. "What will that accomplish?"

"Whatever your imagination and patience can envision. I have taught you, do not sacrifice what you truly want for what you want right now. You all have your own roles in this." Malina pressed her thin lips together. Frankos, her oldest child, had assumed the mantle of CHOAM President, the public face of the enormous company, while Jalma, her only daughter, had married the powerful but senile old Count Uchan, head of a House Major with seven planets under his—*her*—control.

"I need to do more than sit quietly in meetings, Mother. There is work to be done. I have my own network, and we can achieve things of great consequence."

Malina knew he had met with a few outspoken rebellious Landsraad nobles. Sometimes, it was good for them to vent their frustrations and plan audacious protests that would never come to fruition. "When you are ready, I can connect you with influential agitators in the Noble Commonwealth movement. The plan is vast and complex, and we have already accomplished significant erosion over several generations. The foundations of the Imperium are showing cracks, and Shaddam doesn't even realize it."

Jaxson fumed. "The Emperor doesn't realize it because the damage is too little and too slow. You celebrate a quiet refusal to pay Imperial taxes, to conceal holdings and divert resources. I don't want to wait for the slow pace of evolution. We need a *revolution* to bring freedom to the Imperium. Humanity cannot sustain a thousand more years of Corrino decadence. The modern Imperium serves no purpose except for despotism."

Har and Kar looked up at Jaxson, as if fascinated by his speech, but Malina had heard the words many times. "Slogans do not achieve progress. Demonstrate your growth and knowledge." Her voice became harder, and his head snapped up as if she had whipped him. The Bene Gesserit Sisterhood used a similar technique called Voice, but for Malina, it was simply to demonstrate how well she understood every fiber of Jaxson's being. "I will expand your responsibilities, but you must follow my guidance!"

She noticed something that gave her pause, a tempered steel that had been growing within him. He pushed back. "That doesn't serve my purposes, Mother. I spent countless hours talking with my father when he was alive." Even as she began to frown, he raised his voice. "You always disrespect him! Now that he is dead and his grave desecrated on Otorio, you'll never know what an asset he could have been to CHOAM, if only you had let him."

Malina turned away from the smoky, dark sky and faced her son. The spinehounds rose to their paws and stood at her side.

"It is possible to break up the Imperium in my own lifetime," he said. "Your gradual and dithering plan may appear sound to an academic mind, but most people cannot hold on to an esoteric dream that will take centuries to achieve. You and I both know bureaucracy, Mother. Any delay tends to breed another delay, and the end result never arrives. In order to break something, you need more than a slow, gentle nudge. Sometimes a bludgeon is required!"

She shook her head.

He turned back to the door. "I am already packed. I will let you know my progress, because we are indeed on the same side. My efforts will give a permanent public face to our cause."

"This is brash and ill-considered. I will not fund you," Malina warned, suspecting it was a useless threat. "CHOAM accounts are not open to your use, and any expenses must be approved by me."

Jaxson laughed at her. "I have my own sources of funding."

That alarmed Malina even further. "What are you intending to do?"

"You will find out soon enough, and you will recognize its effectiveness. But you can't stop me. The wheels are already in motion."

When does a student stop being a student, or is all of life a continuous lesson?

—CHANI KYNES, comment to her father

Paul Atreides, barely past his fourteenth birthday, took the controls of the military training aircraft. He gripped the directional yoke, getting a feel for the air and wind currents, and the craft responded to the slightest motion of his hands in one direction or the other.

In the seat beside him, Duncan Idaho shut down his instructor's controls, letting the boy operate the craft himself. Duncan was Paul's main protector and trainer, a Swordmaster with many talents, including being a skilled pilot.

This was not the young man's first piloting session in this class of fast-attack flyer. He was familiar with its hybrid operational features, which enabled it to be a comparatively slow ornithopter with articulated wings, or after shortening and fixing the wings, a speedy flyer. Paul liked the combination, since it gave him a good range of adaptability. He shifted to 'thopter mode, lifting and dropping the wings as smoothly as he could.

"Too jerky," Duncan said, his voice stern and encouraging at the same time. "Think of a graceful bird flying, like a spreybird. The flyer won't do it on its own."

Concentrating, Paul calmed himself with a Bene Gesserit breathing exercise his mother had secretly taught him. Once he quelled his anxiety, he understood exactly what Duncan meant, knew how to correct his moves. He loosened his grip on the control yoke just enough to let the craft fly smoothly.

"That's it, boy. Do it the way I taught you."

Paul didn't mention that his mother also deserved credit. Duncan and the Lady Jessica often seemed at odds, strong-willed people both driving the young man to achieve his best. His mother had spoken of it once to Paul, theorizing that she and Duncan were in an odd competition for his attention and affections. But no one else knew the exact Bene Gesserit techniques she was sharing with her son; Duke Leto would not approve. Ironically, Paul knew, neither would the Sisterhood, but Jessica had made up her own mind.

Duncan and Lady Jessica weren't his only trainers, however. Paul also received personal combat instruction from the troubadour warrior Gurney Halleck and from Thufir Hawat, the Atreides Mentat and Master of Assassins. The latter, despite his title, taught more defensive than offensive tactics, instructing Paul in how to avoid trouble, and to survive it.

Duncan, though, was someone special. In addition to being his trainer and protector, he was Paul's best friend. At the command of Duke Leto, the Swordmaster was training Paul in many different fields, and training him *hard*. Today would be no different. According to the weather report, there would be a storm at sea, and Duncan instructed the young man to fly directly into the teeth of it.

The Swordmaster gazed through the cockpit window, assessing the black tempest gathering several kilometers offshore. Ominous thunderheads swelled as if summoned to a cloud convocation.

"Ready for this, boy?" Duncan asked. "Best way to hone your piloting skills."

"'Boy'? Maybe you'll stop calling me that after I fly into this storm." Paul could already feel the winds jostling the aircraft, making it harder to control.

"Maybe. We'll see how you do."

With acute observation skills learned from his mother, Paul detected an edge of worry in Duncan's voice. The storm might be bigger than they'd expected, but Paul did not suggest they change their plans. He was ready.

Flying as Duncan had taught him, he banked toward the storm, leveled out, switched off the flapping ornithopter wings, and drew them in tight against the fuselage. The now-fixed wings were a quarter of the length they'd been. This was a sleek aircraft now, like those used by Atreides patrols, capable of swift attack, although this training vessel had no armaments except for a set of fore and aft lascannons.

Paul pushed an accelerator bar next to the control yoke, and the aircraft leaped forward in the air as if eager to dance with the storm. As the thunderheads grew darker around them, Paul dove toward the cloud cover. Even as wind wrenched the craft, Paul centered down into his inner calmness. The aircraft seemed part of him, an extension of his body, and he nudged the vessel for optimum acceleration.

"Good," Duncan said. "You're improving." Out of the corner of his eye, Paul noted that the Swordmaster's fingers were on the instructor's controls, ready to activate them if Paul should falter.

Below were skirling surges of energy where the clouds touched the water. Though the creatures were rare, he knew what they must be, and he felt a chill of awe. "Elecrans, Duncan! Look how many!"

"Stay well above them, and we'll be all right. Go a little higher."

Paul acknowledged, but he couldn't tear his eyes from the intriguing flashes of living lightning.

The elemental creatures spawned in the sea and needed to remain in contact with the surface of the water or they would dissipate. Sometimes a big wave would send one flying into the air, scattering its water so that it faded into electrical mists. As long as elecrans were firmly connected to the sea, they were extremely dangerous—towers of energy that could discharge dangerous bolts of lightning.

"A trial by fire for you," Duncan said. "A big one."

"Isn't that what you promised?"

They had discussed safe training and dangerous training, and Duncan insisted Paul needed to learn in true high-pressure situations in order to be prepared for real crises. Duke Leto also considered it the optimal teaching method, and it demonstrated his intrinsic faith in Duncan's abilities that he would ask the Swordmaster to let his son take such genuine risks.

But this elecran-infested storm went beyond any planned curriculum. The elemental creatures intensified the storm, building it to a massive squall with hurricane-strength winds.

The lightning strikes did not often rise above the cauldron of the elecrans but skittered out laterally, as if the electrical creatures were firing at one another in some sort of paranormal competition. When a jagged bolt from one elecran struck another, the target creature's tower-shaped body bent, bowed, then straightened before it continued to spark and lash.

For several years now, Paul had been learning Duncan's high-level piloting skills, intricate reflexes, and instant reactions. He admired how confident the Swordmaster always was, but not to the point of hubris. Paul appreciated his friend's style of excellence, flying at the edge of life and death. Duncan thrived on the surge of adrenaline, and Paul had become addicted as well, walking the razor's edge, where any small mistake could be a fatal one.

Right now, Paul felt a thrill that intensified every moment, an infusion of emergency energy, vital for survival, as if his body were rising to its maximum efficiency in the face of great peril. His focus, his tension, his sheer skill and instant reactions were beyond anything he had felt before. Glancing at Duncan beside him, he could tell that his trainer's level of alertness was also elevated.

The tremendous storm was shot through with so many swirling elecran discharges that Paul could not count them.

"Instruments are acting up, too many spurious results," Duncan cautioned. "Do not rely on the readings."

"The electrical energy is interfering." Paul channeled his calm focus again. "I will trust my eyes and instincts."

"Skirt the edge of the storm, so we don't lose sight of the coastline. We still need to find our way home."

Paul altered course, but the tempest was widening fast. Clouds had climbed above them, and heavy sheets of rain lashed the cockpit windscreen. The winds shook the aircraft, threatening to knock it out of the sky.

"I don't trust my readings, but we're definitely losing elevation." As he banked the flyer, he looked out the side window and saw the crackling elecrans less than a thousand meters below, sending out bright flashes of static sparks. Though he had altered course, the flyer still seemed to be heading directly toward them.

The elecrans below snapped out jagged lightning bolts. For a moment, Paul felt entirely disoriented, as if the aircraft had turned upside down, and the skyful of lightning was suddenly overhead. But he'd been in flight training enough to know that he had to rely on his true internal sense of direction. He *knew* up and down, knew where the shore and Castle Caladan were, although he could not see it through the rain and mist.

The aircraft was losing speed as well as altitude, but he encountered a headwind no matter which direction he turned in an attempt to improve conditions. Beneath them, as if sensing prey, the nest of elecrans quested upward, stretching higher and higher. Paul felt a prickle of electricity on his skin, making his hair stand up.

Duncan fired the forward lascannon, disrupting and decapitating several elecrans. But the elemental swirls of energy quickly re-formed.

As the flyer continued to drop toward the ocean, the sizzling entities combined to form a single hydra-like creature with multiple heads of massed lightning, each one thrusting upward.

"This is too great a danger," Duncan said. "I'm taking the controls."

"No, I need to do this." Paul saw a way to survive and escape, the vision as vivid as if he had glimpsed the immediate future. He knew what was going to happen, and what he had to do.

En masse, the combined elecrans extended higher, like a stretched cone of lightning that maintained contact with the surface of the water. The amalgamated creature flared so brightly that Paul could hardly look at it. Images were burned onto his retinas.

Duncan fired the lasbeam again, scrambling the creature's energy patterns and making it recoil. Paul concentrated solely on flying, gripping the controls to adjust the tight wings and stabilize their trajectory, catching thermal updrafts and finding tailwinds that helped them accelerate, but the craft ultimately dropped again.

They were only a few hundred meters above the writhing electrical mass now, and arcs of lightning whipped upward, even as Duncan continued to fire the lasbeam. The aircraft's hull and wings sparked with electricity, and the cockpit's interior seemed alive with static.

Paul recalled his father's tale of being on a boat during an elecran storm. His men had fired lasguns at the waves beneath an elecran, flashing the water to steam and severing the elemental creature's contact with the sea, which turned it into a harmless mist. Now Duncan was firing at the base, but the attempt had very little effect on such a large, combined creature, not generating enough steam to cut contact with the ocean.

Using a tailwind, Paul flew directly toward the top of the elecran.

"Paul, what are you doing? You'll kill us!"

Paul didn't reply, fixing his attention on flying. Duncan did not try to seize the controls but chose to keep firing instead. "I'm targeting the elecran's head, the apex of energy there. It's . . . the nexus of the combined elecrans. Maybe we can break them apart."

"I have another idea," Paul said.

Electricity lashed out in jagged bolts, and one strike rocked the flyer, sending a blast of sparks from the cockpit panel. At the last possible moment, Paul banked hard right and accelerated in a steep climb.

In its haste to reach the pesky interlopers the combined elecrans lunged toward the aircraft and pulled itself higher with such power that it detached from the water in its attempt to reach them. With the connection snapped, the elemental creature dissipated into an expanding cloud of sparkles that flashed and faded.

Heart pounding, Paul flew a circle around where the elecrans had been, and now even the ocean storm seemed a far more surmountable challenge. The elemental creatures were no more than sparking mist that spread back down to the water, where they would eventually re-coalesce.

Paul grinned. "I'll fly us back now. We've had enough fun for one day."

Duncan wiped perspiration from his forehead. "I never doubted you for a moment. I'll never call you 'boy' again."

Loyalty is at the core of my being, and honor is synonymous with the Atreides name. The only matter for debate is to whom do I pledge my loyalty?

—DUKE LETO ATREIDES, letters to his son, Paul

Speak to me of Caladan, Duke Leto," said Empress Aricatha. "After Shaddam and I married, he promised that I could visit many worlds in the Imperium. Should I make Caladan one of them?"

She was nimble, friendly, and when she spoke with guests, she mentioned specific details to demonstrate that she genuinely remembered each person at the reception. Leto was impressed with her.

Her question incited a brush of homesickness, and he smiled wistfully. "Everyone finds beauty in the homeworld of their heart. For me, Caladan will always be a masterpiece of waves and shore. My family's castle is imposing, yet the most comfortable place I can imagine. It has been in the Atreides family for twenty-six generations." He let out a soft sigh. "I like to stand out on a high balcony and watch the seacoast as the tide comes in. On a moonless night, the ocean is phosphorescent and the entire horizon glows faint green. Often my Lady Jessica joins me." He missed her and thought of the private holo-message she had sent along with him.

Aricatha's generous lips formed a smile. "Why, Duke Leto Atreides, you are a romantic."

He had never thought of himself as such. "I am the Duke of Caladan," he said, as if that were an answer.

As twilight deepened outside, lights illuminated the museum complex like awakening fireflies. In the center of his reception, Shaddam—who appeared weary of greeting so many people—made his way toward a set of wall controls that worked the citywide public address system.

The Empress saw him and turned away from Leto. "We must talk at greater length later. My husband is about to deliver a speech to be projected throughout the city. It is meant to be a grand address worthy of the history scrolls." She moved off to be at Shaddam's side.

Most of the crowd fell into an expectant hush, while some applauded to show their enthusiasm. Leto turned to listen.

Before the Emperor could speak, though, the entire tower plunged into blackness.

The power went out as if it had been cut by a headsman's ax. The darkness filled with the gasp of hundreds of attendees who were startled and confused, but not yet afraid, assuming it was some kind of technical failure. A hubbub of indignant questions and complaints swished like waves against a shore.

The broad plaz windows looked out upon a black city shrouded in night, and Leto's eyes adjusted to the darkness outside. To his surprise, not a single light shone across the entire museum complex. Shaddam's new city looked more like an abandoned tomb than a grand memorial.

Leto was instantly alert. Though he assumed Shaddam would be the primary focus of any assassin, his mind assessed the sheer number of targets in this room, himself among them. He instinctively took a step closer to the Empress and Shaddam in the darkened reception hall. Uniformed Sardaukar also swept into position, closing in around the Emperor.

Not far away, Aricatha said in a low, firm voice, "Everything for this event was planned down to the minutest detail! I expect that my husband will find the culprits, and heads will roll."

Shaddam bellowed, "Where are the lights?"

Fenring was there with him, grabbing his arm. "We must assume there's danger, Sire."

Leto remembered the suspicious man he had seen in the alley behind the Serena Butler statue. Had security been able to investigate yet?

The Emperor called, "Protectors! To me!" A temporary handlight came on, held by the colonel bashar of the Sardaukar.

Just then, a wave of shimmering, glowing figures manifested like ghosts around the room. The pale, luminescent figure of a man congealed in the air near the vitrine case that held Faykan Butler's dagger. Four identical projections appeared at strategic points around the crowded hall. The life-sized figures manifested like white smoke. He was a young, powerful man with heavy brows and tight, dark hair like a thundercloud around his head. His expression was filled with power and energy, exactly the same on each image, repeated multiple times.

Leto recognized the watery, lambent translucency. "Holograms." He looked around but could see little by the faint light of the images. "There must be splitters, projectors hidden around the room."

"Who is that man?" one of the attendees grumbled. "Does anyone recognize him?"

The holographic images glowered at all of them, holding everyone's attention without speaking. While the current of surprised conversation grew louder in the reception hall, Shaddam shouted over them all, and the Sardaukar barked orders, organizing and protecting the attendees.

Pressed against the tall windows, other guests pointed through the plaz panes to the city below. Leto now saw countless flickering white lights across the complex like an army of identical holos, appearing among the exhibits, fountains, statues, and auditoriums. Viewed from the height of the Imperial Monolith, they looked like thousands of tiny, pale candle flames, all over the city.

Then the holo-figures spoke in eerie resonant unison, drowning out the background noise. "The city grid has been neutralized. Quiet darkness has returned to Otorio, as it should be. This planet will have one more moment of peace before it is forever emblazoned in history."

Leto guessed that many thousands of holograms were issuing the same statement across the city. Everyone would hear what this man had to say. By an odd trick of projection, Leto thought the shimmering image was looking directly at him. The transmitted voice grew louder. "I have something to say, and you will hear me. The whole Imperium will hear me, because I speak with a thunderous voice."

"He seems quite full of himself," muttered one of the pompous lords.

"You do not know me, but you will. I am Jaxson Aru. My message will be carried far and wide, from planet to planet, because freedom will not be silenced."

"Aru?" Empress Aricatha said. "We know that name."

Leto remembered a Frankos Aru, who was currently the President of the CHOAM Company. Was this Jaxson related to him?

The holograms continued speaking. "The Corrino Imperium has outlived its usefulness, and we must break it apart. The only way to do that is to cut off its head."

The Sardaukar fighters tensed, drew closer to Shaddam.

"You all stand here at a crime scene," Jaxson Aru continued, "one of many Corrino crime scenes. The Emperor stole this world to inflate his ego—just as he has stolen from every single noble family in the Landsraad. We should be kings of our own planets, rulers of our own destinies. The Corrinos have smothered you for thousands of years, and you put up with it! No, you *enable* it. That 'noble' house and the entire core of the Landsraad must be replaced."

The glow of the holograms washed over the audience. Under the pale illumination, Leto saw Shaddam frown. "What do we know about this man?"

Fenring said quickly, "I briefed you about him not long ago, Sire, hmmm? He is the son of Malina Aru, the Urdir of CHOAM, but little else is known about him."

"What does that—"

Jaxson raised his voice from the holograms. "Why do you all tolerate an ancient and corrupt Imperium, monopolized by one greedy family, when we could have thousands of thriving independent planets, each controlled by its own leaders and its own people? That is how the human race survives!"

Across the plaza, the distant crowd was also stirring in the darkness. Leto could see them moving about like angry insects among the countless pale Jaxson Aru projections.

One of the nobles in the reception chamber shouted in a loud enough voice to drown out the projected words. "He speaks treason! I am loyal to the Padishah Emperor."

Leto observed intensely, listening for further explanations as a knot formed in his stomach. Any plot as complex as this would be expressed in more than a simple indignant statement. Jaxson Aru might speak his manifesto and hope to change minds or recruit other rebels, but Leto didn't think he would be satisfied with only that. There had to be something else afoot.

He looked around, increasingly agitated. He knew there were aircraft on the rooftop of the Imperial Monolith—one level above the penthouse reception hall—but if all these people had to evacuate, the accelerated lift was the main means of escape down to street level. What if Aru had sabotaged the reception somehow? Planted a bomb in the tower?

Leto leaned closer to Aricatha. "I do not like this, Empress. We must prepare ourselves for whatever may come."

The Emperor turned to the site-wide communicator he had been about to use. "With this, I can summon security from across the complex. My voice will drown out everything that foolish man says." He waved a hand to activate the speaker, but the system remained dead, all the power out.

Jaxson continued his tirade. "Remember the Noble Commonwealth. Learn our cause. Understand your future. Join us." The holograms paused, then added, "If you survive tonight."

As a rush of angry disbelief washed over the room, the images faded away like sea mist burned off by a hot morning sun. With the holograms gone, the reception area and the city outside fell back into total darkness. The crowd murmurs grew louder, though Leto noticed several people had fallen silent, including Lord Atikk. The Duke remembered some of the guests surreptitiously talking about the Noble Commonwealth. Were they involved in this debacle?

Temporary lights flickered on as technicians restored some circuits in the Monolith. The Emperor stood boiling with outrage, surrounded by a close cordon of Sardaukar. Leto had seen Shaddam furious before, but never like this. Jaxson Aru's rebellious display was not only offensive in its own right, but because it had occurred during the grandiose Corrino gala, it was personally embarrassing.

"Find that man!" Shaddam roared. "Tear up every floor plate and expose the wiring in the walls. How did he accomplish this? Find him. Is he here?"

"I believe that was only a recording, Sire," Fenring said.

"What did he mean, 'if you survive tonight'?" Leto said and pushed closer to the Sardaukar guards, wary. "Is there immediate danger?"

Three Sardaukar pressed forward at a militaristic pace, cleaving through the crowd. Leto recognized the colonel bashar who had agreed to investigate the surreptitious maintenance worker in the plaza. The officer shouldered one lord—Count Dinovo—aside, heading like a projectile toward the Emperor. "We are taking you now, Sire. We must evacuate."

"Evacuate? But this is my gala!"

Showing no deference, the colonel bashar seized Shaddam's arm. "Duke Atreides's suspicions proved to be valid." The Sardaukar looked at Leto. "I'm sorry that it took so long to verify, Sire. There is a plot against the throne."

"Of course there's a plot! We just watched it unfold," Shaddam snapped. "Did you not see the holograms? We have to stop the man from spreading more of his sedition."

The officer reported in clipped words as he urged the Emperor into motion. "The dump boxes and heavy debris in orbit are not empty, as they appeared to be. They are loaded with inert mass and explosives, making each of them a huge and deadly projectile. Their engines have been activated on a swift burn, and three of them are on a direct descent. This museum complex is the target."

Shaddam balked, but the Sardaukar maintained a firm hold on him. "We are evacuating you, Sire. Right now!"

The most important parenting skill is knowing when to exert control and when to let go.

—LADY JESSICA

When the ocean storm swept in, Jessica knew that Paul and Duncan were out training with one of the modified 'thopter-flyers. She bundled herself against the cold wind and rain and hurried out of the castle. Half an hour earlier watching from a high window, she'd seen the two of them take off from the military airfield on the headlands and fly out over the water, undaunted by the darkening storm. Paul would revel in the chance to test his skill in the adverse weather.

But the thunderheads had grown uglier, thicker. Off in the distance, flickers of light at the base of the black cloud suggested something more ominous than lightning. This hazard went beyond anything she wanted her son to face in a routine exercise. All sensible fishermen had returned their boats to dock, but Paul's flyer headed out as if to taunt the storm.

She felt a natural fear for his safety, but she also knew his skill.

Beneath her long coat, she wore an elegant white dress, and her bronze hair was arranged in a bun, studded with rare reefpearls, a gift from Duke Leto. Today was the twentieth anniversary of their very first meeting, and she hadn't forgotten, even though Leto was away at the new Corrino museum. Yet now, realizing that her son could be at risk, she turned her thoughts to more urgent matters.

Leaving the castle grounds, she climbed a rocky path to a high promontory overlooking the ocean. It was not wise to be in such an exposed, windswept place in an electrical storm, but she needed to see. The sounds of thunder and waves drowned out the drone of any nearby aircraft engine. She shielded her eyes against the wet wind and stared out to the ugly line of storm clouds. All those wild flurries of surface lightning suggested this was more than a normal squall.

Glancing along the headlands, she looked toward the landing field where Paul's flyer would return. She told herself that Duncan would keep him safe, but the Swordmaster could also be reckless, and Paul always insisted on pushing his limits.

Even hurrying toward the field, alone out here in the storm, Jessica did not feel isolated. She was an important part of House Atreides, of Caladan. She was so much more than a concubine, a mother, or a Bene Gesserit Sister. Leto had left her in charge when he went away for Shaddam's grand celebration. The Duke and his lady had an unspoken agreement, a bond of trust built over two decades together. Jessica often made decisions in his absence, taking responsibility to ease Leto's burden. She knew the way the Duke thought and what he would decide.

Black clouds clenched like a threatening fist over the sea. Bright and ominous discharges lashed in all directions. As the stinging wind picked up, icy rain splashed across her cheeks. Paul and Duncan were out there, in danger, too far from shore to be safe. Her heart stuttered. Her son was a talented pilot, and no one was better than Duncan Idaho, but even the best could not always survive the wrath of an ocean storm. She hoped Caladan rescue crews would not merely find floating wreckage after the storm. . . .

"Come home, Paul," she whispered.

Before setting off for the airfield, he had stood in front of her, crossing his arms over his chest. "An easy training exercise does not hone my abilities. Only real risk can provide real experience."

She believed in him.

But now as she thought of their fragile craft out in the storm front, Jessica had to use her Bene Gesserit calming techniques. She had survived great risks too in her training back on Wallach IX. Her proctor, Reverend Mother Mohiam, had made young Jessica endure harsh exercises. The Sisterhood was certainly willing to let an unworthy Acolyte die, as a process of sifting out the absolute best candidates. Jessica had passed all those tests, learned all the intense and esoteric skills the Mother School could teach her.

Afterward, she had been sent to Duke Leto Atreides on Caladan, assigned to him as a concubine. Back then, it had been just another mission, a mission in which she excelled. Jessica had never known that it would become her entire life. She doubted many Bene Gesserit assignments turned out so perfectly.

A searing blue-white bolt of lightning struck a high point on the headlands not far away. She tugged the hood down over her hair and ducked as she ran toward the landing field. She could take shelter in the structures there. She thought—or was it just hope?—that she heard an undertone of engine buzzing behind the wind, but she saw no running lights of a returning flyer.

Paul would survive, she knew it. Duncan would not let him die!

As the thunder rumble intensified, Jessica wondered where Leto was right now. On Otorio, surrounded by other ambitious nobles, the Duke was enduring a different kind of test. Even now, he would be engaged in political skirmishes— dressed in finery, enduring the pomp and excesses of Emperor Shaddam's gala. Jessica knew how much Leto disliked those pretentions. Though he did not pander, he was politically adept, with many strong friendships and alliances, making him much more influential than most other one-planet Landsraad houses. Even so, at this moment, he was probably drinking fine Tikal champagne, sampling extravagantly expensive hors d'oeuvres, and making empty conversation with other nobles as he represented House Atreides.

She could have been there on his arm, the Duke's lady, but a bound concubine would not have served what the head of House Atreides required. Because of the tragic death of Ilesa Ecaz just before their wedding ceremony, she knew Leto would resist other marriage prospects, but time was enough to erode any landscape, and politics often outweighed hope. If pressed into a corner, Leto might be forced to put House Atreides before Jessica. Would he ever agree to marry, if the politics were right?

The height of the storm's fury did not last long, and by the time she reached the shelter of the airfield control centers, the winds had already weakened. Over the sea to the east, the sky finally began to clear. Low on the horizon, a bright slash of blue sky peeked through an opening in the clouds.

Standing at the doorway of a low metal hut, she searched the skies and spotted lights above the gray, choppy water, heard the hum of aircraft engines growing louder. She saw the training flyer swoop in, but it wavered in the air. Had the fuselage been damaged? Was the pilot exhausted? Wounded?

She waited at the edge of the field as the craft came in for a less-than-graceful landing, then she hurried forward as the cockpit doors opened. Paul sprang out exuberant, apparently filled with the excitement inspired by a brush with death. Duncan Idaho followed, walking straight and formal; she knew the Swordmaster well enough to see that even he was alarmed by their ordeal.

Jessica chastised in a low voice, "You should not have risked him like that, Duncan."

The Swordmaster clearly had no way to argue. He lowered his gaze and searched for words, but Paul broke in, "We came back, Mother! And I learned so many techniques in that one hour . . ." He wiped a hand across his eyes as raindrops spattered his face. "After all, someday I may have to fly into a terrible storm, and you will be glad I have this experience."

Anyone is capable of committing murder against another person, or against himself.

—THUFIR HAWAT

At the Bene Gesserit Mother School on Wallach IX, an ancient woman lay wheezing on her medical bed, crushed by the weight of visions and age. Lethea, a former Kwisatz Mother of the order, could see the entire gestalt of the Sisterhood's vast breeding program; she understood every thread, bloodline, dead end, and hope, far more than any other Sister.

She lay dying, heavily dosed with the spice melange, kept alive long past her normal life span through horrendous artificial life support. But the Bene Gesserit considered it imperative that she remain alive, for Lethea had a unique and vital talent for the Sisterhood, a skill that was difficult to pass on to others.

The woman was also dangerous, unstable, irrational.

Mother Superior Harishka had just entered the isolated third-floor chamber in the medical wing that kept Lethea safe—and protected other Sisters from her. The Mother Superior passed a young Acolyte guarding the barricaded door, and they exchanged whispers, careful not to disturb the old woman locked inside.

With a silent command, Harishka nodded to the door, and the Acolyte opened the barrier. The Mother Superior entered the rank-smelling chamber, gliding over the dark wood floor toward the expansive bed where Lethea slept. The ancient woman had a surprisingly young face, but the rest of her body was withered and frail, and age spots and wrinkles covered her hands. Harishka had seen images of her friend from decades ago. Lethea was a former breeding mistress who rose through the ranks to head the entire program, and she still retained a shadow of her former beauty.

A stout Sister slid into the room holding a small imaging device. She moved closer to record Lethea's expressions and any words she might utter if she emerged from her catatonic state.

Harishka stood by the bed for several minutes, not rustling her robe or breathing loudly enough to make noise. She would not deprive her old friend of even a moment of sleep. Even before becoming Mother Superior, Harishka had admired Lethea's innate, incomprehensible ability to see the sweeping plan in a way no other Bene Gesserit could.

As if she could sense the Mother Superior's thought, the bedridden woman's eyes opened to slits, then widened. She looked piercingly at Harishka, startling her. "You've been standing there for so long. Are you trying to decide if you should cut my throat and be done with the troubles I cause?"

The Mother Superior responded with an uneasy laugh. "You know I would never consider that, old friend."

"I am not a Truthsayer, so you could well be lying to me." Lethea flinched with a sudden wave of suspicions.

"I did not come here to lie to you. I came to see how you are doing." The Mother Superior added deep sincerity to her words. "The Sisterhood needs you, Lethea. You are irreplaceable."

Peripherally, Harishka saw a tall Sister in a green medical robe approach the bedside. The woman's hair was pinned tightly to her head. Now that Lethea was awake, the medical Sister checked the instruments, then adjusted the diagnostics linked to the patient by wires and tubes.

Lethea snapped at the attendant. "I hate you for keeping me alive." The tall woman looked nervously at Harishka, but held her ground. The other Sister with the imager stepped closer to get a better angle for her recording.

Harishka leaned down and spoke in a soothing voice. "We are helping you. Your body is too weak to sustain itself. This is for your own good."

"My own good?" The Kwisatz Mother half sat up, then slumped back onto the bed. Harishka reached in to prop Lethea, and the medical Sister pushed pillows behind her back. "You mean for the good of the Bene Gesserit."

"Are we not Sisters together? Sworn to uphold and advance the goals of the order? The breeding program is essential to the Sisterhood. *You* are central to the Sisterhood." Harishka straightened. "Therefore, what is good for the Sisterhood is also for your own good."

The ancient woman sulked. "I have no friends, you know. I've never felt even a semblance of affection for any other human being, not even for you."

Harishka laughed. "You are not so unpleasant as you portray yourself to be. I have many fond memories of our conversations."

The former Kwisatz Mother wheezed. "I've had an extraordinarily difficult life, and one that has lasted far too long. So many breeding pathways that proved to be dead ends, so many hopes dashed—I see them all, and countless others that are doomed to failure. What is the point?"

Harishka answered in soft tones. "You can sort out the threads that are not failures. You keep our hopes alive."

"I cannot live forever. You found a Kwisatz Mother to replace me, so let me slip into the realm of Other Memory. She is highly skilled. I have spoken with her. I know she can handle the job."

The Mother Superior gave a consoling nod. "But you have another talent, don't you? One she does not possess? That is why you are so important to me."

"It makes me worth tolerating." Lethea looked at the tubes connected to her, the spice essence flowing into her, the life-support mechanisms that monitored her heartbeat, maintained her respiration. Suddenly, the crone lashed out, "If you care so much, did you bring me something good to eat?"

Harishka reached into a pocket of her robe and brought out a small, compact package that expanded into a portable bowl. She produced a spoon from another pocket, then instructed the tall medical Sister, "Turn off the machines. Leave her in peace for a few moments. She can sustain herself."

The Sister looked dubious, then anxious.

Lethea rasped, "I can control every cell in my body. I will stay alive long enough to eat!"

Though the humming devices fell silent, the tubes and monitors remained connected. Harishka pulled a chair next to the bed. The aged woman squirmed, tried to see the bowl. "What is it today?" Her flicker of eagerness was the most positive reaction Harishka had seen in some time.

"The peppery savoy soup you like so much. It is hard to get." The Mother Superior smiled. "But I found a way. For you."

Lethea looked almost happy, but not quite. "You are the only one who can calm me. Others try, but not like you."

"We both have special skills." Harishka slipped a partial spoonful of the dark green soup into Lethea's mouth. She tasted it and swallowed, so Harishka gave her another spoonful, and another, careful not to let soup dribble down her wrinkled chin. When the old woman had finished, Harishka wiped her lips with a cloth. Lethea refused to let anyone else feed her like this.

Satisfied, the ancient Kwisatz Mother looked sleepy.

Harishka rose to leave. "I will check on you again tomorrow."

Lethea glared at her. "You just want to make sure I'm still alive."

"Yes, I do."

The old woman closed her eyes and pushed some pillows off the bed to lie down again. The medical Sister tried to help, but Harishka took care of making Lethea as comfortable as possible.

As the dying woman lay with her eyes closed, Harishka said to the others, "You can turn the life support back on. Keep me advised of any changes."

AFTER MOTHER SUPERIOR Harishka had gone, Lethea sat up of her own accord. The two medical Sisters remained in the room with their backs turned, conferring in whispers, but she heard every word.

"I go in and out of clarity," Lethea said. "But I am very clear now."

The two Sisters turned toward her, instantly alert. Both showed signs of fear.

Lethea used the irresistible power of Voice, instantly locking her control over the two attendants. "You, with the imaging device, come here."

The stout young woman did as she was told. She stood by the bedside, anxious, but she could not resist.

"Are you recording all of this?" Lethea demanded. "So that my every word, my every action, can be analyzed and discussed?"

The Sister nodded. "I am good at my job."

A soft smile crept onto Lethea's face. "Then do a good job of this." She lowered her voice to a husky whisper, the force of her words directed only to this Sister. "See that stone wall over there, with the one brick that sticks out slightly above the others? See how it's a little bit sharp?" With a gnarled hand, she pointed toward a corner of the room.

The Sister nodded. She held up her recording device.

"Now go over there and bash your forehead into it as many times as you can, as hard as you can." Lethea held out her hand. "Here, let me hold your imager while you do as I command."

The medical Sister cried out and lunged to help her companion, but Lethea stopped her in her tracks with Voice. "Halt! Do not move another step!"

Without hesitation, the stout Sister handed Lethea her imager, and the ancient woman recorded every moment as the hapless young Sister walked to the wall, faced it, and drew herself back so she could bash her head against the stone. After the first impact, she reeled backward from the bloody stain, then lunged forward to bash her head again.

While Lethea recorded and the other Sister watched helplessly, the young woman hammered her forehead several more times into the sharp, protruding stone, until finally she tumbled to the floor. The front of her skull split open, and blood poured down her face.

Exhausted, Lethea slumped back onto her bed again, staring at the brightness of the ceiling, gazing into a white light. She loosened her grip on the imager, but it recorded her words as she drifted off into sleep.

"Jessica . . . Jessica of Caladan! You must take her away from him! Jessica."

Those in the immediate circle around Shaddam recoiled at the colonel bashar's sharp warning. Some cried out in panic. In the dim reception room, Leto thought of all the ships on the nearby diplomatic landing field, wondered how many could evacuate the tower and how much time they had.

As if in a mocking gesture, all the power switched back on, and the full lights blinded the people. Leto ducked away, shielding his eyes. There was not a second to waste. Through the Monolith windows, lights flared on around the museum complex, flashing rainbows, swirling stars, reflective multicolored beams that celebrated Corrino greatness. He realized this was another distraction.

The Sardaukar grabbed the Emperor and forced him toward a discreet door in the back of the reception room. "Sire, you must leave. *Now*." He barked a string of orders to the other Sardaukar in the room. "You as well, Count Fenring, and the Empress. Come with us."

Indignant, Shaddam tried to pull free, but couldn't. "This has already been enough of an insult, Colonel Bashar. I will not run away. My people cannot see me being a coward."

The Sardaukar's face looked deadly, as if the Emperor were no more than an unruly child. He spoke in a low, urgent voice. "These people aren't going to survive to tell anyone, Sire. We are in the impact zone. There is an escape lighter on the roof, a small, fast ship that can take you to safety!"

Without arguing, Fenring swiftly made his way toward a sealed door at the back of the room. "We had better listen, hmmm?" Other Sardaukar cleared the way, knocking noble guests aside as if it were a part of a sports competition.

Leto's tone was terse as he pushed forward. "There are thousands of people in this city, here by *your* command, Sire. We *all* have to evacuate."

Empress Aricatha responded, "My husband is the most important person, but if others can escape, too . . ."

Leto bolted to the site-wide public address system, which was ready to broadcast Shaddam's proud speech, now that power had been restored. He slapped the comm switch. "Attention all citizens! Evacuate the city by any means possible. Get as far away as you can." He doubted they would be able to make it, but he had to give them at least some warning. "Impact imminent!"

Another Sardaukar activated an alarm, and warbling sirens resonated throughout the extensive complex, magenta lights flashing along the web of interconnected streets. The massive dump boxes were already hurtling down through the atmosphere. Leto had no idea how accurate the targeting was or how long it would take, but the mass of the crashing objects and the vaporization of impact would be equivalent to a small atomic.

He saw Archduke Ecaz standing with other nobles. "Armand, get as many as possible into the lifts! Go to the landing field and take any ships you can." The most important delegates would have their fancy ships ready for liftoff. Responding to Leto's command without hesitation, the Archduke herded people toward the lift doors.

Leto shouted into the site-wide address system again. "Evacuate! Evacuate!" His words boomed throughout the huge city and museum complex. He suddenly doubted if he could save himself, and thought of Jessica, of Paul. . . .

The panicked crowd pressed toward the elevators. Armand Ecaz crammed himself into one car already overloaded with nobles. He and Count Dinovo blocked others who tried to force their way in. The etched metal doors slid shut, and the elevators dropped away. Leto hoped his friend would make it in time.

The guests remained disoriented, few understanding the magnitude of the threat. Pushing toward the exit door with the Emperor, the assistant chamberlain bellowed in a loud, deep voice, "Be calm. Everything is under control!"

"And my Truthsayer?" Shaddam insisted as he, Count Fenring, and the Empress were rushed along by Sardaukar. "Make sure she is taken to the roof."

Leto's stomach felt like ice, and he thought of his Caladan pilot, Arko, and the bright-eyed entourage who had come with him here to Otorio, hoping to see amazing sights. The Atreides yacht would be down there . . . and he knew they were doomed.

As uniformed Sardaukar herded the Emperor and his companions through the exit door, others whisked old Reverend Mother Mohiam out a different door. Suddenly, an officer grabbed Leto by the arm. "This way, Atreides." It was the same colonel bashar who had looked at Leto with odd recognition, the one who took his warning seriously. "There is room for you in the Emperor's escape lighter."

With an implacable grip, the Sardaukar rushed him toward the exit door and a narrow set of stairs that led from the reception gallery up to the Monolith roof. Shaddam was ahead of them, climbing swiftly, followed by the Empress and urged along by Fenring. Other attendees swirled after them to the exit door, but the Sardaukar officer knocked them out of the way, pushing Leto at a run.

Leto said, "Why are you saving me? We have to rescue all these people."

"All will not be rescued," said the Sardaukar. "You reported the danger and gave us fair warning. Is that not reason enough to save you?"

"No!" he replied, as if the answer were obvious. "All these nobles, everyone here—there must be some way to help them!"

"Emperor Shaddam gave orders to evacuate you if at all possible. I am following orders. The rest of these are already dead."

Leto was whisked up the narrow, steep stairway to the rooftop platform. He had tried to help the others escape by other means, though he was sure it would be a futile gesture. There wasn't enough time. At least Armand Ecaz had already rushed a group out of the Monolith to street level, and maybe some of the landed ships would fly away.

The Sardaukar officer pushed him. "Faster! We are running out of time."

The Emperor's party burst onto the open rooftop, where several small spacecraft sat ready. Shaddam and Aricatha were just ahead of him. The nearest ship had glowing interior lights, the engines already activated, a pilot preparing for liftoff. The Emperor, the Empress, and Count Fenring ran toward the lighter, scrambling into the cramped passenger compartment. Shaddam stooped and struggled to get inside, while the more nimble Fenring urged the Empress in alongside him.

Nearby, another group of evacuees rushed into a second lighter, which was also prepared to leave. Reverend Mother Mohiam looked like a startled crow in her black robes. The colonel bashar pushed Leto into the Emperor's craft, crushing him against other passengers, then he climbed inside and sealed the hatch.

The Sardaukar yelled to the pilot, "Our Emperor is aboard. Go!" More nobles flooded the rooftop, rushing toward the evacuation ships. Several Sardaukar remained behind, sacrificing their lives so the lighter could take off unimpeded. They blocked more panicked guests who boiled up the narrow evacuation stairway.

The lighter's pilot lurched them into the air on suspensor engines. The alarming acceleration crushed the passengers against the bulkhead. Leto was pressed against the plaz windowport, dizzy and disoriented while the vessel spun, aligning its axis and swooping around the Imperial Monolith in its steep ascent out of the danger zone.

Looking down, Leto saw the bright museum complex below, a smear of images, countless figures running along the bright streets. A flurry of other ships rose into the air like startled dragonflies. Leto was relieved to see some others getting away at least.

Shaddam and Aricatha belted themselves into seats in the crowded passenger compartment. Fenring had squirmed into a corner, pulling his knees up to his chest against the acceleration. Leto and the colonel bashar struggled to situate themselves as heavy thrust crushed them against the deck.

"I cannot believe this," Shaddam said. "My museum complex, my festival!"

Leto forced his words out against the crushing acceleration. "All those people." He looked at the lighter's passenger compartment. "I wish we could have saved more."

"No time." The Sardaukar narrowed his gaze and added a sharp frown. "I made a risky decision to include you, Atreides. I will not hear your objections."

"You said the Emperor ordered it."

"I know the Emperor's *wishes*." The officer fell silent as they streaked higher. What did he mean by that?

Leto's heart ached for his Caladan pilot and crew, remembering how Arko had wanted to buy souvenirs for his sweetheart and his young nephews. The pilot and crew would surely have been out in the city, looking at exhibits, sampling delicacies from food vendors. Even if they had heard Leto's warning over the site-wide comm system, Arko and the others were loyal to their Duke. Even if they made it back to the space yacht, they would have waited for him, refusing to leave without Leto. They would have waited. . . .

He squeezed his eyes shut.

"Is it possibly a false alarm?" Fenring asked. "Are we overreacting?"

"No, sir," said the colonel bashar. "Duke Leto's warning is confirmed. Three sabotaged dump boxes will impact the museum complex."

"Damn this Jaxson Aru!" Shaddam shouted. "I want him found and executed—slowly and painfully."

"We must escape first, Sire, hmmm?" Fenring said. "Let us wait to be vindictive until we are safely back on Kaitain."

"They are simply objects falling from orbit," Aricatha said. "How can the aim be so precise as to strike the Imperial Monolith?"

The Sardaukar frowned, and Leto already knew the answer. "The kill zone from so many explosive, high-mass impacts will extend for dozens of kilometers. They do not need to be pinpoint accurate."

The escape ship lurched to starboard, and the acceleration increased. The pilot called back, "Here they come! I'm giving them a wide berth." The lighter rocked back and forth, buffeted by turbulence.

Leto caught a glimpse of an orange ball hurtling down through the air, a tumbling mass of molten metal like an old-style artillery projectile, with explosives added. Farther in the distance, he saw two more orange streaks, projectiles plummeting toward the surface. Leto had seen these objects from orbit and knew their size and the tons of inert mass in each of them. There was no possible way to stop them.

Shaddam's face was crimson as he stared. Working against the acceleration, Leto shifted his body so he could see through the windowport that faced the planet. The dread inside him felt stronger than gravity. Under the press of acceleration, Leto felt the small lump of the holo-player with Jessica's message. "Jessica . . . ," he whispered. "Paul . . ."

The three massive objects hammered into the surface of Otorio, one after another in quick succession, annihilating the Emperor's new city.

Leto squeezed his eyes shut an instant before the impacts, and the flare of released light still seared through his eyelids. Those sequential flashes had signified the end to thousands of lives.

"Those rare artifacts can never be replaced," Shaddam snarled.

"But we survived," Fenring said, "thanks to the astute observations of Duke Leto Atreides."

"We owe you our lives," said Empress Aricatha.

Leto felt a surge of resentment and strained against the acceleration to sit upright. "Yes, we survived. I survived."

Down below, the blazing light rippled outward. The city complex was a molten scar.

"Breathe easily, dear cousin," Shaddam said to him. "We are safe."

Leto turned back to the windowport and stared at the rising holocaust below.

When do dreams become reality, and when does reality slip into dreams?
—PRINCESS IRULAN, *The Book of Muad'Dib*

I t wasn't the first time Paul had dreamed of the mystery girl. As he slept, his mind's eye saw the young woman standing high on a rock formation, profiled against the sunset, a painter's palette of spectacular colors splashed across the sky. The sunlight was too yellow, the shadows too sharp, the terrain too dry to belong on Caladan.

The young woman wore a strange suit that clung to her form, a tube extending from her collar to her mouth. She moved with light, agile steps down a dusty path as Paul followed her, captivated. She slowed enough to make sure he followed her, and then ducked into a rocky, dimly lit tunnel.

In the dream, Paul wore an Atreides jacket, but it was scuffed and torn, as if he had been in a battle. Recently. The air was hot, dry, and dusty as he followed her inside the cleft, hurrying to keep up. His eyes adjusted to the shadows.

She paused, smiled back at him, and led him deeper into the tunnels and chambers.

He caught up with her inside a cavern and got a better look at her. She looked to be about his age, quite beautiful with an elfin face, dark red hair, and intense blue eyes that gazed at him in a way he'd never seen before. He reached out to take her hand, and she smiled again, in her special way. He knew her in his heart, somehow, but he didn't know her name. He reached out—

The image faded as he woke, gasping. Paul sat up in bed, shivering. He felt lost, longing for the mysterious young woman. He wanted the dream back, but it was gone, leaving him with only a faded image of her form, her face, and a distant recollection of the touch of her hand.

Paul closed his eyes and searched for her in the darkness of his mind, trying to return to the dream. He lay back with a sigh and finally drifted off to sleep again, still looking for her in the haze of slumber. He remembered the hot dryness of the air and tried to bring that back as a door into his vision.

Inside his bedchamber in the castle, he fell into another dream, but she was not there, no matter where he looked. This was different.

Unable to locate her or the distinctive rock formation again, he found his dream-self instead standing in the shadowy corridor of a large stone-walled structure—Castle Caladan? No, that didn't look right. In some large and imposing structure, he was running to warn his father. It was urgent! Somewhere in the darkness ahead, Duke Leto was in danger, real danger, and Paul needed to reach him in time! The corridor branched off in two directions. Which one should he take?

Acting on instinct, Paul chose the one on the left and ran headlong through the ominous shadows, barely able to see ahead. He didn't care about his personal safety, so desperate was he to warn his father.

The corridor brightened, but only a little, and ahead he saw the familiar, powerful, dark-haired Leto standing with his back to him, looking away.

"Father!" Paul called out.

The Duke did not move, did not seem to hear him.

"Father, there is danger!" It was a powerful sensation. His pulse raced, his heart pounded, though he didn't know what the danger was.

Suddenly, a trio of black-garbed assassins leaped out of alcoves and fell upon Duke Leto, stabbing him with knives. His father wore no shield and quickly succumbed to the deadly attack. Paul bounded forward to stop them, but when he threw himself in their midst, the attackers faded.

His father lay on the floor, bleeding, dying. His gray eyes stared at Paul, and he tried to reach out to his son, but did not have the strength. When Paul bent down to touch him, Leto faded beneath his fingertips, just as the assassins had. The wet red bloodstain remained on the floor where the Duke had lain.

"Father!" Paul shouted into the nightmare, then he screamed.

He awoke again and realized that he had actually cried out. Glowglobes in the room surged to full illumination. He blinked, dazzled by the light, and saw a man in the doorway, sword drawn.

"Young Master? Are you all right?" Gurney Halleck, the scarred and burly weapons master of House Atreides, lunged into the room. He looked around, ready to defend the ducal heir. "Gods below!"

Paul sat on the edge of his bed, shaking. "It's not me, Gurney. I'm safe. It's my father! He is in great danger. Right now!"

Gurney looked perplexed, rubbed the inkvine scar on his jaw with his free hand, keeping the sword ready with the other. "He is far away, on Otorio."

"But it's something terrible. The Duke is in great danger."

"How do you know?" Gurney laid a hand on Paul's shoulder.

"I just know!"

I feast on life, I feast on death.
—BARON VLADIMIR HARKONNEN

I n the bedroom wing of his Carthag headquarters, the Baron finished strangling the boy with one powerful hand. He felt dissatisfied and frustrated. Avoiding a twinge of pain from his other, broken wrist, he shoved the scrawny, naked body off the bed. The young man had resisted like a feral cat, even had the audacity to bite the Baron's lower lip, making it bleed. Now he touched his sore mouth, muttering a curse. Another injury!

After the rebel attack on the shuttle, his left hand and wrist ached in their medcast, but they were healing. The wound on his head was better, though a deep gash remained above one ear, inside his hairline. He had not expected so much resistance from his pleasure slave. Next time, he would have to ensure the drugs were stronger.

Nor had he expected such violent audacity from the Fremen rabble. More frustration. He should have been at the Padishah Emperor's gala on Otorio, conducting business, being seen. The Baron worried that Shaddam had noticed his absence, and worried more that he *hadn't*.

He swung his bare feet slowly out of the massive bed and retrieved his suspensor belt from a table. After he activated the device, his enormous body felt lighter, even agile. He liked the way the field made his skin tingle.

Two young men, only a little older than the strangled boy, pushed a curtain aside and hurried in with a towel and a robe. As the Baron stood there, they wrapped a clean white cloth around his waist and between his legs, and secured it with a clasp. They slipped the black robe over his shoulders and cinched it at the waist before backing away with simultaneous bows.

The Baron looked down at the slender, broken body on the floor and flexed his good hand. "Hand me that garbage."

They bent, lifted up the body, and placed it in his reach.

With his good hand, he clasped one of the young victim's arms and walked lightly with his suspensors, dragging the body along to a sealed and armored window. He opened the pane to a wash of dry heat and maneuvered the compliant corpse onto the windowsill. As the other two servants observed in wide-eyed silence, he grunted and nudged the body through the open window. Looking down, he watched it tumble over the side of the headquarters building and thump onto the sand-covered streets.

The Baron usually ordered underlings to do his killing, but on occasion, he liked to feel the brute force himself. The beautiful boys were like fresh flowers he could pick and discard, before selecting another one.

He watched from the high window, knowing what would happen next. Desperate people were so predictable. Poor street rabble appeared, wearing rags over their ubiquitous stillsuits, and snatched up the body, wrapping it and rushing away. According to rumor—which the Baron believed—the poorest scum in the city rendered the bodies down to reclaim water. How desperate their lives must be!

Leaving the contrast of his lavishly appointed chamber, the Baron took a lift down to the dining hall level, where more Harkonnen servants escorted him to his expanded seat at the head of the long banquet table. The other chairs in the dining hall were empty, though places had been set all around the table.

Rabban strode into the hall, accompanied by his lean younger brother, Feyd-Rautha, who was temporarily visiting from Giedi Prime. Rabban moved like an armored vehicle, while Feyd had a liquid grace. The Baron's Mentat, Piter de Vries, slithered and glided behind them, his eyes calculating. The stains of sapho juice on his lips looked like blood.

Nursing his throbbing injured hand, the Baron slumped into his chair, like a king about to hold court. "I am hungry." He called out, "Bring in our special guests."

A procession of twenty servants came forward through the main doors, each carrying a covered platter. They took positions on the long sides of the table, and one stood behind the Baron's chair.

After his nephews and Mentat seated themselves in their customary places, the Baron waved his good hand, knowing this had all been rehearsed. In clockwork unison, the servants removed the covers to reveal severed heads resting on plates—the dead rebels who had tried to commandeer the shuttle. In order to fill all the seats at the table, Rabban had rounded up and executed additional suspicious people in Carthag alleys, whether or not they had anything to do with the assassination plot. It didn't matter.

The eyes of the "guests" were open, staring into eternity.

The Baron focused on the only female among them, the pilot. "Welcome to your first baronial banquet, my dear." As he spoke, more servants hurried forth with additional platters heaped with food for the feast. Shaking with fear, they placed the food on the table and methodically filled the empty plates in front of the severed heads in a mockery of generosity. Meanwhile, other servants put slabs of meat onto the Baron's plate, then served his living guests. Poison snoopers above the table scanned the meal and indicated that it was untainted.

When the plates were full, the servants backed away, exiting quietly through doorways and leaving the Baron to his macabre feast. Rabban and de Vries looked amused, while Feyd-Rautha seemed annoyed, impatient with the spectacle. He made no secret that he would rather be back home in Harko City.

The Baron admired the huge platter before him, a roast wolfbeast haunch and a whole guinsey fowl, although he didn't tear into the meal with his usual enthusiasm. Instead, he lifted his broken hand, frowned at the medcast wrapped around it. But for the attempt on his life, he would have been feasting with all the other nobles in the grand Corrino museum complex on Otorio.

Not waiting for his uncle, Rabban began to eat messily with his hands and a large knife. Feyd and de Vries were more meticulous.

The Baron let his gaze move from severed head to severed head. The dead female's eyes seemed to look directly at him, as if she still possessed a spark of defiance. He would make sure that a full account of this private, vengeful spectacle was distributed throughout Carthag, and maybe it would quiet the simmering unrest among the desert people. His soldiers and security needed to do more.

While recovering from his injuries, the Baron could not allow anyone to see him as weak. He would not report the assassination attempt to Emperor Shaddam or his lapdog Count Fenring, but rather would concoct some other excuse for not attending the gala. He also refused to return to Giedi Prime, because that would look like he was fleeing Arrakis after the attempt on his life.

He finally began to eat, ripping a leg off the roasted fowl, but he had time to savor only one bite before he was interrupted. A uniformed Imperial messenger strode into the banquet hall without introduction. The man carried a sealed, ornate cylinder marked with the Corrino lion. "My lord Baron, I bear news directly from the Imperial Palace."

Wary that the Emperor would rebuke his absence from the gala, the Baron accepted the message cylinder with a greasy hand and unsealed the security ring. He removed the sheet of durable instroy paper and read the message as the courier quickly withdrew. The Baron turned pale.

Feyd-Rautha stared at him, intent and curious. "What is it, Uncle? You look upset."

He read with disbelief, viewing the summary of the disaster on Otorio— complete destruction of the Emperor's new museum complex. "A truly spectacular assassination attempt!" He described the report, and the others seemed both horrified and fascinated.

Piter de Vries sprang out of his chair and hurried to read the message for himself. "Did Shaddam survive?"

The Baron let his Mentat take the paper. "It seems he was evacuated in time, but many members of the Landsraad were killed. They are still counting numbers. Someone from the Noble Commonwealth claimed responsibility."

Rabban stopped chewing. "We were supposed to be there, Uncle. You would have been killed."

The Baron felt a sudden, sharp chill. "Yes! I was ready to depart—" He looked at the gory heads distributed around the banquet table, spoke to them. "Ah, it appears your little attack may have saved my life."

The slack face of the nearest dead man showed no appreciation for the news.

A sudden, unexpected death leaves deep scarring in the hearts of those left behind. The harm caused by unexpected survival, however, is less visible.
—Suk School Investigative Report, Psychological Division

Caladan welcomed Leto home with expansive oceans, rich, moist air, wild and fertile lands, and warmhearted people.

During the frantic evacuation from Otorio on that terrible night, Leto had been forced to leave everything behind except for his life. Most of those who had come to celebrate the Corrino memorial had lost even that. Now, after long delay, he traveled on a commercial transport from Kaitain with Imperial passage and papers. He could not get back home fast enough. The court chamberlain, tall and funereal Beely Ridondo, urged Leto to wait for more luxurious diplomatic-class tickets, but the Duke insisted on boarding the first ship heading out with Caladan on its route.

Leto still felt disconnected, swept up in the tragedy and the ever-growing repercussions. His mind was filled with the panicked evacuation, all those doomed people left behind while the Sardaukar hustled him aboard the escape lighter. The fiery impact of the three gigantic projectiles, the smear of incandescent devastation as he had watched from high above. . . .

Upon reaching Otorio orbit, Shaddam had commandeered the waiting Heighliner and ordered its immediate departure for Kaitain. The Guild Navigator delayed only long enough for a small flurry of escape ships to limp up out of the atmosphere. Leto's heart had ached when he saw how few vessels made it away. Sadly, his Atreides yacht and its small crew had not managed to evacuate. They had been wiped out with so many others in the blast.

In the reckoning of casualties, he was glad to learn that his old friend Archduke Ecaz had escaped along with a small crowd of nobles. In all, barely a hundred had gotten to safety—most of them because of Leto's urgent warning across the site-wide communication network. He tried to take heart from that, to grant himself a small measure of peace. Those souls were alive because of him. And he, Duke Leto Atreides, was alive.

But all those others . . .

Reports of Jaxson Aru's attack spread like shock waves throughout the Imperium, but many details were confused and uncertain. At first approximation, and surely inaccurate, 84 important Landsraad nobles had been obliterated, as well as 241 additional high-ranking family members, and uncounted locals, support staff, guards, service workers, numbering as many as ten thousand.

Once back on the capital world, with the Imperium in chaos and crisis, Leto was easily lost in the shuffle. Empress Aricatha wrote him a personal note, applauding his alertness, which had saved them. Chamberlain Ridondo provided everything he needed—clothes, money, supplies—but seemed in no hurry to help Leto arrange passage back home.

While Leto had waited, seeking travel alternatives, Reverend Mother Mohiam approached him in a side hallway of the Imperial Palace, once more offering to provide suggestions of suitable mates for Paul, many of whom had Bene Gesserit training. He found the old woman's statement intrusive and inappropriate, especially in such turbulent times. Paul's eventual bride was far from his greatest concern right now. He brushed her aside and made arrangements to leave Kaitain, glad to be gone within the hour. . . .

When the Guild ship arrived at his beautiful ocean world, Leto was in range and could finally use direct communication systems to speak with Jessica. It was the first uplifting moment he had experienced in days. On the screen, he saw the expression of joy and relief on her lovely face. Until that point, she had not even been sure he was alive, having heard only fragmented rumors of the disaster.

As the passenger shuttle left the Heighliner and landed at the Cala City Spaceport, Leto felt as if a great weight had lifted from him. The hatch opened and the ramp extended, but the other passengers and merchants held back, deferring to the Duke. He stepped forward, feeling intensely alive. He drew in a quick breath of the fresh salt air. Scudding clouds overhead presaged afternoon storms.

A crowd stood beyond the demarcation zone, wearing familiar Caladan garments—fishermen, boatwrights, innkeepers, craftsmen, wealthy merchants, and quiet servants. They let out a resounding cheer. The response buoyed him up, and tears stung his eyes, but he did not let them show.

Jessica and Paul stood at the front of the crowd, flanked by his Mentat Thufir Hawat and Gurney Halleck, with Duncan Idaho just behind them. Leto's heart swelled as Jessica locked her gaze with his, and Paul ran forward, a fourteen-year-old full of energy with coal-black hair so similar to Leto's.

Leto bounded down the shuttle ramp to meet his son, and Paul crashed into him. The young man cried out, "I had a dream you were in terrible danger!" His raw emotion unsettled Leto, who was not a man to show boundless public affection. Even with Lady Jessica, he opened his heart to her only in the privacy of their chambers.

He grasped the boy's shoulders in a hug, then held him at arm's length to look at him. "I am safe, Paul, but my injuries are here." He pressed a hand to his heart. The memories would haunt him for a long time.

Jessica glided forward with perfect grace, and Leto saw that she was using Bene Gesserit control to keep from throwing herself into his arms, as Paul had done. "My Duke," she said, her eyes sparkling like Hagal emeralds.

"My Lady." He could not remain frozen any longer, and he wrapped his arms around her in an embrace that provoked another round of cheers from the welcoming crowd.

Thufir, Duncan, and Gurney gave him a few moments with Jessica and Paul, then greeted their Duke. The broad smile on Gurney's face made the inkvine scar wriggle like a bloodworm.

As if a dam had broken, other people pressed forward. It seemed as if everyone wanted to clap him on the back, but Thufir, Gurney, and Duncan took up protective positions, giving the Duke his space.

A bearded man in heavy brown robes parted the crowd with majestic grace. The man wore a square cap embroidered with a simple fern frond. He had heavy eyebrows, bright eyes, and a smile that broke through the thick nest of his beard.

"I came to see you in person, Duke Leto Atreides, my Duke. I do not often come to such a crowded place." He looked around at the spaceport and the city, discomfited. "These . . . mountains of buildings make me uncomfortable."

"You honor me, Archvicar," Leto said.

Archvicar Torono led the ancient Muadh sect on Caladan, and he was popular and well respected in the northern agricultural reaches. Countless pundi rice farmers belonged to the introspective, untroublesome religion. The Muadh revered the land, preached peace, and concerned themselves with the bounty of the harvest, as symbolized by their colors of brown for the soil and green for the thriving rice plants.

Torono gave another bow. "When we learned what happened at the Emperor's festival, I had to bring word from my followers. We prayed for you, Duke Leto, our Duke. I came in person so that you would know. The Muadh rejoice that you have returned to us safely. The Duke of Caladan *is* Caladan, who walks among us." He spread his fingers and bent to touch the ground, then rose up as if pulling invisible lines from the world itself. He spread his hands again, dispensing the bounty. "I bring you our blessing."

When the solemn moment was broken, the people cheered again. Leto looked at his son, at his beloved concubine, and replied to the religious leader, "Thank you, Archvicar. I am truly blessed."

AT THE EVENING meal in the dining hall of Castle Caladan, Duke Leto wore his own clothes again, glad to be out of the garments provided by the

Imperial chamberlain. He took comfort in sitting with his family in his ancestral home.

Caladan was in his blood, and sea breezes were entwined in every strand of his genes. After so many generations, so many fallen ancestors whose remains lay buried on the land or distributed out to sea, how could it not be so?

He gazed across the room at the painting of his father, the Old Duke, dressed in a matador costume. The portrait showed the characteristic overconfident lilt in his smile, the superior air he flaunted because his people loved and expected it. At the opposite end of the table, Leto sat beneath the mounted head of the Salusan bull that had killed Paulus. A transparent fixative had preserved the bloodstains on the beast's sharp horns.

Lady Jessica sat at his side in a formal banquet gown, looking at Leto instead of the mounted trophy. Paul wore the uniform of a young Duke, the presumed heir. At Leto's request, the kitchens served a feast of traditional Caladan fare— honey-glazed moonfish, seasoned pundi rice, and slices of sweet paradan melon. Leto basked in the sensations of home.

Duncan Idaho joined them at dinner, as did Hawat, Halleck, and a number of advisers, ministers, and trade representatives, all celebrating the return of their Duke, though Leto did not have his mind on business, not now. Even so, the business of Caladan still needed to be done, and Leto could not let his surrogates do it alone.

Hawat ate his meal mechanically, his mind always turning with Mentat processing. His lips were stained deep red from the sapho juice he consumed to increase his mental acuity. As the first-course plates were taken away, the old veteran spoke up. "Caladan is secure, my Duke. While you were away, your staff and ministers handled everyday details. Let me take this opportunity to brief you on certain matters so you are fully aware of the state of your holdings."

The Mentat glanced down at his hands, as if reading imaginary reports there. "Pundi rice remains Caladan's most lucrative export, both in volume of shipment and solaris earned. Crop output has been stable for generations. As a longer-term strategy, we may wish to consider upgrading agricultural operations to increase yields from the terraced paddies."

"The pundi rice farmers are traditionalists," Jessica said. "They have done things the same way for generation after generation. They may take offense if we try to . . . improve things."

Thinking of the loyalty the Archvicar and his followers had demonstrated, Leto agreed with her. "I am content with our pundi rice operations as they stand. We don't always have to increase what we have. The Harkonnens may try to squeeze more and more out of their people and planets, but that is not the way of House Atreides."

Hawat conceded the point and changed subjects. "In other exports, moonfish shows the most significant uptick in outside demand." He produced reports, which Leto had no intention of reading at the moment. "The northern fisheries have expanded so we can deliver more tonnage of fillets and less-expensive by-products. Demand throughout the Imperium increases as our customer base grows. Many Landsraad nobles have acquired a taste for moonfish."

Leto muttered, "Let us hope they weren't all killed on Otorio." His comment brought a moment of awkward silence.

Hawat glanced at a man dressed in formal business attire two seats down the banquet table. "Commerce Minister Wellan has more insight into the moonfish market. He recently visited the fisheries himself—"

"Then let the man speak, Thufir," Leto said with an edge of impatience, "and let him be done with his report so I can eat in peace."

The minister seemed agitated, nervous at being put on the spot. His eyes were bright, as if a thin film of cracked glass had been laid over the irises. "Yes, our fishery operations have expanded. They are privately owned but regulated by the ducal norms imposed by your father, my Lord. The facilities are extensive— rustic but effective. The fragile nature of moonfish breeding and the unique spawning grounds present serious challenges for large-scale production, but with sonic panels providing the proper soothing harmonics, the moonfish breed as much as we could want." He brought forth a thick stack of papers, set it on the table next to his plate. His hands had a faint tremor. "Everything is detailed here."

Leto looked at his half-finished meal, closed his eyes for a second—as long as he dared to withdraw—then opened them again. "I will review it later. For now, I would like time with my Lady and my son." Realizing his words sounded like a rebuke, he gathered his calm and pulled the invisible mantle of leadership around him. "I apologize, Minister. I find the business of Caladan reassuring, and on the morrow, I will study your findings thoroughly."

Gurney Halleck reached down beside his seat and raised his baliset, balancing it on his lap and striking a brief musical chord. "Perhaps a tune is what you need, my Lord."

"Indeed, Gurney. I've been too long without music."

Jessica touched Duke Leto's forearm, letting him know her heart and thoughts were with him. He smiled softly, looked from face to face around the table. "After the spectacle on Otorio and the flashy glory of Kaitain, Caladan is much more to my liking."

*A news report is based on fact, fiction, or a combination of the two, and
is presented from a certain angle. Truth belongs to those who control that
perspective.*

—COUNT HASIMIR FENRING

All the Imperial glory around Count Fenring could not distract from the
shock waves and turmoil after the attack on Otorio. Emperor Shaddam
considered himself at war against the violent rebels.

Fenring swept into the Imperial audience chamber accompanied by a small,
thin man with an oversized head. Unfortunately, it was not the most impressive
of entrances. The other man had a distracted way of walking, sometimes veering
away and then catching himself. Fenring grabbed one of the man's spindly arms
and led him toward the throne.

The Padishah Emperor sat on a massive blue-green throne cut from Hagal
quartz. Empress Aricatha occupied her own smaller throne beside him, her eyes
intent and interested, and nearby lurked an aged woman in dark Bene Gesserit
robes, the Truthsayer Mohiam, who had also barely escaped from Otorio.

Though Shaddam brooded on his throne, he brightened to see Fenring. "Ah,
Hasimir! We have many important plans to discuss." His brow wrinkled with
impatient concern. "I see you brought your failed Mentat with you. Is he . . .
functional enough?"

Fenring motioned for his tottering companion to remain off to one side,
while he approached the dais and made a perfunctory bow. "The peculiarities
of Grix Dardik are something I must tolerate in order to obtain the full benefit
of his genius." He smiled. "For the sake of the Imperium, we need his insights.
After all, he is the one who found records of Otorio lost in the dusty archives."
He glanced at the strange little man, who seemed preoccupied with his shoe.
"And if he can discover a whole missing planet for you, Sire, what else might
he find? The Noble Commonwealth is hiding somewhere, and we must root
them out . . ."

From his throne, the Emperor regarded Fenring's peculiar companion.
Shaddam's new wife leaned closer and spoke in low tones, so that Fenring could
not make out all the words, something to do with an Imperial assignment she
wanted. Fenring knew Aricatha was constantly pressing her husband for more

responsibility and meaningful things to do. Other Empresses had rarely been allowed to sit with him in the throne room at all.

Their interaction was remarkably different from how the Emperor had treated his previous five wives, a couple of whom Fenring had tolerated, while others he had loathed. He hadn't yet decided if Aricatha would be a useful ally or a hindrance. She certainly had the powerful ruler wrapped around her finger.

While Fenring waited, the Emperor listened to his wife coax him about new duties. "Now that so many Landsraad representatives are gone, you need someone you can trust," she said. "I am capable of carrying out more extensive diplomatic assignments."

"Trust is a very difficult thing right now, my dear," Shaddam said. He looked at Fenring and raised his voice. "How widespread is this Noble Commonwealth movement? How do we find the vile Jaxson Aru and bring him to justice?"

"That is what we must discover, Sire." Glancing over at the tottering Mentat, Fenring saw Dardik's gaze wandering around. He had to pull the man back to reality, or he could drift off for hours. Count Fenring needed the Mentat to be useful right now.

He spoke Dardik's name sharply, noticed a slight jerk of his head, a rolling of the eyes. He spoke more sharply, and the eye rolling stopped. "We are here to make an important report." The Mentat returned to reality with a sudden snap. "I need you to help us with this grave political crisis."

Though brilliant, Dardik needed constant management. The slender man had failed to become a full Mentat because of his difficult personality and social maladjustment. In the Mentat school, he'd had a disturbing habit of starting arguments, debates, and even duels to the death.

But Fenring enjoyed a good debate to keep his own mind sharp, and though the eccentric genius might outthink him, Fenring could easily defeat him in personal combat. He had injured Dardik often enough to make his point, and the two men had managed to achieve a peculiar balance.

Now that he had his companion's full attention again, Fenring turned him to face the throne dais and addressed the Emperor once more. "Sire, my Mentat will talk with you directly, but I will interject the, hmmmm, niceties of conversation, if he forgets himself. He has few social graces, but his brilliance makes up for that."

"I want to hear what he has to say," the Empress said.

Shaddam waved a hand at his wife. "I have my own court Mentats, Hasimir, and this one has not even earned his basic certification. In our response to the urgent matters before us, I need only the best advice."

Fenring pursed his lips. "Sire, he was right about the existence of Otorio, wasn't he? Let us hear him out."

The Emperor sighed. "Speak to me, Mentat, and be efficient with your words. My time is valuable."

"A Mentat is always efficient with words," Dardik retorted. "My time is valuable as well."

Fenring considered killing him right there. "Issue your new findings and prove your worth!"

The failed Mentat straightened. "Background summary: More than a year ago, I discovered the supposedly lost planet of Otorio, which you then commandeered as the site of your new Imperial museum complex. In light of recent events, I researched the world even more thoroughly. Jaxson Aru's violence struck me as more than a mere political statement. It had a personal component as well."

"A personal component?" Shaddam asked. "It's clear the madman wanted to kill me and destroy the Imperium."

"The attack was also about Otorio itself, not just you," Dardik said, then after a momentary pause, he remembered to add, "Sire." He blinked, as if reassessing his calculations. "I found clear evidence that the supposedly lost planet was an unacknowledged holding of the extended Aru family, used as a quiet retreat for several generations. After being removed from his duties for the CHOAM Company, Brondon Aru, Jaxson's father, was sent to Otorio in effective exile. Jaxson spent much time on Otorio as a ward of his father."

The Mentat hummed, as if he had forgotten to include important information. "Jaxson's mother is the prominent Malina Aru, the Ur-Director of CHOAM, and his brother, Frankos Aru, is the public face of CHOAM, serving as President. Malina Aru has a third child, a daughter, Jalma, married to Count Uchan on the planet Pliesse. An interesting side note: Count Uchan is listed among the casualties in the Otorio massacre."

As the failed Mentat rattled off the string of details, Shaddam tried to absorb the connections. "Are you saying that the insignificant world I chose for my Corrino museum is actually a CHOAM stronghold?"

"Possible, but not proven. Still, Sire, it is likely that Otorio was occupied by the Aru family, personally, and your museum paved over their ancestral holdings."

Shaddam reddened. "One of the wealthiest and most powerful families in the Imperium hid an entire planet from our notice and paid no Imperial taxes on it? For how long?"

Empress Aricatha interrupted, "It was pointed out at the reception that CHOAM representatives were conspicuously absent. Did they know about the plot ahead of time? Did they stay away for their own safety?"

Fenring had heard the conclusions already, but still tried to grasp all the intricacies.

Shaddam struggled to remember. "I have met the CHOAM President at diplomatic functions, of course, and even Ur-Director Malina Aru. But Jaxson Aru? I did not recognize him from the projected holo-image. Am I supposed to know him?"

Fenring was not surprised the Emperor had forgotten. "Yes, Sire, but, hm-mmm, it likely made little impression on you."

"I seem to recall him as a boy, hyperactive and nervous," Shaddam said. "His mother had a physician tending him to calm him down. He was very intense."

Dardik continued, "Jaxson was a black sheep, sent away to Otorio with his father, presumably so he could cause no problems."

The failed Mentat gave more details about how he had arrived at his conclusions, a smattering of his supreme mental gymnastics, but the Emperor was no longer listening. Shaddam slouched back in his enormous throne and stroked his chin. He raised a hand to silence the Mentat, but Dardik kept talking.

Fenring nudged him hard in the ribs. "Enough!"

The Mentat looked confused, and a few more words sputtered out before he stopped speaking.

The Emperor dismissed them both. "Go now, so I can consider this."

Fenring bowed, then had to drag Dardik out of the chamber. The failed Mentat was already so lost in thought, he could barely walk on his own.

*There are few more terrible times in life than when a son faces the reality
of his father's death.*

—DUKE LETO ATREIDES, introduction to the authorized
biography of Duke Paulus Atreides

Not all of Duke Leto's noble duties were joyful. Today, he had a painful obligation to fulfill, and it was his own responsibility. He could not delegate it. His heart ached, but his shoulders were strong.

The wife of Arko, the pilot of Leto's space yacht, looked weary, aged by fresh grief and a hard life. Leto remembered that the pilot had referred to her as his "sweetheart," though they had been married for many years.

In addition to her sadness from losing her husband in the Otorio disaster, she seemed intimidated to be in Leto's presence in a private withdrawing room in Castle Caladan. She bowed her head in a brief greeting that made her gray-flecked hair swing forward and back. "You honor me, my Duke. This meeting was not necessary. I . . . understand."

Gently, Leto placed a hand on her shoulder and felt hard muscle and bone; she was shaking. He said, "Your husband honored me with his loyal service. I brought him to Otorio as a reward, and he lost his life because of it."

She looked up quickly. "Not through your fault, my Lord! I knew Arko all my life, and the trip to Otorio was the most excitement he ever experienced. And he was so proud to be chosen. Even if he'd known the risk, he would still have wanted to be your pilot."

Leto's heart felt heavy, knowing that the members of his retinue had been trapped, maybe hoping Leto would find a way to rescue them. They had been left behind. They had died in the fiery impact.

"The first responsibility of a Duke is the safety of his people," Leto said, breaking her gaze. His father had taught him that, an intentional shift in the words of the Landsraad code. "I failed in that duty. I will make sure that you and your family are well taken care of."

He had already met with the other surviving family members, but saved this unfortunate woman for last, knowing it would be the hardest conversation.

Arko's wife began to weep. "You've been so good to us, Duke Leto."

He wanted to insist that he didn't deserve such consideration, but those words would ring hollow, maybe even sound dismissive of the pilot's loyalty and sacrifice. Now was not the place or time. Leto would provide whatever this valiant woman and her family needed, and he would try to do better. "I will host a ceremony two days hence at Crescent Cove, to honor your husband and the others we lost on Otorio. The moon will be full."

The woman took a deep breath. "Thank you, my Lord! My children and I will be there." She left, still grieving, but somewhat uplifted.

Leto felt the weight of those deaths on his heart. *The first responsibility of a Duke is the safety of his people.* He thought of Arko and his companions, how their eyes had sparkled with eagerness as they left Caladan with him, how amazed they had been to see the renovated planet, with its Imperial museum complex, fine foods, and dazzling sights. Arko's widow had been right. The trip to Otorio might well have been the high point of their lives. Leto had meant the assignment as a reward for them, and yet . . .

Two days later, Leto, Jessica, and Paul attended the honorance under the pale white light of the full moon. The tide had come into the perfectly formed Crescent Cove, a sheltered and serene inlet north of Cala City. The bereaved families gathered for the somber celebration, along with friends and acquaintances. Hundreds had made the short journey north, crowding into vehicles or even walking. The respectful mourners gathered along the gray gravel of the cove at the waterline.

The families stood together, heads bowed. One tall, thin man, the young brother of a retinue member, stood by himself, shaking and weeping. Leto made a point of going over, putting an arm around his shoulders, and giving him a firm embrace.

Leto had ordered beautiful lily wreaths interwoven with white starflowers, one for each of the men lost on Otorio. The wreaths rested on the planks of a low fishing dock that extended into the cove. Accompanied by Paul and Jessica, Leto walked to the end of the dock and turned to look at the gathered people.

He drew a breath, ready to call on his renowned speaking ability, but the words caught in his throat. He stood for a few seconds in anticipatory silence. Paul looked up and nodded at him. Jessica's face was filled with strength and warmth. She took Leto's hand.

Leto drew support from them, as well as from the somber crowd. These people were *his* people, mourning their own. The rebel leader Jaxson Aru was to blame for all of the death and destruction. Arko and the others had merely been collateral damage, gone in the flash of impact. So unfair! The members of Leto's retinue had cared nothing for Imperial politics, but they had died nonetheless.

"I remember and appreciate every individual we are here to remember. Each of them was special to you, and to me as their Duke." He named each man aloud, making sure the mourners understood the depth of his feelings as well. This was an Atreides expression of care for his people. It was not an action that the Padishah Emperor could comprehend.

He looked down at the beautiful lily wreaths. "Paul, would you help me?" His son came forward, and together they picked up the first woven wreath. Leto spoke Arko's name, set the wreath in the water, and nudged it to drift out into the moonlit cove. Paul picked up a second one without Leto prompting him, spoke a second name, and they set the wreath adrift. Leto smiled proudly at him.

Jessica named a third person who had been lost. Working together, the three of them placed all the wreaths on the water. The flowers drifted gracefully away on the gentle ripples. The full moon lit the somber group and somehow lifted them up.

A few moments later, Leto heard a muttering sound and turned, gazing out at the calm waters of the sea, where the wreaths continued to float. This protected cove was home to many luminous jellyfish that now swam forward, drawn to the floating flower wreaths. Like a galaxy of pale blue stars, the glowing creatures clustered around the flowers and escorted them out to sea, as if souls were wafting away into the deep currents.

The people at the honorance gasped, and Leto even saw a few smiles among them. He loved these people. He never wished to do them wrong. He looked at the silvery jellyfish and whispered, "Thank you."

Then he glanced at Paul and Jessica beside him, the other two pillars of his strong family. He turned to face his people and raised his voice.

"Thank you."

YOUNG PAUL WAS consumed with sudden thoughts of mortality. In the great dining hall of Castle Caladan, he stared at the monstrous bull's head and the blood of his grandfather still on the horns. Years ago, Leto had told him the story. "It is an Atreides tale for you to know and never forget, but do not cry when you think about it. Remember your grandfather's strength, and one day, you will be strong, as he was."

Though he was just a boy at the time, Paul had promised to be strong. "Yes, sir."

Now the mounted head was a striking reminder that *his* father had almost died, too. Countless innocent victims had been killed on Otorio. If Duke Leto had been in a different part of the reception hall, if that Sardaukar officer hadn't rushed him to the escape lighter—almost on a whim!—Leto would have been vaporized along with the rest of the complex.

A chill ran down the young man's back. Although his father had gone to the Imperial gala without enthusiasm, he had done it to fulfill his political obligations, representing House Atreides and Caladan. And he had nearly died, an innocent victim of a terrorist attack. Such a thin line of mortality!

Thinking back, Paul couldn't even remember if he had said goodbye to his father before the Duke set off for Otorio. It was likely just a casual farewell without any notion that it could have been the last time he ever saw Leto.

If the Duke of Caladan had died, where would that have left Paul and his mother? He was the only son, the heir apparent . . . but did a fourteen-year-old boy have enough political acumen to hold House Atreides against what would surely have been strong political maneuvers in the Landsraad? Sensing weakness, would some other family have tried to oust the illegitimate Atreides son?

He realized that same situation must be happening on scores of worlds even now, in the wake of Otorio.

Paul took a long breath, his gaze unfocused. He felt frustrated. Duke Leto wanted the best for his family fortunes and for his son. He made sure that Paul trained hard, with the most intense instructors, and the young man did his best to meet expectations. His father placed a heavy burden on him, and Paul placed the same on himself.

As the young man stood unobtrusively in the dining hall, the chief server, a dark-skinned man in formal castle livery, tested the spiderlike poison snoopers dangling over the long table. Humming quietly to himself, the server held a plate of carefully measured poisonous powders and liquids beneath each detector. Small indicators turned red as he moved down the length of the table, and then reverted to green when he passed. All the while, Thufir Hawat monitored the calibration from the doorway with a dour expression, plainly not satisfied, but that was the way of the chief of security.

One of the snoopers failed, and Hawat barked orders to a man in work clothes. "Replace this entire unit, and I want to see it tested again."

The man hurried out of the hall to get a replacement.

Paul appreciated their attentiveness. Even here on Caladan, they could not let down their guard and had to worry about a new War of Assassins, like the one he and Duncan barely survived a year ago. There were rules governing inter-House warfare, and each noble knew them, but mistakes happened, excuses were made, exceptions slipped through the cracks. . . .

Paul took nothing for granted, knowing full well he would be the primary target for any enemies, because he represented the future of House Atreides. Duke Leto had once told him the harsh truth. "To lose my son is to lose our future." Thus, he insisted that Paul always remain alert, practice situational awareness, and never fail to have a contingency plan. Disturbing words, and hard to hear, but Paul would rather know the truth than be left in ignorance of it. His father's next statement, though, stood out like a beacon in his memory: "Prepare to live."

Paul faced other challenges appropriate for the son of a Duke. In the strict nobility rules of the Imperium, he was still only a bastard, an "assumed" heir.

Leto had named Jessica his bound concubine, which provided some security, but everything could change if political expediency required his father to marry some other noble daughter, as he had almost done with Ilesa Ecaz. Leto had promised Jessica that would not happen again, that he did not intend to accept any other offer of marriage. Paul wanted to believe him.

If Leto had died on Otorio, Paul knew that Thufir, Gurney, Duncan, and the Atreides troops would remain loyal to him as the Duke's son, but Emperor Shaddam IV could easily reassign the fief and deliver Caladan to some other noble house. It was unsettling to consider.

Though he loved and even revered his father, Paul also resented him for not marrying his mother. The decision was wise in one way, foolish in another. As Thufir might have said during one of his intense thought exercises, Paul was not an objective observer in such matters.

Finished with calibrating the poison snoopers, the chief server and his companions departed, leaving Paul alone in the hall. On a side table, he found paper and a stylus and took them to his customary place at the table, to his father's right-hand side. He needed to organize and record his thoughts. He stared at the blank surface, trying to will his emotions into words.

He had barely sketched out a few unsatisfactory lines before Leto himself entered the hall. When Paul looked up and saw him, he slid the paper aside to conceal what he was doing.

Leto frowned. "Secrets between us, son?"

"No secrets. I was writing you a letter. I thought it would be best to be logical and judicious about my words."

Leto at first seemed amused, then noted his son's seriousness. "Oh? And the subject?"

"I would rather write it out, choose my phrasing, but—" He inhaled a deep breath. "I might as well get it off my chest right now."

"This sounds serious." Leto took his customary seat, placed his elbows and hands on the table, and regarded Paul as if he were an important diplomatic visitor.

Wrestling with his thoughts, the young man expressed his uncertainty, his concerns for himself, his future, and the future of House Atreides, and his mother. After a brief pause, while Leto listened intently, he also revealed his fear—and anger—at how close he had come to losing his father. Duke Leto had indeed escaped, by mere good fortune, but the brush with death had chilled Paul to the core.

Leto did not interrupt. When Paul had said everything that was on his mind, sure that it must be a jumbled, irrational mess, he finished by saying, "That's what I wanted to write in the letter." His hands and voice shook with the passion of his emotions, and he tried to compose himself using Bene Gesserit techniques, but it did not work well.

Leto considered his response for a long moment. "You are my son and heir, Paul, and everyone knows it. Your opinion is valuable to me, but Imperial politics place certain obligations on a person of my station."

A ball of ice formed in the pit of Paul's stomach. What was his father saying?

Leto continued, "You have studied history and politics, the Landsraad code, the Great Convention, the rules of conflict and alliances between houses. House Atreides is a Great House, but not a particularly powerful one, and that is fine with me. My peers in the Landsraad accept me well enough, but after the Otorio massacre, I fear that a large part of our social fabric could shift, maybe even unravel. We are facing a time of turmoil, and many conditions may change."

Paul felt his cheeks grow hot, wondering if his father was once again considering a political marriage, which would shift his role and that of his mother. Assailed by unaccustomed insecurity, the young man rose to his feet, not wanting to hear any justifications his father might offer.

"If you will excuse me, sir. I'll return to my room to reflect on what you said." He tried not to let Leto see his distress, but could not hide it. "I will do my best to understand."

I have faced the most extreme conflicting loyalties. And I made my decision.

—LADY JESSICA

The next morning, Paul faced off against both Duncan and Gurney in shield fighting. They put him through more than the customary exercises, attacking from two directions in one lesson. As always, his trainers fought to their utmost and expected Paul to do the same.

"A real assassin would show you no mercy, lad," Gurney said, striking harder.

Wiping sweat from his brow with his free hand, Duncan was especially complimentary of Paul's technique. "Excellent work today. You're close to passing a threshold that's been holding you back. For two months, you've been at a plateau in personal combat, and we need to push you beyond it. Even if it takes two of us."

"Aye, a true statement," Gurney said. "I saw the same thing. There's something . . . more about you now."

Paul beamed, glad that they had noticed. "I practiced a couple of specific techniques over and over, just as both of you taught me to do." His mother had also been quietly teaching him Bene Gesserit skills, helping him master muscular control beyond any ability Duncan or Gurney possessed. He grinned at his two opponents now. "Every aspect makes me a better fighter. Learn each method slowly and get it right before moving on to the next."

Gurney laughed, a deep roar. "So now you think *you're* in charge of these lessons and not us? You decide when you move on, and when you hang back?"

"Ah, but if I'm doing what you tell me to do, doesn't that mean you're still in charge of me?" Paul asked.

"And a slippery lad you are, fighting with both words and blades."

Though it was designed to prepare him for life-or-death encounters, Paul enjoyed his training, was proud of his progress. But he did not let himself grow overconfident, because each stage of improvement only pointed to some higher rung he needed to reach. Always more to learn, always more to know.

The trio clasped arms as they did at the end of a particularly good session, then parted. Paul showered and changed into a simple tunic and trousers, then went back to his quarters, which were like a museum of his young life—sports and fencing equipment, an assortment of projectile weapons, framed images of his parents and Paul on his fourteenth birthday the previous month.

He stood at the center bank of windows and gazed out on the Caladan Sea, which stretched to the horizon. Looking down the sheer cliff beneath his window, he saw the white spray of surf hitting the rocks. Out on the waves, fishing boats bounced around in the whitecaps. An ornithopter buzzed overhead on its security patrol, like one of the scout craft Thufir Hawat liked to fly, keeping watch over House Atreides.

The thought of the Mentat teacher and his frequent admonishments made Paul suddenly self-conscious. Thufir insisted that he never sit or stand with his back to a door. Situational awareness. As part of this, the young man always knew where doors were, where threats could arise, what direction a potential assassin might use, and what Paul's escape routes were. His room had a second door that led to his private bedchamber, where he could take refuge in an attack. He had even practiced escaping through the balcony door and climbing down the castle wall, or up to other balconies.

He turned to face the closed door with one hand on a dagger at his waist. He'd heard a small noise out in the corridor, but at the sound of a soft knock, a *familiar* knock, he let himself relax. "Enter, Mother."

Jessica opened the door and stepped through. She looked regal with her bronze hair secured in a formal wrap with a blue sapphire pin on the front. It had been a gift from Duke Leto on a special occasion. Her expression was serious, concerned. "I heard you and your father having a tense conversation yesterday. I sensed the uneasiness in your words, maybe more than he did. Is there anything I can do to help?"

Paul looked at her for a long moment. She was also one of his teachers. Thanks to her lessons, he could adjust his breathing, his pulse, his reflexes. Jessica was far more advanced than he was, could even control her metabolism, alter some of her biochemical processes.

He had tried to use those Sisterhood techniques to steady his own doubts, but he had not entirely succeeded. He was disappointed in himself, though he refused to admit it to her.

Jessica saw his expression, recognized the Atreides pride not unlike that which she often saw in Leto. She stood before Paul now, saw that he was hurt, trying to show her support. She wanted to reach out and hug him, but held back. "You still seem distressed, but if you don't want me here—"

"I didn't say that." He smiled a little. "I'm still processing."

She touched his arm. "Will you talk about it?"

He disengaged. "I always appreciate your concern for me."

"My *love* for you," she corrected him.

"I already talked with my father about my future and his plans for House

Atreides." He turned to the window. "But he is the Duke." That single phrase raised, and answered, so many questions.

She moved to his side and stood gazing out at the ocean with him. Jessica understood Paul's pride, his streak of independence. She watched him, but did not pamper him. Leto would not want his son to seem weak. Paul was finding out who he was, growing up and breaking free of his parents. It was a normal process.

With all her Bene Gesserit responsibilities and training, Jessica had stepped into a role here far more complex than she had ever anticipated. Though she still had unbreakable ties to the Sisterhood, she had become a vital part of House Atreides, a true companion to Leto. But her most important job was to be a mother to Paul. The Sisterhood, however, might disagree. . . .

She considered all the Bene Gesserit around the Imperium, the Sisterhood's unspoken but widespread agenda, how they watched noble houses and pulled the strings of government. Even though Jessica had been raised in the Mother School, she was not power hungry. She was content, even happy, as the bound concubine of Leto Atreides and the mother of Paul. She had found love, despite Bene Gesserit warnings against emotions. The Sisterhood's paramount command was to put the order above her personal interests. Jessica was doing both, walking a fine line and succeeding.

She gazed sidelong at her teenage son and thought of his potential. When Paul was just a child, she'd often watched him at play, but now he had turned to more serious pursuits, training to become the next Duke of Caladan. No longer a boy, but not quite a man, either. She wished he could enjoy what little freedom and innocence he might still have. He had no friends his age, no flirtations or dalliances with local girls. At least he had Gurney Halleck and Duncan Idaho as his trainers, protectors, and friends.

She said, calm and firm, "As the Duke's son, you must decide and define your role, your identity. How will you handle yourself?"

As he stared out to sea, he showed no sign that he'd heard her. Jessica could see he was deep in thought. Silently, she slipped out of the room.

DISTURBED AFTER THE previous night's unexpectedly weighty conversation with his son, Leto consulted Thufir Hawat. The warrior Mentat had been Leto's own mentor and trainer when he was young. Hawat had just returned from copiloting a patrol aircraft on its rounds, verifying that House Atreides security was being performed to his satisfaction.

The two met in the Atreides family museum, a small collection of valuable artifacts that was open to the public twice a month. Earlier in the morning, a burglar had been arrested by Hawat's guards, caught trying to steal one of the first Atreides hawks, a small metal sculpture several centuries old. The very attempt had exposed an unusual lapse in watchfulness, which concerned Leto more than the attempted robbery. The old Mentat quickly vowed to review all household patrols and external security measures.

Leto was distracted by his racing thoughts, though. "I am certain you will get to the bottom of it, Thufir." After the conversation with Paul, he had finally come to a decision. He remained silent for a moment, and then because Hawat was such a close personal friend, he brought up the other matter that had been troubling him.

"My son is concerned about his role in House Atreides, his future as my heir." He inhaled. "And he is correct to worry. Two years ago, everything was thrown into doubt when I agreed to marry Ilesa Ecaz. His stability vanished, and he's never forgotten. If I ever formally married, a legitimate heir would call his own succession into question. Now, after the attack on Otorio, there will be much upheaval in the Landsraad, and many more marriage alliances will be available—and required." He shook his head. "Though I have asked the Emperor for nothing, I've had to publicly keep my options open, at the expense of my son and the woman I love, I fear."

"Politics change," Hawat said. "Someday a wedding to another House might become necessary."

"But what about the people I am hurting?"

Hawat drew his heavy eyebrows together. "It is a political reality, my Lord, and all you can do is diminish the damage. Show Paul and Jessica the love they seek, but hold your ground. Lady Jessica is fully aware of this fact. As is Paul."

Leto looked up at him. "I do not intend to set Jessica aside. If a marriage alliance is required, we must bow to political necessity, at least for appearances' sake. But I have another solution."

Hawat straightened, intrigued.

"Paul is now fourteen," Leto said. "If the Landsraad demands that House Atreides consider a marriage alliance, then let us approach the matter from a different direction, one that will at least keep them talking and distracted."

"How can I help, my Lord?"

"I want you to research and suggest candidates for a possible marriage to Paul."

Standing beside the Golden Lion Throne while the Emperor held court, the Sardaukar commander remained motionless. He could not allow outsiders to see that he was simmering and alert for danger.

Colonel Bashar Jopati Kolona had been at Otorio and investigated Duke Leto's warning of suspicious activity. He himself had ensured the evacuation of the Emperor and his immediate retinue. He would never allow such a threat to happen again.

Now Landsraad nobles came forward into the Imperial audience chamber to express their concern for their beloved Shaddam IV, making certain they were noticed and remembered. They mourned all those killed in Jaxson Aru's heinous attack, but the Sardaukar guard could tell that every one of these people also had their eyes on the empty seats, vacant holdings, and wealth that might be up for grabs. . . .

For most of his life, Jopati Kolona had watched how Imperial politics shaded reality, changed the recording of history, and swept disfavored noble families into obscurity. Jopati's own Great House had been overthrown many years ago in a scheme concocted by Emperor Elrood and Duke Paulus Atreides, an act of treachery that the man would never forget or forgive.

Shaddam's father had somehow convinced, or blackmailed, Paulus Atreides to launch a surprise attack on the House Kolona homeworld of Borhees, killing some of Jopati's family members, driving the young man, along with his father and brothers, into hiding. Eventually, Duke Paulus had tracked down the guerilla fighters, with—Jopati knew now—the secret aid of Imperial Sardaukar disguised in Atreides uniforms. Young Jopati Kolona and his brothers had been captured, then exiled to the prison planet of Salusa Secundus, where they were recruited and trained as Sardaukar themselves.

After a lifetime in the ruthless military corps, the colonel bashar had no remaining House, but he did not forget. He had excelled among the Sardaukar, rose to become an officer, and now served directly at the Emperor's side. He was loyal, but always remembered that his family had been wiped out, their holdings stripped away. It left him with perpetual dark feelings, an enmity that he concealed from everyone.

The people who had committed that terrible betrayal were gone, dead for years, but House Atreides and House Corrino remained. On the other hand, the colonel bashar could not forget how young Duke Leto Atreides had surprised him with an unexpected act of generosity and honor. . . .

EXHAUSTED AFTER HOLDING court for hours, Emperor Shaddam retired to his quarters to rest and ponder. He had not slept well since the Otorio mess, wrestling with his many possible responses and reactions—if only he knew where to strike. He had appointed several commissions to dig deeper into the Noble Commonwealth movement, to uproot further sedition. Was Jaxson Aru just an impetuous lone wolf with a personal grudge? How widespread was this supposed uprising whose goal was to end millennia of Corrino rule?

Empress Aricatha went about her own activities to discuss the remodeling progress with a construction crew supervisor in the north wing of the palace. Though Shaddam wanted to mount a dramatic response to the rebels—wherever they might be—his wife insisted that the work of the Imperium must continue for the sake of appearances. She even advised downplaying the disaster on "that minor planet."

In his plush apartments, Shaddam reclined on a daybed, propping himself up on pillows, but knowing he wouldn't sleep. So many problems! He realized he was not well liked among the nobles. Much of the Landsraad would even applaud the breakup of the Imperium, but he could not believe they would engage in an outright civil war, as Jaxson Aru advocated.

He had noted the names of the most outspoken nobles, but Fenring advised—and was probably correct—that the loudest ones were likely the least problematic. The quiet, insidious traitors would cause far more damage.

He had a complete list of those who had come to his celebration on Otorio, and none of them could have known what Jaxson intended to do. It would have been suicide. Conversely, he knew which noble families had made excuses and chosen not to attend. For now, Shaddam had no hard evidence that all those families had actively joined the rebel movement. Only suspicions.

Fenring had helped him compile a list of those he considered loyal, as well as a maddeningly large group of those who remained ambivalent—nobles poised to go in either direction. Could anyone be a bystander in a civil war? Shaddam would watch them closely, having his associates note every move they made, every word they said. After the massacre on Otorio, there were many Landsraad seats to fill, and he needed to choose the right people.

As expected, he did not sleep, but managed to rest a little. Ever since

ascending to the Golden Lion Throne, he'd had so many worries. Shaddam recalled how he had longed to become Emperor, all those years of waiting and
scheming, how he and Fenring initiated the long, slow poisoning of Elrood. And
now this. . . .

He stepped out onto a north balcony from which he could look across the expansive garden courtyard. He saw his lovely wife speaking with the construction
supervisor accompanied by lanky Chamberlain Ridondo and Aix Nibs, a small,
feisty man responsible for monitoring the remodel. Nibs always carried a rubber
truncheon with him to emphasize his decisions.

Aricatha and Ridondo both had offices in the wing where the remodeling
was taking place, and the two often met, even shared meals as they discussed
long-term plans for the Imperial Palace. Shaddam knew their friendship was entirely innocent; he'd sent investigators to make certain of that. He was glad,
hoping his sixth wife would last longer than the others. Aricatha had a way
about her. . . .

The remodeling work seemed like child's play compared to what Shaddam
had to do from the Imperial throne. The Empress led the supervisor to an area
where three workers were laying tile, and she seemed dissatisfied with something.
Moments later, the men began tearing out the tiles to redo them. Aricatha had
a good eye.

Leaving Nibs to supervise the work, the Empress departed with Ridondo.
As if to impress her, the little man shouted at the construction supervisor and
waved his truncheon. The supervisor backed up, and the fearful tile workers
bolted, but Nibs whacked two of them on the backs of their legs as they ran. A
man stumbled, and Nibs landed one more blow on his back before he managed
to get away. The workers hovered in the shadows, waiting for Nibs to calm down.

Before long, Aricatha returned from the construction site to join Shaddam
in his Imperial suite. She smiled at him, but he was troubled with what he had
just seen. "You say you would like more responsibility and diplomatic duties. Was
that little episode diplomatic? Sending Nibs after those men with a truncheon?
A bit barbaric." He made it clear that he did not necessarily disapprove.

Frown lines formed on her forehead. "I believe it was effective. They know I
am a stern taskmaster, and you will see the results soon."

"My dear, are you certain you have the patience or finesse to be a diplomat?"

Her expression hardened. "Give me the chance, and I will prove it."

He admired her toughness. "Then . . . we will have to find something for you."

THAT EVENING IN his private study, the Emperor decided to take bold
action. He issued a proclamation that declared Jaxson Aru an outlaw and placed
a huge price on his head, the largest Imperial bounty in the historical record.

As he sat in his office signing the pronouncement, Shaddam studied preliminary reports from his investigative commissions, disturbed that they had found evidence of the Noble Commonwealth movement dating back at least two centuries. It now appeared the sedition was spreading, albeit quietly.

There was nothing quiet about Jaxson Aru's attack on Otorio, though. He wondered why the rebels had made such a drastic change in their tactics. They had not previously resorted to violence.

Angry, the Emperor looked for some way to respond to the Otorio attack, to make everyone understand how serious he was. The sheer *cost* of the Otorio debacle enraged him! How would he pay for all that destruction?

Obviously, he needed to implement some kind of surtax to pay for his expensive museum, as well as the cost of increasing security and swelling the ranks of his Sardaukar. He would have to dredge up the money from somewhere.

The solution came to him as he realized who could, and would, bear the burden of such a substantial tax. Since everyone in the upper classes used the spice melange, and would never give it up, he would immediately impose a spice surtax, with the funds to be devoted to increasing Imperial security.

It had not escaped his notice that Baron Harkonnen—his siridar-governor on Arrakis—had conveniently found a way to avoid the gala on Otorio. Was the Baron part of the Noble Commonwealth movement, too? How insidious was this unrest?

He summoned Count Fenring again, but his mind was already made up. As the Imperial Spice Observer, Fenring would go back to Arrakis to impose the new surtax. What better way to affect everyone in the Imperium, generate enormous revenue, and make them pay attention?

The proper selection of a marital partner is critical for the people involved, individually and collectively. It affects more than just the future of the couple, and can have a bearing on galactic politics.

—DUKE PAULUS ATREIDES

The message cylinder from the Bene Gesserit Mother School—an innocuous-seeming note, but marked with a special sign—was delivered directly to Jessica. The words came from Mother Superior Harishka herself, wishing her well and offering bland news about the Sisterhood.

Jessica felt a chill, knowing the message was far more important than it appeared.

The raised dots on the paper, that would look like imperfections or flyspecks to most, formed a complex code that her special proctor, Reverend Mother Mohiam, had taught her. Jessica went to her private withdrawing room, sat, and ran her fingers over the paper, carefully reading the Mother Superior's coded words again and again.

The hidden message was disturbing. "It has come to our attention that Leto Atreides is considering marital matches for his son, Paul. Upon thorough assessment of our breeding program, we must cut off specific undesirable bloodlines now. Certain names are likely to come up as candidates.

"By order of the Sisterhood, you are to remove the following names from consideration, by any means necessary. The Bene Gesserit cannot allow the bloodline of Paul Atreides to mix with these Houses. We have other plans. Do as you are commanded."

The names followed, also in dotted code, and Jessica committed them to memory. Some of the family names were familiar, and others were completely unknown to her. Nir Piriya, Selenity dar Okun, Maria Sydow, Noria Bonner, Maya Ginia, Tarisse Cambour, Sun-Mae Brandenberg, Hecate Dinovo.

Jessica was troubled. How could they have known so quickly? Then she remembered that Leto had mentioned the idea among the Landsraad nobles, and he had seen Mohiam there. After surviving Otorio, he had been waylaid on Kaitain for a few days until he found passage back to Caladan. He might have floated the possibility, beginning to build the framework for Paul, and if her old teacher had heard even a whispered hint . . .

At first, she was angry to receive such a brusque command from the Bene Gesserit. Not only were they meddling in Landsraad alliances and House Atreides matters but interfering in the choice of a future mate for her son.

Yet why would she be surprised? She had been raised and trained by the Sisterhood, and still had a strong loyalty to them. Though those bonds and obligations did not often come up in daily life here on Caladan, they were always present and in her awareness. Jessica could not forget. While she knew of the existence of the extensive breeding program, and she herself hoped for great things from Paul, she did not know the details of the Sisterhood's vast plans.

Completely oblivious to such machinations, Thufir Hawat was presently studying the family trees of Landsraad members and developing a list of suggestions for Paul. Jessica had no personal stake in any of these names, and if she defied the Mother Superior's wishes, the Bene Gesserit had invisible strings they could pull and subtle ways to punish her if she refused. How could she possibly eliminate all of these names from consideration? Would she have to lie? Leto was a proud man, and if he ever learned of the Sisterhood's interference, he would probably choose one of the excluded women on purpose, just to spite them.

No, Leto could never know the instructions had come from the Mother School. He already harbored a deep resentment toward the Bene Gesserit, even though she was training Paul in important Sisterhood techniques.

Jessica considered resisting, but the Bene Gesserit had a hold on her. Technically, they could still command her and she had to obey, although they had been wise enough to use a soft touch in the years since she had been contracted as concubine to Leto Atreides. This was one of the first blatant requests they had ever made.

She drew a deep breath, remembering all she had learned on Wallach IX. Her first inclination was to resist their message of command just because she resented it—and secretly her love for Duke Leto overrode any obligations she held to the Sisterhood—but if culling out some candidates was so vital to the Bene Gesserit, she was obligated to at least research the names.

She had to find a way to serve both loyalties.

WHEN THUFIR HAWAT finished his list of suggested candidates for Paul, Duke Leto met with him as well as Jessica to discuss his son's future wife. There were many political, financial, and personal considerations. As head of House Atreides, Leto had to make the best choice balanced among many alternatives, while also doing right by Paul.

He remembered his father's strained, decaying relationship with Lady Helena from House Richese. Certainly, on paper, that match of two noble houses must have seemed ideal. It was not, and Leto wouldn't fall into that trap. Hawat was analytical, but Jessica would help him make the right decision using her heart.

He decided to hold the discussion down in his fishing shack, a place he usually preferred to go by himself. Old Duke Paulus had built it as an isolated, rustic sanctuary where he could get away from his sharp-edged wife, and Leto also found the place relaxing, much less formal than his private study or the war room in the castle. He felt it was a better place to talk openly about such matters.

A mechanical lift connected the shack to the cliff above, but Leto preferred to use the steep stairs. He found the open air invigorating, and the view inspired him, looking out to sea and back up at the high towers of Castle Caladan. Leading the way, Leto descended a wooden staircase made slick by the moist air, and Jessica followed with graceful steps. Reaching the private structure in a sheltered cove at the base of the cliffs, Leto opened the door with a disconcerting creak and gestured gallantly inside. "After you, my Lady."

Leto activated the warm glowglobes inside the main room, while Jessica tended to the thermal heaters to dispel the damp chill. No one had been here for more than a month. She glanced around. "This place is even more . . . austere than the last time I saw it."

"It's hardly a romantic hideaway, but I like the simplicity. When we get back, our castle suites will look much more comfortable by comparison." He heated a pot of fresh water on the small stove. "I have tea, so we are not entirely without amenities."

Jessica set out mugs. "I understand why you like it, just as you and Paul enjoy your rugged camping expeditions each year."

They heard the mechanical noises of the lift as it descended the cliff tracks. Leto opened the door of the shack as Hawat arrived. Muttering, the grizzled old Mentat walked out onto the dock, favoring his left leg, which still bore scars from being gored during one of the Old Duke's bullfights, years ago. He carried a leather valise, which he guarded as if it contained the codes for the family atomics. When he saw Leto, he tried to walk normally. Out of respect, the Duke pretended not to notice and gestured him inside.

Nets, poles, and other angling gear hung on the shack's wooden walls, along with mounted trophies. Hawat looked at the largest stuffed fish, which had iridescent scales, bulging eyes, and ferocious-looking spines. "Ah, I was with your father when he caught that. The battle exhausted him as much as any bullfight. He said it was the best fish he ever tasted, though. Lady Helena declared the meal . . . adequate."

Leto laughed. "I should invite you here more often, old friend."

Hawat set his valise on the table. "That will not be necessary, my Lord. I am perfectly content with a drafty castle."

Jessica handed mugs of steaming tea to both men and took one for herself.

Leto motioned the Mentat toward a sturdy chair at the table, a chair he himself usually sat in. Hawat set the leather case in front of him. "As you requested, my Lord, I have compiled a report on your son's prospective marriage alliances. These are the names I feel would be most beneficial for House Atreides."

"In a political sense," Jessica said. "But there is more to picking a mate. We are curious to see which choices you think would make a good wife for our son."

The Mentat glanced at her, then turned his attention back to the Duke. "I analyzed many factors and organized them for your consideration. You can of course give additional weight to subjective personal matters." He displayed a long list of names. "No ordinary match will do for the heir to House Atreides, the future Duke of Caladan."

Leto leaned forward to scan the list, with Jessica close beside him. He breathed in the faint honeysuckle scent of her hair.

Hawat produced documents from the valise and removed a small holoprojector, but did not activate it. "Searching through the Landsraad houses, I identified families with viable daughters within a reasonable age range. I had to establish my own parameters, since you did not specify how soon you would wish Paul to marry."

Leto frowned. "We are merely exploring possibilities right now. He is still young." He looked at Jessica, and she nodded in appreciation.

Hawat opened the dossier. "Given the limitations, I found nearly thirty possibilities. It is only the first sifting, so as to provide as many viable options as possible."

There were so many Major and Minor Houses in the Landsraad, Leto was surprised even Hawat could remember all their names. Some were familiar to him, others completely new. Octavia Tootu, Danielle Kronin, Cae Norn, Rondi Constance Urda, Junu Verdun, Hecate Dinovo, Nir Piriya, Maya Ginia, Noria Bonner, Greta Naribo, and many more. After glancing over them a couple of times, they stopped having meaning. Jessica scrutinized the list, and Leto saw her briefly stiffen, then hide her reaction.

He sighed, unsettled even to discuss the matter. "Paul still seems too young, but I know we must face political reality. I have borne this burden for too long, dangling the possibility of a marriage alliance to *me*. By letting the Landsraad know we are open to considerations for Paul, we divert the attention and pressure from me. I do not intend to marry." He looked at Jessica. "I am content with my Lady."

She touched his hand. "I am also watching out for Paul. Even though we may evaluate these suggestions, we are not required to accept just any betrothal. For the present, this is a pro forma discussion. It will keep the gossips talking, however." Her green eyes sparkled. "What do we know of these young women? And how can we be sure Paul would even find them attractive? If their personalities are compatible?"

"Is that a primary factor?" the Mentat asked, as if the question itself intrigued him.

"It is still my decision," Leto said, "but I would prefer not to make Paul miserable." He drove back a brief flash of memories of shouting behind his parents' closed door, the friction that oozed through the castle halls, the separate bedchambers they had maintained for the last decade of their marriage. "But I think he will do his duty for House Atreides."

"That he will, my Lord," Hawat said. He spread papers on the rough surface of the old table. Each sheet held a printed image of a different young woman, along with reports on their families, holdings, the parents, Landsraad rankings, and past voting patterns of the Houses. "Each candidate has advantages and disadvantages, which I attempted to quantify. You want to negotiate the best dowry alliance possible."

He showed names, turning the pages to reveal the candidates. Jessica said, "That one, Nir Piriya, I have heard she is a shrew and thoroughly unpleasant."

Leto was surprised. "And how have you heard that? Some Sisterhood whisperings and backstabbing?"

She flinched, but chuckled quickly to cover it. "I am the Duke's lady, and it is my business to monitor other noble families. You think it is a new idea to imagine who might eventually become a wife for Paul? I have even looked at Princess Irulan. Maybe only a daughter of the Emperor would be good enough for him."

Hawat grunted in surprise, and Leto smiled at her. "You like to dream!"

"I have extraordinarily high hopes for our son." She turned back to the list and offhandedly suggested Hecate Dinovo be put on the bottom of the names while Hawat paid particular attention to Maya Ginia, Octavia Tootu, Cae Norn, Greta Naribo, Junu Verdun, and Noria Bonner. Jessica found many of them acceptable, though she expressed reservations about Ginia and Bonner. Leto gave them due consideration.

"I want my son to have more than I ever had," he said. "I remember hearing my parents arguing about my own marriage prospects, but I never got to meet any of the young women they considered. I was only fifteen when my father was killed, and that process was disrupted." His voice trailed off. "Can Paul not have a woman he likes and respects, who is also a solid political match?"

"There is more involved in the decision than family statistics," Jessica said. "A true life partner cannot be based merely on numbers."

Hawat frowned, seeming to take her comment as criticism. "We are advisers, but this is ultimately the Duke's decision."

She gathered her pride. "Who better than his concubine to help choose a wife?"

He looked at Jessica, remembering his promise to her after the murder of Ilesa Ecaz. "I will set aside any possibility of a political marriage of my own. You are the only woman I love, the only woman I will *ever* love, but Paul has a duty to

House Atreides. We will make the best choice for him." Leto activated the holo projector to view more detailed profiles of the candidates.

Hawat's projector flashed images of a young brunette and her family estate. On the recording, she strolled along with grace, walking a large dog. The young woman read documents, she studied mathematics, she gave a well-received speech in a university setting. "This one is Greta Naribo, scholarly, somewhat serious, and from a wealthy, influential family."

Leto nodded. "I've met her father. He's in the transport business, shipping specialized goods across the Imperium under an arrangement with the Guild and CHOAM. Lord Naribo is a little stuffy, but I've seen worse." He paused, then added as an afterthought, "And the girl is quite pretty."

Jessica added, "She seems to be a pleasant young woman who does not put on airs."

Hawat moved on. "The next candidate is Junu Verdun, youngest daughter of Duke Fausto Verdun. I was quite interested in her and her family. House Verdun rules the planet Dross and has been working hard to expand its reach."

"'Dross'?" Jessica asked. "Doesn't that mean 'something worthless'? Not an auspicious name for a holding."

Hawat recited from his Mentat knowledge, "The planet was named in the early days of the Imperium. It is not overly rich in resources, nor is it a harsh or difficult place. It is remarkably . . . average."

"Perhaps the world's name explains Duke Verdun's ambition to add more worthwhile holdings to his House," Leto pointed out. "That could work in our favor. I've met him. Our House is equivalent to his, except Verdun has a CHOAM Directorship—an unusually important one, apparently—that was grandfathered in from earlier days of prominence. Although House Atreides has no CHOAM Directorship of our own, perhaps he could help us push for one as our moonfish industry expands."

The images showed a teenage blonde strolling through a garden, riding purebred horses, swimming laps in a large pool. According to the biographical report, the young woman was charming, musically talented, and performed volunteer work at a hospital.

"Bear in mind," Hawat added, "some of this information may be slanted by Duke Verdun to make his daughter a more desirable marriage candidate. He does not know we are considering her for Paul, but he has made it plain he expects to use her for a solid marriage alliance."

"And this was before Otorio," Leto said.

They spent the next hour reviewing other young women Hawat had selected for consideration. Leto lost track of the number, but the Mentat had been thorough. Jessica added occasional comments and objections about which girls would be poor personal matches for Paul, deflecting some names but willing to accept most of them.

The meeting was interrupted when servers descended the cliff on the rail-lift to deliver a lunch Leto had arranged. When the food was certified free of poison and spread out—giant Caladan mussels in a seafood stew for the main course—the three of them sat around a small buffet table, sharing the meal while continuing to discuss candidates. They had gone through the dossier three times before they ate small pastries to finish the luncheon. After reviewing holo-reports and detailed supporting files, they kept coming back to Junu Verdun.

Finally, the Duke made his decision. "I will extend an offer to Duke Fausto Verdun and suggest that we formally begin discussions for a marriage alliance between our Houses. If our negotiations are satisfactory, we could announce a betrothal, with an extended time frame."

"As you wish, m'Lord," Hawat said.

Satisfied with the choice, Jessica looked at Leto. "Let me be the one to tell Paul."

Thinking of the uneasiness the young man had shown recently, the tension of their discussion in the dining hall, Leto nodded. "He might find that reassuring." He softened his voice. "At least he will be glad to know that I myself don't plan to marry."

Jessica gave him a resigned smile. "I can make him see the advantages of this Junu Verdun—at least for the sake of discussion."

"It's settled, then," Leto said. He wished it could be different, that he could marry Jessica after all, and Paul could marry for love . . . and they would all live happily on Caladan.

I must stay the course, he thought, *no matter how difficult it is.*

Dressed in a black Bene Gesserit robe, Reverend Mother Gaius Helen Mohiam accompanied the Emperor into the cavernous Landsraad Hall. An emergency meeting of nobles after the Otorio disaster had been called into session.

The stately chamber had never looked like this before, draped with black mourning banners from the walls and ceiling. Eighty-four painfully empty seats indicated the members killed in the most monstrous terrorist attack in modern history, and countless flowers symbolized the hundreds of family members and tens of thousands of support staff and locals also obliterated in the crash when the dump boxes crashed into Otorio.

After Shaddam took his ornate chair at the side of the stage, the Truthsayer seated herself on his right like a silent conscience. A dozen high-ranking Landsraad dignitaries filed in and took seats subordinate to the Emperor. They had gravely important roles in this emergency session, including elderly Speaker Tilson Xumba and even the dignified Ur-Director of CHOAM, Malina Aru, who rarely appeared in public. As the mother of the mastermind behind the Otorio massacre, Malina Aru faced a wave of anger and scorn. Nevertheless, showing remarkable bravery, or audacity, she had come to face the Landsraad in person. Mohiam was curious to hear how the Urdir would frame the situation.

She also feared the Landsraad nobles might tear Malina Aru limb from limb.

In initial statements, the Ur-Director had insisted that neither she nor the CHOAM Company had anything to do with Jaxson Aru's fanatical act and denied any involvement in the Noble Commonwealth movement. Malina and her other son, Frankos, the CHOAM President, had publicly disavowed the violent actions. Mohiam could not analyze the Urdir's written statement with truthsense, but she believed the woman's claims. How could allowing such ruthless devastation possibly be in CHOAM's best interests? Malina Aru had a sterling reputation, was a vocal supporter of the Imperium and its traditions, and surely wasn't part of the resistance to bring it all down.

Gazing across the restless noble members in the long banks of seats,

Mohiam noted faces that were red-eyed and shadowed with grief. So many close friends, associates, allies, and family members had been lost in the carnage— larger-than-life personalities and important voices that were now gone forever. Repercussions would continue throughout the Imperium for generations, and fundamental power shifts would occur.

Those eighty-four empty seats had to be filled, all at once, and ambitious nobles would be attracted like carrion birds to a fresh corpse.

As the simmering crowd settled, Speaker Xumba caught the eye of the Emperor, who nodded. The Speaker, a tall mahogany-skinned man of advanced years, walked slowly to the podium, where cones of light shone down on him. His eyes were red and moist, his expression downturned with grief.

He gripped the lectern and stood in silence, staring meaningfully at the empty seats as if reciting each individual name in his mind. No one made a sound. The Landsraad Hall had become like a graveyard for the noble dead.

Xumba gazed up at the ceiling, as if grasping for appropriate words for such a solemn occasion. "Funerals for our dead have been held, eulogies spoken, remembrances shared, and tears shed." He wiped his cheeks. Mohiam detected sincerity in the Speaker's words, genuine grief.

He waved an arm in a slow horizontal arc to indicate the empty seats, the vacuum left in the political landscape of the Imperium. "All those passionate voices silenced, dedicated noble rulers seeking to keep the Landsraad strong. How can we ever replace them? The Emperor will consider candidates for those positions, and soon, he will submit names to us for our review."

Shaddam leaned to one side and whispered to Mohiam, "The balance of power has shifted, since so many of my allies were killed at Otorio. We will need to rectify that."

She knew the truth of it. The Emperor's closest loyalists had attended the gala celebration, while lesser sycophants, possibly even Noble Commonwealth sympathizers, had made excuses not to attend on Otorio. "So many seats, Sire. But you had a majority before, and you will arrange to install only true loyalists in their places. At a time like this, the Landsraad would not dream of weakening the Imperium further."

Shaddam frowned at her. "Would they not? It seems the rebels might use our perceived weakness as an opportunity to fracture our very civilization."

She considered. "I will use truthsense to vet any candidates and make sure that each one is truly loyal. You will reward your real allies, and leave the false ones out in the cold."

"I like that approach."

As Speaker Xumba finished his speech and stepped back, the Emperor rose in the weighty silence and took his place at the podium. He waited for the amplification fields to adjust. "This is a vital and serious matter. I will never forget my loyal comrades who were murdered at Otorio. Eighty-four of the finest, most loyal nobles. It will not be easy to replace such qualified, talented members, but my committee will work day and night. I will give due consideration to new candidates who can fulfill those tragically empty seats."

A few members of the audience called out in support. One shouted, "Long live the Imperium!" Sitting quietly, Mohiam knew Shaddam would have preferred to hear "Long live the Emperor!"

Nevertheless, he accepted the praise. "Things will get better," he promised. "Things will get much better." Shaddam spoke for several minutes, naming the Landsraad members who had been lost, one by one in a solemn recitation, highlighting those with the most significant accomplishments. He ended with a vow. "We will find and punish the criminals responsible for this terrible attack. The violent nature of the Noble Commonwealth has been exposed for all to see. My Sardaukar will not rest until Jaxson Aru is brought to justice." He basked in a thunderous standing ovation.

Mohiam felt tension in the air. Ur-Director Malina Aru would speak next, and Shaddam had just lit a funeral pyre for her.

An awkward, hushed ripple traveled through the room when the proud woman approached the speaking zone. She walked without shame, though muttered insults and accusations were hurled at her like sharp barbs. Malina Aru stepped up to address the noble families of those whom her son had murdered.

Without flinching, she waited for the angry undertone to subside. Many gave her only numb stares, silenced by their own disbelief. Mohiam could hear the underlying venom in the audience, though a few seemed slightly more sympathetic toward an innocent mother blindsided by her son's crimes.

As a Bene Gesserit, Mohiam admired the Ur-Director for the power she held in CHOAM, although Malina's work was far different from the Sisterhood's. Few women ever achieved such prominent, visible power in the Imperium. Malina Aru had been brought in to salvage the less-competent administration of her husband, who had been quietly retired from his position. As Urdir, Malina's record of CHOAM profits and influence was unimpeachable.

Today, though, the woman was not here for her business acumen but for an accounting of Jaxson's terrible act.

At the podium, Malina Aru looked as if she wished she were somewhere else, *anywhere* else, and finally her strong, stoic expression cracked. She appeared uneasy—uncharacteristically so. From what Mohiam knew, the Urdir had always been extremely self-confident, sure of herself in life and business; when seen in public, she even carried herself with a certain swagger. Now Malina had something to say beyond her carefully worded written statement.

Facing the Landsraad, the Urdir's posture slumped. With a visible effort, she gathered herself and turned to the side of the speaking zone, waiting. Three men in formal attire entered from the perimeter, and then another three from the opposite side, and another trio came from the front, each group bearing a large and impressive display of exotic flowers from all across the Imperium. They placed the lavish bouquets on the stage around Malina.

"These flowers are to honor the victims of the horrendous tragedy on Otorio, blossoms from the worlds that each fallen noble called home," she said, then added steel to her voice. "No memorial can possibly make up for the loss of so many significant lives."

The audience grumbled in dissatisfaction. Reverend Mother Mohiam knew that the Urdir needed to say more, or do something, to bring them around to her side.

Malina's gesture activated a set of images. Holos of the dead Landsraad members shimmered throughout the audience in the great hall, appearing in their proper empty seats, like ghosts. The Reverend Mother was eerily reminded of the display Jaxson Aru had unleashed just before the impact from orbit.

The audience gasped in unison. Some members sobbed.

The holos did not move, mere projections of the dead, each one depicted in official Landsraad robes, sitting stiffly with hands clasped on their laps.

Malina continued, "I was not able to attend the gala on Otorio, and for that I have formally apologized to the Emperor. I survived, but only by happenstance. I did not know what my son intended to do."

Some members wiped tears from their eyes, and waves of sobbing passed through the chamber. A few angry grumbles of disbelief rippled through the tiered seats.

Malina added an edge of real anger to her voice. "If I had known, I would have stopped him. I would have killed him if necessary! I denounce what Jaxson did. CHOAM does not support his actions in any way, nor do I . . . his mother." She drew in a shuddering breath.

Reverend Mother Mohiam listened with her truthsense to analyze how much of this woman's emotions were real and how much of her grief and indignation was manufactured. Surprisingly, she couldn't entirely tell. The Ur-Director had remarkable control of herself.

"From my personal holdings, and by assent of the CHOAM board, we will donate a significant sum to help the noble houses harmed by my son's reprehensible act, and also the families of the other victims, the commoners, the retainers, friends, and support staff. Not every casualty came from a wealthy House—countless workers helped build the Corrino museum and the Imperial Monolith. For their laudable achievements, CHOAM wishes to honor their memories."

Polite applause went through the chamber, but did not last long. The audience was still resentful, still suspicious of her. Mohiam could read their mood.

Malina Aru faced them, letting shame descend upon her like a mourning cloak. "I find this difficult to say. _Impossible_ to say. I know . . . I know . . . I gave birth to a monster." Tears streamed down her face.

The audience fell silent, listening to her every word, watching her every movement and gesture.

"I renounce my son, sever all ties to him. Emperor Shaddam has declared him an outlaw, as do I. I grieve with you, but not for him. I hope never to see Jaxson again . . . except when he is brought to justice."

She left the speaking zone to a stunned silence. The holoprojections of the dead Landsraad members remained for a few moments longer before they flickered out.

As Speaker Xumba closed the meeting, Mohiam pondered what Malina Aru had just said, trying to decide whether it was an incredibly brave act or merely a measure of self-preservation, designed to protect CHOAM. As Truthsayer, she had listened closely. The Urdir carefully shaded the truth, interweaving it with oblique falsehood, but Mohiam could not identify outright lies.

When the crowd dispersed, the Emperor lingered in the vast hall, engaged in conversation with several nobles who had rushed up to make their case for some of the now-vacant Landsraad holdings.

While Shaddam was preoccupied, a Bene Gesserit messenger slipped up to Mohiam, one of the trusted Sisters also assigned on Kaitain. Her words were carefully modulated so that only Mohiam could hear her. "Reverend Mother, you are summoned back to Wallach IX. It is an urgent matter regarding one of your former students. The message comes directly from Mother Superior Harishka. You must obey."

Even though she was the Emperor's Truthsayer, Mohiam responded to a secret, higher calling. "I must obey. Arrange immediate passage to the Mother School."

In his developmental years, many people said of Paul Atreides that he was destined for greatness.

—Imperial histories

Paul enjoyed his training sessions with Duncan Idaho more than with any of his other instructors. Sometimes at the beginning of a session, the Swordmaster just gave him an intense look that told Paul it would be a tough and demanding workout.

Now he raised two large, heavy blades, one in each hand. "Today, young Master, we train with a different weapon. Broadswords."

Paul frowned, knowing the weapon was unwieldy and inappropriate for someone of his small stature. "Not our usual type of swordplay."

"All the more reason to train." Duncan tested the broadsword, swishing it in the air. "This one is for you. It's easier to handle, though longer than your arm. A good weapon to start with. Use your shield."

"Ah," Paul said, activating the controls at his belt. "You want a larger weapon than mine because you are afraid of me."

"Not unless you give me a reason to fear you."

They fought with the overlarge two-handed swords and body shields, using traditional thrusts and parries, along with combat variations Duncan had learned on Ginaz. Paul also applied some of Gurney Halleck's defensive tactics, which Duncan easily recognized.

During the practice fight, Duncan teased the young man by calling him Gurney, which distracted Paul and threw him off balance. In the heat of combat, he lost the nuances of what he'd been taught and instead resorted to instinctive fighting, relying on the quick footwork of his youth.

After a loud and vehement clash, Paul stepped back, panting. "So is it better to fight instinctively, as animals, or constrained by knowledge and rehearsed techniques, as humans often do? Natural versus the trained, animal versus human?"

Duncan raised his heavy sword, ready to fight again. "We are basically animals, so that's our instinctive side. The other side, the human one, involves

socialization, learning how to find our way in society and excel in our pursuits."
He sliced the air, pressed closer.

Paul parried, grunting with the effort of lifting his blade, and then Duncan
paused. "We use learned fighting methods to overcome obstacles and danger,"
the Swordmaster said. "Our human side is more polished and refined, an advantage over lower animal forms. We can call upon a larger arsenal of actions to
remain dominant." He nodded to himself, pretending to relax, but Paul could
sense he was prepared to lunge. "Ultimately, the goal of our lives is to become as
human as possible, to advance as far as we can."

When Duncan suddenly sprang forward, Paul danced out of the way, and
spun to face him with the broadsword raised. "On the other hand," the young
man said, "we can never abandon our primal ways, never allow our basic senses
and inborn traits to atrophy." Duncan swung hard, and Paul used his shield to
slow and block the blow, then stepped away, hefting his own broadsword.

"Well said, young Master." Duncan laughed, a deep chuckle similar to Gurney's. "Words are an effective weapon for the human to use. You just used them
on me."

"Effectively?"

He raised his sword in a salute to Paul. "You're the young Master, and I shall
never forget that, but in the world of the classroom, I am the master, and you will
do as I say . . . for your own good."

Their sparring was interrupted when Jessica appeared at the door of the
training room. Duncan lowered his sword, giving Paul's mother a deferential
nod. Paul could sense that uneasiness hung around her like a shawl; she herself
had taught him how to read the signs. "When you are finished with your session,
Paul, I must speak with you."

The young man wiped sweat from his forehead. "I think I have exhausted
Duncan enough for one day."

Jessica turned to the Swordmaster. Her tone was polite, but firm. "If you
would be so kind as to grant us privacy?"

"Of course, my Lady." Duncan returned his broadsword to the rack and left
the chamber while toweling himself off.

Though his trainer had shown the proper deference to the Duke's concubine,
Paul had seen a hardness in his eyes when he looked at Jessica. He didn't understand why his mother and Duncan were often at odds. Paul wanted to use every
technique, along with the ones Gurney and Thufir showed him, to become as
skilled as possible. They all wanted him to be the best Duke, and he appreciated
that.

Jessica's expression seemed both warm and sad at the same time. "There is
something you must know . . . plans your father is making." Paul returned his
broadsword to the rack, and he and his mother took seats on a hard bench.

She framed her words carefully. "Leto is the moral foundation on which House Atreides stands. He is my anchor and my love. After looking at many marriage possibilities, he has reached a decision, an important one for our future—in consultation with Thufir Hawat and me."

Paul read into what she said, the nuances of her voice, her flicker of expressions. He dreaded what she would say next.

Jessica handed him an image plate bearing the face of a beautiful young blond-haired woman. "Who is this?" he asked, suddenly wary.

"Her name is Junu Verdun, the daughter of Duke Fausto Verdun, an influential Landsraad noble. Joining their House to ours in a marriage alliance would significantly strengthen House Atreides. Your father has sent a proposal to Duke Verdun, suggesting negotiations for a possible betrothal."

Paul's anger flared toward his father, as well as a deep hurt for his mother. Duke Leto had promised he would not marry. "She looks my age! And my father intends to marry her?" He felt dizzy.

Surprised, Jessica let out a quick laugh, which perplexed him. "Oh, Paul! No, your father is suggesting Junu Verdun as *your* future wife."

Now Paul reeled in sudden confusion, even astonishment. Searching for words, he finally said, "I'm only fourteen! When does he expect me to marry?"

Jessica's eyes bored into his, and she reached out to touch his hand. "When I look at you, I often forget how young you are, even though you have wisdom and fighting skills beyond your years."

He took pride in that, but felt disoriented. "A betrothal . . . for me? When does he propose that the wedding happen?" In his mind, he was shouting, wanting to know how much time he had to be a young man, instead of a future Duke.

"We are exploring options, and this is merely a suggestion of a proposal, for now, an exploratory idea that will nevertheless set the Landsraad buzzing. If accepted, however, it could become a legally binding pact between our two Houses." She drew a breath. "We can draw out the negotiations, if need be. And I will insist that you meet her yourself. The timing is still up for discussion." Her voice took on a lighter tone. "Several of the other candidates Thufir suggested were far less compatible. I will make sure those are never again considered."

Though his thoughts were spinning, he smiled in gratitude. Suddenly, his entire world was uncertain.

She handed him the image plate so he could look at Junu more closely. "You don't know the girl, of course, but you can review the information we have compiled about her. If we receive a positive response from Duke Verdun, we will arrange for the two of you to be introduced."

He looked down at her features, found her pretty. He rolled the name over in his mind. *Junu Verdun.* Paul would be expected to take her as his formal, legal wife for political reasons. One day, she could be the Duchess of Caladan.

Jessica regarded him for a long while, and he worked hard to control his breathing, his pulse, exactly as she had taught him. She did not guide him in the technique but let him work through the exercise on his own. Finally, his heartbeat calmed, his breathing slowed, and he gathered a sense of stillness about him.

He opened his eyes again and stared sadly at the image of Junu Verdun. "But this isn't right. She is not the girl I see in my dreams."

The comment drew Jessica's interest. "Your dreams? You see a girl?"

"Often the same dream again and again. I'm sure it will come true—sometimes I can tell." He explained about the young woman in the cave and the vast desert, her all-blue eyes, dark red hair, and elfin features. He set the image plate aside on the bench, then picked up a drawing pad there among the records and training logs. "I've dreamed of her enough that I know her features. And it is not the daughter of Duke Verdun." To the best of his ability, he sketched an image of the dream girl. "I think this is the person who will be my wife and my love."

"Those two are not always the same thing." Jessica's voice had a quick undertone of bitterness from her own situation. "And dreams do not always come true."

"Maybe we need to listen to dreams, though," Paul said. "Remember the dream I had not long ago, one that terrified me in my sleep? I dreamed my father was in danger." He paused. "I consulted the Ixian chronometer in his study and confirmed what I already suspected. My dream occurred at the same time as the Otorio attack."

Jessica was alarmed. "That is strange indeed. Prescient dreams are of great interest to the Sisterhood." She had always known there was something special about Paul, and now she felt more certain than ever that her son had an important future. But she worried about him.

THE MESSAGE CYLINDER came from Lord Atikk. From their brief conversation on Otorio, Leto remembered the loud and blustery man. Now when he unsealed the cylinder and read the words, Atikk's sheer venom and fury struck him like a physical blow.

"The Landsraad has heard of Atreides honor, Duke Leto, but now I know it is a lie to cover your hateful corruption. Have you no inkling of the harm and suffering you caused? Damn you and your drug operations."

Leto felt as if he had been impaled by an icicle. The unexpected condemnation from this stranger did not even seem real.

"Your Caladan drug killed my son! At first, the drug seemed less harmful than some of Raolin's other vices, but you know the truth, don't you? You lured him with a peaceful release, but it was like a hidden bomb. Now he is dead because of you. Dead! I held him in my arms as his life drained away in horrible convulsions from the vile drug you sell on the black market.

"I should declare a War of Assassins against House Atreides, here and now, but you saved my life on Otorio. That places me under an obligation to my own honor. I managed to escape on one of the only ships, along with Archduke Ecaz. Therefore, you have me under an unwilling life debt. But the Landsraad will know what you are, Duke of Caladan."

A coldness seeped and spread within Leto, and he couldn't fathom what he was reading. He did recall Atikk's odd mention of "the Caladan drug" during the Imperial reception, but Jaxson Aru's attack had swept the detail from his mind.

The message concluded. "You are forever the enemy of House Atikk, Leto Atreides. It will not be forgotten."

That was all the letter said. No further explanation.

"Thufir!" he shouted. "Thufir Hawat!"

Leto rose from his desk and read the damning letter again, but it still made no sense. His immediate instinct was to pour out a message of sympathy, to somehow offer reparations for the loss of Raolin Atikk, but he did not dare. So much vengeful outrage dripped from the letter!

What was this Caladan drug, and how could Leto not know about it? Caladan was his planet, and he ruled it under the mantle of morality and reliability, and now his own reputation had been undermined. Clearly, he needed to get to the bottom of whatever this illicit activity was. The son of a Landsraad noble was dead. How many others had been harmed?

The Caladan drug?

The warrior Mentat strode into Leto's study, flushed. He'd come running when he heard the summons. "Yes, my Lord Duke?"

Leto handed him Atikk's vitriolic message. Hawat's brow furrowed deeply as he read. The Duke stepped away. "Find out what is going on, Thufir. Identify this Caladan drug—who is manufacturing it, who is distributing it? How does it get offworld? Why did we not know about this . . . and how am I to blame?"

Hawat straightened, handed the letter back. "I will begin an investigation immediately."

Suspicions have a way of becoming "facts," even if they have no basis in truth.

—PRINCESS IRULAN, *The Book of Muad'Dib*

After he returned to Arrakis, Count Hasimir Fenring traveled to Carthag in the early evening. After the sun set, the air was cooler, the desert not so menacing, although the central Harkonnen city was still an ugly place. Fenring had spent enough years on this harsh planet to know when best to leave his lovely Arrakeen Residency. His mission to the Baron Harkonnen would be difficult enough.

Fenring stepped out of the overland flyer that had brought him from the spaceport wearing a pro forma stillsuit, but he refused to wear a face mask or inconvenient nose plugs. He inhaled a dusty breath, smelling the unpleasant fumes that the Harkonnen troops and equipment seemed to exude.

Fenring already missed Kaitain, but Shaddam had sent him back to his duties as Imperial Spice Observer, and he understood the importance of the task the Emperor had set for him. Though he liked to care for his lovely wife, Hasimir Fenring was not a man who needed to be pampered.

Moving quickly, he stepped into a waiting groundcar on the edge of the landing field and breathed a sigh of relief when the door sealed behind him. Since the Baron had dispatched the vehicle for him, Fenring did not need to give the driver instructions. Without a word, the man rolled the groundcar across the paved area and into the city.

Fenring hated the megalopolis where Baron Harkonnen maintained his headquarters. This crowded city, with its roadways and blocky buildings, was a magnet for heat and grime, making the place seem even more unpleasant. The air reeked of oil, sweat, and industrial odors, of filthy smoke mixed with dust. After the Richesian governors had left eighty years ago, the Harkonnens had brought their brute-force sensibility and manufacturing methods from Giedi Prime, leaving a stain that would last for centuries.

Fenring much preferred the older, more stately city of Arrakeen, where he had made an acceptable home for himself and his dear Margot, but he reminded himself this was not a pleasure trip. He had to deliver the Imperial decree about the new spice surtax, and the Baron would not be pleased.

In the downtown core of Carthag, the taller buildings rose above the hazy smoke of fabrication and repair yards for spice-harvesting machinery. The governor's mansion was not as tall as the central Guild Bank structure, but stockier and more fortified.

As the escort car pulled up in front of the mansion's guarded gates, Fenring saw two desiccated heads on spikes. Their darkening skin had blistered in the heat, and now in the gathering darkness, glowglobes spotlighted the gruesome trophies.

After being ushered past guard stations and inside the main structure, Fenring strolled into the fortified mansion with his Imperial credentials, in case anyone needed a reminder of his importance.

Baron Vladimir Harkonnen greeted him from the suspensor chair behind an ellipsoid desk in his spacious private office. The desk was made of jade-pink elaccawood, a replica of the original in his Giedi Prime office. He also kept a relief globe of the desert world here. Scrolls and filmbooks lined the walls.

Fenring sauntered forward, taking a seat without being invited. As he settled into the guest chair, though, he noted that the Baron had staged the furniture so he would be a head taller than any visitor. Fenring did not like to be in a subordinate position to this unpleasant man.

Baron Harkonnen was intimidating in his girth, with uneven discolorations on his face from a persistent, incurable malady. He wore a bandage on his forehead and a medcast on his left wrist and hand. Fenring immediately noted the details, confirming what he knew.

Shaddam was deeply suspicious of the Baron's failure to attend the grand gala. After Jaxson Aru's screed about breaking up the Imperium, the Emperor had begun to see signs of treachery everywhere, secret members of the Noble Commonwealth, sympathizers with the rebellion. Were the Harkonnens part of the brewing rebellion?

House Harkonnen had governed Arrakis with its lucrative spice industry for eighty-odd years. The Baron's father, Dmitri Harkonnen, had ruled for years until his death, followed by the disastrous tenure of the Baron's half brother Abulurd, before Vladimir Harkonnen himself took over the operations. By long tradition, a noble family was assigned to the desert planet for a century, although the Emperor could remove them at any time. But the profits—both on the books and under the table—were so extensive that few families willingly relinquished their siridar-governorship.

Seeing Fenring's scrutiny, the big man lifted his med-wrapped arm. "I have not been feeling well. A minor accident left me with this injury. That is the reason I could not attend the Emperor's gala on Otorio."

"And such a fortunate coincidence, hmmm? How convenient you were away from Otorio when the attack happened." Fenring leaned forward. "Exactly how were you injured?"

The Baron sniffed, then waved his wrapped hand dismissively. "Oh, just a little household accident. My suspensor belt failed me at a most inopportune time, and I fell on the stone stairway. Alas, for a person of my size, gravity is not my friend." The fat man's gaze drifted off, as if he were pulling a fanciful story out of the ether. "You can reassure the Emperor, though, that I am feeling better every day, and my work here has not suffered one bit."

Fenring knew he was lying; he had his own sources of information. "Interesting. Hmmm-ahh . . . a household accident, indeed."

The Baron squirmed, but gave no additional details.

Fenring had done his own investigating and compiled a thorough intelligence report. The real reason had not been difficult to determine at all, nor did it appear to have anything to do with Jaxson Aru or the attack, but it was certainly no clumsy household accident. As planetary governor, Vladimir Harkonnen did not want to admit unrest or violence on Arrakis. The assassination attempt made him look weak.

Fenring would not let him believe his clumsy deception had succeeded. "Did you really think the Emperor would not know about the malcontents who attacked your shuttle? The assassination attempt on your person?" His voice had a razor edge. "You did not consider it relevant that desert rabble nearly killed the designated governor of one of the most important planets in the Imperium?"

The fat man began sweating profusely. "It was . . . an internal matter, and it has been dealt with."

"Yes, ahhhh, I saw the heads outside the gate."

"House Harkonnen takes our spice operations seriously, and we will defend them against outside interference or internal unrest." Now the Baron looked smug. "I ordered my nephew Rabban to increase security, and I brought in additional troops from Giedi Prime. I assure you that melange production is secure." He visibly swallowed. "We are even rooting out nests of highly organized smugglers in the desert, which will further cut down our losses. Emperor Shaddam will be pleased."

The Count tapped his fingers together. *This is a man of lies,* he thought. But Fenring understood him. He had gotten the answers he needed, and would report to Shaddam that Baron Vladimir Harkonnen did not appear to be involved with the rebels or the attack on Otorio. Clearly, the Baron had *intended* to go to Otorio, so he'd possessed no knowledge of the planned massacre.

But that was only one reason the Emperor had dispatched Fenring here. He stared at the Baron in silence, waiting to deliver his decree, making the other man uncomfortable.

Finally, the Baron cleared his throat with a rumble. "And what is it you want of me? You said the Emperor had an important message? I have a busy schedule tonight."

"Yes, mmmm, I will be brief. In light of the costly devastation from the recent terrorist attack, the Emperor is forced to seek an unorthodox remedy. In order to pay for that damage, as well as the costs of significantly increased security and enhanced military forces in key positions, the Padishah Emperor commands that you impose a surtax on all spice production and distribution. This surtax will be painful but necessary, and you will make sure that it is implemented."

Spluttering, the Baron raised himself up on his suspensor belt. "A surtax on top of our costs? But that would cause serious harm to the market! Our profit margins are already narrow, with the amount of equipment that gets damaged and lost in this hellish place! The customers will balk at paying more—"

"And yet they will pay, hmmm?"

The Baron fumed. "Yes. Some of them will pay, but others will buy less." He struck his desk with his wrapped hand and winced in pain. "Tell the Emperor this is unacceptable! We already endure extreme Imperial taxes on melange, and this will take us beyond the breaking point."

"With all due respect, my dear Baron, if you have a response for Emperor Shaddam, you will have to tell him yourself. I am not your messenger. I am *his*." Fenring smiled thinly, rather like he smiled at people when he slipped a knife between their ribs.

As Fenring turned to leave, Baron Harkonnen lowered himself back into his expanded chair under the weight of his new obligations.

BACK AT THE Residency, Count Fenring found his Bene Gesserit wife in the conservatory, a room she loved more than any other. This lush garden chamber in the south wing seemed out of place on the arid planet. Lush, verdant plants were a luxury that only the wealthy and privileged could afford to keep, an extravagance that consumed so much water.

Once he passed through the door seal, Fenring approached Margot, standing so close to her that their elbows touched. Both of them smiled, adoring each other's presence. They spoke in voices so low that the white noise of the splashing water from a small fountain would disrupt any covert listening devices.

Fenring always confided in his wife. "The fat man told me two lies—about how he was injured and why he skipped the Otorio celebration."

"Do you believe he knew about Jaxson Aru's plans ahead of time? Is House Harkonnen involved in the rebellion?"

"No, he is merely trying to protect himself from embarrassment. He had his own security incident, which he wants to hide from the Emperor. If the Otorio massacre had not occurred, few would have noted his absence, but the fact that he conveniently survived has drawn unwanted attention."

"So the Baron is actually innocent?" Margot sounded surprised.

"Oh, Vladimir Harkonnen is far from innocent, my dear! But he is not guilty of conspiring with the Noble Commonwealth."

She stroked his forehead with a fingertip. "How much sleep have you been getting? You look tired." She kissed him on one cheek. "Poor darling."

"Mmmm, I feel refreshed simply being in your presence. Tomorrow, I return to my official duties as Spice Observer and my unofficial job as liaison to the smugglers. Much will change now that the Emperor is cracking down. It may push people to . . . inappropriate actions."

Margot remained in the conservatory, tending her plants, while Fenring retired to their private chambers, heeding her suggestion about getting some rest. He lay on their spacious bed, covering his eyes with a cloth.

He thought about his sweet wife, as he often did when she was not in bed with him, not in his arms. Some considered the two of them to be complete opposites, but they had quite an endearing relationship. Margot didn't have his reputation as a killer, but he knew his wife was deadly in her own right. She possessed an arsenal of Bene Gesserit fighting techniques, although she had never admitted to killing anyone herself.

Still, Lady Margot had more innate goodness than he did, and her gentle ways brought out a greater measure of good in him. He appreciated that. Her loving attentions were a nice respite from his professional work.

Through fervent beliefs and secret revelations that are denied to others, religions can easily be manipulated. They can also act as a stabilizing influence by creating a community united by a bond of beliefs.

—Bene Gesserit internal document,
"Analysis of Uncontaminated Religions"

Each Guild ship that arrived at Caladan delivered news updates about the confusion echoing throughout the Imperium. Duke Leto carefully studied the reports, read the minutes of Landsraad emergency sessions, watched the Emperor's responses. He saw a recording of the speech in which CHOAM's Ur-Director denounced her own son Jaxson Aru.

He was glad to be far away and at home on Caladan.

The Duke was not like the ambitious nobles who saw opportunities in the tragedy, ways to enhance the stature of their Houses. Even as they expressed dismay and grief about the fallen nobles, the family leaders bribed, argued, and jockeyed for position to fill the empty seats. As a respected Landsraad member himself, Leto could have gone to Kaitain and used his influence to expand the Atreides power base, but he felt it would be ghoulish, like plucking coins from a dead man's eyes. He would not lower himself to such nonsense for the opportunity to rule other planets he did not need or want.

After surviving the Otorio disaster, Leto had remained on Caladan to focus on governing his own people, strengthening the holding that had belonged to House Atreides for so many generations. And Paul would take on that mantle when it was his time.

But because the repercussions of Otorio would affect his son as well, Leto included Paul in the intense council meetings, discussing each new report and the consequences resounding throughout the Imperium. He told the attentive young man, "You need to be well informed. Soon enough, you will have significant responsibilities on your shoulders."

"I will do my best to understand Imperial politics, sir," Paul said. Beside him at the council table, Hawat nodded sagely, proud of his student.

"Understanding Imperial politics may be beyond any of us," Leto said. "But we try to make what sense of what we can."

In more public business, the Duke held court in the main audience hall, where he heard petitions, received gifts, granted favors, and dispensed justice.

Unexpectedly, Archvicar Torono arrived late one morning after traveling from the northern pundi rice fields. Standing before Leto's imposing seat, the religious leader spread his hands and dispensed another blessing. "The Muadh serve you and pray for you, my Duke. House Atreides has ruled on Caladan for centuries, but my followers have been here even longer than that, making a peaceful home where the All-Seeing intended us to be."

Leto responded with a warm smile. "You have always served me well, Archvicar, and your people ask for little. What is it I can grant you?"

Torono spread both palms. "I come not with a request, my Duke, but with an invitation."

"And what is this invitation?"

"Come north to our main Muadh temple near the Arondi Cliffs. Each month, our members conduct a centering and purification ritual. The Muadh have performed this sacred ritual for thousands of years. It is the core of who we are. The essence of the barra fern enhances contentment and our place in the universe." He smiled. "I ask you, your lady, and your son to join us."

Leto leaned forward with a solemn nod. "Thank you for the gracious invitation, Archvicar. As Duke, I wish to know my people better, and ever since you came to greet me when I returned home safe, I realized that I do not know your people well." He paused. "Tell me more about this ritual and what it entails."

"Yes, we harvest young ferns in the deep forest, dry them, and share them in a community gathering." He brushed his palms down his bushy beard. "The essence is called ailar."

Leto frowned, suddenly recalling the unsettling angry message from Lord Atikk. Could this have something to do with the mysterious Caladan drug? "I would not be willing to consume a mind-altering substance, nor would my son . . ."

The Archvicar did not seem to understand the problem. "But we have done it for thousands of years, my Duke. The ailar binds us in its gentle embrace. We come to no harm. The All-Seeing would not condone it."

"Circumstances are different for me as Duke." When Leto saw the deep disappointment on the religious leader's face, he added, "Would it be acceptable if we attend your ritual but merely observe? We can offer our support, but we are not members of your religion."

The Archvicar bowed again. "We would be honored to have you join us, in any manner you prefer."

Leto sat back in his ornate chair and mused, intrigued that there were still things about Caladan he needed to learn.

All the gold, jewels, and colorful gowns that surround an Empress cannot reveal whether her heart is a sparkling gem, or the coarsest stone.

—PRINCESS IRULAN, *In My Father's House*

As far as the CHOAM Ur-Director was concerned, Empress Aricatha served a clear purpose, even though no one else realized it. The opportunity was unexpected now, but the Emperor's charming young wife could help Malina Aru in the wake of her son's debacle.

Malina had debased herself in the Landsraad Hall, disowning Jaxson and letting him be declared an outlaw. It needed to be done. Many in the Imperium would be skeptical of her personal motives, but she could also use the lever of heart-wrenching sympathy. Despite running the most powerful company in human history, she was still a mother shamed and disgraced by her own child, a bad seed. . . .

Yes, it needed to be done.

After her speech before the Landsraad, Malina accepted a gracious "invitation" from Empress Aricatha—a meeting that Malina herself had arranged, surreptitiously. Even so, their meeting did not go unnoticed.

On Kaitain, the Empress had many showy duties. Her social ministers, secretaries, and schedulers made all of her movements and conferences public. As instructed, the glowing Empress received the Urdir on the palace grounds for quiet conversation and a walk through the gardens outside the newly remodeled northern wing.

Malina wanted all the observers, spy-eyes, gossips, and courtiers to see her as she entered. On cue, Aricatha came forward, a smile curving her generous lips, a warm flush on her dusky skin. Her blue-black hair fell in lovely tresses. The guards watched cautiously as the Empress gave the Ur-Director an embrace.

"I am so sorry, my dear Malina. I cannot imagine the pain a mother must feel in such a circumstance. It tugs on the strings of my heart. You have my support in this trying time, and the support of the Imperium as well."

Malina bowed, letting the numerous hungry eyes absorb her obvious discomfort, her grief. "Thank you, Empress. That means a great deal to me."

Aricatha took her by the arm. "Come, let us walk on the terrace. I have been anxious to show it off, now that the contractors are finally gone. The tiling has been redone, and the remodel is complete."

The Imperial guards made certain that inconvenient observers did not follow beyond a certain point as the two women left the palace proper and went out to the lavish terrace, with its flower displays and calming fountains, as well as the noise-dampening fields and cones of silence that offered complete privacy.

Malina's demeanor changed when the observers faded back. "This is import-ant, Aricatha. It goes a long way to repaying your debt."

Now that she was Empress, the young woman had become more than a mere puppet, and she no longer maintained her meek demeanor. Aricatha had always been an avid and ambitious student, but Malina Aru still controlled her.

"I consider it an exchange, Ur-Director," the Empress said. "You have helped me, and now I help you. It is a perfect business relationship."

Malina replied with a cold smile. "Exactly as I taught you."

Empress Aricatha was Shaddam's sixth wife. His first one, Anirul, had been a strong Bene Gesserit, who bore him five daughters before being assassinated. Wanting someone more pliable, the Emperor then went through several vapid beauties who had been trained to fawn over him. His preceding wife, Firenza Thorvald, lasted only six months.

Aricatha, though, was something else. She was indeed a beauty, and she had spent years analyzing Shaddam's concubines and previous lovers, cultivating her-self to catch and hold his attention like an invisible fishhook. She had realized the plain, pear-shaped Firenza wouldn't last long.

Now as Aricatha walked with the Urdir, the glint in her eyes grew cloudy. "Is it true that Count Uchan died on Otorio? I do not recall seeing him there."

"It is true that he died," Malina said guardedly. "And the records will indicate that he was among the Otorio casualties."

The Empress walked along the path of prismatic gravel, tossing her dark hair. "He was a poor and distracted lover, but he had a kind heart."

"My daughter will say all the appropriate things about her husband," Malina said. "But Jalma has now taken complete control over House Uchan. Everything fit together perfectly."

"So the attack has a silver lining." The Empress looked wistful. "You always taught me that advantages can be seen if one expands the view wide enough."

Early in her vibrant, beautiful youth—under a different name and slightly different appearance—Aricatha had served as a valued concubine for House Hagal and then House Uchan on Pliesse, where she had come to the notice of CHOAM.

Malina Aru had seen the young woman's potential, and while Aricatha was in the court of Count Uchan, CHOAM gave her secret lessons, training her aggressively in business interests and personal manipulation. CHOAM had thousands of years of influence on market conditions, trade interactions, and personal alliances.

When it became clear that Shaddam IV would soon be wanting a new wife, Malina Aru began to pull strings behind the scenes, and Aricatha was the perfect subject. CHOAM would control the Empress's throne as well.

When her daughter, Jalma, married old Count Uchan, who had not serviced his beautiful young concubine for a year anyway, Aricatha was whisked away from Pliesse. All records of her duties as a concubine were expunged. A past identity was created for her, along with impeccable (fabricated) noble bloodlines, and she was infiltrated into a neutral Landsraad House. When Shaddam chose to remarry again, after curtly disposing of Firenza, Aricatha was the obvious and perfect candidate.

Now that she sat on the throne, Aricatha did not forget that Malina Aru's manipulations had helped put her there.

The two women paused by a mirrorlike pool in which swam hungry golden fish. On a pedestal beside the pool sat a small aquarium filled with crickets. Aricatha reached in, pulled out one of the black insects, and tossed it to the water. The golden fish swarmed and fought, devouring the cricket.

Malina reached in and took a bug of her own, tossed it into the pool, and watched the ensuing frenzy. "That reminds me of the Landsraad as nobles fight over the empty seats."

"My husband will be adamant about choosing only those who swear blind loyalty to him."

"And he will find them," Malina said. "We know the hearts of the nobles."

Whenever Aricatha heard something significant to CHOAM, she was instructed to dispatch a secret message to Frankos Aru in the Silver Needle, who then forwarded them to his mother on Tupile.

As an offhand report a year earlier, Aricatha had let Malina Aru know that Shaddam intended to annex a minor world called Otorio, where he would raze part of the landscape and commence construction of an unprecedented Corrino museum. Aricatha had not known the significance of that backwater planet, simply reported the information as a matter of course. She had no idea what Otorio meant to the Aru family.

Malina now regretted that she had chosen not to tell her son Jaxson about it immediately. She had miscalculated just how mortally offended he would be when his father's burial shrine and the sacred olive grove were desecrated.

"I am also trying to expand my role here in the palace," Aricatha continued. "So far, my dear Shaddam has given me only empty activities for a pretty Empress at silly events. I cut ribbons and place wreaths, but I am qualified to do more than that."

"Of course you are," Malina said.

With the exception perhaps of Anirul, Shaddam's other wives had been untrained and unequal to the task or the opportunity. Aricatha would play her role perfectly, and Shaddam would underestimate her, as would most of the Landsraad. They would see only the jeweled, elegant lady and not begin to imagine the sharp and dangerous ambition she concealed inside, like a razor-sharp dagger hidden in a jeweled sheath.

"I will find a way to make him appoint me as a diplomat, an ambassador to some important world."

"That would be quite advantageous," Malina said, "but don't belittle your role as Empress. You can continue to give me the information I need."

"And my dear Shaddam will keep providing it," Aricatha said. "It will be a most beneficial relationship."

Euphoria can be produced through a variety of means—emotional, edu-cational, religious, or chemical.

—Suk Doctor Handbook

The prospect of the journey north to the Muadh temple delighted Paul. Although the Duke often traveled alone and unguarded here on Caladan, and he and Paul went on their annual wilderness expeditions accompanied by only a few companions, the current uproar in the Imperium necessitated additional security for the trip.

Duncan Idaho joined the entourage as Paul's personal bodyguard, and a contingent of Atreides house guards escorted Duke Leto and Lady Jessica. The Atreides entourage was led by Lieutenant Nupree, who had specifically asked to travel to the tiered pundi rice paddies and flooded farmlands. Since the young lieutenant had a clean service record and performed his duties well, Duke Leto allowed it. When pressed for a reason, Nupree had admitted, "I've always wanted to see the Arondi Cliffs, m'Lord. I hear they are quite remarkable."

The Duke, Jessica, and the rest of their group set off in a sedate and luxurious processional frigate, while Paul and Duncan flew separately in a shielded escort flyer.

As the flying procession approached the pundi rice fields after four hours in the air, Paul was impatient. "You and I could have flown faster, Duncan! We should show off what these engines can do."

"We could, but there is no need to rush. Sometimes waiting for a thing is part of the enjoyment. Is your mother not teaching you patience and control? I have seen you sit motionless for hours as you think about one muscle at a time."

Paul was surprised Duncan had seen their private training. "That's different. It enhances my skills. It helps me become a better fighter. This is just a . . . a trip."

"When I was at the Ginaz School, the Swordmasters would make us sit motionless for hours, sometimes a full day, without explanation, without giving us a goal. We learned to understand and accept futility."

At the piloting controls, Paul glanced over at him. "You speak as if that's a good thing."

"Even a Duke or an Emperor cannot always control the universe, young Master. It is best to be prepared for that eventuality."

Paul looked down to see the landscape dotted with a web of silvery canals, shallow pools, irrigation sluices. In the sides of a deep river valley, the farmers had excavated spectacular terraces, lush steps in precarious vertical layers, each one covered with extensive rice paddies that were harvested, then planted again. The intensity of the green made Paul's eyes ache.

Though the terrain around the terraced valley was mostly flat, a startling buttress of rock lurched out of the ground like a mountain in the middle of a wet plain. Before the trip, Paul had studied the geological anomaly with Dr. Wellington Yueh, the Suk doctor for House Atreides and one of his teachers. The Arondi Cliffs were two thousand meters high, sheer granite that looked as if a seismic knife had sliced half of a mountain away. Rubble lay around the base from rocks that continued to slough off.

Paul pressed closer to the windowport. "I never expected it to be so big! That is enormous."

"Considered one of the most difficult and treacherous climbs on the planet. Much harder than the sea cliffs you ascend for sport."

"The sea cliffs are difficult, but I have mastered them, as well as the castle wall outside my balcony." Paul studied the sheer rock face, tracing fault lines and imagining ascent routes. He looked at Duncan. "And you know I don't just climb for sport. It teaches me skill, balance, concentration. It will help me escape from a trap if need be."

"You'll hear no argument from me." Duncan stared ahead through the cockpit. "See the Muadh village there at the base? It will provide a good enough view of the cliffs, for certain."

Well ahead of the more ponderous and showy Atreides processional frigate, Duncan circled above the village and landed in a flat clearing away from the cluster of dwellings. After the engines hummed down to a low throb, Paul climbed out and waved as the villagers came to greet them.

Before long, the rest of the Atreides escort ships landed like a flock of mechanical birds while the main diplomatic craft approached. Even though this was a relatively brief expedition, the Atreides protocol ministers had made preparations as if it were a military invasion.

Lieutenant Nupree and the Atreides guards fanned out for a quick security inspection of the Muadh village. When Nupree transmitted that the landing area was ready for the Duke, the stately ship lumbered in on suspensor engines. Paul knew the Duke's formal processional barge was not all for show. With fast and powerful engines, it could streak away should danger arise.

Paul had seen ducal processions and state ceremonies before. Right now, he was more impressed with the sheer rock wall of the Arondi Cliffs. He stared at the vertical expanse of stone, the cracks and lines of igneous hexagonal columns that rose high, like sharp-edged straws packed together.

After his father disembarked from the larger craft, Paul and Duncan hurried to join them, but Paul kept staring at the cliff face, intrigued. Seeing his son's fascination, Leto gave a wistful smile. "Ah, the Arondi Cliffs. Do you see all the rubble strewn at the base? If you look closely, you will find as many bones as rocks. Hundreds of climbers have attempted that insurmountable face. Fewer than fifty have successfully scaled it."

"I'm a good climber," Paul said, reluctant to admit the danger he took upon himself even by climbing outside his castle window or on the sea cliffs.

Leto's face tightened. "Your abilities are superior, Paul, but this . . . no. When your grandfather was young, he made the attempt and had to turn back. The experience frightened even Paulus Atreides."

Paul knew many tales about the Old Duke. "From what I hear, my grandfather was so brave he laughed as the Salusan bull trampled him."

Leto took his son by the shoulder, turned him away from the cliffs. "There will be no climbing of that rock face. We have come here to meet these people, attend their ceremony, and make a good impression. Surely that is a difficult enough task for today."

HURRYING TOWARD THEM from the village, Archvicar Torono arrived with several junior deacons. Crowds of rice farmers worked the fields for the day's harvest, while their families had remained behind to prepare for the purification and centering ceremony.

Although it was a normal routine for the locals, Paul was surrounded by a feast of new experiences. The villagers wore homespun clothes and had no extravagances, but he was struck by how calm and content they were. The Muadh were satisfied with their homes, families, and work. After all the hubbub in Castle Caladan, the astonishment and fear he had experienced when he learned about his father's brush with death at Otorio . . . after the constant meetings, reports, political intrigues, and backstabbing Landsraad nobles, he was happy to see the quiet, self-contained lives of these farmers. Paul envied these people for knowing their exact place.

While Duke Leto and Lady Jessica spent the afternoon meeting with village leaders, prominent rice farmers, and Archvicar Torono, Paul and Duncan explored the comfortable settlement. Lieutenant Nupree dispatched guard teams to lock down the village for security purposes. Though Nupree had expressed his desire to see the Arondi Cliffs, the man did not seem overly interested now that he was here. The lieutenant spent much of his time in quiet conversations with certain villagers. Paul wondered why.

That evening, the villagers gathered in the central square and ate a meager meal, bland rice and squash from their gardens. The Archvicar apologized to Leto for the sparse hospitality. "It is traditional that we fast for the centering and purification ceremony, my Duke, avoiding most foods and beverages. The ritual is a difficult ordeal, yet also an immensely gratifying one. You will see."

"We honor your traditions," Leto said. "Pundi rice and vegetables from Caladan soil make a fine enough feast for me." He, Paul, and Jessica sat at a wooden table in the open, sharing bowls with villagers, after the Duke's ministers verified each dish with poison snoopers. Attentive Atreides guards stood outside the feast, not eating. Lieutenant Nupree and the others would dine later in shifts.

Archvicar Torono's eyes shone, for he was enormously happy to have such important guests. "After tonight, you will understand us much better, Duke Leto."

"My Duke," the people muttered, as if it were some kind of a chant and response.

After darkness fell under the shadow of the Arondi Cliffs, anticipation built in the village. The rice farmers' murmured conversation grew more animated. Paul looked all around, listening, concentrating.

Jessica's eyes sparkled. "Learn what you can, Paul. This is a new experience for all of us."

The people rose from their long tables and gathered in front of the rustic Muadh temple that rose higher than any village dwelling.

Leto looked up at the stars sparkling overhead and spoke to Paul as they waited for the ritual to begin. "We are far from ocean mists and the glare of city lights. Look at all those stars. You can see the universe."

Deacons in rough-spun robes emerged from the temple carrying hand-woven baskets filled with dried brown organic material, little nubs that looked like bent, mummified fingers. Paul watched curiously, his senses alert.

"Ailar unlocks our minds and hearts," droned the Archvicar. "Ailar grants us peace and clarity. Ailar gives us energy. Ailar gives us calm."

The Muadh followers muttered something in a language Paul didn't understand. Torono reached into the basket and held up one of the dried brown curls. "The barra fern grows wild in the forests north of here, very rare. Our village hunters comb the wilderness to harvest them at exactly the right time. A little sprig such as this . . ." The Archvicar held one of the brown objects between his thumb and forefinger. "Perfect potency."

With reverence, he extended the dried brown fern to Leto, who took it in his palm. Paul leaned closer, fascinated, but his father gave him a cautioning look. He turned the dry, airy object and let Paul hold it. The young man felt his fingers tingle, but that may have been his imagination.

"We do not ask that you partake," Torono said. "But observe and join us with your hearts."

Nupree stepped closer, accompanied by his guards. The tension rose in the air, but Paul was neither afraid, nor suspicious. He sensed no danger among these people.

The woven baskets were passed around the crowd of reverent villagers, each person taking one of the shriveled brown curls. They nibbled the dry plant, savoring each tiny morsel. As they chewed, the rice farmers and their families began to hum, at first individually, then as the sound grew louder, they resonated, coordinating their voices.

A shiver went down Paul's back. He looked at his mother and father, saw Jessica memorizing details, while Leto stood with erect posture, observing. Paul felt the buzzing grow in the air, and the majesty of the ritual.

The participating villagers sat cross-legged and close together on the ground, consuming the nubs of dried fern. More baskets were passed around. The people reached out to touch shoulders and arms, stroking adjacent faces as if in wonder and admiration. Their eyes and their smiles grew brighter.

"Thus, we are unified," said the Archvicar. "Thus, we are part of Caladan and the universe."

The humming became a background drone like that of summer insects. Paul felt sleepy, lulled into a sense of peace, and his eyelids drooped. The Muadh deacons returned the empty baskets to the temple and then came back outside, each one holding a bent brown fern, which they were the last to consume. They sat among the other followers who were already being affected by the ailar.

In the back of his mind, Paul sensed a glow, as if he could join the clarity and celebration experienced by these people. He glanced at his father with a silent question, seeing many other teenagers, young men and women his own age, participating in the ritual.

Leto shook his head and whispered, "No, we will not."

Paul accepted the decision and watched the others. The euphoria was thick in the air like mist on a cool morning.

"These are my people," Duke Leto said, then turned to Paul, "and they are your people, too."

Paul watched these villagers wrapped up in their own world, their own lives, and shared a measure of their satisfaction.

In the universe of Imperial politics, it is necessary to take actions that are not made public. In fact, far more remains unseen than seen.

—PADISHAH EMPEROR SHADDAM IV

After flying low, beneath sensor records, Fenring landed his unmarked 'thopter at the designated coordinates, near a distinctive rock formation below the Shield Wall. Alone at the controls, he remained inside the cab as the craft clicked and cooled. Looking through the plaz screen, he scanned the rendezvous point, always alert for treachery. Although he expected to find none today, he never let down his guard.

He'd been to this spot in a previous covert meeting with the smugglers, but he saw no one now. Still, he knew Esmar Tuek and his crew were watching him. It was a delicate dance of trust and suspicion. His interactions with these fringe people were valuable, and no one could know of his involvement.

He continued waiting in the landed aircraft, knowing he was vulnerable. Fenring climbed out of the 'thopter and stood next to the insect-like craft. Warm, yellow sunlight reflected off the dusty fuselage. Finally, as he stared at the outcropping in front of him, a portion of the rock shifted to reveal an opening, a false front for their secret base, an electronically veiled entry. Three smugglers stood inside, wearing desert robes. They gestured for him.

He followed them into the revealed rock cleft, and the guards opened a moisture-sealed door that led into the tunnels of the hidden base. Though the smugglers tried to lead, Fenring strode ahead, since he knew the way to Tuek's office. He intended to move at his own pace. Fenring could only infer the size of this hidden base; in his previous meetings, he had seen only a few of the passageways.

Esmar Tuek, the scar-faced leader of this smuggler band, waited for him in the rock-walled cave office. Gazing at his visitor with the deep blue eyes from a lifetime of melange, Tuek sat back at a metal desk with the demeanor of a king taking his throne. He signaled the others to leave. Fenring declined the offered chair across from him.

Tuek scowled, heavy brows overhanging his eyes. The smuggler's face had angles and planes, as if he were a creature carved out of Arrakeen stone. Though an outlaw, Tuek lived comfortably here with his cohorts, reaping extravagant profits from his illicit spice operations. "You said you have an important message, Count Fenring? My wife and son will join us. They are heavily involved in our work here."

"Hmmm, then they need to hear my report as well. It will affect all aspects of spice distribution from Arrakis, both through legal channels and the black market. Emperor Shaddam has instituted certain changes, after Otorio."

Rulla Tuek entered with a haughty toss of her head, accompanied by Esmar's adult son, Staban. Fenring had met them before. Staban, perhaps thirty-five, had the thick eyebrows of his father and a similar craggy face. Esmar's new wife, a dark-haired Fremen, was about the same age as his son. Inside the smuggler base, she wore an eclectic outfit that consisted of a colorful scarf, a feminine blouse of offworld design, and loose trousers such as were normally worn by a man. Here behind the moisture seals, she did not wear a stillsuit, and Fenring could see that she was obviously pregnant, her abdomen rounded. Perhaps seven months, he guessed.

Esmar had once told Fenring privately that Rulla was vain about her appearance, one more way she pushed back against her Fremen traditions. Esmar would have preferred her to dress more conservatively as a woman of the desert, uncomfortable to have her so relaxed and even flirtatious around his rough smuggler crew. Esmar's first wife, Staban's mother, had been entirely different.

He had married his ambitious second wife seven years ago, had given her gifts, wealth, and influence, and now Rulla was in charge of certain aspects of his smuggling operations, along with Staban. Through her Fremen contacts, she was especially adept at setting up spice caravans with domesticated kulons, selecting routes through the desert that were not harassed by territorial sandworms or by Harkonnen patrols.

Rulla and Staban sat next to each other on a rock bench to the left of the metal desk. Fenring sensed tension between the woman and her husband and a well-concealed awkwardness with the son. The Count wanted to understand their personal complications, because they might affect his business relationships, but right now, he was here on the Emperor's behalf.

The smugglers would not like the news.

"I bring tidings from Emperor Shaddam IV," Fenring said. "There is a significant, hmmm-ahhh, change in policy that you will have to accept. And it will cost you. The Emperor has imposed a new spice surtax, which directs a much larger portion of all melange income to the Kaitain treasury."

The smuggler leader frowned. "We do not operate within Imperial rules. We have our own commercial network."

"That is the reason for our existence," Rulla interjected. "We won't pay any more."

Staban remained silent, listening.

Fenring's expression darkened. "You operate under a certain, hmmm-ahhh, understanding of the rules. Shaddam tolerates your activities, as do I. I can destroy all your operations with a single message to Kaitain—or to Carthag, if I decide to let the Baron take credit."

Esmar flinched. "We already pay a significant bribe to the Emperor! That was our agreement."

"And in return, he looks the other way. From now on, he has decreed that you will pay him more. All operations need to recognize and absorb the new spice surtax. Even smuggling operations. I will be keeping a close eye on you."

"Do these words come from the Emperor or from you, Count Fenring?" Rulla demanded in a tone that irritated him. "Will you pocket a part of the profits for yourself?"

She seemed to realize he disliked her, but didn't seem to care. Though he was a deadly assassin, the woman apparently felt protected here. But it was not wise to make an enemy of Count Hasimir Fenring, and he decided that Rulla would bear closer watching. He tamped down his indignant reaction. "It makes no difference. I speak for Shaddam."

Esmar shot his wife a sharp glance, then turned back to Fenring. "This will hamstring us. The Emperor needs to give us more leeway."

"The Emperor has made clear what he needs. So far I have convinced him it is in his best interest to ignore your operations, because I personally find you useful—at times. But your freedom is merely an illusion." He glanced pointedly from Esmar to his wife. "I can cancel your trading network whenever I wish." Under his sharp gaze, Rulla looked away.

"The smugglers perform a unique service for the Emperor," Staban, the son, interjected. "We provide crucial information on the Harkonnen fief-holder, report whispers from the edges that even you did not know about."

Fenring smiled. "And because your information has proved valuable in the past, we are lenient with you, as a cost of doing business, although it greatly frustrates Baron Harkonnen." He narrowed his gaze. "But there is a limit to what the Emperor will allow. Never forget that, and never try to take advantage of him, or of me. You *will* meet the additional surtax. I will require even more detailed and doubly verified accountings of all your production and shipments."

While Rulla glowered at him, keeping a hand on the curvature of her belly, Esmar gave a reluctant but deferential nod. "Is this surtax temporary? Our normal operations can resume when this crisis wanes?"

"The tax will last only until it pays the deficit in Shaddam's treasury after the expense of the Corrino museum and the expansion of his Sardaukar corps."

"How long will that be? When has a temporary tax ever remained temporary?" Rulla asked, sounding shrill. "What do the cost analyses and projections say?"

"Hmmm-ahh, it will take as long as it needs to take." He hardened his voice. "And the smugglers will pay what they need to pay."

He saw the remark hit home. Rulla looked fearful, for only a moment, but that was enough.

IN HIS CARTHAG office, Baron Harkonnen watched as his twisted Mentat entered.

Piter de Vries moved forward with mincing steps that made him look both effeminate and predatory. "You summoned me, my dear Baron?" His voice was more lilting and musical than usual.

"That is a stupid question," the Baron replied as the Mentat folded his lean body into a chair in front of the ellipsoid desk. "I am not happy—no, I am *outraged*—about the spice surtax the Emperor expects me to pay. I will pass the costs along, but the price can only be raised so much. We have already pushed our customers close to the limits of what they can pay, and I cannot squeeze more without losing some accounts. Many of those not addicted will simply turn to other drugs. I need a way around this! Find me an answer, Mentat."

"Ah, a challenge!" De Vries removed a vial of sapho juice from his pocket and swallowed the red liquid. After a moment, his gaze grew distant as he pondered the challenge. "The obvious solution is for us to produce more spice. And sell more spice."

The Baron growled his displeasure. "If we produce more spice, we will be taxed more! The Emperor profits, but House Harkonnen does not."

The Mentat's eyes took on a calculating look. "Not if we produce spice that appears in no accounting records, my Baron. This planet is vast, and the deserts have much melange. No one can keep track of it all."

The Baron puffed his cheeks. "You mean operate like the dirty smugglers? Perhaps work with them to sell more spice? I suspect the smugglers already have secret connections with Count Fenring, and thus the Imperium—though I can't prove it. Give me a different projection."

De Vries fell silent again, and the Baron felt he was taking too long. This problem needed to be solved now.

The Mentat blinked. "Move a step beyond the smugglers. Our official operations produce and sell melange, which is administered by the Imperium. Such operations are already heavily taxed and monitored closely. That sanctioned melange is distributed through the CHOAM Company. Through special contract, the Spacing Guild receives its direct allotment of spice, which is also heavily taxed. The smugglers move their spice offworld, presumably also through CHOAM, and therefore they must pay significant bribes . . . which go back to the Imperial treasury."

"And still Shaddam claims he needs to wring more money from us!" The Baron snorted. He remained impatient. "I understand basic economics. What is your suggestion?"

"Create another independent channel, a new and secret path to get undocumented spice off-planet. We could sell a certain amount of spice directly to CHOAM, which would appear on no balance sheet, a private closed-loop distribution. That would eliminate the middle tier and be financially beneficial to House Harkonnen and to the CHOAM Company."

The Baron hesitated. "That is taking a tremendous risk." But he needed to survive this abominable new surcharge. . . .

De Vries continued, "I suspect CHOAM would be happy to have an alternative that does not depend on Imperial oversight. If we create the plan, I believe they would welcome it."

The Baron let this idea sink in, then smiled craftily. "Piter, I believe I will let you live a little while longer."

Unfortunately, in extreme cases, a medical treatment can be as fatal as the ailment itself.

—Suk Medical Practicum

The sky of Otorio was smeared with smoke and ash. Fires continued to burn through the devastation because no one was there to put them out. Eventually, the isolated planet would quell itself.

Weeks after the impact, Jaxson Aru had to observe with his own eyes the results of what he had done. Not caring about the resulting horror, he allowed himself a faint smile.

In the aftermath of the attack, some humanitarian aid and salvage operations went to Otorio, and Jaxson managed to infiltrate them. The do-gooders who came to help "those poor injured people" did not realize that Otorio had done just fine for centuries without Imperial interference. As a purported aid worker, Jaxson obtained a private short-range flyer and traveled to the outskirts of the impact site.

Even though the heavy dump boxes had partly vaporized in the air, shock waves had ripped across the Imperial structures, uprooting and flattening them. Scavenger camps surrounded the rim of the crater, groups sifting through the rubble for anything of value. Maybe he would purchase some material from these scavengers: lumps of impact glass as souvenirs to mark his great victory, the first real blow for the Noble Commonwealth. He had jolted the Imperium awake, that was for certain.

The blackened, wrecked landscape was not how he wanted to remember this peaceful, beautiful place. He closed his eyes and brought to mind images of the serene Otorio where he had spent so many years. His mother had sent him away when he was young, disturbed by his volatile nature. Of Malina's three children, Jaxson was the least known, considered unfit for diplomacy like his brother and sister. Rather than thinking of it as an exile, Jaxson had been happy to stay with his father, with whom he had a very close relationship.

Brondon Aru was the last member of his long-standing dynasty, but considered incompetent by his business associates. His wife, though, understood the necessities of the vast company, and Malina was able to wrestle the complex business interests into line, whereas her husband simply had no talent for it.

CHOAM wanted to sweep Brondon under the rug, keep him in a quiet place where he could cause no harm through ineptitude and disinterest. Much later, Malina also used Otorio as a place to hide her impulsive younger son until she knew what to do with him.

Jaxson had spent every summer at their secret estate on Otorio, away from Imperial politics and business complexities. Even so, his mother had insisted that he receive an intense education, strictly through textbooks and theoretical treatises rather than direct experience. Though the young man was intelligent, his knowledge of politics and history was idealistic rather than pragmatic.

His preoccupied father listened to Jaxson's ideas about breaking up the Imperium into a more democratic commonwealth. There was no fire in Brondon's belly to bring about change, but he nevertheless encouraged his son's dreams of a system far superior to the corrupt Emperor and his cronies.

From a distance, Malina supported her son's passions, encouraged him to keep studying how to undermine the system. She revealed with great pride that the Noble Commonwealth movement, sparked in the early years of Fondil Corrino III, had secretly been growing and gaining momentum for generations. Malina had finally found something she could share with her son, an assignment for him that would be as important as the roles of her other children.

Meanwhile, she had encouraged Jaxson to remain out of sight, unnoticed. She would work with him to keep building the quiet but widespread rebellion. Eventually, they could achieve their dream, maybe in the time of Jaxson's great-grandchildren, according to long-term projections. The creaking old Imperium would at last crumble.

Meanwhile, Jaxson and his father kept themselves busy on Otorio. They were active in sports, riding genetically enhanced thoroughbreds, swimming and diving in the calm inland sea, flying together in glide suits over the plains.

One evening, Brondon suffered a devastating stroke at dinner, which left him nearly paralyzed, barely capable of speech. As he lay under the care of local doctors, Brondon wept for his lost life, and Jaxson wept for all the lost time and opportunities with his father.

As it rained outside and he sat with his slack-faced father, Jaxson talked about all of the things they had done together, things that Brondon would never do again. Struggling to form words, the older man slurred to his son, "Don't waste your life, Jax. I did. Now it's over. Never gave it a thought. But you . . . do great things. Do what you must. And people will remember for ages to come."

Fearing the inevitable decline of his functions, Brondon begged Jaxson to assist him. The young man eventually procured a euphoric poison that helped his father end his withered life.

Jaxson buried his beloved father in an ancient and majestic stand of olive trees that covered acres on the old estate. This sacred grove was where he and Brondon had talked about improbable dreams. This was a personal sanctuary for him.

After the funeral, Jaxson left Otorio to stay with his mother on Tupile, where she engaged him in more vigorous political and commercial training. He even visited his sister, Jalma, on Pliesse, and they made jokes at the bedside of comatose Count Uchan, her husband, even though the helpless old man reminded Jaxson too painfully of his own helpless father.

Next, Jaxson had traveled to the Silver Needle on Kaitain, the official headquarters of CHOAM, and sat in on formal Directors meetings chaired by his brother, Frankos. But he found the ponderous bureaucratic pace frustrating, and he could only remember his father's last words insisting that he do something to make his mark on history.

Then Shaddam rediscovered the "misplaced" planet of Otorio and chose it as the perfect site for his gaudy Corrino museum. He had razed the landscape and erected his eyesore.

During the disruptive construction work, Jaxson had slipped back there, unable to file any protest because the Aru family holdings were secret and held in blind corporations. Aghast, he saw that Shaddam had uprooted and cleared the entire olive grove, desecrating his father's grave shrine.

That was the point at which Jaxson realized that the slow work of the Noble Commonwealth was simply not good enough, and he decided to do something about it. . . .

Now he stared at the glassy wreckage of the impact site, where the lovely olive grove had once stood, the peaceful, sacred area where his father had been buried. The wanton destruction from the crash pained Jaxson, but his beloved home had already been destroyed by the hated Shaddam Corrino.

His eyes and lungs burned from the lingering smoke in the air. He had seen enough.

When the Noble Commonwealth succeeded, the people of Otorio could make their own choices, just as all worlds could choose. Jaxson would make them choose, whatever the cost in blood.

The most insidious enemy is one that resides in your own household.
And not all such enemies have a human face.
—DUKE PAULUS ATREIDES, "Counsel to Future Dukes"

Creaking with age and dignity, Castle Caladan was like a favorite suit of clothes, worn but well cared for. The stone walls emanated a cool dampness, with an occasional film of salt collected from the sea air. Nighttime clouds had rolled in across the ocean with a light but steady rain, but Leto was warm and at home in his private office.

Distracted and restless, Leto settled down alone to read reports that had piled up in his absence. The visit to the Muadh village had been satisfying and necessary, but he still had much outstanding business to attend to. The hour was late, Paul long in bed and Jessica off in private meditations.

Dark wood trimmings and crowded bookshelves provided a stately setting, befitting the Duke's station. Glowglobes near the ceiling were tuned to warm orange, which triggered a deep primitive response of comfort, as if from a family hearth or a cave fire. A decanter of honey-colored Kirana brandy rested on the corner of his hardwood desk, and as he perused his reports, Leto poured himself a splash.

He reviewed the comprehensive summary Minister Wellan had prepared regarding Caladan's moonfish industry, which included projections of the market share and suggestions to expand fishery operations in the north. Leto looked at images of the linked breeding ponds, read proposed leases and tithe contracts with various offworld customers, even several futures investors. Wellan had appended a solicitation from CHOAM agreeing to an increase in distribution and a list of the associated fees.

As he flipped through Wellan's numbers and projections, something caught his eye. He studied the reports, compared dates, and saw that the minister had inspected the fishery operations personally, not just once but multiple times—a surprising number of times, in fact. Leto flipped through receipts and travel manifests. On several trips, though, the minister had also diverted his itinerary inland, even skirting some pundi rice villages, including the one Leto had just visited for the Muadh ceremony.

That was odd. A fishery minister should have had no business whatsoever with pundi rice farmers. Was Wellan making side investments of his own? An influential man with knowledge of the commerce of Caladan might expand his private holdings, but he should not have masked such things as part of his work involving moonfish exports.

Leto glanced at the Ixian chronometer on his office wall, a fancy model once given to him by the exiled Prince Rhombur Vernius. It displayed the time on multiple worlds across the Imperium. Although the hour was late, Minister Wellan was known for his irregular schedule.

In addition to household staff and close retainers, many of the primary government offices of Caladan were located in a separate wing of the castle. Newer administrative buildings in Cala City housed minor officials and handled general bureaucracy, but the fishery minister had offices in the castle itself, even a small sleep chamber for when he chose to work at odd hours. The Duke decided to try to see him.

Leto picked up the questionable report and left his office. Even if Wellan was not there, he intended to leave a note, requesting an immediate conversation.

The halls were empty as Leto walked to the administrative wing. As expected, most of the offices were dark, the doors closed, but a yellow glow shone from the fishery minister's rooms. Leto stepped toward the office door, ready to ask uncomfortable questions.

With his leadership style and long-standing connections to the people of Caladan, the Duke always tried to think the best of his staff and officials. He led by example with the hallmark Atreides code of honor, but he was not naïve. Such trust had to be earned. Wellan had served him well enough over the years, and Leto would let the man explain the anomalies. Perhaps there was nothing to worry about.

When he rapped on the door, his ducal signet ring struck the hardwood as loud as the report of a projectile weapon, but no one answered. Despite the lights inside, he heard no one stirring, saw no shadows moving through the hazed plaz window. Perhaps the minister had gone home after all.

Leto found the door unlocked, which troubled him. The records stored inside the ministry offices contained sensitive information and should not have been left unsecured. He pushed open the door and entered the outer chamber, which would normally be guarded by a receptionist. "Wellan? I need to speak with you."

The office had a sour heaviness, as if it needed to be aired out. The front desk sat empty—not surprisingly, since Wellan was the only one likely to work so late. The door to the inner office, though, was wide open. Inside, the glowglobes were tuned bright, giving off a harsh white glare.

Leto found the minister slumped over his desk, his arm extended forward, palm up, fingers curled around a dried brown object. Wellan had not just fallen asleep; his mouth was slack with drool oozing out, his eyes half-open and bleary with startling scarlet hemorrhages. His face pressed against paper documents strewn across his desk, and his other arm hung down like deadweight at his side. He looked as if some giant hand had swatted him like a bug.

Leto dashed forward. "Wellan!" The man didn't react, even when the Duke grabbed him by the shoulder. Leto bellowed into the empty antechamber and the unoccupied office wing. "Help! Someone bring assistance." He looked down at the man, peeled his eyelid open farther, and saw only a blank blur behind his red eyes. Wellan still didn't stir.

Leto found the comm speaker on the man's desk and pounded down on the pickup, yelling into the grid. "I need help in Minister Wellan's office. Send Dr. Yueh!"

He pulled the man up, worried that Wellan might choke on his own vomit. Then he recognized what the minister held curled in his hand, a shriveled brown thing like a bent finger—exactly what Leto had seen during the Muadh centering and purification ritual. He plucked it out of the twitching grip. The dried remnant of a supposedly innocuous barra fern, half of it gone. Wellan had taken the drug ailar, but his reaction was unlike what Leto had seen among all the pundi rice farmers when they partook of the consecrated substance.

The anguished words of Lord Atikk's message suddenly came back to him. *Your Caladan drug killed my son!*

Leto touched Wellan's temple, then his throat. The man was barely breathing, his pulse thready. Previously, the minister had exhibited a frenetic demeanor, a sharp, fractured look in his eyes. But during the Muadh ceremony, ailar had made the people peaceful, content, and more alert . . . not this!

You lured him with a peaceful release, but it was like a hidden bomb.

The Caladan drug?

Thufir Hawat burst into the offices accompanied by three Atreides guards, all of whom had their body shields activated and weapons drawn, ready to fight.

Minister Wellan began to twitch, then went into extreme convulsions.

The warrior Mentat charged forward, blocking the Duke protectively in case Wellan lashed out in a frenzy. "Are you safe, my Lord?"

"He has taken some kind of drug. Help me with him! Where is Dr. Yueh?"

"On his way." Leto and Hawat wrestled the minister, attempting to hold him flat and still, but his body writhed. His eyes flew open, and the white scleras were now completely red from internal hemorrhaging. Two guards pressed forward to help hold down the thrashing man.

Leto spoke through clenched teeth. "I came to see him because of some anomalies in his report. I did not expect this. Look what was in his hand."

Hawat glanced down at the curled brown shred. "Is that a barra fern? You asked me to look into rumors of a new Caladan drug, my Lord. I found some hints, but nothing conclusive. There have been reports of ailar use as a drug."

"I never heard of it before the Muadh ceremony," Leto said. "Is it not just used for religious purposes? What we saw appeared to be mild and euphoric, not deadly. Why was I not informed?"

Hawat's expression was stern. "I would not expect you to know of a low street drug, sir."

"Wellan made trips up north to inspect the moonfish pools and the processing fisheries," Leto said, making connections in his mind. "But it seems he also made unscheduled appearances inland near the pundi rice paddies in the northern wilderness."

Hawat assisted the Duke, but his eyes had a faraway expression. As a Mentat, he was always at his best, alert, organizing details in his mind. "I have not applied my thoughts to Minister Wellan before, but certain data points do not align. I should have been suspicious sooner."

The Mentat's eyes became distant again, assembling additional connections, conversations, and encounters with unexpected personnel. "Perhaps a review of the house guard is in order. I recall three instances in which I witnessed Wellan speaking to a certain lieutenant . . . someone with whom he should have had no direct business."

Dr. Yueh finally rushed in, disheveled. Wellington Yueh was a small-statured, intense man with a drawn face, sallow complexion, and lips the color of bruises. His long, dark hair was bound in a single ponytail held by a silver ring. He was a doctor of the Suk School, formerly in service to House Richese. In recent years, Yueh had remained on Caladan as the House Atreides personal physician. A diamond tattoo in the middle of his forehead indicated his deep Imperial conditioning.

The Suk doctor rushed to the convulsing patient. He slapped an injector against Wellan's neck, glanced down at the brown remnant of barra fern on the desk, recognized it. "Oh no."

"It is some kind of rustic drug called ailar," Leto said. "He is reacting badly."

The minister's convulsions grew worse, and his staring eyes became as red as a demon's and filled with blood.

"I have seen this before, my Duke. An extraordinarily potent strain of the barra fern that releases a high concentration of ailar. At this stage, there is little—"

"Do something!" Leto said.

Yueh opened his medpack, touched monitors to the patient so he could read his biological functions. When Wellan's thrashing slowed, Leto thought the minister had improved, but in fact, his condition was declining. Wellan's entire body slumped, as if melting.

The doctor stood back, dark lips downturned in a frown that etched the lines deeper in his face. "He has a severe brain hemorrhage that I would not be able to relieve even with immediate surgery, I'm afraid. We are merely here to watch him die, my Lord."

"How can you be so sure, Yueh? Don't give up like that!"

The Suk doctor pressed his lips together. "Because no more than an hour ago, I treated an identical case in the guard quarters, and I have noted a rash of ailar overdoses in Cala City, especially in the low-town, the taverns, and boathouses. All were fatal."

Leto couldn't believe what he was hearing. "Such deaths are commonplace?"

"Alarmingly so, Sire. And spreading farther."

The words of Lord Atikk echoed in his mind. *Your Caladan drug killed my son!*

"How is this drug here in Cala City? *And in my castle?* How has this drug infiltrated my people?"

Yueh stepped away from the dying minister. "I am merely a doctor, my Lord. Those are answers I cannot provide."

"Who was the other victim?" Hawat demanded. "You said you just lost another person from ailar. In the guard quarters?"

"That is why I was slow to respond here." Yueh's long, dark mustaches emphasized his deep frown. "Apologies, but it would not have made any difference to Minister Wellan."

The man twitched one more time and let out a long gurgle, a death rattle. Yueh touched his hand and closed his red-stained eyes.

"Who was the victim in the guard quarters?" Hawat asked again.

The Suk doctor glanced up. "A lieutenant named Nupree. He died in the same way."

The Caladan drug . . . Leto knew of only one source of the ailar. "Barra ferns are used in a Muadh ritual, growing wild in the deep northern wilderness. Minister Wellan went up there on several trips that did not make sense. By his own request, Lieutenant Nupree led security on my recent expedition to the pundi rice farmers. There is a clear connection. They all went up to the area of the Muadh village."

Hawat's expression was grave. "Nupree is the officer I spoke of, my Lord. Minister Wellan and Lieutenant Nupree were observed meeting several times, but I could think of no reason they would have any business together. There was no explanation."

"Until now." Leto looked at the shriveled remnants of the half-consumed fern. "How is this happening among my people?" He thought of the Archvicar and his deacons passing around baskets full of the shriveled plant. "I want it stopped at once."

The Silver Needle thrust above the skyline of Kaitain with liquid metal curves. The CHOAM administrative building was a prominent landmark, drawing so much attention that no one thought to look for the company's real center of power hidden on Tupile.

After her necessary speech in the Landsraad Hall, and then the meeting with Empress Aricatha, Malina Aru had withdrawn to the Silver Needle, where she could seal herself behind plaz doors and pentashields.

No one challenged the Ur-Director when she entered the soaring complex. With the speed of a projectile, an accelerated lift took her to the pinnacle, and she emerged unruffled in the headquarters of CHOAM's figurehead President.

Frankos stood waiting for her when the lift doors slid aside, as if he had anticipated the precise second of her arrival. "The others are here, Mother." He bowed slightly. "They await your guidance."

"My guidance will come after I hear their input," she said, stepping briskly forward. "The upper-echelon Directors of CHOAM are selected for their wisdom and imagination. I am not an autocrat."

"Of course, Mother." Frankos gave her a knowing smile.

Her older son had an air of maturity and respectability. Dark hair salted with silver gave him a distinguished look, while his smooth, tanned face and sharp blue-gray eyes implied confident energy. His appearance matched the role he had to play. Frankos had served as CHOAM President for a decade, and he performed exactly as Malina had taught him to.

As President, he made the public appearances his mother did not want to make. Standing in front of the yellow CHOAM banner with its red-and-black circles, he would issue public announcements about company policy. He occupied offices at the apex of the Silver Needle and held the highest rank of the thousand CHOAM Directors across the Imperium.

Because Malina enhanced her health and slowed her visible aging through a steady diet of spice, the mother looked the same age as her son. Both had been crafted to exude power through training, expectations, and poise.

Frankos gestured her toward the closed onyxwood doors of the main conference room. Two monolithic guards stood motionless outside, staring down the hall.

Malina led the way. "Are Har and Kar inside? You've cared for them?"

"Of course, and they are content, though they will be glad to see you." His voice took on an amused undertone. "I think Duke Verdun is intimidated by them."

"He should be." Warmed by the thought of seeing her pets, she approached the guards in front of the closed onyx doors. The men looked like boulders with arms and legs, but they moved nimbly to open the door for her. She entered the conference room, where several other key allied Directors sat around the mirror-polished table. As soon as the doors opened, the high-ranking men and women rose respectfully to their feet.

"Welcome, Urdir," said old Rajiv Londine in his reedy voice. The elder lord wore intense red-and-violet colors, as if to show his verve for life.

Viscount Giandro Tull bowed as he rose. "Urdir." In contrast to Lord Londine, he wore brown-and-charcoal formal business attire. He was a young and handsome man, only recently installed in his position after the unexpected death of his father.

Duke Fausto Verdun took a step toward her, smiling. He had long, wavy hair and a stylish Vandyke beard and mustache, artfully pointed and waxed. Four others also stood to acknowledge her arrival. It was a tight inner circle.

Malina, though, turned her attention to the bristling silver spinehounds crouched beside her daughter, Jalma, who remained seated holding their krimskell collars. Har and Kar were eager to see their mistress, but well enough trained that they waited for her to stroll toward them. Malina gently stroked the hard gray needles that comprised the animals' fur, scratched behind the spikes in their upright ears. Such beautiful animals, created and perfected by Tleilaxu breeding and genetic manipulation. Their long and terrifying teeth could rip a human apart in seconds, but Malina was not afraid.

With one command, she could turn the spinehounds loose on everyone in this room, but she didn't have to. That was why she had summoned these important men and women to the secret CHOAM meeting. The Noble Commonwealth movement needed them and trusted them.

After she had paid appropriate attention to her hounds, Malina finally acknowledged the rest of the attendees in the room. The seven high-echelon Directors remained standing out of respect, each wearing the colors of their Houses and the garment styles of their planets.

As if they had all held their breaths until the Urdir's arrival, the conversation flooded back louder, overlapping voices trying to get her attention. She took a seat next to Jalma, and in doing so became the anchor that defined the head of the irregularly shaped table. The two spinehounds came to take up positions next to her. She was pleased to see that they looked healthy and eager.

Jalma wore a dress overburdened with ornate but prim finery, as was the custom on Pliesse. Over her years of being married to the wealthy and frail old Count Uchan, she had adopted the local customs and now wore such constraining clothes as if they were her due.

Duke Fausto Verdun leaned forward and spoke as if he intended to earn points from the Ur-Director. "Before we begin, let me express my deepest sympathy to Lady Jalma at the loss of her husband on Otorio." He shook his head, made a soothing sound. "So many nobles died there. The Landsraad will be reeling for generations."

"Indeed, a terrible tragedy," said Lord Londine.

Jalma's face remained impassive, showing not a hint of grief. "Thank you for your condolences. The Pliesse government remains stable. With my husband's long-standing ailments, I myself had to conduct more and more of the daily affairs."

Malina gave her daughter a respectful nod, affirming the story they had concocted. "It was your husband's last wish to see the lovely new Corrino museum on Otorio. I'm glad he got that opportunity before he died."

She knew full well that Count Uchan had never even left his deathbed in the old family mansion on Pliesse, but falsified records now showed that he had traveled to Otorio, where he'd perished in the explosion. None of the survivors would remember whether or not he had attended the gala reception, and his body would never be found. Everything for a kilometer around the impact point had been vaporized.

Years ago, Jalma had married Count Uchan, an older, powerful Landsraad noble who controlled seven planets, including Pliesse. Soon after the marriage, Jalma dominated House Uchan, received a power of attorney that enabled her to speak for her increasingly frail and confused husband. The Count had not been seen in public for the past five years. Malina knew that the doddering old man had actually fallen into a coma, unable to interfere with Jalma's work.

Upon learning of the Otorio disaster, Jalma had reacted swiftly, manufacturing the story and the evidence, which became an effective way to erase the pustule of a husband she endured for so long. Jalma had killed him herself, erased his remains, and secured her power over the House.

Malina approved, though she wished her daughter had asked permission before taking such impulsive action, but she understood there had been no time. At least that was one silver lining from Jaxson's outrageous act. The Aru family had learned to be flexible, to seize opportunities.

Now in the meeting, Frankos also expressed insincere condolences to his sister. He knew, of course, what had actually happened. He took the seat beside Jalma and deferred to his mother as the leader of the meeting.

Malina called the group to order. "We begin by stating the obvious. We must discuss and understand what my foolish son Jaxson has done. What do we say, how do we respond? And how can CHOAM benefit from it?"

"Benefit?" asked Duke Verdun. "He has eviscerated the Landsraad, disrupted commerce across hundreds of systems! We are Landsraad nobles, each of us, but we are also CHOAM Directors. Your son's act unravels the fabric of the Imperium."

"Our *objective* is to unravel the fabric of the Imperium," said Rajiv Londine. "Is that not the stated purpose of the Noble Commonwealth? Is that what you mean, Urdir? Can we use your son's act to expand our work?"

"We have the same goal as my foolish son, but fundamentally different methods," Malina said.

"The Noble Commonwealth has worked steadily for generations," said Viscount Tull, "but now our careful plans are ruined." He groaned deep in his chest. "Through constant, gradual pressure, we have weakened the underpinnings of the Imperium and continued to spread our ideals."

"It was taking hold," Malina said, "but now we must survive and adapt. What Jaxson did is already done." She should have planned better, should have anticipated her younger son's outrage and impetuous behavior, but she had not grasped how deeply the desecration of the family estate would affect Jaxson.

A crack finally showed on Frankos's businesslike expression. "I remember my brother sitting in this very room, listening in on official CHOAM meetings." He shook his head. "Jaxson always seemed unstable, out of place. I thought we were beginning to rein him in, make him see the bigger picture. But what he just did . . ."

"When Jaxson decides on a goal, he is as focused as a lasbeam," Jalma said. "He saw only a hot red targeting cross in front of him instead of the whole plan."

"We cannot undo the attack on Otorio no matter how much we complain," Malina repeated. "But we must be careful to mitigate what we can. Shaddam is already volatile and capricious. After such destruction, if the Emperor becomes reactionary, that would harm us. We must deflect him."

"He's already imposed a heavy new spice surtax!" groaned one of the more introspective upper Directors, Earl Leeper. "Even I cannot afford it, no matter how desperate my need for melange may become. People are going to die of withdrawal. They are not able to live without spice."

"We will find a way around it," Malina said.

"Your son has exposed the Noble Commonwealth, set back all the progress we made!" huffed Fausto Verdun. His voice was so loud that both spinehounds began to growl, and the Duke sat back, looking nervous.

Malina extended her hands on either side of her chair, and Har and Kar took solace in licking her palms. "You Directors understand the intricacies of commerce—supply and demand. The Otorio disaster disrupted normal trade routes, and with so much uncertainty in the Landsraad, the markets are falling. We must find a way to arrest the economic collapse."

"We should arrest your son, bring him to justice. Then the markets would calm," Verdun grumbled, then clamped his lips shut as the spinehounds growled again.

"I do not know where he is," Malina said, and it was a true statement. "He has cut off ties with me as well."

Old Rajiv Londine, a quiet and reserved man despite his garish colors, expressed his frustration. "Our forefathers developed a long-term plan for the independence of thousands of planets. Now Jaxson's attack not only provokes the Emperor, it also turns countless potential sympathizers into enemies."

Viscount Tull nodded, tugging the sleeve of his charcoal suit. He was still uncertain of his position in the inner circle, but he filled his father's shoes well. "For a long time, rumors about the Noble Commonwealth were dismissed or ignored. We were very careful! But Jaxson's manifesto shone a beacon on all our work, and the fool Shaddam is paying close attention. He sees it as a personal affront. We are not ready to unravel the whole Imperium yet."

"By design, Jaxson killed only those nobles who are *not* allied with our cause," Malina pointed out, reluctant to entirely disown and destroy her son, despite her words in the Landsraad Hall. "No one from CHOAM officially attended the museum ceremony. All of our secret loyalists were instructed to make excuses— even without knowing what my son intended." She sighed. "I had meant it as a quiet snub of House Corrino."

Jalma's face bore a pinched expression. "Many have dual loyalties between CHOAM and the Landsraad, Mother. Our movement did lose some allies."

"Then they made their choice," she said, resting her elbows on the mirror-polished table. "I suspected Jaxson might do something unwise, but I never guessed the sheer magnitude of his violence." She braced herself, squared her shoulders. "Yet we are resilient. In fact, my son's blatant violence helps us camouflage the Noble Commonwealth's true work. We can make use of this."

Frankos sat up straighter, looking at his mother with surprise and even a glint of hope. "How so?"

"Your brother is unpredictable, but at times, he serves a purpose. His action was like a red flag in a bullfight, and he will draw the full attention of Shaddam and his Sardaukar forces. They will be busy hunting him down." She rose from her chair, and the two spinehounds climbed to their feet, shaking themselves vigorously so that their silver spines fluffed out like the thorns of a thistle.

Malina swung her gaze around the irregular table, looking at her children and the inner-circle Directors. These were only a handful of the secret supporters of the Noble Commonwealth. "You heard my address in the Landsraad Hall. I personally disavowed Jaxson, broke ties with my own son, although that was merely a formality. He is my son and will always be my son. I believe Jaxson will come back into the fold, and we can use him. For now, he will draw attention while we continue to quietly dismantle the Imperium."

Jalma tapped her fingertips on the polished table surface. "Shaddam's reactionary policies will result in driving a greater wedge between himself and the Landsraad. The nobles will certainly rebel against the higher melange prices, even if some can afford it." She gave a nod to Earl Leeper on the other side of the table.

"Markets rise and fall. Supply and demand," Malina said. "We are CHOAM. We are the suppliers, and we encourage the demand."

"But how do we get around the surtax?" asked Duke Verdun. "I use a lot of melange myself, and now it will be significantly more expensive." He pouted, and Malina knew that spice was a status symbol for him. "Almost more than I can afford."

"Perhaps we have another supplier, a completely separate channel from the melange regulated by the Imperium." Her lips quirked in a small smile, and she saw she had their full attention. "With a surreptitious and untaxed flow of spice, we can supply our own network, our loyalists, the people who continue the vital work of the Noble Commonwealth. Meanwhile, those who suffer from the burden of Imperial taxes will grow ripe for our cause. We can work with this."

"The situation will not turn out well for Shaddam Corrino," said young Viscount Tull.

Frankos brushed imaginary lint from his sleeve. "And where will we get such an unexpected supply of spice, Mother? Melange is under the tightest control."

She paused to look at each of her Directors. In unison, Har and Kar lay down at her feet. She smiled and mused aloud, "I just received a very interesting communiqué from Baron Vladimir Harkonnen. He thinks he has a channel to provide the spice we need."

Accompanied by his warrior Mentat and Suk doctor, Leto summoned a contingent of Atreides guards to head north to the Muadh village. Some of the Atreides soldiers were shocked and shaken at the sudden death of Lieutenant Nupree. Duke Leto insisted on going to the known source without delay.

He took his secure diplomatic frigate, though not in its customary slow and pompous procession. It flew swiftly, like a gunship, and raced up to the pundi rice paddies, the lush terraced valleys and silvery irrigation pools. The Arondi Cliffs rose abruptly like the blade of an ax, marking the location of the farming village and its religious center.

Leto wrestled with his anger and disbelief at what Archvicar Torono had done. The religious leader had boldly distributed the insidious ailar right in front of the Duke, even tried to tempt Leto and his son into trying it. The audacity! Was the man flaunting his drug, so confident in his power that he could dare Leto to do something about it? Did he think the Duke would remain oblivious to the spread of something so deadly, a poisonous substance implicitly tied to House Atreides?

Your Caladan drug killed my son!

He could better comprehend the personal dagger of Lord Atikk's grief. Even if the spread of ailar had been done without Leto's knowledge, the people of Caladan were his people, and the Duke's reputation was his own. No enemy could take away his reputation, but he could lose it much more quickly than it had been gained. . . .

Approaching without escort or warning, the Duke would demonstrate a swift, firm response. His processional frigate settled down at the edge of the main village, blocking the central path into the clustered houses. Atreides soldiers emerged from the ornate airship, body shields already activated. They lined up as an impressive, intimidating honor guard.

Hawat marched out ahead of the Duke and surveyed the area like a prowling gazehound, then signaled Leto that it was safe to emerge.

When he activated his own body shield, the Duke felt the thrumming ozone around him, saw the faint distortion in the air. Though he doubted these meek Muadh villagers would attack him, his knowledge made him suspicious. Were they all involved in the drug trade, processing and smuggling deadly ailar to Cala City and then offworld? Even if they claimed innocence, they would have to earn his trust again.

As he surveyed the confused pundi rice farmers coming forward, his expression was intimidating. He let his anger show. The Atreides hawk was proudly displayed on his breast, the green-and-black cape flowing behind him. The Muadh villagers milled about, unsettled to see the mood of the important visitors.

He turned his gaze to the majestic Muadh temple, ready to demand explanations from Archvicar Torono. But how could he believe whatever the man said? He knew Minister Wellan had surreptitiously gone to this area over and over again. He knew Lieutenant Nupree had just been here, probably obtained the last shipment of ailar during the recent visit. He knew both men were connected . . . and it all traced back to here.

As Dr. Yueh disembarked behind him, Leto glanced over his shoulder. "Help me find answers, Yueh. We know where the drug ferns come from and who uses them. We have to stop this, uproot it like a noxious weed."

The temple doors swung open, and the impressive Archvicar emerged in his formal brown robes and cap embroidered with a barra fern frond. Despite all the soldiers in the Atreides honor guard, the religious leader looked peaceful and benevolent, warmhearted as always. But Leto viewed the bearded man differently now.

Had Torono's respect merely been a ruse? But to what purpose? Why would the religious leader go out of his way to draw attention to the ailar and its euphoric properties? Leto had been unaware of the "low street drug," as Hawat called it, but the Archvicar had made sure Leto witnessed the purification ceremony, watched all those people drugged with the barra ferns.

If this ailar, this poison, were being developed and quietly smuggled throughout Cala City, killing his people, and distributed offworld extensively enough that other nobles talked openly about the "Caladan drug," Duke Leto could not abide it. How many others had died and silently blamed him?

With an innocuous smile, Torono opened his hands expansively to draw a blessing out of the air. "Duke Leto Atreides, my Duke, we did not expect to see you again so soon. You honor us with a return visit."

Leto took two steps forward and stopped abruptly, facing the religious leader. "Let us not discuss honor here. I come to discuss victims. You must know why we've returned."

The anger in Leto's voice disoriented the religious leader. "Why, no, my Duke. We do not know."

"Two members of my staff are dead from drugs that could only have come from your village. At least one noble son has also died from your ailar, and now I learn that many other Caladan people have been killed, because of your barra ferns! Did you think we would not find out?"

The Archvicar looked confused. He took a tentative step back, then paused, glancing nervously at the Atreides honor guard, the glowering face of Thufir Hawat. "What do you mean, my Duke? I do not understand." Torono made strange gestures, tracing and pulling intangible strands as if plucking an unseen web of lines.

"We saw your ritual," Leto said. "We know the source of ailar. You showed it to us yourself."

"Yes, we shared it with you. We offered you the chance to partake as well."

"It has killed many people, not just in Cala City, or in my own staff, but off-world as well."

Hawat turned slowly among his soldiers, signaling to prepare them as if he expected the frightened villagers to turn into a mob.

Torono remained calm. "We did not kill anyone, my Duke. I swear by the All-Seeing, by everything the Muadh consider holy, by everything you hold dear. You have seen our ritual."

Leto could not dispel the memory of Wellan in his death throes, writhing, hemorrhaging. "Yes, I have seen what it does."

Despite his anger, though, Leto felt a twinge of uncertainty. The Archvicar was quite convincing. The Muadh villagers looked alarmed, but they did not act guilty. The Atreides soldiers remained at attention.

Hawat addressed the religious leader, rattling off the evidence again. "Our fishery minister died of an overdose of ailar. We found one of your dried ferns in his clenched hand. Our military officer Lieutenant Nupree, who visited here with us to witness your ceremony, likewise died of the drug." He glanced at the Suk doctor standing next to Leto. "Dr. Yueh has further information."

The Archvicar kept shaking his head. "No, that is not true. Ailar is gentle and enlightening. We have all gathered barra ferns, used them for generations."

Yueh said, "The drug is exceedingly potent. I would not characterize it as either 'gentle' or 'enlightening.' At my Duke's request, I ran a medical search through the records of Cala City." The doctor's brow furrowed in deep concentration. "There are many medical practitioners, small clinics, local doctors. I discovered numerous accounts of ailar use, a black market in barra ferns, but there has been a recent surge of deaths, ugly overdoses. Many local physicians did not know what they were dealing with." He paused, looked at the Duke. "In the past several months, one hundred twenty-three reported fatalities have occurred, all overdoses from ailar. There could be many more, unrecorded."

"My Duke, that is not possible!" the Archvicar cried. "The Muadh have partaken of the ferns for generations. It is not dangerous."

"I saw the dried fern myself in Minister Wellan's hand as he died," Leto said. "I know what it was. The connection comes from you, your people, and this area."

The Archvicar stroked his thick beard as if he thought that keeping it under control might keep this situation under control. "But I know nothing of this. Hundreds of my people partook before your very eyes. No one suffered ill effects." The rice farmers muttered, and the Archvicar continued, "We comb the forests and marshes up north. We find where the wild ferns grow and harvest the nubs. It is a bonding activity for our community. We dry them here in the village for our own supply. But we do not sell the ferns, not to anyone."

"Someone does, and I will get to the bottom of this." Leto knew he could not be lenient. How many other anguished letters would he receive from grieving nobles who had lost children to the scourge? "Effective immediately, I forbid further usage. Burn it all."

Now the Muadh cried out in dismay. Torono stiffened. "But it is a key component of our religion. You can't take this away from us!"

"People have died! Caladanians have died. Nobles have died!" Leto said. "And I don't want any of your people to die, either. Maybe you have been lucky? I don't think so. Where is the supply? Who sold the ferns to Lieutenant Nupree, to Minister Wellan, to all those other victims? Who runs the black market in Cala City?"

"I do not know, my Duke. Honestly, I do not."

Leto paused, seeing the sincerity and desperation in the Archvicar's face. As Duke, he did not interfere with the religious practices of his people, but he knew the danger here, the innocents who had died. He had seen the agony Wellan suffered, and knew how many others had already succumbed. *The first responsibility of a Duke is the safety of his people.* "Burn all the remaining ferns so they do not end up in the hands of other victims."

Trembling, the Archvicar looked at the Atreides guards, the Duke's implacable expression now that he had made up his mind, and knew he couldn't resist. Sullen, Torono clapped his hands, and deacons rushed into the temple to emerge carrying baskets. "Our remaining supply is minimal, my Duke," the Archvicar said. "We used most of it in the recent ceremony. We need to gather more ferns."

"From now on, you will no longer have your ceremony," Leto said. "That is my decree. I outlaw the practice, due to the demonstrated danger the drug poses."

The deacons dumped the shriveled curls onto the ground, and the rice farmers backed away, forming a wide ring.

Yueh approached the mound of ferns, fascinated. "We should keep some samples for testing, my Lord. We know very little about ailar, not just the effects of the drug but how the ferns grow naturally in the wild. I have seen a record that the special fern grows on no other planet. If we are going to stop this drug epidemic, we must learn everything we can about the source."

Hawat agreed. "The Suk doctor is correct. Simply burning this supply will not end the problem. I advise we keep samples for research."

Leto understood the need. "Yes, keep what you require, Yueh, and destroy the rest."

The villagers beseeched him, and the Archvicar looked deeply hurt, but before he was tempted to be compassionate, Leto thought again of Wellan's face flat against his desk, drool puddling from his slack mouth . . . remembered the grieving letter from Lord Atikk.

Dr. Yueh gathered a handful of dried specimens from the pile on the ground, but only a few. Leto looked at the Archvicar. "My Mentat will engage in a full-scale investigation. If the fern grows only in the wild north, how does it find its way into the streets of Cala City? How are your people distributing it?"

Torono shook his head. "My Duke, our followers do not go to Cala City. The Muadh are simple people. We stay here." He stretched out his arms. "The rice fields and these cliffs are all we need."

"And the drug," Leto said.

"We gather only what we require for ourselves. It is a harmless substance."

Seeing the mound of shriveled brown ferns, Leto recalled sitting happily among these people as they passed around baskets of the drug, offering it to Leto, to Jessica . . . to his son!

What if Paul had taken some of the tainted plants and died in horrific convulsions?

"Burn it," he said.

Two guards came forward, doused the pile of ferns with accelerant, and ignited them.

The Muadh people bowed their heads. Leto avoided the curls of greasy smoke that rose up, inhaling only shallowly. He looked around at the rice farmers, knowing they had revered him, and had honored so many previous generations of the Atreides Dukes.

Hawat lowered his voice as they watched the conflagration. "One point to consider, my Lord. If these ferns grow wild, and the Muadh truly gather only what they use for their ceremonies, then others could be harvesting the barra fern for a different purpose entirely."

A DAY AFTER the party returned from the Muadh village, Dr. Yueh delivered his analysis to Leto in Castle Caladan. The Suk had brushed his long, dark hair and bound it neatly in its silver ring, and the diamond tattoo on his forehead stood out because his sallow complexion seemed paler than usual. Thufir Hawat accompanied him, but stood in silence as the doctor presented his results.

"I studied the fern samples, Sire. The remnants we retrieved from the Muadh temple do contain ailar, but the potency is quite different from the samples found on both Minister Wellan and Lieutenant Nupree. That one is a different strain of the fern, with a vastly higher concentration."

Leto frowned. "Not the same as the drug used in the ritual? Is it a subspecies of barra fern?"

"Maybe, my Lord. But deep cellular analysis suggests it was organically modified. I suspect with the intent of increasing the concentration."

Leto studied the Suk doctor's cool analytical expression, though he himself felt deep anger and disgust in his heart. "So anyone expecting the normal, milder ailar could easily have overdosed."

"Indeed, my Lord." Yueh held up one of curled brown objects. "The type of enhanced fern consumed by Wellan and Nupree—and presumably by the hundreds of victims in Cala City—would have proved fatal in the same quantity the Muadh used in their ritual."

Leto's cheeks flushed. He nodded. "Lord Atikk's son discovered the same thing."

Yueh deftly removed another packet from his pocket, a slightly different specimen. "But this is what we found on both victims in Castle Caladan, and it matches samples from other overdose casualties in Cala City." He extended the second fern curl to Leto. "As you can see, my Lord, the pigmentation is a little different, slightly mottled. I believe this type of genetically modified fern is now being sold in Cala City, and offworld." He bowed and stepped back, his report complete.

Leto stared down at the fern remnants on his desk as if they were coiled vipers. "The Caladan drug," he said, feeling the personal affront to his reputation, his honor.

Hawat added information. "I have discovered that smuggling operations are far more significant than I first imagined." The Mentat wiped at his cranberry-stained lips and gazed away. For a moment, the old Master of Assassins looked genuinely old. "I applied Mentat analysis to trace connective strands through manifest documents in the Cala City Spaceport as well as uncategorized launches from smaller spaceports up and down the coast." His heavy eyebrows drew together, and Leto heard something change in his voice.

"Sire, I believe this drug has spread across the Imperium—right under our noses."

Some people want to know the future so they can prepare for it. But I pre-
fer not to know. I would rather prepare myself for eventualities and move
forward with the confidence that I am strong and ready to face whatever
may come.

—GURNEY HALLECK

O n the morning Reverend Mother Mohiam arrived on Wallach IX, a
thick mist lay over the Mother School, turning the day into gloomy twilight. Across the complex of old red-roofed buildings, interior glowglobes shone
through the windows, and bright lights illuminated the outside common areas.

The Emperor's Truthsayer walked briskly across the central quad to the main
school complex. Mohiam did not expect warmth and sunshine on Wallach IX,
but this day felt less welcoming than ever. She passed young Acolytes huddled
beneath layers of dark clothing. Mohiam drove back the bone-chilling cold by
adjusting her pulse, her body heat, her nerve responses. Even so, she experienced
a different kind of shiver as she stepped up to the tall doors of the administration
building.

Mother Superior Harishka stood at a balcony railing on the second floor,
looking down at her. She said, "Hurry inside. Waiting for you in this weather
does not improve my disposition."

Mohiam entered the main foyer and met the Mother Superior as she glided
down the stairs. Three young Acolytes scurried out into the cold, bracing themselves. Mohiam said, "Many Sisters are having trouble staying warm."

"Winter is a time of testing," Harishka said in a clipped voice. "But this cold
snap comes early, and no one is ready for it." She motioned with one arm and
walked with surprising quickness for a woman of her age. "We have an urgent
situation . . . questions that must be answered immediately. We need your wisdom and experience."

Intrigued, Mohiam accompanied the other woman down the central corridor past a residential wing, then took a lift to the third floor in a secure section
of the enormous building. Mohiam felt a chill when she realized where they were
going. She had been here before. "You are taking me to see Lethea, the Kwisatz
Mother."

"Yes. She has grown worse. Much worse."

Just ahead, a woman's scream, high-pitched and bloodcurdling, rolled down the corridor. "That's her!" Harishka said. The door to the Kwisatz Mother's room was open, but the Mother Superior hesitated before both of them rushed inside.

Ancient Lethea lay on her bed in a large room, her sticklike arms flailing as if fighting invisible ghosts. Five medical Sisters tended her, two of them trying to hold her down, one monitoring instruments that jittered alarmingly; another woman attempted to give her an injection, while the last recorded her unintelligible jabbering. Lethea thrashed her head from side to side and tried to bite one of the Sisters holding her, but another Sister smoothly and forcefully pulled the old woman's head away, just in time.

Lethea cried out a name that turned Mohiam's blood to ice. "Jessica! Jessica of Caladan! Take her away! Our future depends on it." She choked, then spouted more words around spittle in her mouth. "I have seen horror . . . bloodshed! Disaster! The end of the Sisterhood! Take her from the boy."

Jessica? Mohiam was surprised. *So that is why I'm here?*

One of the women, Reverend Mother Terta, looked up with relief when Harishka walked in. Terta had auburn hair and round, anachronistic spectacles. The careworn medical Sister shook her head in dismay. "She is worse than ever. She continues to call out that name, and her vital signs are going downhill at an alarming rate." As another Sister performed medical tests, Terta spoke in a hushed voice to Mohiam and Harishka. "Who is this Jessica of Caladan? Why is she significant? And who is the boy?"

Mohiam answered, though she reeled at the onslaught of unexpected memories. "The Lady Jessica, consort of Duke Leto Atreides. I was her mentor and proctor at school here. The boy Lethea refers to is likely Jessica's son. But what does she mean by it? Take her from where?" She was careful to say no more, though she considered.

Mother Superior Harishka was not so circumspect, and her response indicated that Terta was to be trusted. "As a Kwisatz Mother, Lethea understands all the intricacies of our breeding lines. Jessica bore a son to Duke Leto rather than a daughter, as she was commanded. A male child creates complications, as well as possibilities."

Harishka did not, however, reveal that Jessica was also the natural-born daughter of Reverend Mother Mohiam by the Baron Harkonnen, a fact known to only a select few. Mohiam kept that knowledge to herself and said instead, "But Lethea wants Jessica separated from the boy? She says our future depends on it?"

"She rants," Terta said. "Often she makes little sense." She lowered her voice. "And after the destruction she has caused, I would not be confident that Lethea thinks of the Sisterhood's best interests."

Harishka nodded. "That is why I called Mohiam, on the chance that she can help us understand before we disrupt our other carefully laid plans."

Mohiam asked, "Why not just bring Jessica here? To be safe? You know where to find her. Send her a summons, and she must obey. Take her away from Caladan, as Lethea demands. Then you will have your answers. Jessica was raised in the Sisterhood and would never defy a command from her Mother Superior. Why go to all the trouble of bringing me here first?"

"Lethea's actions are volatile and dangerous. We felt caution was warranted." Harishka seemed hesitant to say more.

The chill deepened inside Mohiam's heart. In having a son, Jessica's act of defiance had caused great turmoil to the extensive Kwisatz Haderach breeding program. Empress Anirul, a previous Kwisatz Mother, had been directly involved in the birth, and treachery had cost her life.

Take her from the boy . . . Our future depends on it.

Mohiam remained skeptical. "I also question the wisdom of separating a Sisterhood-trained mother from a boy with such potential. I know the preliminary reports. Do we not need Jessica to continue instructing him in Bene Gesserit ways, just in case?"

She looked toward the writhing crone on the bed. The boy, Paul, had been born fourteen years ago. What would have triggered Lethea now?

Leto Atreides was already considering possible marriage matches for the boy, and although the Duke had been ambivalent to her direct offer of assistance in choosing a mate for his son, the Sisterhood had issued instructions to Jessica. Mohiam hoped she would do as she was told. With marriages being considered for Paul Atreides, perhaps that was the catalyst that had increased the dementia of the old Kwisatz Mother.

Terta shook her head. "We want to be careful. We know Lethea's value as well, even if she is dangerous."

Mohiam's brow furrowed. Lethea looked no more than a wisp of a person. "How is she dangerous? She can't even leave the bed."

"She is irrational, vindictive, and powerful," Harishka explained. "She used Voice to compel an unfortunate Sister to bash her own brains out, and forced another to record the whole thing."

Mohiam was stunned. "You think she wants to kill Jessica if we bring her here?"

"Unknown," Harishka said. "We have Lethea under constant surveillance, with layers of checks and balances. While medical Sisters tend her in person, others observe from the next room, shielded, ready to spring into action if necessary. We must protect Lethea from herself."

"And protect us from her," said Terta.

Disaster! The end of the Sisterhood.

Was the ancient Kwisatz Mother prophetic, or just insane? Mohiam knew about Lethea's special skills of focused prescience, which rendered her too valuable for the Sisterhood to lose. They had kept her alive through artificial means far longer than they should.

The medical Sisters finally managed to calm the old woman down, and she lay on the bed breathing fitfully, wheezing and coughing. She looked enraged, frustrated, and then as if a switch had been thrown, defeated.

From her years in the order, Mohiam knew that after Lethea began to grow mentally unbalanced, a Bene Gesserit council had held an emergency session to appoint a new Kwisatz Mother. Even as her mind faded, though, Lethea was still consulted when she was not lost in a combination of dementia and spice trance. Enhanced by the consumption of melange, the ancient woman could see the near future of the breeding program. On her more rational days, Lethea had provided invaluable advice and guidance for strategic decisions. Now, though . . .

"Her moments of clarity are diminishing," Harishka said. "She used to be lucid every other day or so, but it has been more than a week since we've had a glimpse of her real mind." She looked away. "When I summoned you here, I had hoped you could penetrate her fog, speak to her about Jessica."

Mohiam drew a breath. "The information is there, inside her head. And she cannot live much longer. Has anyone tried to transfer her memories, as dying Reverend Mothers do?"

The Mother Superior shook her head. "We are worried about damaging the information . . . and killing Lethea. I kept hoping she would become clearheaded again, so I could make the attempt myself, before she relapsed into gibberish. But it has been so long . . ."

Harishka glanced at the medical Sisters adjusting the intravenous lines, checking and rechecking the readings. Lethea began to twitch and gurgle. Mohiam rushed closer, alarmed. "I think she's dying."

Terta rechecked some of the vitals and shook her head in dismay. "You may be right."

Mohiam grew determined. "If she's dying anyway, we should attempt to transfer her memories. They will be lost regardless."

Harishka hesitated. "It is too dangerous."

But Mohiam felt the urgency. "If Lethea dies, we lose whatever is inside her head! There may not be time to call Jessica all the way from Caladan, and I do not see how that would help anyway. We might try to use the energy of another Reverend Mother to capture and transfer the contents of Lethea's mind. It might be our last chance."

"She could have only hours left," said one of the medical Sisters. "Or she might last years more. Her resilience has been incalculable."

"There are three Reverend Mothers in this room right now," Mohiam said. "You, Terta, and myself." She gathered her courage. "I could do it."

Harishka recoiled. "You are the Emperor's Truthsayer! The Bene Gesserit could never risk losing you. On Kaitain, you are the Sisterhood's highest political placement."

"And we cannot risk the Mother Superior," Terta said, squaring her shoulders. "Therefore, if we make the attempt, the choice is clear. It should be me."

As if she had overheard, Lethea convulsed on the bed and clawed at the air, drawing the attention of her attendants. Medical alarms rang out. Harishka flashed an urgent glance at Mohiam, as they both realized that Lethea could perish in a matter of minutes.

"It has to be me," Terta insisted. "And I should make the attempt now, before it is all lost."

Harishka nodded reluctantly. "Go ahead."

The other Reverend Mother pushed her round glasses against the bridge of her nose, shook her hair loose, and cupped her palms against the papery skin on the old woman's temples. Taking a deep breath, she leaned down and touched her forehead against Lethea's.

Terta's worried expression smoothed as she concentrated, extending her thoughts in an attempt to draw out the old woman's vault of memories.

Mohiam watched, absorbing details.

"I'm getting something," Terta whispered, her eyes closed behind her glasses. Her voice grew excited. "Yes, I've broken through. Oh, incredible! This is fantastic!"

The other women in the room seemed to be holding their breaths.

Then Terta whimpered and shook. She tried to pull away from Lethea, but was unable to do so, as if her brow had fused to the old woman's forehead. The medical Sister grimaced, struggled, gasped.

Mohiam and Harishka grabbed her arms, pulled her away, and broke the physical contact, but Terta screamed, staggered backward, and wailed. "The voices! Voices overwhelming me!" she howled. "I'm drowning in them!"

The other medical Sisters rushed forward to help her, but she pushed them away and ran blindly, still screaming. With unexpected strength, Terta knocked the other women down, tore herself away, and bolted toward a balcony door.

Seeing her intent, Mohiam shouted, using Voice in an attempt to stop Terta with a command. But even that had no effect.

Reverend Mother Terta crashed open the balcony door, vaulted over the railing, and dove out into the cold winter air. She screamed all the way down.

On the bed, old Lethea fell back into her catatonic state, a cruel smile on her face. . . .

As a doctor and a scientist, I have studied the intricacies of nature and the mechanisms of the human body. Yet sometimes I wish I did not know the answers.

—DR. WELLINGTON YUEH, private journals

He walked a fine line between being the Duke and being Paul's father.

As Leto considered the tensions on Caladan, he grew more worried about the depth of corruption implied by the illicit distribution of the now-deadly ailar drug. The ferns were supposedly wild, but this new subspecies was considerably more potent. And the increasing use of "the Caladan drug" implied a lack of leadership and responsibility on his part, which he could not allow.

At home, Leto still felt a reticence from Paul, which came from the boy's inner turmoil after his father's brush with death and learning that he had been offered up—at least provisionally—for a political marriage.

Leto wanted to strengthen the relationship, but could not help who he was. He had been raised in a similar fashion, taught to wall off his emotions when he observed Paulus and Helena in their cold and loveless marriage. Neither of his own parents had shown much warmth toward their only child but Leto had not treated Paul like that. In wistful moments, he imagined he could be a father like some of those dockside fishermen who would take their boys out to the boats, let them play with the fishing lines, and help unload the wriggling catch.

As a father—and a Duke—Leto rarely spent such casual, carefree moments with his son, although each year, they did take several days to go on a rugged wilderness retreat, father and son. Otherwise, he and Paul did not laugh or play games. As the head of a House Major, Leto was expected to be formal, serious, and political, and Paul was not allowed to be a rambunctious boy. He had too much to study and practice in preparation for his noble responsibilities. There were other teenagers in Cala City, but the Atreides heir was sheltered. He did not stay out late with friends, didn't get in trouble with other boys. While Paul devoted hours each day to education that would make him a respected Landsraad leader, he had little chance to experience life.

It was time for them to go away again on an adventure, to make them remember some of their favorite times. Leto needed this, too. He could fulfill two roles, as father and Duke, and do it well.

An hour after dinner, as sea mists rose beneath the cliffs, Leto approached Paul's quarters, but paused when he heard laughter ahead.

"That move is not allowed, Gurney!"

"Gods below, it certainly is allowed! Who taught you to play cheops?"

"My father did, and he is not a man to be loose with the rules."

Halleck laughed. "You'll get no argument from me there, young pup. The Duke is a man who lives within a fortress of rules."

Paul chuckled. "And in Castle Caladan, my father's rules are law—even his rules on pyramid chess."

"Then take my piece, damn you, boy, and I will still win the game."

Leto stepped through the door and saw Paul and the troubadour warrior seated at a table, facing their game of pyramid chess. The young man's hand wavered on the third level, hesitating over a game piece.

Startled, Halleck was on his feet in a flash, one hand reaching for the blade at his side, but when he recognized the Duke, he straightened, abashed. "Sorry, my Lord. I did not mean to be so jumpy."

"It is reassuring, Gurney," Leto said. "You make me confident that not even a biting fly would get close enough to bother my son."

Paul rose to his feet in stiff formality. Leto could see the boy wanted to bound toward him, but he held himself back. "Good evening, sir."

The restraint was exactly what Leto had taught, but now it made him sad—such a formal response even in his private quarters in a relaxed moment. Leto sighed. Was this how he wanted his son to treat him? He softened his voice. "I came to see you. We do not spend enough time together in informal settings."

Halleck picked up his nine-stringed baliset from the side of the table and prepared to go. "I will leave you two together, my Lord."

"Stay, Gurney. This concerns you as well. I think you'll like the invitation."

Paul brightened. "Are we having a banquet? I will represent House Atreides to the best of my abilities." Then he tensed. "Or is it a reception to introduce me to marriage prospects?"

Leto again felt the heaviness in his heart. "No, it is a bit more relaxed than that, something you'll enjoy. It's time for us to go out on another wilderness expedition. You always like our retreats."

Paul did smile. "I didn't expect to go for several months yet. The weather will still be rainy."

"We'll bring warm gear," Leto said. "But I think we could use some time away from being a Duke and the Duke's heir. Don't you agree?"

"I would like that," Paul said. He almost added "sir," but caught himself. "Where are we going this time?"

Wearing a more serious expression, Leto said, "To the northern wilderness beyond the pundi rice fields and the Arondi Cliffs." The words raised immediate questions, and he added, "Our little expedition can serve an additional purpose, if we keep our eyes open."

Gurney was instantly alert. "I will arrange a full security escort, Sire, as well as porters and support staff. What is the purpose of this expedition?"

"Not a full escort. We'll remain in contact, but the purpose is for us to get away from all this—as Paul and I have done before. But you'll accompany us, Gurney. And Dr. Yueh."

"Yueh?" Halleck looked surprised. "I suppose it would be good to have a doctor with us, but I cannot picture that man camping in the wilderness."

"Neither can I," Leto admitted, "but I need his expertise, and he needs specimens. While we are out in the forest, we'll have a chance to investigate the barra ferns. Thufir Hawat tells me ailar is a rough and primitive drug, easily collected and shipped in its raw form without extensive processing." Leto added in a bitter tone, "*The Caladan drug.* The Muadh followers simply go out in the forests and collect wild ferns for their rituals. Others could be doing the same." He frowned. "I may have overreacted with Archvicar Torono. I imagined those people were flaunting their access to the drug, to provoke me somehow. I ignored the obvious possibility that others could be harvesting ferns in the wild."

He directed his attention back to Paul, who showed an eager smile at the possibility of adventure.

Leto continued, "Yueh wants to search for native ferns and test them, see if he can find this new strain. It has been documented that the plant grows nowhere else but Caladan. The ailar that killed Nupree and Wellan might have been genetically altered, and that raises many more questions. Who is behind such a sophisticated, hidden operation? Something is happening in our uncharted forests, and I want to find it."

Halleck slung the baliset over his shoulder. "I can put together a dozen scouting teams, my Lord. We'll turn them loose in different rugged areas to look for signs of fern-growing operations."

Leto thought of the time he needed with his son. "Not dozens of teams, Gurney, at least not yet. That would not serve my purpose as a father." He rested a hand on the boy's shoulder. It felt good. "Just the four of us."

"I would enjoy that very much," Paul said.

Leto intercepted Halleck's objections before he could speak them. "Obviously, we will establish tracker signals and backup support teams, and we'll have our weapons, and shields. We've done this before, Gurney, and never had a problem."

"Times are different now, my Lord. I do not understand why you enjoy these primitive outings! As a young man when I made my way across Giedi Prime in search of my sister, I spent too much time sleeping on the hard ground, staying hidden, avoiding Harkonnen patrols." He shook his head, lost in a reverie for a moment. "One doesn't do such things as a lark." Then his grin made the inkvine scar dance. "Ah, but I don't suppose there are Harkonnen patrols in northern Caladan, and a rugged campsite is better than Beast Rabban's slave pits. I will be there at your side."

Leto saw his son's open joy, which bridged some of the distance between them. A boy's emotions were much more pliable than a hardened man's, and Paul was quick to forgive. "When do we leave?" he said. "Have you told Mother yet?"

"I will let her know." Leto realized he was anxious to go himself. "We leave as soon as Dr. Yueh is ready."

THOUGH WELLINGTON YUEH had been part of House Atreides for years, his quarters were small and austere. He lived in the main part of the castle so he could be available to respond whenever a member of the household needed medical attention.

As he prepared for the expedition, the Suk doctor moved with precise gestures, not a wasted twitch of muscle. From his infirmary and adjacent laboratory, Yueh had gathered instruments, sample boxes and jars, specimen pouches, test vials. When Leto stopped in to see him, he found the doctor packing plaz tubes, lenses, fine-point calipers, thin pipettes, and a chemical analysis kit. He included scanners and logbooks, shigawire spools with reference volumes on Caladan, though the information was sparse.

"Such a lack of data on the flora and fauna of this world is quite a failing, my Lord," Yueh said with an undertone of disappointment. "Over the centuries, why has no dedicated naturalist explored the landmasses, overturned every leaf, and catalogued each species of plant, insect, bird, or fish? Has humanity forgotten our need to answer questions?"

"Obviously, it wasn't a priority for previous Dukes," Leto said. He had read his ancient history. "The Butlerian Jihad snuffed out our drive to know all the answers. Long ago, with that unbridled curiosity, we created thinking machines that enslaved the human race. Brash overextension of science with no consideration of consequences led to the Time of Titans, the creation of the cymeks, and so many centuries of oppression." He pursed his lips. "Maybe it is better that we don't look everywhere or answer every question."

Yueh arranged his instruments, wrapping them in protective cases against exposure to the elements. He picked up a magnifier, then a lasknife for specimen cutting. "But as a result, we know almost nothing about the barra ferns. Do we not want to find answers to the ailar drug operations?"

Leto frowned and let out a heavy sigh. "I make an exception when my own people are being harmed."

The doctor mused, preoccupied. "Alas, the lack of general research is not restricted to Caladan, my Lord. It is a flaw in our current mindset. We don't even know much about the spice from Arrakis, which is one of the most important substances in the Imperium. The Spacing Guild needs it for their Navigators, and many nobles are addicted to it. Think of how many would die if their supply were suddenly withdrawn? And yet we know very little about the substance and where it comes from on Arrakis. With the Emperor's new spice surtax, melange has grown much more expensive, causing hardships."

"That makes me even more glad I do not use the stuff." He thought of Lord Atikk's son, Raolin, and his many addictions. His expression tightened. "There is clear danger in something so costly, so important, so alluring. It is a weakness."

Yueh continued, "One can wager that House Corrino has extensive data about melange in their secret records." His eyes took on a faraway look. "I wonder . . ."

Leto cut him off, anxious to finish preparations for their expedition. "For now, let us concern ourselves with questions closer to home. We will find the source of the ailar, and deal with it."

Colorful camouflage can be used to hide secrets. Look closely, not just out
of the corner of your eye but at what is directly in front of you.
—The Mentat Book of Focus and Diversion

As they traveled north in a flyer that skimmed low over the treetops, Paul admired the pristine Caladan scenery. For this primitive expedition with his father—their first outing to the northern wilderness—the young man had reviewed filmbooks of the various landforms, trees, birds, insects, and even unusual fungi encrustations that grew taller than a human. So many things he wanted to see!

Paul also asked Yueh countless questions, and the Suk doctor was patient with him, as always, while maintaining a certain coolness. Yueh had never joined their rugged retreats before, and Paul could not imagine the prim doctor in the cold, wet discomfort. "My service to House Atreides has been limited to the castle, and I served House Richese before that. This is the first time I have researched anything about Caladan wildlife." His faint smile twitched his long mustaches. He seemed eager, yet a little nervous.

Leto piloted the flyer himself. He called back to Paul, raising his voice over the thrum of engines. "It is important for the future Duke to see the heart of Caladan. Personal experience is far superior to filmbook learning."

Paul leaned forward to ask, "And did you see it yourself when you were my age?"

"Alas, no. The Old Duke was not a man to explore the countryside, though he wasn't afraid to get dirty or sweaty. I missed many opportunities to get to know him. I hope to make that up to us, Paul."

Sitting in the back of the unmarked Atreides aircraft, Gurney lounged against the bulkhead, strumming his baliset. He seemed uninterested in the scenery, willing to stay at the Duke's side, wherever they went.

Before flying into the deep wilderness, Leto announced they would detour for an unexpected visit to the moonfish pools. In investigating Wellan's death, Thufir Hawat had tracked the minister's activities, which confirmed the Duke's suspicion that he was connected with the black-market ailar operations. The man had visited a particular fishery too often.

"One installation should not need more inspection visits than any other, and yet Wellan kept going there. I suspect there is something more to it." Leto's expression was stern. "What if the fishery has some connection with the drug smuggling? That's why I want to have a look with my own eyes."

Gurney's fingers jangled on the baliset and stopped the flywheel. He snorted. "We will find out."

"I want to see the fishery village and the spawning pools for their own sake," Paul said. "Moonfish are interesting creatures."

"You eat enough of them, lad," Gurney teased.

"It is good to know where one's food comes from," Yueh said.

The flyer took them north along the sparsely populated coast and then inland into marshy territory, where tributary rivers drained into shallow inlets. Artificial rectangular ponds were connected by canals. Paul could see the demarcation of spawning pools, holding ponds, and transport troughs bridged by low metal walkways.

As the sun lowered in the late afternoon, Leto circled the flyer, then came in for a landing on a raised metal grid. The Duke did not announce their arrival until his aircraft was right on top of the fishery.

The settlement was a factory complex but with a pastoral character. The processing buildings were lines of boxy structures for cleaning, cutting, and packaging the fish. Homes built from planks of raw wood stood on stilts, balanced above the mud flats. Clusters of glowglobes drifted like fireflies only a meter above the spawning pools, shining a warm, constant light beneath the cloudy sky.

With expert maneuvering, Leto settled the flyer on the crosshatched metal platform. Fishery workers looked up as they waded in the muck below or stood in shallow canals and crosswise ditches. Wearing waterproof gear, thick gloves, and bandannas in the humid air, they bent down and reached into the water.

One worker, apparently the crew boss, hurried to the landing platform to meet the unexpected visitors. Leto shut down the engines and stepped outside in casual dress, wearing an old fishing cap. His long, dark hair hung down around the edges of the hat. Paul, Gurney, and Dr. Yueh joined him.

The crew boss clambered up rungs to the upraised platform and stomped his sturdy boots on the metal grid to get rid of the mud. His pants were wet and dirty, his sleeves rolled up. Several days' growth of whiskers covered his cheeks.

The man regarded the flyer and the strangers. "Are you . . . are you our Duke? Duke Leto Atreides?" He seemed cautious, afraid to believe the idea. He touched an earpiece. "I was working, but heard the transmission just before you landed."

Leto said, "Yes, I am the Duke. We are on an expedition to the north, and this is our stopping point. My son wants to see the moonfish operations." He hardened his voice. "As do I."

The boss, who introduced himself as Hylie, seemed disconcerted. "I wish we could have prepared, my Lord. Surely Minister Wellan delivers his reports to you? Everything is in order, sir."

Leto remained unmoved. "I did not suggest otherwise. Yet."

Looking at the crew boss, Paul could see the man was unaware of Wellan's death.

"Aye, moonfish is a substantial part of Caladan exports," Gurney said. "It is important for a Duke to understand where he makes his money."

Hylie brightened at that, but Paul detected unusual mannerisms—anxiety, maybe. It might have been just discomfort at being so close to his Duke, but Paul didn't think so. Jessica had taught him many subtleties of observation.

"I like to see my people as they go about their regular duties rather than in a prepared reception," the Duke said. "It helps me to understand them."

"We will gladly give you a tour of our operations, but the day's work shift is nearly over." Hylie fidgeted. "It is a hard life, and the crews are weary by the end of the afternoon."

Paul said, "I understand that the moonfish thrum at night. Will we be able to hear them?"

Leto gave him an indulgent nod. "Yes."

"Then you will need lodgings, Sire?" Hylie glanced over at the rugged shacks on stilts in the mud. "We don't have much, but we can find guest quarters for you. Minister Wellan never stays."

"We'll see," Leto said. "Maybe we will."

Paul glanced back and forth between his father and the crew boss, and knew Leto wanted to find out more about the illicit ailar operations. Were the fisheries somehow connected to the gathering or distribution of the wild ferns? Minister Wellan had certainly been involved here at this particular fishery. Hylie would require watching.

The crew boss stomped to the edge of the landing platform and dithered there. He turned and said apologetically, "We are not at our best right now, Sire. One of our workers was found dead in her dwelling last night. A terrible tragedy! She was young, but we've lost several already this year." Hylie scratched his stubble. "Perhaps you could dispatch more workers from Cala City, my Lord? Expand our labor force? We need help up here. Minister Wellan keeps promising some assistance."

Before Leto could answer, Yueh interrupted, "How did she die?"

Hylie shrugged. "She was dead when we looked in on her this morning. It is the way of life."

"Death is indeed a part of life," Gurney said, "but not all deaths are the same."

"We don't have the facilities to perform medical analysis or autopsies," Hylie said. "The question is beyond me."

"I would like to see the body," said Yueh. He glanced up at Leto, who nodded.

Now the crew boss looked alarmed. "That would . . . not be possible. We celebrated the return service today, the funeral. Shedai's body was . . ." He shrugged again, more jerkily this time. "It is no longer available."

"Your people believe in cremation?" Leto looked dubiously around the marshy area.

"Her body was not consigned to fire but to the water, Sire." Hylie nodded toward the canals and troughs. "There are moonfish. She went to them. That is what we always—"

Paul understood. "You placed her body in the water so the fish could feed on her."

Gurney lowered his voice, sounding suspicious. "A very good way to dispose of a corpse if the evidence needs to be gone."

The crew boss was confused. "Evidence of what?"

Paul could sense the man's anxiety growing, more than just discomfort at discussing the body of a fallen worker. The young man said quietly to Leto, "He is hiding something, Father. I can tell."

"As can I," Leto said. "We will take that tour of your operations now, Hylie. I want to see this body, whatever remains of it."

Down in the shallow holding ponds, wading through the muck, the workers used nets to catch moonfish fingerlings and move them into growth pools. Other suited workers stood thigh-deep in wide canals, counting and marking larger fish that bumped and jostled one another until workers flung them out into harvesting bins, where the fish flopped and struggled.

Hylie stammered as he tried to give them the tour. "At night, we activate sonic membranes. The resonance frequency calms the fish, helps them to breed. We've greatly increased output in the past five years, as I'm sure you know, my Lord."

"I do," Leto said. "But I was not aware that people were dying."

The fishery workers paused to stare at them. As the sun moved toward twilight, the glowglobes drifted along like ghosts over the water. Hylie led the visitors over raised metal walkways. The crew chief pointed down into the murky water, more a slurry of mud than an actual canal. Contented moonfish swam there, crowded together. "Shedai is . . . she is here in this trench, my Lord. We placed her there this morning, and the fish have been busy for hours. She will not be a pleasant sight to see."

"Death rarely is," Yueh said. "But there may be enough left for analysis. I only need a tissue sample."

Leto stood on the raised metal walkway with Paul beside him, both of them looking down into the rich-smelling water. Gurney barked orders, and Hylie called his workers closer. A group of suited men and women waded back into the canal, looking up to the walkway, uneasy with the instructions.

"Do as he says. Find Shedai down there," said the crew chief. "These men want to see her body."

"She's dead," said one of the workers. "Why would they want to see her?"

Another man sneered up at the visitors, said nothing.

Hylie reddened. "Follow my orders! Duke Leto is an important man."

"But why do they want to see Shedai? What did she do?"

"Do as you're told or I'll reduce your wages," Hylie said.

That proved to be an adequate threat. The workers stirred the shallow water, groping with gloved hands, moving along through the slurry until they found the corpse. "Here she is!" They pulled up the dripping body and flopped it onto the metal grid so that the water and mud dribbled through.

Paul was fascinated, though the corpse's expression was horrific. Shedai's eyes were gone, her nose and ears nibbled away, her skin bloated.

Yueh picked up the woman's limp hands, rubbed at her fingernails, and looked at the cuticles. He bent close to study her face, undeterred by the grotesqueness. "If the eyes were intact, I could inspect the scleras for hemorrhages." He glanced up at Leto. "I know what you suspect, my Lord. I do have the chemical analysis kit aboard the flyer. It will not take long to detect traces of ailar, if that is what killed her."

Paul had already put the clues together, but Yueh's blatant statement alarmed Gurney. The troubadour warrior whispered to Leto, "Shall we call in reinforcements, my Lord?" He looked around, as if expecting an attack. "We can have Atreides forces here in a couple of hours."

Leto shook his head. "This is just an expedition, and we hope to discover the answers to our questions. Hylie here can help us." The Duke's politeness held an undertone of razors. "If necessary, I can call in Thufir Hawat and a security team from Cala City."

Yueh extracted a tissue sample from the corpse while the uneasy crew boss looked on in fascination and disgust. Other workers waded in from side canals.

Throughout the intense activity, dusk faded into a curtain of twilight. The tall hills around the narrow cove made the shadows lengthen farther. Hylie grew more agitated as Yueh worked. "My Lord, let us take you to quarters for the night, where you can be comfortable. We will prepare a meal. There are obligations that—"

"I am quite content here, out in the open," Leto said. "We stay until we have answers."

"Yes, my Lord." Hylie stood without moving, yet appeared to be squirming.

YUEH'S TESTS QUICKLY revealed that the dead woman had succumbed to the toxic substance in the ferns. "Her muscles are permeated with ailar," he said. "She must have used the drug for a substantial time, but if she ingested the new strain without knowing, it would have been far too much even for one who had built up a tolerance."

Now Hylie began to make excuses. "Why, yes, those ferns are known around here, especially in the deep forests. Some of our workers use them occasionally, to relax and find a bit of peace. It is harmless."

"Harmless?" Leto growled.

"Looks like she found more peace than she was seeking," Gurney said.

The Duke became a thundercloud of command. "I want each dwelling searched, every one of these workers questioned. We will lock down this fishery and keep everyone in place until I am satisfied we've found all of the ailar and uncovered any connection to the smuggling operations. Gurney, call in Hawat and all the security and investigative troops he needs."

Hearing this, the fishery workers reacted with alarm. Some rushed back to their raised dwellings, and Gurney bounded after them, seizing one man and tossing him into the muddy canal. "You will do as your Duke commands."

Leto and his companions spread out, now armed with weapons from the flyer while they waited for the larger crackdown team.

Paul could smell the fish and mud all around. On their automatic schedule, the underwater sonic membranes began to thrum, and countless moonfish rose to the surface, adding their pulsing music in response, filling the air with vibrations that both calmed and rattled the observers.

The fishery workers were agitated for their own reasons. Gurney's adept search uncovered five more people who possessed dried ferns, a handful for personal use, but two with large sacks of the mottled potent strain—obviously to be delivered somehow to black-market dealers.

Leto spoke into the flyer's comm as his Atreides troops arrived to lock down and occupy the fishery. They swiftly seized all of the ailar in their crackdown. The search and inspection continued long into the full dark, and glowglobes drifted around the fishery site, illuminating the place with an eerie glow.

The workers were terrified, and Paul detected a deep uneasiness among them. "Chaen Marek will not like this," one muttered.

Paul heard the name repeated.

Duke Leto shouted to the gathered workers who had remained standing aimless and nervous outside. "These are my Atreides fisheries, and Caladan is my world." When he looked at his son, his implacable expression was angry and terrible, then Paul watched it shift to become his father's softer side. "I won't let this spoil our time together, Paul. Tomorrow, we will go farther north and do what we intend to do. Thufir can handle the rest here."

Politics and war make for strange bedfellows.
—Ancient Terran philosopher

Though his position as siridar-governor of Arrakis conveyed great political influence, not to mention wealth, Baron Harkonnen was pleased to be back in his comfortable, industrial, *civilized* home on Giedi Prime. Despite all the business he conducted for the strategic plots of House Harkonnen, he would not stay here long. Arrakis demanded his full attention, especially now.

First, he had an important meeting, one that might mitigate the Emperor's infernal spice surtax, which had already begun to stifle melange use.

With his bulk supported by suspensors, the Baron met his visitor in front of a military manufacturing facility, his largest such complex on Giedi Prime. Black streaks caused by acid rain ran down the front of the factory building, like drying tears. Nearby, two workmen stood on a platform, scrubbing a stained statue of his father, Dmitri Harkonnen, which graced the factory entrance.

Ur-Director Malina Aru emerged from a groundcar, accompanied by her pet spinehounds. The predatory animals looked deadlier than any Harkonnen guards, but the Baron knew the Urdir was far more dangerous than her pets.

Malina was a slender woman who exuded unflappable professionalism, clearly not prone to excess. Her brown eyes had the intensity of a raptor. She wore a dark business jacket, trousers, and a white blouse. A small CHOAM guard force emerged from a separate vehicle that pulled up like an armored troop carrier.

The Baron wore his own version of business attire, a loose orange tunic and billowing trousers, with a gold Harkonnen medallion on a chain around his neck. He greeted her, and she granted him her attention, although without warmth. He had met the Ur-Director in passing at Imperial functions, and he understood what a shrewd businesswoman she was, how efficiently she ran the CHOAM Company. Now, thanks to Piter's suggestion, House Harkonnen and CHOAM might do lucrative business together, secret and dangerous business. Such an arrangement required mutual trust and a recognition of each other's power.

Balanced, even graceful with his suspensors, the Baron loomed over the small woman. Malina Aru was not intimidated. Her spinehounds padded forward and regarded the Baron as if he might become a feast. The armed CHOAM entourage followed her, but he had snipers stationed in unseen places.

The Baron indicated the armed escort. "You can leave your guards out here, Urdir. You're perfectly safe on Giedi Prime."

"No one is perfectly safe." She narrowed her eyes and looked to his arm, where the medcast was covered by the loose orange sleeve. "I hope you have recovered from your injuries on Arrakis? I was shocked to read the detailed report of that assassination attempt from desert brigands. And aboard your own shuttle! That must have been quite a lapse of security." She clucked her tongue. "I assume you have reassessed all Harkonnen protective measures."

Her comment astonished him, because he thought he had covered up the incident, except for what Count Fenring's local spies had reported. A thrill of fear shot through him. Was Malina working with Fenring? And thus connected with the Emperor?

He recovered quickly, knowing it would do no good to dissemble in front of this woman. Instead, he said, "I am completely healed from my accident, and the perpetrators have been dealt with." He still felt occasional throbs of pain, and the knitted bones of his left wrist were still weaker than he liked, but he would not show it. "Yes, I have enhanced security measures across all Harkonnen holdings. I assure you, our meeting is perfectly safe." He again looked at her security escort, lowered his voice. "For such matters as we need to discuss, the fewer ears the better."

The Urdir responded with a thin smile. "My associates can remain nearby on call, but Har and Kar go with me." She gently patted the silver bristles of her spinehounds.

"Yes, you may bring your . . . interesting pets." He turned toward the entrance of the munitions factory. "We will share a meal and talk in private inside the complex. I have a special room where we can be completely candid as to our needs and expectations."

She gave orders for the escort to fall back, then strolled alongside the Baron's light, bobbing steps into the burly factory. The spinehounds trotted behind her like well-trained soldiers, never taking their yellow eyes off the Baron.

As she accompanied him into the factory foyer, she said, "Your message described an interesting business proposal regarding CHOAM's access to spice." She seemed eager to start their discussions as soon as they entered the building. "I am interested, but skeptical—pending details."

"First things first," he said. "I'm hungry. We have plenty of time."

The Ur-Director cut him off so efficiently that he didn't at first react to the rudeness. "Time is valuable and should not be squandered."

"I assure you, Urdir, that this will not be a waste of time." They stepped onto a lift large enough to accommodate his size and rose to the second level, where windows and walkways looked down upon the immense factory floor below. The manufacturing bay hummed with activity.

With suspensor-enhanced steps, the Baron led her to a catwalk that extended out over the factory floor to an isolated annex chamber that hung like an island over the activity. His fat body barely squeezed between the metal handrails that bordered the walkway. Below, new Harkonnen military equipment was being assembled for shipment to Arrakis. Showing no anxiety, Malina followed him across the high catwalk.

They entered the annex chamber, which had no other access point, and when they were inside, a waiting servant sealed the door, enclosing them in a blanket of silence. The floor of the isolated room was made of thick, transparent plaz to show the manufacturing activity below. Malina and the Baron seemed to be standing on air as they approached a long table in the center of the room. "Our meal will be along presently," he said.

The spinehounds glanced at their paws on the transparent floor. They looked up at the Ur-Director, drew reassurance, and took positions on either side of her chair. "I will sit with you for the meal, Baron, so long as we engage in concurrent discussions."

"Efficiency saves money and time. We discuss my proposal while we eat." He tried to sound casual, but noticed her calculating gaze as she took her seat. Har and Kar rested on the invisible floor.

A parade of servants marched across the catwalk, each bearing a tray of food. They entered and placed platters on the table, a selection of sliced meats, glistening sauces, roasted vegetables, large steamed crustaceans. One servant draped a bib across the Baron's orange tunic, and he selected several of the largest crustaceans, cracking the shells with his fingers and stuffing seafood into his mouth.

Malina politely tasted a small serving of food. The spinehounds pricked up their thorny ears, then relaxed again. "In CHOAM, I have enough wealth to do as I like, and I am not easily impressed," she said. "Please provide more details about your proposal. How will you implement it, and what will you need from me? Have you brought me here to ask for a secret loan? Has the Guild Bank turned you down?"

The Baron roared with laughter, a deep belly laugh that shook his entire body. "With my income from spice operations on Arrakis, I assure you House Harkonnen has no need of a loan from CHOAM, or the Guild Bank, or even a generous benefactor such as yourself." He nodded toward slices of meat in a brown glaze. "Try the rukka fillets. Highly intelligent creatures, and delicious."

She did so, pronounced the taste satisfactory, and waited for him to continue.

The Baron tried to crack through her stony, professional demeanor. "I would like us to be friends, Urdir."

"If I thought of us as enemies, I would not have come here with such a small personal guard." She fed morsels of meat to her spinehounds.

Before they could begin their deep discussions, a handsome young man glided across the catwalk to the isolated meeting room. The Baron looked up with a flash of pride and delight. "Ah, my nephew Feyd-Rautha!"

Feyd sauntered in, looked at the feast, then at Malina. "Pleased to meet you," she said, in a formal tone. She did not rise from her seat. "But this is a private meeting." She repeated the Baron's own words, "The fewer ears the better."

The Baron covered his flicker of annoyance at the interruption. "Are you not needed for monitoring the floor operations, my dear nephew?"

Feyd did not seem concerned with his uncle's displeasure, but focused his attention on the two spinehounds. "I saw the animals when I looked up from the factory floor." He inched closer, extending a hand as if to pet one. Har and Kar growled, which seemed to delight the young man more than intimidate him. "How might I purchase some for combat in a gladiatorial arena?"

"They are my own special breed." Malina frowned. "The Tleilaxu developed them to my exact specifications."

"Tleilaxu?" Feyd seemed disappointed. "Please let me know if any more become available."

"Perhaps something can be worked out, my dear nephew, pending the outcome of our negotiations," the Baron said. "For now, the Ur-Director and I have significant matters to discuss. Please leave us to our meal." Dismissing his nephew, he took a mouthful of rukka meat. Feyd continued to look at the silvery predators, then left with an insouciant glance at Malina.

She folded her hands in front of her, clearly finished with pleasantries and distractions. "You offered a way around the burden of the Emperor's excessive surtax. CHOAM is suffering under the onerous requirement, as are many of our best customers. I am sure that House Harkonnen revenues have been hurt as people turn to less effective, but less expensive recreational drug alternatives. Let us begin negotiations and see if there is a deal to be made." She looked through the transparent floor, saw how they were unsettlingly suspended high above the manufacturing bay. "And if we disagree, will you touch a button and drop me to the manufacturing lines below?"

"Preposterous. There is no such mechanism!" He chuckled. "I like you, Ur-Director."

"I will hear what you propose, Baron, and then decide whether or not I like you." The spinehounds continued to watch him disconcertingly.

"Very well, no more preamble." He sealed the door so that the servants would no longer disturb them, then shifted his attention to another tray heaped with melange in various forms. "My Imperial-class chef has prepared various recipes with spice . . . pure and uncut, or mixed into beverages, biscuits, tarts, and other desserts." He took a pinch of rust-colored powder from a bowl, inhaled it, and rocked back on his suspensors. "Nothing like pure, fresh melange."

Malina took a small pinch of powder and sniffed it, then nibbled at a biscuit. "And your business proposition?"

"You are consuming it. Just a small gesture, a proof of concept." She watched him with intense eyes, and the Baron explained. "The Emperor knows nothing about the shipment of spice from which these samples were taken. All melange operations on Arrakis are closely monitored, all exports taxed—now more heavily than ever. Some smugglers use a separate channel to move illicit melange and sell it on the black market, but their freedom is illusory. The Emperor monitors them and expects them to pay as well."

He took a thick honeyed wafer, consumed it in a single bite. "With my influence, however, I could procure a completely isolated supply of spice, a secret between me and you—it would be just a trickle, to start, but in these days of excessive costs and crippling taxes, it might be worthwhile to certain customers."

The Baron saw he had her complete attention. "But I must have a discreet, completely confidential way of distributing it. Even though the Emperor's surtax is ridiculously high, my head is worth more to me."

"CHOAM has absolute discretion," Malina Aru said, "and our distribution network is not entirely visible to Imperial spies." She looked down at her spine-hounds as if consulting them. "Your offer does have merit, Baron. Provided you can achieve what you promise."

The Baron smiled. He inhaled a large pinch of spice, and then another, until he began to feel euphoric. "I am absolutely certain of it."

Caladan, oh Caladan! I have tried to write songs, but thy beauty beggars all music. My memories are all the songs I need.

—GURNEY HALLECK, *Collected Songs*

Atreides crackdown troops swarmed over the fishery complex, uncovering more hoarded barra ferns hidden among moonfish shipments, ready to be sent off to the main city. Leto turned the investigation over to Thufir Hawat, knowing the Mentat would get to the bottom of the matter.

They spent the night in quarters provided by the crew chief, protected by Atreides soldiers, and flew out the next morning into the rising light, with Gurney Halleck at the aircraft controls. The flyer cruised over small fishing villages and docks, and then over more rugged terrain.

Higher up the uninhabited coast, they found an isolated inlet with a broad expanse of gravel, where Gurney landed the craft. "This should be safe, my Lord. Thufir has the tracker, so he will be able to locate us. We also have emergency communicators to call for help, if necessary. A response would be only an hour or two away."

He glanced at Yueh, and the Suk doctor nodded. "I have a full medical kit."

After disembarking, Duke Leto looked inland toward the rugged forests and rock outcroppings. The land looked tantalizing and mysterious. "We are prepared, Gurney, but we won't need any rescue party. Paul and I want to get away from the comforts of noble life."

Gurney scoffed. "You say that now, my Lord."

"I will say that in a few days as well."

After securing the flyer and activating shields to keep wildlife away, they took their packs and headed out. Forging their own trail, they followed the streams up from the coast, heading into the tall conifers. Paul could sense his father's stubborn determination.

Even here in the wilderness, Leto wore his ducal signet ring, and Paul wondered if he would ever wear it himself. He didn't want the ring as a symbol of personal power or to increase his wealth or holdings, but he understood the games of the Landsraad, the positioning of Great and Minor Houses. Out here in wild and beautiful Caladan, political problems seemed so far away.

Objectively, he understood why his father had approached Duke Fausto Verdun about joining their Houses in marriage. It was a necessary move, an exploratory idea. Paul had seen images and read reports about Junu Verdun, who seemed intelligent and pleasant enough, certainly pretty, although she was not the girl he kept seeing in his dreams. . . .

Surrounded by the glorious northern forests, Paul marveled at the lush fir groves, the moist air laden with the spice of evergreens. The thriving foliage and buzzing insects gave him a sense of untapped bounty, an urgency of life that made him feel smaller, a mere part in an interconnected web of nature.

A biting fly landed on his cheek and tried to draw blood, but Paul swatted it instantly, a reaction of his training, and the squashed fly fell dead to the ground.

The drizzle had been intermittent as they trudged into thicker forests. They found a place to stop on a wide sandbar next to a twisting, sluggish stream, where the moss-draped conifers offered some shelter.

As Gurney went about the work of setting up the campsite, Paul surveyed their surroundings, never letting down his guard despite the tranquil isolation. This time, after what they had found at the fishery complex, he felt more alert than on previous wilderness retreats with his father.

"We have a polymer tarp for the rain," Leto said, glancing at the sky. "We'll be dry and comfortable enough." The man's dark hair glistened in the mist.

"This trip isn't supposed to be about comfort," Paul said in a light tone.

"Part of your training is to be miserable, lad," Gurney said as he unfurled a fabric overhang. "And to learn how to endure it."

Their packs rested against thick trees, and Paul could hear the flow of the stream. "I've been miserable before, Gurney. I've heard your singing, remember?"

The troubadour scowled and turned to Leto. "The young Master has no taste."

Leto chuckled. "I have heard your singing, too."

In mock indignation, the other man finished setting up camp. Dr. Yueh was already poking around the area, studying specimens, taking images, collecting small samples for later analysis. "I would not expect to find rare barra ferns on our first day, but I will use this opportunity to extend our knowledge. There are many gaps in our understanding of natural science on Caladan."

When the drizzle subsided and a brisk wind pushed the clouds away, the air had a pervasive chill. Gathering a warm cloak around him, Paul went to the sandbar and gazed up at the clearing sky through a wide gash in the trees. He made a pile of driftwood on the pebbly beach. "Let's build a fire here."

He and Gurney pulled dry weeds and stacked them with twigs and larger branches, and soon they had a crackling fire that produced a prodigious amount of smoke. As Paul hunkered down, the flames offered an atavistic, primal cheer. He felt it inside him, creating a sense of his ancient forefathers. He looked at his father with a spreading warmth. "I am glad we came here."

Duke Leto rose from adjusting their bedrolls under the dry tarp and came to stand next to his son, his usually formal expression melting. "I'm glad too, Paul."

Paul closed his eyes, basking in the raw sense of nature, the snap of the smoky campfire. It was good to be far away from political considerations, but he knew his father was still pestered by the details of what awaited them back at Castle Caladan, just like the black biting flies that buzzed nearby.

A large twisted log had washed up on the sandbar, and Paul sat on it, gazing into the curling stream. Gurney found a spot beside him, rested his baliset on one knee, and flipped out the multipick. "Some music, young Master?"

Paul smiled. "You know I love your singing, even though I teased you."

"Criticism only makes a minstrel work harder," he said.

"Is that from the Orange Catholic Bible? You like to quote verses."

"No, that is what an innkeeper said when he didn't like my songs." Gurney strummed and began to play, humming to himself as he randomly picked out notes and sought words. He was not a Mentat like Thufir, but he did have an amazing repertoire of folk tunes as well as his own compositions.

He sang in a voice that was surprisingly beautiful in contrast to his rough features.

> My woman stands at her window,
> Curved lines 'gainst square glass.
> Uprais'd arms . . . bent . . . downfolded.
> 'Gainst sunset red and golded—
> Come to me. . . .
> Come to me, warm arms of my lass.
> For me. . . .
> For me, the warm arms of my lass.

Yueh joined Paul on the weathered log, while Gurney continued with his music. Paul gazed at the stream by the sandbar and was startled to see several large fish—moonfish!—in the water in front of him, as if drawn by the chords Gurney strummed. These wild moonfish were larger than the ones kept in the holding pools and troughs at the fishery. They had large copper scales surrounding a thin drumhead membrane that vibrated in harmony with the music. The moonfish floated there as if mesmerized.

Leto retrieved a long, flat net with a telescoping handle from the fishing gear he had brought. He scooped the net sideways, easily flipping several dazed moonfish onto the sandbar. Gurney stopped his music and set aside his baliset. "Once again, I sing for my supper. We shall eat well tonight."

"I heartily approve," Leto said. "My stomach is rumbling." He and Paul pushed the moonfish higher onto the soft sand. "We will have a countryside feast unlike the ones in the banquet hall in Castle Caladan." He laughed. "And I wager the fish will taste better."

Gurney tossed a small knife into the soft ground at Paul's feet. "Take that, pup. You can help me gut and skin these fish."

One of the moonfish looked different, with dark swirls on its coin-like scales, its stretched membrane covered with small bubbles. When he gutted it, Paul found a sack of pearl-like eggs filled with tiny twitching larvae.

"A female after spawning," Yueh said with keen interest. "That one was about to give birth."

Paul scooped the shimmering eggs and wriggling larvae back into the water, thinking they might survive and grow to be more moonfish. "I would rather not have killed a mother, but I cannot undo it. I shall eat this one, then."

Gurney said, "Don't go soft on us, lad. It is only a fish." But Leto looked at Paul with respect.

Yueh silently took notes. "I am interested to see the life cycle of the moonfish up close, since it is such an important product of Caladan. I found little about them in the filmbooks I studied, and Minister Wellan did not document much."

They roasted the fresh fish on the driftwood campfire, and Yueh supplemented the meal with edible plants and berries he had gathered, even though they had brought enough pack food to feed them for more than a week. Paul admitted that the fresh-caught moonfish did have a different, gamy flavor that he found a little odd, but not unpleasant. He ate all of his fish.

When full night had set in, they relaxed around the fire, and Gurney sang more ballads, but soon, the deep darkness told them it was time to sleep. Paul felt weary and his stomach was queasy, possibly from all the turmoil in the past few days. They lay back on their bedrolls, Leto closest to his son.

As the Duke stretched out on his blanket and stared up at the stars, he said quietly, "This is deceptively peaceful. It almost lets me forget the dangers of the Imperium."

There is great skill in violating an essential rule, and in being the only one to get away with it.

—COUNT HASIMIR FENRING

With Leto and Paul far to the north, Jessica performed the necessary work of Castle Caladan, made administrative decisions, managed the household staff, and quietly did what she could to alleviate any concerns the Duke would have to deal with upon his return. She had been with Leto so long, she made many small decisions on her own, and she knew he trusted her.

With her Bene Gesserit training, she knew how to see both the large picture and the small intricacies. While not a Mentat, she could meditate and focus on problems that remained to be resolved. She needed to be active and alert.

On a clear, breezy morning, she left the stone walls of the castle and began with a slow walk along the nearby cliffs, inhaling the sea air. Observers might have seen her as a lady at court without a care in the world, strolling out along the grassy headlands, her skirts blowing around her legs, but in her mind spun many wheels and many details.

She could fathom why Leto so enjoyed going out to the wilderness with their son, but she also had to mull over the various marriage candidates that had been suggested for Paul, not just the political considerations that Leto and Thufir Hawat weighed but also the stark instructions the Mother Superior had sent her. Jessica had been indignant that the Sisterhood would meddle so blatantly, but she had been raised and trained on Wallach IX, and knew full well their longstanding breeding schemes.

She had to thread a fine needle, balance the needs of House Atreides with the needs of the Bene Gesserit, and what was best for her son. But Leto could never know. Fortunately, with the initial choice of Junu Verdun, they had sent a letter of invitation to a young woman acceptable to both sets of needs.

Alone, but crowded with thoughts, she walked gracefully down the narrow path along the cliff edge. Despite the sheer precipice nearby, she had always been sure-footed and hyperaware of her surroundings. She paused at a viewpoint guarded by a metal railing, where a flagpole flew the green-and-black Atreides banner.

She looked over the edge, a perilous drop-off to the crashing surf below. Twenty meters down the cliff, she spotted a ledge that held the nest of a giant spreybird. The gray female huddled on a reinforced pile of flotsam and dried weeds, while the white male soared smoothly above his mate, then landed next to her, tucking in his wings.

Looking closely, Jessica saw that the egg had already hatched. The nesting female lifted a wing that had been sheltering a fuzzy baby spreybird. The mother positioned herself to shelter the chick from the wind and from potential attackers.

Watching this, Jessica thought there could be nothing more natural than the love of a mother for her offspring. She could not always shelter Paul, though. He was growing into a man right before her eyes, leaving his childhood ways behind at an astonishing pace.

As she continued walking, she looked up into the bright sky to see an Atreides patrol glider soaring out over the water, riding updrafts and gusts of wind. A man worked the controls, enclosed in the plaz control cockpit that did not impair visibility. Though this surveillance was the work of a low-ranking scout, she recognized Thufir Hawat himself, only just returned from the moon-fish operations to the north. The warrior Mentat had flown often in his younger years, and he still took discretionary shifts on the watch gliders.

Standing on the open grass of the headlands, she watched the patrol craft circle the tall stone towers of the castle, then glide toward her. Thufir was a master of the nuances of gusts and breezes. Jessica was impressed by how he used aerodynamics and worked the craft's geometry to cruise above the sea cliffs as he kept a sharp eye on the surroundings.

Spotting Jessica out in the open, he approached, made a tight circle, and landed gently on the grasses. She hurried to greet him as he struggled to anchor the lightweight craft.

The old Atreides Master of Assassins had taken charge of the drug investigation at the fishery, at Leto's command. After two intense days, he had left cleanup crews and security forces who continued to monitor the situation, while he returned to watch over Castle Caladan.

With the light craft anchored, he unhooked his harness and stepped free of the small flying machine. The old veteran was still quite nimble, but Jessica noted the stiffness he hid. A great warrior in the days of Duke Paulus Atreides, Thufir Hawat refused to admit that he might be growing older and slower. Nevertheless, Jessica knew the Mentat's loyalty was without question.

He bowed and smiled with his stained lips. "Always on duty, my Lady, always vigilant. Flying up there gives me a chance to think as well."

He called for a retrieval crew to move the lightweight craft back to the military landing field, and they walked together back toward the castle, leaving the anchored glider shifting restlessly behind them.

"I understand the drug investigation is in good hands," she said. "You have cut off one of the black-market channels?" She had already learned much of what had happened there, but Thufir had not presented a formal report yet.

"My team was thorough," the Mentat said. "We began to unravel the drug operations, although we have not yet located the primary barra fern crop, but we did cut off some of their smuggling routes and seized a fair amount of product. For that, at least, some of the people of Caladan are safer. I have reviewed Minister Wellan's travels and which other fishery operations he inspected."

Jessica nodded. "Yes, those might also be parts of the smuggling network."

"Someone is moving the Caladan drug through the moonfish supply chain. The distribution network is like a weed with roots extending in all directions." Thufir paused, silently summarizing his report before he spoke again. "As we interrogated the frightened moonfish workers, one name came up repeatedly—Chaen Marek. Apparently, he is in charge of the illicit operations."

"And who is this man?" Jessica asked. "Have you uncovered further details about him?"

"Marek is an enigma, my Lady, but he certainly struck fear in the workers. He is apparently an offworlder, with intricate connections that allow him to distribute his deadly drug around the Imperium. That must be how Lord Atikk's son received his supply." His brows drew together. "I am still investigating the extent of interplanetary spread. The fishery workers revealed nothing else, and I am convinced they knew no more. They were not the type to . . . resist my probing."

He and Jessica had a formal relationship, distant but respectful. She rarely gave the Mentat compliments, but now she felt he deserved one. "Leto will be proud of your work, Thufir," she said.

The veteran looked troubled. "I do not do it to make him proud, my Lady. I do it because it is my job."

"You do your job well, as we all strive to," Jessica said, thinking of all the quiet, subtle operations she herself did to balance her obligations and keep the complicated wheels turning. "And that is how we make House Atreides strong." Musing, she spoke up, "We have a rivalry, you know, Thufir."

He remained stiff and formal. "My Lady, I do not oppose you in any way."

"But we compete for the attention of my son. You with your deep training methods, and me with another form of training. I have taught my son—all for his own good."

"You use *Bene Gesserit* training," Hawat said. She detected an undertone of distaste in his voice.

"That, and more." She smiled. "And we both know you've been teaching my son the ways of Mentats. I approve."

"My specific training is strictly to help his thought processes, my Lady." They exchanged knowing glances. "Even if such training is frowned upon by others, strictly speaking."

"Paul has a great eagerness to learn and a great capacity for absorbing information." A gust of wind caught a strand of her hair and whipped it about. "I appreciate what you're teaching him, Thufir. You are preparing him to survive the political battles he is bound to encounter in Imperial life. You equip him against the difficulties he might face."

The Mentat paused in his stride. "The son of a Duke will face mental, physical, and political challenges. The young man must be ready for all of them." His stained lips turned downward in concern.

Jessica thought of Paul's future. "Has there been any response from Duke Verdun about a possible betrothal? I am glad we found at least one name we could all agree on, but we dispatched the inquiry some time ago."

"No response at all."

"Strange. Why the delay, do you think?"

Thufir pondered as they approached the side of the castle. "Difficult to say. With the turmoil in the Landsraad and the many open holdings after Otorio, perhaps Verdun isn't so quick to marry off his daughter." He added with a hint of unguarded pride, "Duke Verdun could not find a better match than young Master Paul."

Jessica smiled. "You'll get no argument from me."

Together, they reached the northern wing and entered through a side doorway to avoid drawing a flood of attention.

The Mentat bent down to rub his scarred leg. "I sense something very different about Paul, my Lady. As he learns more and more, he has a kind of inner balance, a deep calmness beyond his years."

She had noticed that herself, not just as a mother seeing her son through a fog of expectations. "Yes, Paul is extraordinary, and our guidance can make him even more so."

The difference between delirium and insight is only a matter of perspective.
—DR. WELLINGTON YUEH, private medical journals

Paul awoke out in the cold wilderness, twisting in pain. In the darkness, he heard the sounds of buzzing insects and night-hunting birds, though they were drowned out by the roaring in his head and the pain of cramps. The sickness struck him as swiftly as the charge of a maddened bull.

Paul rolled off his cushioned blanket, curled into a fetal position, then pushed himself to his hands and knees on the sandy ground. Waves of pain jabbed his guts like a serrated blade. He rolled and began vomiting violently.

The driftwood campfire had burned down to dull red embers. Gurney Halleck was instantly alert, springing from the ground. "Young Master! What is it?"

"Paul!" His father lurched up from the blanket beside him. "Yueh, get over here!"

Paul sensed something toxic was inside him. A poison. His body rejected whatever was in his stomach, and he vomited again. He tried to speak, but only a ragged gasp came out. He choked. His mind was aflame. He felt people grabbing his shoulders and shaking him. Someone, perhaps Yueh, touched his forehead.

Paul began to shake and thrash. He dropped and rolled onto his back, staring upward. The stars grew brighter, then dimmer, like diamonds burning out. As his eyes filled with tears of agony, he squeezed the lids shut, went inward.

He lost more and more awareness of the world around him . . . the trees, the shouts, the forest shadows. A roaring in his ears reminded him of the grumble of the ocean, but there was no ocean here.

Paul shivered and opened his eyes to see pounding sunlight and sinuous dunes that extended like a different kind of sea. He'd seen long expanses of beaches before, but nothing like this. He convulsed, but his mind seemed far away, barely aware of his body.

As he looked at the barren landscape that was gentle and stark at the same time, he saw people moving, lines of hooded figures in mottled tan capes. Paul was able to see them through his third eye, which had now opened even as his physical eyes clenched shut with pain. The figures ran forward and struck an outpost. He heard the piercing screams of the dying, saw blood and orange flags, emblazoned with stylized griffins . . . the sign of House Harkonnen, mortal enemies of the Atreides.

Scouring sand blew in his unreal face and obscured the images. Paul felt a rumbling beneath him in the sunbaked sand, not the forest floor of Caladan.

The dunes split open as a rolling wave crest shuddered across the expanse, and an enormous monster emerged, like a lamprey with a mouth the size of a massive sea cave. The creature roared upward in an explosion of sand that engulfed the view, the vision, and Paul himself.

"WHAT IS HAPPENING to my son?" Leto stood ready to fight any foe to protect Paul, but there was nothing he could do. "Give me answers, Yueh!"

The Suk doctor held down the convulsing young man, who had vomited several more times until his stomach was empty. Yueh had already injected him with stabilizers from his medkit, strapped on a fluid pack. With instruments in hand, he worked with whipsaw movements, like a battlefield surgeon. "I am running tests, my Lord. I can treat the symptoms, but I cannot cure him until I know what's wrong. I am confident this will help in the meantime."

"Seven hells, he's been poisoned somehow," Gurney said. He had drawn his kindjal. Leto felt confident in Gurney's ability to protect them all against an overt attack, but this was not an enemy that any sword could defeat.

"How could he have been poisoned?" Leto demanded. "How is that possible? We caught our own fish, have not touched the pack food."

Gurney turned slowly as if expecting assassins to sweep in out of the wooded darkness. "I am not an imaginative man, Sire, but even I can think of ways— something slipped into our equipment perhaps, contact poison sprayed on his bedding."

Leto resisted the urge to deny each possibility, but saw Paul shaking and pale, his eyes red. He had wanted to get away from countless retainers and guards, for this time of bonding with Paul on their customary retreat. And now . . . "This has to be part of some plot. He looks like Wellan when he died from the ailar. Save him!"

Yueh continued to work at a measured but frantic pace. "There are some similarities in the symptoms, my Lord, but there are many possibilities."

The young man's back arched as if he were trying to throw off a crushing weight.

"Paul—" Leto gasped. He meant it as a shout, but the word came out as a desperate whisper.

Gurney said, "I'm activating the emergency comm to summon rescue ships. They can be here in . . ." His voice trailed off.

Leto looked at him in stark silence. It would probably take much too long for help to arrive. "Yueh, will he be all right?"

The Suk doctor continued to work. "I do not know, Sire, but we'll know in the next few minutes if my treatment has any effect. If not . . ." He peeled Paul's eyelids back, took his pulse. He'd taken blood samples, and the chemical analyzers were already offering a first approximation. "I see no traces of ailar in his bloodstream. He has not been drugged, that I can tell."

"Some other poison, then!"

"How can you give him an antidote if you don't know what the toxin is?" Gurney asked.

"I have already done the obvious—fluids, electrolytes, saline," Yueh said. "In the past few minutes, his pulse has already slowed, grown more stable. That is a good sign. His body reacted violently to some substance, but he is driving it off." He glanced at where Paul had vomited on the ground. "Because we all had the same food for dinner, I have to assume it's not anything he ate."

Leto struggled to understand. "But how could someone have slipped poison in—" He looked at Yueh and Gurney. Could either of these men have done something so treacherous? And why out here? Both of them had had ample opportunity to poison Paul for years if they were going to do so. Such suspicions were insane.

"We did not all eat the same thing," Gurney pointed out. "We caught moonfish, but we each ate our own. And Paul's was different . . ."

Yueh looked up, blinking. "The spawning female! A moonfish in the reproductive stage could well exude unusual hormones or toxins." He rummaged in his medkit, found another autoinjector, and slapped it against Paul's neck. "Food poisoning can cause such a violent reaction. Perhaps we were looking too hard for an insidious answer."

Leto knelt and rested his hand on Paul's shoulder, stroked his son's dark hair away from his forehead. Beads of sweat glistened there, but Paul had calmed, was resting more easily. His breathing was even.

Yueh took another set of readings. "Temperature returning to normal." He breathed a long, slow sigh of relief. "We may be past the crisis. Let the boy rest, and we'll watch him closely."

Leto stared down. Every planetary leader, every head of a House Major or House Minor was always on guard for his or her life. Poison snoopers and shields, self-defense, and spies were a way of life in the Imperium.

Could it truly be possible that Paul's sickness had nothing to do with treachery or an assassination attempt? Just tainted fish?

Yueh looked up at him. Gurney stood guarded, alarmed, and watchful, but he had allowed himself to relax his imminent killing stance. The Suk doctor double-checked his readings. "I cannot say with absolutely certainty, Sire, but sometimes a fever is just a fever, and food poisoning is just an accident."

"Thank you, Yueh." Leto let out a shuddering sigh. "I will leave Paul's life in your hands."

Unfortunately, the most evil personalities often possess extraordinary intellectual skills that enable them to advance their dark agendas.
—PRINCESS IRULAN, *In My Father's House*

Two men stepped away from the Harkonnen ornithopter onto loose, sparkling sand. Heat devils wavered over the desert, but Rabban was most interested in the rusty red stain of melange on the landscape.

He and Piter de Vries stared at a battered spice harvester, a dangerous and groaning wreck that should have been removed from service long ago. It lumbered its way across the open dune field, scooping and sifting sand to separate out melange. The harvester would work here until its vibrations summoned a worm, and then it was supposed to be lifted out of danger in the nick of time. The giant machine had done this many times before.

The crew, however, did not know that this particular unit had been removed from all Harkonnen equipment records five runs earlier. Any spice it produced now would not appear on production manifests or tax records, because this particular factory no longer existed on any inventory.

It was a ghost. A profitable one.

Rabban saw spotter aircraft circling over a wide range of the sky, pilots ready to call out wormsign. This harvester had been dropped down onto the spice sands by a carryall only minutes before his own 'thopter landed.

The noises of closer aircraft thrummed in the sky as a squadron of secret mercenary craft hovered directly overhead, awaiting a signal from Rabban. Operated by men secretly transported here from Giedi Prime—outside of the Baron's normal staff and military—these were pirate vessels, ready to snatch a load of spice and whisk it to safety.

It was a special operation that the crew of the doomed harvester knew nothing about. For several weeks, ever since the old wreck had been officially decommissioned, the crew had not been allowed back into Carthag, but rather were billeted at isolated Harkonnen outposts or the revived Orgiz processing facility, which also appeared on no maps.

The factory crew complained about terrible conditions aboard the barely functional spice factory, and had begun to disbelieve promises of higher and higher bonuses. Rabban knew the crew was played out and needed to be disposed of. He also judged that the factory would not last beyond today. Time to scuttle the whole operation—for real this time. Six full, undocumented loads of spice made a worthwhile profit.

Burly Rabban, a personification of brute force, looked to his Mentat companion, a far thinner, jittery man. Piter de Vries was a weapon of calculated plans, proud of his acuity and insight. Rabban found him annoying, though, with his wild hair, effeminate face, and acidic insults. His uncle tolerated the twisted Mentat only so long as he proved himself useful—as with this particular operation. Sooner or later, though—just like this lumbering factory—de Vries's usefulness would end.

Rabban glanced at his nemesis. *If my uncle decides to kill Piter, I hope he lets me do it.*

He activated a headset, heard static and the chatter of voices over the line, the harvester crew, the supervisor urging his workers to keep the factory lumbering along for just a little longer. Rabban changed channels, heard his pirates talking, preparing for their part of the operation.

The twisted Mentat watched with clear distaste as the crippled, creaking factory wheezed forward. "Even my most generous projections did not envision the equipment lasting this long. The manufacturer is to be commended."

"That harvester is even older than you are," Rabban quipped. He chuckled at his joke.

The Mentat grimaced. "Perhaps it will last longer than you, unless you show me proper respect and recognize my worth." His voice had a melodic, threatening quality, which managed to make Rabban feel inadequate.

Rabban flushed, inhaling deeply of the hot, dry air. "Your worth, in comparison to me? I am the Count of Lankiveil, recently named the Baron's governor-designate of Arrakis."

"And I am a very expensive Mentat, specially indoctrinated by the Tleilaxu per Harkonnen specifications." He paused, sniffed. "The Baron has not told me about you being appointed governor here, official or unofficial."

One day, Rabban would lose his temper and break Piter de Vries. "My uncle named me in his place when he went back to Giedi Prime on business, but even when he returns here to Arrakis, I will still be your superior."

"Oh, my superior?" A cruel smile worked around the edges of his sapho-stained mouth. "A moment, while I try to visualize that."

Rabban dismissed the insect. He had more important things to do, with the pirate operation here reaching its peak. He had to be more subtle, more patient.

"As I've told you before, life is a chess game," the Baron had counseled. "You must think several moves ahead."

Good advice, although not so easily heeded in the heat of the moment. This time, Rabban decided to ignore the Mentat's provocation. Instead, he stared at the noisy, shaking harvester. "I prove my superiority each time our pirates slip away with another load of undocumented spice." Continued successes like today would guarantee Rabban's designation as the Baron's heir. In that position, he would have plenty of time to dispose of the annoying twisted Mentat as he saw fit.

De Vries wisely held his tongue, for now, and the two watched from a distance while the machine crawled ahead to a better vein of spice, where it resumed harvesting. Rabban smelled the burning odor of dusty cinnamon, as well as smoke and sour exhaust from the laboring engines. At one time, this harvester had been considered lucky. Now it shook and clattered so noisily that Rabban's ears ached, even from a safe distance.

One of the unmarked mercenary craft landed on the rocky flat adjacent to their 'thopter. A tall, grizzled man disembarked with the aircraft engines still thrumming. Though he wore no uniform, he saluted. "This is a good vantage from which to observe our operations, Count Rabban."

This was the chief of the mercenaries the Baron had sent from Giedi Prime, pirates who would steal the spice from this ghost factory and sell it off the books to CHOAM. Not only were these rugged men separate from the harvester crew, they were not connected with any smuggler bands on Arrakis, unknown even to Count Fenring.

Rabban smiled to hear the man use his formal title, especially after de Vries's insult. The pirate chief brought out a handheld screen tied to the doomed factory's interior sensors. The image showed the level of spice in the harvester's hold. "We are currently at satisfactory levels. I don't expect that wreck will be able to gather much more."

"It has reached the end of its service lifetime," Rabban said.

"Wait another three minutes," de Vries said. "That would be the optimal time to swoop in."

Rabban ground his teeth together, but recognized the Mentat's abilities, and looked at the mercenary. "No approaching worm yet?"

The pirate chief shook his head. "Not yet, which is a surprise, considering all the noise and vibrations."

"Three minutes," Rabban grudgingly agreed with the twisted Mentat. "Then take the haul."

The pirate chief ran back to his craft and lifted off. Shortly afterward, the squadron of mercenary 'thopters dropped down like bloodsucking insects, in armored cargo vessels that attached themselves to the factory hull and ripped open the melange compartments. Wide-mouthed vacuum hoses dropped into the open bins of fresh spice, roaring like old-style spaceship engines as they siphoned off the reddish powder.

The spice crew, astonished by what was happening, pulled in their groundcars. Dust-covered men waved and shouted at the raiders, who continued to move about efficiently, ignoring the irrelevant workers.

On the channel in his headset, Rabban heard the factory supervisor howling for assistance, but the escort ships, even spotters, had been sent away. No one else needed to see this culminating event, the final gasp of the old factory's long years of rough service.

Within minutes, the wormsign alert sounded, triggering what would normally have been a breakneck wrap-up and evacuation. But this operation was different in every way, the last haul from the old harvester. The handpicked pirate commandos engaged in their own mission.

Members of the doomed spice crew scrambled out of the big machine, trying to defend their positions. Hatches opened, and burly workers boiled out, brandishing any tools they could turn into makeshift weapons. With cold-blooded efficiency, though, the pirates stabbed them with long blades and dumped the bodies over the hull of the lurching machine and down into the churned sand.

"Worm inbound!" one of the pirate spotters reported over their private channel. The chief acknowledged, and the team went about their tasks with a greater urgency. "Four minutes."

The mercenaries took three minutes to transfer the rest of the spice cargo and leave the harvester broken and exhausted on the dunes. By then, the great worm rushed closer with a visible ridge of sand rolling ahead as a precursor.

The desert monster came fast, while Rabban ran for his observation 'thopter with the Mentat scrambling behind him. The rocky terrain of their vantage should have kept them safe enough, but neither man wanted to take the chance. Once they were aboard the craft, the articulated wings flapped and lifted them into the air, carrying them high enough to circle the site.

Rabban watched as the worm crashed blindly into the harvester, engulfing it. Sprays of sand erupted into the dust-laden air. Even from a distance, he could hear the roar and groan of the enormous metal hulk being ripped apart. The sandworm seemed to take malicious glee in helping Rabban destroy all remaining evidence.

"Well, that operation went smoothly," de Vries said. "My compliments to our mercenaries. We were perfectly justified in decommissioning that dangerous hulk, and yet it still produced five more loads of melange." He smiled with his stained lips. "Now it is well and truly scuttled."

On the desert below, the worm thrashed about, burying the remains of the harvester.

"Yes, my uncle devised a clever plan," Rabban said, knowing the barb would sting the Mentat.

"Indeed he did," de Vries replied, not challenging him. Rabban realized that both of them were learning to pick their battles, and battlefields.

There is joy in discovery, an intellectual euphoria that comes from grasping a complex concept or uncovering a thing previously unknown. But some discoveries bring with them a burden and a curse. Be careful what you seek.

—The Mentat's Handbook

When Paul awoke in the camp, it was still dark. His stomach roiled, and his mouth tasted worse than the insides of old military boots. His muscles ached as if he had undergone two days of combat training with both Gurney and Duncan.

Dr. Yueh was already there, checking him. Leto came to his side, steadying the young man as he tried to sit up. "You gave us quite a scare, son. We've already called the retrieval crew, but they are still more than an hour out. With the tree cover and the rugged terrain, we have to wait for daylight."

"What happened?" Paul tried to remember where he was, vaguely surprised to find himself on Caladan rather than surrounded by empty sand, as in his dream.

"You reacted badly to tainted moonfish," Yueh said. "I ran a chemical screen with some of the scraps, and I found evidence of a potent toxin."

The words were a jumble in his ears. "Someone poisoned me?"

The Suk doctor stroked his long mustaches. "I believe it is a natural hormone produced by the female moonfish during the breeding cycle, and your body rebelled against it." Yueh rapidly explained palliative treatments he had pumped into Paul's bloodstream, the medications and hydration. "The substance should all be purged now."

Leto shook his head, disgusted. "Why didn't anyone at the fisheries warn us that a spawning moonfish is poisonous?"

"We know they were covering up things," Gurney added. "After all, they hid their involvement in the barra fern smuggling."

Yueh was more clinical. He had made notes during the night, documenting Paul's symptoms. "I told you that we have many gaps in our understanding of Caladan. The fishery workers could not have guessed we would catch and eat one in the wild. The fisheries likely do not harvest females full of fertilized eggs. It would not make commercial sense. The workers might have known about the toxin and considered it common knowledge. Why would they go out of their way to tell us?"

"And we did not exactly ask them for such details," Leto admitted. "Thufir Hawat was a bit more preoccupied with shutting down the ailar operations."

Paul sat back, feeling weak, but strengthened by the drugs Yueh had used. At the back of his mind, like a jumble of shadows, he thought of the powerful vision he had experienced. "I saw a desert, warriors . . . a monster. It was real, or it will be."

Leto frowned in concern. "Was it one of those dreams of yours that interest your mother so much?"

"I . . . I don't know." Paul's head was still fuzzy. He could just see the gray light of dawn leaking into the sky.

"Likely just delirium," Yueh said, offering him a bowl of bland breakfast meal. "This will calm your stomach and help you regain your strength."

"We'll be heading home soon enough," Gurney said. "I just received word from the rescue craft, and they have reached our landed flyer. They'll work their way out here a little after daybreak." He looked around the primitive camp at the slow-moving stream, the sandbar, the rugged mountains in the distance, the cold, damp mist in the air. "You picked a most inconvenient place to be sick, young pup."

Leto looked up at the thick canopy of trees. "Just rest, and we'll get you home. We never should have gone so deep into the uncharted terrain."

"I thought that was the point," Paul said with a wan smile. He ran his fingers through sweaty hair and felt a new determination. "But we can't go back yet, Father. You promised me several more days."

Leto said in a stern voice, "You need to get to where you can recover, in a comfortable bed with people to tend you. What if you have a relapse?"

"Then Dr. Yueh would treat me. He has his medkit."

"It is not the same," Yueh said. "Although, I would indeed be doing the same treatment back at the castle, my Lord."

"I'm already much better. We came on this expedition expecting discomforts," Paul insisted. "But what we are doing is important, and I can be resilient. I have to be. If I am to be Duke, I can't just give up." He struggled to his feet, though his entire body felt as shaky as the dwellings on stilts near the moonfish operations. "Besides, we have to find the barra ferns."

Leto looked at him, clearly unconvinced. "The rescue craft are already inbound."

"Then recall them. Have them turn around." Paul forced himself to stand straighter, as if to exude power. "You can call them back if I do feel sick." He thought he saw a hint of pride on his father's face, and he took it as an opening to continue. "Gurney always says not to pamper me. If it was only food poisoning, as Dr. Yueh says, then it's over. I'm much stronger already, and I want to explore. We can look for barra ferns in the wild. Dr. Yueh needs fresh specimens."

Yueh nodded slowly. "That would be useful for my research."

For some reason, Paul felt it was important for him to be out here to prove his strength, his independence. It would demonstrate his fitness to be the next Duke of Caladan.

The vivid desert dream, though—was it more than just delirium?—still disturbed him.

Gurney offered unexpected support. "The lad is right, my Lord. We still haven't found the illicit ailar operations. They must be growing the ferns somewhere. Too many questions unanswered."

Leto turned his hawkish gaze on the Suk doctor. "What do you say, Yueh? You are Paul's physician."

The sallow man stroked his chin. "His body has been through quite a strain, but his vitals are acceptable. While I do not recommend vigorous activity yet, I can give him vitamin shots and stamina enhancers." He gave Paul a long, analytical look. "I suggest we rest here in camp for the day and see how he does. Once he has recovered more, I can make a better assessment."

"Please, sir," Paul said to his father. "This is part of being a leader, too."

Leto regarded him with smoke-gray eyes. "Your mother knows Bene Gesserit manipulation techniques, but you seem to be using them yourself."

Paul gave Leto a half-hearted grin. "Is this one working?"

"Send the rescue craft home, Gurney," the Duke said, and turned back to Paul, sinking down to sit beside his son. "We will rest today and see. Once we start exploring the wilderness, we will go at your pace."

"I can keep up, sir." Paul's lips quirked in a smile. "And if not, Gurney can simply carry me."

The troubadour warrior responded with a snort.

BY THE NEXT day, Paul felt good enough to move out, and Dr. Yueh gave his provisional approval. The Suk doctor had explored the area around their camp, acquiring interesting biological samples, adding images to his naturalist's catalog, although he had not found any barra ferns.

Breaking out their transmitter, Leto communicated with Thufir Hawat, further explaining—and downplaying—what had happened to Paul. The Mentat was back at Castle Caladan now, after leaving Atreides troops to occupy the moonfish operations and continue investigations of the ailar smuggling.

The group set off into the misty forests, where majestic firs stretched skyward and their boughs trapped the rising fog. Paul hiked in sturdy boots as the group forged a trail through scattered brown needles, climbed over rocks, and worked their way between thick trunks mottled with lichen. Spectacular shell fungus crawled up the bark of one evergreen titan. Trudging along, they kept alert for any sign of the unusual barra ferns.

Gurney documented their route by placing small signal beacons at strategic points, and they could always track their way back to the flyer landed on the open beach. The four hiked close enough together for conversation, but ranged far enough apart to broaden their search.

They traveled and camped for two days until they were grimy and tired, though Paul felt cleansed of lingering effects from the moonfish toxin. Now his exhaustion came from the genuine hard work of climbing through trackless wilderness.

One afternoon, Gurney ranged well ahead of them toward a distant ridge. Paul stepped over a fallen log, pushing his way through underbrush, and bent down to see a bright green curl, the delicate frond of a fern poking up from the mulch, spiraling like a tight prehensile tail. "Dr. Yueh, I think I found one!"

The Suk doctor crashed his way over to Paul through bushes and brambles. The normally reserved man grumbled at being scratched by thorns. Leto also joined them, slipping on moss and debris, pushing saplings aside.

Yueh bent down to inspect the pale green nub. "A barra fern, indeed, young Master." He opened his pack and removed his analysis kit. "We achieved an important goal. Now I have a fresh comparison sample. I can test to see if the ailar content matches the ones that caused those deadly overdoses."

Leto shouted, "Gurney, we found one of the ferns!"

The troubadour warrior was nearly out of sight, working his way uphill to a crest where the trees were thinner. Paul could see his figure through the slatted forest shadows. Hearing the Duke's call, Gurney topped the rise, but remained silent for a long moment. Finally, he turned back to them, waving his arms. "God's below, why would you stop at finding just one? Look up here!"

Yueh plucked the fern specimen from the underbrush, wearing a glove to avoid getting the substance on his skin, and stored it in one of his sample vials. When Gurney kept shouting, the three fought their way up the slope to the top of the ridge, panting hard.

The ridge was actually a high, open expanse with pines interspersed with towering fern trees, some of which rose five meters high. Yueh looked up, craning his neck. The fanlike fronds of the mature ferns were like lacy veils screening the watery sunlight.

In his calf-high boots, Gurney stalked ahead across open ground covered with a carpet of pale green ferns, tender nubs each the size of a curled human hand.

Paul felt a sense of wonder at all the growing plants. "These ferns are about the same age, and they have a more mottled appearance than the young one I just found in the forest." He bent down, found a snipped stem, but did not touch it. "Look, they've been cut and gathered before they could grow any higher."

"Not only that, lad." Gurney gestured, and the young man instantly saw what he meant. "*They are in rows.*"

Paul scanned across the evenly spaced planting. "Not wild growths at all, then. Someone cultivated these ferns."

"And harvested them." Leto strode forward, scanning the tall fern trees and the pines that helped camouflage the growing area. "How extensive is this field?"

"Too many barra ferns for us to uproot, my Lord," Gurney said as he stomped one of the nubs and ground it under his heel. "I imagine we'll find similar fields adjacent to this one. It's a large growing area."

Paul looked beyond the large fan-shaped fronds and spotted silvery threads that interconnected the tallest trees. "What are those? A web of some kind?"

Leto ran his fingers along the thin wires. "A camouflage net. It can scramble sensors to hide the ferns from aerial surveys."

Gurney ranged farther along, scanning the forest of towering mature ferns. Flicking his glance from side to side, Paul estimated perhaps a thousand young, mottled ferns awaiting harvest.

Yueh observed, "If these were planted and harvested, then someone must be tending them regularly. How often do you think they inspect their fields?"

"Maybe someone is still here." Gurney drew his blade and loped along. "Here, my Lord! Over here!"

They followed his voice, pushing aside weeds that helped mask the rows of ferns. Duke Leto got ahead of them while Paul and Yueh hurried to catch up.

When they broke through a stand of fern trees, Paul spotted a prefabricated hut erected along with several rectangular storage units. Bulky mechanical equipment was covered by polymer tarps.

A thin, sunken-eyed man in drab clothing burst from the hut, alerted by the commotion. He stared at them, his mouth agape, before he lunged back into the structure, panicked and confused. A moment later, he returned carrying a long fern-harvesting pike with a curved blade.

Gurney was upon him with his own kindjal, hacking at the harvesting pike. The man flailed, unable to defend himself against a skilled fighter. He jabbed the point at Gurney, but the man was a mere harvester, and Gurney easily deflected the blow, avoiding the inartful attack.

Yelling, the worker retreated into the hut and slammed the door. By the time Leto, Paul, and Yueh joined Gurney, the man had barricaded himself inside the flimsy structure. Paul looked around for other workers at the site, but the man appeared to be alone, like an isolated shepherd tending a flock.

Gurney's face was flushed, his inkvine scar beet red. He grabbed the discarded harvesting pike and pummeled the hut's wall. He called over his shoulder to Leto. "We'll pull him out, my Lord, and then he'll give us some answers."

Thrusting and twisting with the pike, Gurney finally staved in the wall. From the shadows within, they heard the worker's dismayed whimper. Pulling the polymer material wider, Gurney pushed his way inside, with Leto pressing close behind.

They found the worker on the packed dirt floor, curled into a ball, shivering and convulsing. He had stuffed his mouth full of the curled green barra ferns. Spittle and foam trickled out of his mouth. His eyes were already scarlet with hemorrhages.

Leto roared in frustration. "Yueh, save him!"

The Suk doctor stared. "With that dose, my Lord? Not possible." He nevertheless dropped to his knees and whipped out his medkit.

"Why would that man kill himself?" Paul said. "He doesn't even know who we are. We could just have been hunters."

The worker's eyes were red, filled with blood. Yueh had cleared his mouth, knocked the half-chewed ferns aside, but the victim had already swallowed too much raw ailar.

"Why did you do this?" Leto demanded. "Give us answers! Who is responsible for these operations?"

Yueh's ministrations had no effect.

Even as the worker died, he managed a hoarse, rasping cackle. The man coughed and spat out words. "I fear Chaen Marek . . . more than you!"

Since our founding, the Bene Gesserit have always found ways to slip into the corridors of power.

—MOTHER SUPERIOR HARISHKA

After Reverend Mother Terta's violent death, an undercurrent of sadness and fear ran through the inner halls of the Mother School.

"I genuinely thought Lethea was dying at the time," Mohiam said. "Maybe I was too impulsive, but it might have been our last chance to retrieve her memories and skill . . . Now poor Terta is dead."

Harishka shook her head. "By connecting with her mind, Reverend Mother Terta was only trying to help her."

"And help the Sisterhood—but it was a trap." Mohiam considered. "Does Lethea hate us? Is she warning us of a disaster to the Bene Gesserit, or is she causing it?"

The two women entered a large greenhouse where white-robed Acolytes silently tended flowers and leafy plants, trimming and potting them. "We need her ability to predict the near future of the breeding program, but at what cost? She has left a swath of victims in her wake." Her voice grew hard, angry. "Lethea is more than a liability—she is a genuine danger to all of us."

The rich, moist smell of plants in the enclosed building did not dispel Mohiam's uneasiness. "Is Lethea even conscious of what she's doing?"

"She is aware of more than we suspected, and has shown herself to be malicious and vindictive. How can we trust what she wants to do to Jessica, if we bring her here?"

After expending so much mental energy to drive the medical Sister to suicide, the ancient woman had settled back down and now rested calmly in her isolated chamber. Spy-eyes transmitted Lethea's every movement into other rooms, but the Sisters were now too terrified to tend her personally. The Mother Superior had ordered the attendants to stay away.

They walked among rows of green plants, surrounded by earthy aromas of mulch, the mist of watering systems, the perfume of blossoms. Harishka paused and took a calming breath, bending over a burst of colorful blue flowers. She made an odd, distracted comment. "I find this place relaxing. Years ago, a younger Sister taught me that being surrounded by plants could be restorative to a troubled spirit. We certainly need that now."

Mohiam smiled, remembering the same thing. "Sister Margot said that, I presume? She always had such a fondness for her conservatory. I see her and Count Fenring often in the Imperial Court. An interesting marriage that benefits each of them, as well as the Sisterhood." She frowned. "I fear she cares a bit too much for that awful man, though."

Harishka's voice grew stern. "Too many Sisters allow themselves the vulnerability of love. It distorts their perspective."

Mohiam tried to be more understanding. "They are human."

"But the goals of the Bene Gesserit must remain paramount in their minds and in their hearts. No matter where they go or what assignments they receive, all Sisters belong to the order."

Mohiam had never let herself feel giddy emotions for any of the lovers she had taken during her long life. Per the Sisterhood's instructions, she had given birth to daughters, and had felt no fondness for their fathers. She shuddered as she recalled coupling with the loathsome Baron Harkonnen, back before he was fat. But at least that union had resulted in Jessica . . . *Jessica of Caladan.*

What did Lethea want from Jessica? Why was the Sisterhood's future at stake? And why was it so important that the mother be torn from her son?

Thin sunlight shone through the plaz panes, heating the humid enclosure. Wearing a surprising, unguarded smile, the Mother Superior led Mohiam to another row in the greenhouse. "Here is something you haven't seen yet."

A long, slender leaf floated free in the air, carrying tiny winged creatures on all of its sides, as if the hovering leaf were an airborne troop transport. The air was alive with the sound of fast-beating wings. Mohiam squinted to see the creatures fly away to pollinate flowers.

"The smallest hummingbirds in the Imperium," Harishka said, "smaller than bees."

Mohiam smiled as the distraction gave her momentary respite from the Lethea crisis. Other leaves carrying minuscule hummingbirds drifted through the air, and the tiny creatures buzzed along, working in concert, as if controlled by a single brain.

Some of the creatures perched on Harishka's shoulders, and her voice took on a tinge of wonder. "They have no fear of humans. They make a purring music."

Other hummingbirds settled on Mohiam, then flitted away. They also flew off from Harishka. The Mother Superior sighed. "It is said they can sense good people."

Mohiam considered the terrible things she had done in the name of the Sisterhood as she watched them buzz about. "They seem ambivalent toward the two of us."

"Nothing is so simple and clear-cut for a Bene Gesserit of our rank and experience," Harishka said. "I doubt they would come near Lethea." Walking under a gentle irrigation mist, the Mother Superior continued to muse aloud, "And what to do about Jessica? I keep wondering why Lethea would demand to see an obscure Sister who was assigned to a world of little note. But two separate Kwisatz Mothers have focused on her now. Mother or child must be relevant to our extended breeding program."

"Jessica forgets herself. I believe that in her arrogance, she imagines she might have produced the Kwisatz Haderach," Mohiam said, shaking her head. "Perhaps the boy does have significant potential."

"There is that possibility," said the Mother Superior. "I, too, reviewed the materials Anirul left us years ago, and the bloodlines are indeed reaching a long-anticipated convergence, but breeding is never an exact science. Our program has produced numerous candidates who could be the Kwisatz Haderach, and all have disappointed in one way or another. Some remain under observation. Jessica will bear closer watching, though." She grumbled in her throat. "I hate to accede to Lethea's violent demands, but we also ignore her words at our peril."

The hummingbirds continued to buzz around, darting away from the two women as if both attracted and repelled.

Harishka took a few moments to ponder, having a debate with herself, with Mohiam there as a sounding board. "But if Paul Atreides does have the potential to be what we have long sought, do we dare take Jessica away from him? Does the boy not need to be molded and shaped under her guidance? Does he not need to be controlled?" She turned her intense eyes to her companion. "Will Jessica raise him and indoctrinate him as we wish?"

Ever since coming here, Mohiam had wrestled with the same questions. "Even if she is important, Mother Superior, my daughter may have forgotten her obligations to the Sisterhood. Remember, she was told to bear only daughters with Duke Leto Atreides, yet she gave him a son. That defiance has done significant harm to our plans. But if Lethea calls for her, maybe there is a way to salvage something? We should take her away from Duke Atreides, transfer her here. To be safe."

Harishka paused before a row of animated blossoms that puckered and shifted as if to attract attention. She abruptly changed the subject to more mundane matters. "Now that I have the Emperor's Truthsayer here, we can also discuss broader Sisterhood politics. We must exert our influence as Shaddam considers candidates to fill all the vacancies among the noble houses."

Mohiam nodded. "The well-established families have designated successors, but many weaker Houses will likely fall or be replaced. More ambitious nobles will seek to make advantageous moves." She felt a sense of relief, even happiness. In the wake of Lethea's horrific acts, it seemed so comfortable to be talking about the Sisterhood's usual schemes.

Mohiam listed candidates the Emperor had already proposed, and the two women reviewed what they knew of the personalities and characters of these likely new members, how a clever Sister could exploit them through the arts of seduction, Truthsaying, and statecraft. They discussed particular Sisters who might be suitable for specific nobles—exactly as the order had done when assigning a very young and pretty Jessica to Leto Atreides on Caladan.

Harishka said, as if broaching a difficult subject, "When you return to the Imperial Court, we will need your eyes and ears even more than usual. There is a certain situation at a major noble house, one that is in flux. The Sisterhood has lost influence with House Tull, one of the most powerful in the Landsraad."

Mohiam took a moment to recollect what she knew of House Tull, details she had seen on Kaitain. "We have a Sister there already . . . Zoanna? Doesn't she have the Tull patriarch wrapped around her finger?"

"Not anymore. A month ago, the old man died in bed with her, and he was succeeded by his son, Viscount Giandro Tull. Giandro was not present at the Otorio disaster, because he was planning the funeral ceremony for his father. But that is not our difficulty now. In the wake of the old Viscount's unfortunate death, his son declared Sister Zoanna unwelcome on his planet. Worse, he is suspicious of Bene Gesserit influence and refuses to allow a replacement Sister into his House. He is bitter toward our order."

Mohiam thought of a handful of other noble families that had spurned assistance from the Sisterhood, though it was rare. "Even if he wants no concubine in his bed, a Viscount still needs the services of a Truthsayer. Bene Gesserit political counsel is unparalleled."

"He doubts our motives and has rejected all overtures. Now he refuses to respond to us. We need to get a Sister back into his court."

Mohiam could see the Mother Superior's deep concern. "When I return to Kaitain, I will investigate. We can find a Sister acceptable to the new Viscount, though it may take time."

Suddenly, a young, flushed Acolyte rushed into the greenhouse. "Mother Superior! Lethea is awake and speaking!" The young woman looked like a startled rabbit.

Harishka and Mohiam hurried back to the ancient woman's medical chamber, where several Sisters remained outside the door, hesitant to go inside. One Reverend Mother stood guard, waiting for the Mother Superior.

Even from the corridor, Mohiam could hear the old woman bellowing from her bed, "Bring me Jessica! Jessica of Caladan!"

Allies, business associates, and friends are three entirely different catego-
ries. Do not confuse your definitions or your feelings. The results could
be disastrous.

—MALINA ARU, CHOAM Ur-Director,
Private Administrative Briefings

An unpleasant man, an unpleasant place, Malina Aru thought. *It is difficult
to decide which is worse.* Even so, she needed to verify that Baron Harkonnen was true to his word.

After roundabout, secretly arranged transport, the Ur-Director reached Arrakis hidden aboard a regularly scheduled Guild Heighliner. From orbit, the great
ship dispatched dump boxes with supplies for the Harkonnen garrisons, and Imperial merchants shipped down ridiculously expensive luxuries. New spice crews
arrived, wide-eyed dreamers believing false promises of riches, or disillusioned
workers clinging to scant hope, knowing Arrakis was their last chance.

Malina was unaccustomed to the survival culture among the locals, who
went to great lengths to hoard even the smallest breath of water vapor. In the
past, she had seen hollow-eyed beggars so desperate for money that they squabbled and prostrated themselves for a few micro-solaris tossed in the gutter. The
people of Arrakis treated water in much the same way. Each day's existence was
like a suffocating person sucking in one last breath.

In a sense, the Urdir found it affirming to see just what humans would do to
stay alive. People always wanted something, and someone could make a profit by
providing it. That was what kept the CHOAM Company in business.

After the commercial cargo and transport ships disembarked from the
Heighliner hold, Malina traveled down in an unmarked lighter with a CHOAM
security escort. Her pilot had the coordinates of the Baron's surreptitious meeting site—out in the middle of nowhere, completely unobserved.

She considered the fat man arrogant and disgusting in countless ways, and it
offended her that he would demand that she come to see the specialized operations with her own eyes. As a concession to the harsh desert environment, she
wore a tan scarf over her hair, a long-sleeved airy blouse, a lightweight long skirt.
She rarely saw the necessity of doing things in person, did not understand why
her physical presence was required now.

Nevertheless, she was here.

The pilot headed across the hostile desert of undulating dunes broken by lava outcroppings and irregular mountain ranges. They flew too high to spot any spice-harvesting operations on the great open sands.

After flying for more than an hour, the pilot raised his voice to say, "We are approaching the precise coordinates, Ur-Director, but I see nothing. Nothing at all."

"The Orgiz refinery complex is out here somewhere. Use scans."

The line of rough mountains consisted of black striated rocks, jagged and sinuous peaks. Her pilot dropped lower and talked to himself, perhaps forgetting he had left his speaker on. "Why would they place a refinery so far from any transport lanes? No one could ever find it."

"You answered your own question." Malina peered down at the razor-edged cliffs as the lighter continued its descent. When they circled overhead, she saw cracks between the mountains, gorges and narrow defiles that might have been river canyons in ancient times, if there had ever been water on this planet. "Those are the mountains on the chart. A landing area is down there, somewhere, but the Harkonnen operations take great pains to remain unseen. Find it."

She had studied the unreliable charts of Arrakis because, as Ur-Director, she preferred to know everything about her most important accounts. By long-standing tradition, or flaw, the maps of this world were sketchy and inaccurate, with no Guild surveillance available from space, no detailed weather satellites or accurate topographical images. The absence was so blatant it had to be intentional. Why?

The arrogance of a ruler who chose to be willfully oblivious about vital facts had always bothered her, but the Padishah Emperor accepted this sort of ignorance. Shaddam IV was a singularly incurious man. Not knowing the details of the spice melange—one of the most important substances in the Imperium—seemed a critical failure to her. Someday, if the Noble Commonwealth did break the Imperium into countless thriving, independent worlds, Arrakis might be governed by someone more knowledgeable. For now, CHOAM was just a customer.

After her pilot narrowed the search with a scan, the Orgiz refinery became visible. The sheltered basin in the rugged mountains was like a fortress surrounded by high rock walls, accessible only by air and with superior flying skills.

The pilot braked his descent, tilted the lighter, and slid between the towering walls. The refinery's landing zone was demarcated with low lights. Using suspensor engines, he dropped to a precise landing on the hard field among several 'thopters and Harkonnen gunships.

Once the craft was secured, her CHOAM security guards emerged first, fanning out to form a cordon. Malina stepped out into the pounding heat. Her nostrils and lungs crackled as she breathed dry air that was saturated with the cinnamon odor of melange.

A Harkonnen reception committee waited at the edge of the landing zone. With suspensor-lightened steps, an enormous zeppelin of a man came forward to meet her. Though she had seen the Baron recently on Giedi Prime, he seemed out of place here in the bleak spice refinery complex, weaker than in the more civilized surroundings of the Harkonnen homeworld. Even as he stood upright, flanked by personal guards, the Baron seemed vulnerable in the stark desert.

He grinned and bowed before her, overly friendly. "My dear Ur-Director, I am pleased we could meet in this very special place. Let me show you our newly reopened complex. The potential for our cooperation is great."

Malina did not smile back at him. Instead, she looked around at the cliff walls, the sand scattered everywhere, the pipes and pumps of the refurbished complex, the tall storage silos, the gleaming metal conduits already corroded and covered with dust. "Why did I need to come here in person, Baron? This wastes my time. We are in basic agreement, and images would have sufficed."

"Ah, but images could be falsified." His forced laughter rumbled like an out-of-tune musical instrument. "More importantly, for a scene as magnificent as this, images would never do it justice. Look around you." He raised his hands as he turned, and his suspensor belt took him in a slow, ungainly pirouette. "My father, Dmitri, made Orgiz a thriving refinery complex, but nearly forty years ago, under my incompetent half brother, Abulurd, it was destroyed by desert rabble.

"Orgiz lay ruined and abandoned until recently, when we secretly reopened and brought it back to full production." He lowered his voice. "And everything is completely off the books. This refinery is no longer subject to monitoring by the Emperor or his Spice Observer Fenring. As far as they know, it is no more than ruins."

Malina surveyed the substantial and impressive facility, where cargoes of raw melange from spice harvesters could be filtered, distilled, packaged, and even disguised. The Orgiz landing field held unmarked supply ships ready to launch for the Heighliner above.

Malina frowned. "And the refinery was this extensive years ago? How is it possible that some desert band could shut such a place down? What kind of weapons do they have?"

The Baron looked uncomfortable. "As I said, my brother's governorship here was disastrous, his security systems astonishingly lax."

Malina scrutinized the Harkonnen soldiers standing at attention. "Even so . . ." She shot him a piercing glare and waited for an answer.

The Baron seemed to realize he would be required to provide more detail. "The rabble, ah, somehow drove one of those giant worms into the canyons. The creature was trapped inside this walled basin, unable to find its way out. It went berserk and spent days in a frenzy, destroying everything." He rumbled a deep, dissatisfied grunt in his throat. "One worm. It was years before anyone would even go back to the site, because we could not be certain the monster had gone."

Malina's face pinched. "Now you have rebuilt the refinery in secret—and you pass along the cost to me. That is why your spice is so expensive."

"Urdir," he said, "with this facility, we can produce an entirely separate stream of spice. Plainly, the cost of these operations requires that I charge a premium without the surtax on all of the *discretionary* melange we provide."

Around them, the Harkonnen security detail was as expressionless and rigid as statues, but she was sure they could turn deadly in a moment.

"We will work out any additional details," the Baron said, "but I believe we have a meeting of the minds. Orgiz is a functional platform for us to ship an agreed-upon amount of spice through CHOAM distribution channels." His round, fat face darkened with concern. "So long as Count Fenring and the Emperor never get wind of what we do here. Shaddam could strip House Harkonnen of the Arrakis governorship, just as they did to House Richese before us."

"Oh, you certainly have my agreement, Baron, but since I came all this way, you will now take the time to show me your operations in detail. I want to understand the process flow and every aspect of your business." Malina pressed her lips together. They were already dry and cracked. Amazing how rapidly this planet stole water from the body! "The alliance is acceptable—so long as you do not demand that I come to this godforsaken place again."

The most honorable course of military action rarely wins the battle.
—SUPREME BASHAR CORREA DOBLÉ

With elite Sardaukar standing on each side of his immense throne, the Emperor shouted to his assembled aides. Even after making revisions to the list, he remained dissatisfied with the current candidates to fill the Landsraad vacancies.

Throughout the morning, Chamberlain Ridondo had ushered in numerous advisers and scribes, and Shaddam had read summary after summary. He didn't recognize most of the names, though his dear Empress likely would. So far, the dossiers did not impress him. He needed to know that all Landsraad replacements he approved would be loyal to him, even with the brewing unrest fostered by Noble Commonwealth sedition.

"I need more names. I eliminated half the ones you submitted based on their private sentiments and public statements." He glanced at Ridondo, then down at the Imperial functionaries. "You should never have wasted my time with them."

The advisers cowered, which was the appropriate response.

"Not only is this an emergency," Shaddam continued, trying to make them understand, "it is also an opportunity. I intend to fill the vacancies with those I can rely on to carry out my policies and to support me against any controversy. We must be absolutely certain that none of them are involved in Jaxson Aru's heinous insurrection. Am I clear?"

"Very clear, Sire," said Stef Ibbon, a career bureaucrat who led one of the research teams.

"We will consult with a broader group of experts and deliver new candidates by the end of the day," said a young woman. He couldn't recall her name, but knew she was a recent graduate of a top university. The Emperor frowned at her, as did Stef Ibbon, both of them aware that the young woman should not have spoken up in front of others who had far more seniority.

Then Shaddam looked at her again. Unlike many of these others, she seemed to have confidence, intelligence, and stronger convictions than her colleagues. He recalled that the candidates she had put forward were satisfactory, and many of them remained on the Emperor's list. "Clearly, I need to disrupt my old focus groups to get better results." He struggled to remember this young woman's name. Ah, now he had it! "You are Aina Tere, correct? From this moment forward, I place you in charge of the candidate search." He glowered at Ibbon. "You will follow her orders from now on."

The career bureaucrat paled and lost his voice for a moment, before he managed to reply, "Yes, Majesty, as you wish. We will strive to do better."

"Provide her with all your research. Aina Tere will vet the names more carefully, dig deeper to identify the Imperial loyalists on the list, and separate out the traitors."

DEDICATED AND READY to sacrifice his life should any threat arise against the Emperor, Colonel Bashar Kolona stood beside the throne and listened intently. Shaddam IV was justifiably angry and frightened about the violent assassination attempt, but he was just as concerned by the quieter aspect of the Noble Commonwealth rebellion, the slow advance of planets secretly slipping out of his iron grip.

The Emperor was beginning to see traitors everywhere, most of them imaginary, but some were genuine rebels. As his Imperial spies dug deeper and exposed evidence of some noble houses that promulgated independence and advocated the breakup of the Imperium, Shaddam refrained from exposing them in public, since that would give them an open platform to air their indignation and grievances. But he began making his list.

The Sardaukar officer observed, but he kept his thoughts to himself. Many Landsraad nobles were treacherous, and yet some surprised him, Leto Atreides in particular.

Not long after becoming Duke, young Leto Atreides had discovered his own father's unwitting participation in the downfall of House Kolona. Even though the seized Kolona holdings had been transferred to House Atreides, Leto's sense of honor would not allow him to keep assets that had been gained by such means. Years ago, though it cost the wealth and stature of his House, the Atreides Duke had come to Kaitain and voluntarily surrendered his inherited Kolona holdings to distant surviving relatives.

Because he said it was the honorable thing to do.

The young colonel bashar had been attending Shaddam at the time and had witnessed Leto's unexpected generosity. From that point on, Kolona had reconsidered his original low opinion of the Atreides. Now he refused to believe Leto was involved in the Noble Commonwealth rebellion, especially after what he had seen on Otorio. The Sardaukar had immediately taken Leto's warning with due seriousness, though he was certain the Duke of Caladan did not know who Jopati Kolona was.

Shaddam's suspicions, though, ranged widely.

Now that the Emperor had the attention of young Aina Tere, he continued lecturing his search committee. Shaddam held up the paper. "On this most recent list, I see the name of Count Trum Vichon, a man who has spoken out in favor of planetary rights. Though he did not cite the Noble Commonwealth by name, does that not give any of you pause? In order to build a strong and unified Imperium, do we dare give power to a man who idealizes the very concept of breaking it up?"

The advisers quickly consulted their notes. One heavyset woman spoke up in a surprisingly high voice. "Vichon has never criticized you or the throne, Sire. I read his speech. The Count merely proposed a political thought experiment, about the challenges of governing such a large star-spanning Imperium, given the time lags and communication delays across vast distances. We thought you only wanted to exclude those who had openly agitated against you."

Shaddam was not in an open-minded mood. "Think about what you are saying! The core of the Noble Commonwealth's argument is planetary rights as opposed to Imperial rights, scattered independence versus strong unification. A nobleman who is in favor of planetary rights might be an enemy of the throne."

The aides responded with dead silence.

Kolona remained at attention, listening as the Emperor's rant gained momentum. Though he was a loyal Sardaukar, Kolona had mixed feelings about this man. Shaddam Corrino had demonstrated the utmost cruelty in the service of maintaining his firm hand of leadership. Fifteen years ago, Shaddam had executed his own half brother in the Imperial Plaza after declaring him a traitor. He was not averse to hard decisions or extreme acts.

Yet Kolona had also seen Emperor Shaddam show surprising kindnesses. He recalled a day when Shaddam had been walking in the gardens with Princess Irulan, his favorite daughter, when they noticed a commotion at the West Gate. Several dozen people clamored at the edge of the palace grounds, begging for food. Some of the Imperial guards had begun taking the ragged people into custody, but Shaddam and Irulan intervened before the beggars could be hauled away. Irulan had charmed her father into feeding the beggars from the palace kitchens. The Emperor personally handed out food, despite the security risk.

Of course, the moment Shaddam and his daughter walked into the palace, the Sardaukar had roughly escorted the people away, then set up procedures to keep them from ever getting so close to the palace grounds again. Even so, the Emperor had made the gesture to help them . . . an impulsive act, perhaps, but it said something about the man's heart, and about Irulan as well.

Despite the deep-seated loathing Kolona felt toward House Corrino for

Elrood's part in bringing down his own noble house, Jopati Kolona couldn't help but respect this Emperor.

Similarly, despite what Paulus Atreides had done, he could not help liking Duke Leto himself.

Now Shaddam waved his hand, dismissing the scolded advisers. They bowed in near unison and backed out of the chamber. Kolona remained at attention, staring straight ahead, not moving a muscle.

Freedom of choice implies that one is willing to make a given choice. But what if every option is disastrous? Is it better to make no choice at all, or to choose and then face the consequences, whatever they may be?
—The Mentat's Handbook, "The Paradox of Leadership"

Paul was glad to be back home in Castle Caladan after their wilderness expedition, but Thufir Hawat gave him little time to rest. Within a day, the Mentat teacher resumed his intense mental training.

Feeling confined in the castle, Paul asked Thufir if they could go into Cala City for their discussions and mental exercises. His teacher did not object. "So long as you continue your learning, the environment is irrelevant. You must not become stagnant." His red-stained lips smoothed in a smile. "We will go to Cala City, have a fine meal in one of the restaurants, and ponder difficult matters. If we dress in plain clothes, maybe they will think you are just a boy with his uncle, having a bite to eat."

Paul laughed. "After all the years you've served House Atreides, you think no one will recognize the Master of Assassins?"

"And you are well known and loved as the Duke's son, but because these people respect House Atreides, maybe they will allow us our little fiction and give us a few hours of normalcy while you study."

CALA CITY WAS a mixture of historic homes and newer structures. Thufir led them to an outdoor café on the waterfront, from which they could watch fishing boats out in the harbor and aircraft skimming up and down the coast to land in the open field above the city.

Paul and the old veteran sat across from each other at a small wooden table outside, facing the harbor. The café proprietor let his gaze linger on them, but did not remark on who they were. The two were served strong, bitter coffee and a large steaming bowl of frilled Caladan squid laced with stringy cliff greens.

At the end of the harbor, Paul could see the promontory of rock on which towering statues held ever-burning flames, the equivalent of a lighthouse. The titan-sized figure of bearded Paulus Atreides guarded the harbor, as prominent in his stone-and-steel form as he had been in his flamboyant days as planetary leader. The Old Duke's hand rested paternally on the shoulder of a young boy—Victor, Leto's first son, tragically killed in an explosion. Both statues looked out to sea.

Thufir followed Paul's gaze to the statue of the young boy, Paul's half-brother, whom he had never met. His expression became warm but calculating, as if he could read his ward's mind. "You are Duke Leto's son, too, and like Victor, you were born of a concubine, not a wife. But you are the heir to House Atreides, and your father loves you." He narrowed his eyes. "Yet you worry that the situation might change."

Paul was unsettled by the Mentat's incisive comments. "You taught me to think for myself, Thufir, but now you express my thoughts even before they occur to me." He took a sip of strong coffee, winced, and swallowed. "Not so long ago, my father arranged to marry Ilesa Ecaz, and though my mother understood the political necessities, she was hurt by the idea. My father's decision changed everything in my world. If the marriage had succeeded, any child born to Duke Atreides and Ilesa Ecaz would have become his true-blood heir. I would be a mere bastard son."

Thufir's brows knitted together. "The Duke would not discard you so."

"My father is guided by the rules of politics. He did promise me and my mother that he would not marry, but now he has put me on the market for betrothal instead. I think any promises are made of paper."

"A properly worded document on paper can be as binding as plasteel cuffs," the Mentat said. "Your father was presented with untenable choices, and no answer was acceptable to him. As always, Leto will do his best by you, just as you will be the best son to him, whether you are the next Duke of Caladan, an important trade minister for House Atreides, or even the Emperor of the Known Universe."

Paul forced a laugh. "That's a wide range of possibilities."

Thufir removed a vial of sapho juice from his pocket and gulped down the cranberry-colored, mind-enhancing liquid. "I want you to consider impossible choices, young Master. That is today's lesson. Recall the classic example of the Bridge of Hrethgir at the end of the Butlerian Jihad—the impossible choice that formed the basis of the long-standing feud between House Atreides and House Harkonnen."

"I learned all about the Battle of Corrin," Paul said. "The last stand against the thinking machines, where my ancestor Vorian Atreides won the day and Abulurd Harkonnen was convicted of cowardice. Humanity almost went extinct because of that man."

"That's a nice story." Thufir's eyes had a piercing intensity. "But the reality is not so simple. The Bridge of Hrethgir became a classic conundrum, a situation with no acceptable outcome, no correct choice. The planet Corrin was the last stronghold of the evermind Omnius and his fellow thinking machines, and after centuries of Jihad, it would be the final battle. Human forces led by Vorian Atreides and Abulurd Harkonnen surrounded Corrin, intending to eradicate the machine scourge no matter the cost. But Omnius had encircled the planet with metal stations filled with hundreds of thousands of innocent human hostages, all of whom would be killed if the humans attacked. Abulurd Harkonnen valued the innocent lives too much, but Vorian paid the price without counting the cost."

Paul was troubled. "But the Harkonnens are murderers. They are evil."

"Many of them are, young Master, but over the course of ten thousand years, perhaps some of them had hearts and souls."

"So what really happened at the Bridge of Hrethgir?" Paul asked. "The thinking machines were obviously defeated, and Abulurd Harkonnen was banished for cowardice."

"I will let you read your histories, Paul. Think about other impossible choices now. Before you blame your father too much for his decisions about marriage, or for putting you forward in a possible political union, let us conduct a Mentat exercise." His eyes had an intense sparkle. "This is not a set of esoteric facts. It is an *experience*. Look at me, deep into my eyes. Make it real in your mind."

The young man followed his trainer's instructions, as always. Thufir's gaze fixed on him, and Paul felt the surrounding sounds fading away. Disoriented, he felt as if he were falling into those dilated pupils. The warrior Mentat continued to stare. "Imagine. Place yourself in the scenario. *Believe*."

Paul believed.

"You have been captured by Harkonnens. Picture yourself in a box, a prison, close plaz walls around you, pain amplifiers strapped to your body."

Paul knew it was just his imagination, but his surroundings grew fuzzy, and he envisioned himself in a plaz-walled chamber like a coffin. He felt the needles and barbs, the cuffs, the electrodes piercing his skin. He was trapped, confined, and about to be tortured. He thrashed, but could not escape.

"Next," Hawat continued, "there is another chamber. Your mother and father are both there—also held prisoner, also connected to pain amplifiers. And they will not survive the torture. You know the truth of it."

"I know it." He saw Jessica and Leto distraught, their clothes tattered, their hair tangled. Their eyes were shadowed, their cheeks hollow. Clearly, they had been tortured already. Damned Harkonnens! Jessica pounded on the plaz wall, but sound dampeners muffled the noise. He saw her lips move. She was saying something to Duke Leto, pleading with him. He shouted commands to his son, but Paul couldn't hear them.

Thufir's voice jarred him again. "And a third thing you must know in your heart. The Harkonnens have found the Atreides family atomics, seized them, and planted them in Cala City and all the main cities on this planet. The warheads are linked to a single trigger. With one gesture, the Baron can detonate the warheads and annihilate three-quarters of Caladan's population."

"No!" Paul exclaimed.

"Now you have a choice. The Baron has granted you one favor—only one. You have three choices but you may make only a single request. You can save your parents, set them free with a simple appeal. Or you can save the population of Caladan. The Baron will surrender the nuclear triggers, and all those people will be safe—but he will surely torture your parents, and you, to death. Or third, you can save your own life. The Baron will free you. Your parents will die in agony. The people of Caladan will die. And you can only choose once."

Paul was engulfed by the provocative experience, trapped in the scenario. In his mind, he pounded on the plaz walls, shouted to be released, but nothing happened. He saw his parents desperately trying to break free of their own prisons as the pain amplifiers increased. At the same time, he was aware of the atomics everywhere and the devastation those warheads would cause, millions of people dead if he made that choice.

"Decide!" Hawat insisted. His command lashed out like a whip. Paul jerked. "Do you save your parents? Do you save yourself? Do you free all the people of Caladan, or do you let them die in a nuclear holocaust? Do you watch the Duke and his lady writhe in agony as they are flayed before your eyes? Or do you face that death yourself?"

It was so real that Paul felt caught in the hypnotic scenario the warrior Mentat had triggered within him. "No. I won't choose."

"But you must. If you do not choose, then you all die."

"No!" Paul said.

"You must choose!" Hawat shouted. The roar of his voice penetrated the illusion around him.

Paul focused his thoughts, snapped himself free, and stared out at the statues at the edge of the harbor, the flames shining from the lighthouse. As he sat at the outside table, Cala City seemed so peaceful, the blue skies scudded with fluffy clouds. "Thufir, don't make me . . ."

"You see, young Master. It is a simple choice, is it not? The parameters are perfectly clear. Why not just select an option?"

"There must be another way," Paul insisted. "I'll think of a different idea."

"I gave you none," Thufir said. "There may well come a time when you are faced with such an impossible choice."

Rattled and breathing hard, Paul gazed at the people moving along the streets, simple Caladan folk, merchants, fishermen, boatwrights. A teacher with a dozen children in tow walked along the byway toward the promontory park. Paul's heart pounded as he let the magnitude of the experience sink into him.

I won't choose! It was the fourth choice available to him, no decision. Giving up his parents and his own life was not a victory, even though he knew what he would choose.

"I refuse."

"Then all will die," Hawat said.

Frustrated, Paul refused to accept the terms. "There must be another perspective, some negotiation—"

Suddenly, his attention was riveted by a young woman strolling toward the corner. He saw her, recognized her features—dark reddish hair, large eyes, elfin face. She reminded him of the young woman in his recurring dreams, but this was not a desert, not some hot cave or canyon. Still, he watched her move, and his attention was jarred from his confusing thoughts. Startling the Mentat instructor, he lurched to his feet. He had to know who she was.

He left the table and began to hurry after her, but Thufir lunged up, seized his wrist, and pulled him back. "I did not give you leave to go."

"But, Thufir, that's the girl! The one I saw in my dreams. The one I sketched."

Anger flared in the Mentat's eyes. "I did not give you leave to go. Sit down!" His command was sharp with rebuke, and Paul reacted almost as if his mother had used the Voice on him. "Even here, my class is still in session."

Paul looked longingly as the girl vanished around a corner. He stared after her in disappointment.

Thufir rapped his knuckles and pushed him back into the chair. "I require your *undivided* attention, young Master."

Paul sighed and looked back at his teacher.

No matter how compelling the argument, an evil justification is still evil.
—DUKE PAULUS ATREIDES, private letter about the Kolona Affair

The towering lighthouse statues of his father and his first son reminded Leto of the greatest pain he had ever suffered, but the monuments also calmed and reassured him.

On the spit of rocks at one end of the main harbor, huge boulders formed a jetty, and Leto walked along the gravel path alone. On this sunny day, more than a hundred people had gathered in a wide park around the base of the colossal statues. Fishermen sat on the outer rocks and dangled lines in the water, families held picnics, and children flew colorful kites.

He looked up at the stone face of Paulus Atreides in his matador outfit. Yes, the Old Duke had always been larger than life, and this great statue made him even more so. The lighthouse fire in his hand blazed bright, flames fed through fuel tubes so the light was never extinguished.

Leto had grown up knowing his mother was stern and humorless, and he understood that the marriage between Paulus and Helena was loveless and political, but when had it become murderous? How could Lady Helena have killed her husband?

His eyes stung as he saw the flash of a reflector kite dancing across the face of the taller statue. Leto remembered when young Victor had done that, playing with reflective strips that flew in the air caught on salty updrafts. Oh, the little boy had laughed and laughed!

He paused in his step and closed his eyes as he remembered the flare of fire in the airship, the horrendous explosion that had killed Victor . . . and the even greater pain when he later learned who had set that tragedy in motion. How could his concubine Kailea have hated him so much?

Both Kailea and Helena had wanted the impossible, demanded something their men could not give, and they had responded with bloodthirsty personal violence.

Leto could never imagine Jessica doing such a thing. He loved her deeply, and he was sure that Jessica loved him as well, despite her Bene Gesserit training. He did not trust the Sisterhood, but he knew Jessica better than he knew anyone else, and could not conceive that she was capable of the bitter violence Helena and Kailea had shown.

Or was he only being naïve? As Duke, he had made hard decisions and shown iron fortitude. He had faced treachery and defeated it. He knew every person close to him, his family, and his staff. He trusted them, and earned their trust in return by showing an unwavering sense of honor.

Shrieking seabirds wheeled overhead, excited by a young couple tossing bread crumbs into the air. The birds fought one another for scraps. A similar thing was happening now in the Imperium as Landsraad survivors squabbled over the holdings left vacant because of Jaxson Aru's terrorist attack. Leto was glad to be out of that scheming nonsense.

On the smaller stone figure, Victor's cherubic face stared out to sea with a wistful smile. The Old Duke's face, though idealized by a sculptor, was etched with timeworn experience and hard realizations. When Leto looked in the mirror, his own face often wore a similar expression.

The weight of concern had increased since he and his companions had rushed home from the northern wilderness. They had found at least one field of barra ferns, and tomorrow, Leto would send in flyers to wipe out the growing area, a firm and clear retaliation against this Chaen Marek. Then he would dispatch survey parties throughout the wilderness, combing the rugged landscape to find other fields. Duke Leto Atreides would be thorough and unwavering.

The first responsibility of a Duke is the safety of his people.

There would be no more ailar deaths on his watch, on or off Caladan, if he could help it. He would eradicate the illegal drug operations. He doubted Lord Atikk would ever forgive him for the death of his son, but it was the right thing to do. There would be no more *Caladan drug.*

Meanwhile, as the preparations were made, he came out to stand under the statues and be at peace. His people knew he was a private man and granted him space. His thoughts were far away when a stranger stepped up to him. "As Duke, you hold the planet in your hands. Will you do what is best for all these people?"

He turned to see a man dressed in a common fisherman's outfit, high boots, a vest with many pockets to carry tools, a waterproof gray cloak. His thick eyebrows were like dark caterpillars on his brow, his hair black and curly with just a hint of silver, like a cloud of black smoke. But the face and skin did not belong to a man who had endured sea weather all his life. To the contrary, his features looked patrician.

Leto froze as he recognized the face. He had seen only a solido-hologram of the man, hundreds of identical images projected across the Corrino museum complex on Otorio. Jaxson Aru!

His hand instantly went to his personal shield and dagger. "I know who you are."

Jaxson responded with a hard laugh that held no humor. "Just as I know you, Duke Leto Atreides! That is why I came here, because we have much to discuss."

"You're a butcher. So many innocents died on Otorio! I barely escaped with my own life . . . and so many didn't."

The terrorist did not act the least bit disturbed. "I'm glad you survived, and you should know you were never a target, not specifically. You are not part of the corrupt Corrino web that has to be destroyed. House Atreides is known for its honor. That's why I've paid special attention to you." Jaxson spoke just loudly enough to be heard over the nearby surf, the conversation of families, the laughing children. "I think you could be an important member of the Noble Commonwealth. We need planetary leaders like yourself."

Appalled, Leto took a half step back. His cloak whipped around his shoulders in a gust of wind. "I would never agree. I witnessed what you did."

Jaxson showed no guilt. "It was necessary action, part of a cleansing process."

Leto clenched the hilt of his dueling dagger. The rebel leader could not be allowed to get away with his horrific crime. From what he could see, Jaxson Aru did not even wear a personal shield. Leto could call his guards, summon Atreides security, and bring this man to Imperial justice.

Jaxson noticed his shift, raised his eyebrows. "Leto, I came here to have a conversation. Don't even think about trying to attack me, or have me arrested. I've taken precautions." He gazed wistfully at the towering statues, the families picnicking on the grass, the fishermen dangling their lines in the water, the children running about. He seemed so calm, so confident.

"What precautions?"

"Before I approached you, I spent considerable time and effort planting explosives in these statues and in numerous places around Cala City. I can detonate some or all of them, however I wish." He paused for a tense moment. "Would you like to see your own people massacred just like those ridiculous nobles on Otorio? All I ask is a few moments of your time."

Leto felt ice down his spine, and he did not move. "This is how you attempt to recruit me to your cause? By threatening the wholesale slaughter of my people?"

His mind raced to understand how so many bombs could have been planted without being detected by Atreides security forces. Thufir Hawat would never have allowed such a lapse. Was the terrorist just bluffing?

Jaxson's eyes crackled with intensity. "Listen to me carefully, and don't misunderstand, or underestimate, our cause. Caladan is a perfect candidate to stand against the oppressive and stagnant Imperium. You could have your own planetary defenses, your own commerce, your own independence. Why should you pay your share of an exorbitant spice surtax just because Shaddam is incensed at me? Why should you pay for that ridiculous and extravagant eyesore on Otorio in the first place?"

Leto hardened his gaze even more. He had indeed felt the burden on the Caladan treasury when the Otorio construction began.

Jaxson's heavy eyebrows drew together. "You know what the Noble Commonwealth hopes to achieve, and you know in your heart we are right. House Atreides has been a pawn of Corrino schemes more than once. Oh, here on Caladan, you give a cold shoulder to Imperial politics and machinations, but you know how corrupt, petty, and manipulative Shaddam Corrino can be."

"I saw you murder thousands just to draw attention to yourself." Leto noticed a pair of city guards, but they were a distance away, talking with a couple who seemed to be asking them for information. He could wave, signal them to come running. . . .

Jaxson was dismissive. "They were all sycophants to the corrupt Corrino Imperium. Even you, Leto, went to Otorio to bow before Shaddam IV, a man with the blood of countless millions on his hands." His lips folded into a wry grimace. "The nobles may think they are innocent, but each is complicit by supporting a system that has lasted ten thousand years."

The city guards hadn't noticed Leto yet, or if they did, they were giving him space. With the threat of the hidden bombs, the Duke did not dare summon them. Did Jaxson have the detonator there on his person? This madman had already proved himself to be capable of extravagant violence.

Standing close, as if they were just two men talking about the weather, Jaxson made a passionate entreaty that did not sound rehearsed. "Think of all the inter-House warfare and family feuds over the centuries resulting in countless deaths. House Atreides versus House Harkonnen, House Ecaz versus House Moritani. You know about the extermination of House Kolona when you were young—your own father participated in that plot." He lowered his voice. "And I admire you for trying to rectify that injustice after you became Duke. It shows what kind of man you are. I admire your core principles."

Leto remained guarded. He remembered the scandal and uproar, the overthrow of House Kolona, the extermination of the family. Duke Paulus had always regretted being blackmailed into the ignoble deed. After his father died, Leto had discovered that the entire scheme originated with Emperor Elrood IX, and Leto had returned the stolen planetary holdings to distaff cousins of House Kolona, removing the stain from Atreides honor.

"The Noble Commonwealth is a fanciful notion that bored people discuss in drawing rooms," Leto said. He remembered Armand Ecaz and several nobles discussing it in the Imperial Monolith. Lord Atikk had been part of that small group. "But what you did on Otorio proved the movement is brutal and shameful. Why should I want anything to do with what it stands for?"

Jaxson laughed. "Then you do not know what we stand for."

Oddly, there was something appealing about the man's manner, his charisma. He seemed almost convincing, although Leto considered him as dangerous as a viper. Leto said, "Even a Duke cannot simply declare independence for Caladan. The Emperor's Sardaukar would slaughter everyone on this world."

Leto did not like what he had just heard himself say, but at least the rebel was listening, rather than threatening to detonate the bombs and kill more innocent people. And Leto was buying a moment of time.

Jaxson shrugged. "Shaddam does indeed have that capability, but if Caladan declares independence along with a thousand other worlds, and if the Spacing Guild cooperates by delaying certain Heighliners to sidetrack Imperial troop movements, the Emperor could never put out so many brush fires at once. The Imperium would fall apart before he could do anything about it." The rebel's eyes took on a deeper intensity. "But we must begin by setting all those brush fires! The Noble Commonwealth needs you, Duke Leto Atreides."

Leto could only think of all those who had been killed on Otorio, the indiscriminate destruction. Before he could speak, the other man pointed out in a reasonable voice, "There is no such thing as a peaceful, bloodless civil war."

"I don't want a civil war of any kind."

A flash of disgust crossed Jaxson's face. "You do not even know what you want! Consider my offer, Duke Leto. Isn't the promise of true freedom and economic independence worth expending a little effort, enduring a little pain?"

Leto hardened his own response. "I am a citizen of the Imperium and a member of the Landsraad. I will not join your movement. It is my duty to turn you in."

Jaxson sniffed and turned to watch a whitecap that crashed into the end of the promontory. "Come now, Leto. I have done my research. You are not a person who scrambles for wealth or fawns over Imperial favor. You are a respected man of independence. That is why I came to present you with my proposal. And I know that you, a man of good conscience, will give it due consideration."

Leto had gone out here to be alone, to look at the memorials to his father and his lost son, but apparently Jaxson Aru knew he would be alone. Like a confidence man finding a mark. Troubling thoughts roiled through the Duke's mind. "You are an outlaw. The entire Imperium is searching for you. If Emperor Shaddam knew you were here, a legion of Sardaukar would descend on Caladan."

Jaxson seemed amused by the idea. "But the Emperor does not know. He has no idea of my movements or whereabouts, and you will not tell him. Would you really want the Emperor's special forces to swarm over your lovely planet?"

"If that is what justice requires," Leto said.

"I came here meaning no harm to you." The rebel leader shrugged. "I just want to talk."

"Talk? While you threaten my people with bombs?"

Jaxson pouted. "Only to get your attention. My visit was not wasted, because I have begun a dialogue with you. I gave you things to think about. You don't know it, but I find myself on Caladan on occasion. We can speak again later, after you have had time to consider."

"You need to face justice for what you did."

"Justice, yes, that is what I seek. Just remember what I said to you."

When Leto bristled, Jaxson swirled his fisherman's cloak around him and prepared to leave. "You have a choice to make, a difficult but important choice." He gave a rakish laugh in parting. "If you wanted only simple choices, perhaps you should have been a fisherman instead of a Duke."

Jaxson stalked off, folding himself among the other people gathered there.

We operate on the fringes of rules and of Imperial law. In these nether regions between destruction and success the most money is made.

— ENGER RISTOS, Guild Banker

Shaddam Corrino IV received many briefings in various forms and from numerous sources, but this morning, he read a report so disturbing that he skipped breakfast with his dear Empress Aricatha.

The initial report of income generated by his new spice surtax had proved disappointing. He had established the surtax to fill the hole in the treasury left by the gigantic, expensive, and now-vaporized Corrino museum complex, but the increased income was far less than he had expected.

He was upset with his financial experts and their now-useless projections. Hasimir Fenring had clearly warned him of the risks of such a high surtax. The price of melange was already prohibitively high, due to the outrageous cost of production. The Arrakis environment wrecked equipment regularly, destroying expensive harvesters and spice factories. Baron Harkonnen had reported five harvesters destroyed or scuttled in just the past month, due to sandworm attacks and an exceptionally heavy storm season.

His surtax had pushed melange above the price where anyone but the wealthy could afford it, which had resulted in a precipitous decline in use. Worse, the tightening market was causing great unrest among nobles, merchants, and businessmen who consumed spice but could no longer purchase what they needed. Instead, as a poor substitute, they turned to alternative, illicit euphoric drugs.

Because of the disruption and inconvenience, they were also less reticent about voicing complaints about House Corrino, and that, in turn, played directly into the hands of the Noble Commonwealth rebels who were busily spreading sedition. Violent scoundrels like Jaxson Aru must be laughing at his conundrum.

Shaddam needed time alone in his private contemplation chamber to review the report. His young daughters Josifa and Rugi came to him dressed in colorful gowns. They asked permission to throw a party in the palace orchards, which were just now blossoming, but he sent them away, telling them to consult with Aricatha. He knew the Empress would do the right thing.

Sighing, he concentrated on all the information in the surtax summary, a dizzying roil of numbers. A forensic accounting traced spice sales and distribution, along with careful records of all harvesting and processing on Arrakis, tracked almost down to the kilogram. As his Imperial Spice Observer, Count Fenring watched every Harkonnen move with a careful eye, and he had even interrogated his smuggler contacts. The melange records seemed to be accurate. But off.

The Mentat accountants insisted that they saw something missing, a gap where there should have been none. Some of the tracked *usage* of spice did not have corresponding *sales* channels. Their conclusions were fourth- and fifth-order projections, subtleties beyond subtleties, and Shaddam simply could not follow it all. He tightened the sash of his embroidered formal robe and carried the rolled instroy parchment of the report as he left his contemplation chamber and strode toward his throne room.

Reverend Mother Mohiam stood waiting at the entrance to the audience chamber. He was surprised to see her back from Wallach IX. He had not seen his Truthsayer in some time, not since she had rushed off—without requesting his permission—on some errand back at the Bene Gesserit Mother School. She had left an apologetic message claiming that in this emergency her obligations to the Sisterhood superseded any duties for the Emperor, and she was gone before he could argue with her. He had keenly felt her absence.

Seeing him, Mohiam lowered her eyes in a respectful manner. He resented the fact that she had been gone when he needed her to help review candidates for the empty seats in the Landsraad. Now he confronted her. "You and your damnable witch Sisters. What have you been up to?"

The Reverend Mother was reserved, deferential. "We exist only to serve, Sire. Our Sisterhood furthers the cause of humankind."

"And does it further the cause of this throne?"

She bowed again, even deeper. He was surprised the old woman was so limber. "The Imperium represents humanity. The Sisterhood has never done anything to hinder your rule, Sire. How may I assist you now?"

She followed as he entered and climbed to the shimmering throne. Despite his frustration, he was oddly comforted to have his Truthsayer at his side again. Count Fenring also waited for him in the audience chamber, having just returned from his own trip to Arrakis and prepared to give a report on spice operations. With Mohiam and Fenring here, at last he would receive good, reliable advice. They could get to the bottom of this damnable report.

Dressed in a white lace tunic with billowing sleeves and black trousers, Count Fenring approached the throne with supple moves like a dancer. Though he was glad to see his childhood friend, Shaddam thrust the instroy pages at Fenring. "There are serious shortfalls, Hasimir. I suspect that someone is cheating me, somehow. My Mentat accountants have raised a faint specter of impropriety. I must know the merits of their suspicions."

Fenring scrutinized the report and the veiled conclusions. With eyes flicking back and forth, he absorbed the summary, then reviewed the original data. "Ahhh, hmmm, they suspect that melange is somehow leaving Arrakis without being accounted for. There is a leak in some distribution channel."

"Your smugglers are getting out of control. I will no longer tolerate it."

Fenring was taken aback. "Hmmm-ahh, the smugglers are carefully monitored, and they know their place. We choose not to notice their operations in exchange for information they provide. We would not want to lose that source of valuable data."

"They are cheating us." Shaddam looked down at the report. "It is clear that they are selling spice elsewhere without reporting the income, or paying the agreed-upon bribes."

"Esmar Tuek is aware of his tenuous position, Sire. He keeps his crew under tight scrutiny, mmmmm, and I keep them all under careful observation. It may not be them."

The Emperor didn't believe it. "Obviously, they have another channel of spice export, beyond your purview. We must learn what they are doing and punish them accordingly."

Fenring perfunctorily studied the report again, but he did not seem surprised by the results he saw. "I, ahhhh, received a copy of this an hour ago. I have already enlisted Grix Dardik to analyze it as, mmmmm, a check on your own Mentat accountants. I expect he will have insights."

Shaddam frowned at the mention of the odd man. "You depend too much on that failed Mentat. You could afford someone better."

"Hmmmm, 'better' is a subjective term. I am attracted to his unorthodox methods and conclusions. I salvaged Dardik from the trash heap of Imperial history."

"Then let us see if he can provide a satisfactory explanation." Shaddam leaned back to wait. The two men knew each other too well.

One of the court functionaries hurried away and soon returned with a hesitant, jittery Dardik, who seemed confused. His oversized head lolled to one side, and his gaze wandered, as if the man were trapped inside his body and wanted to escape.

The Count took him by the arm, and led him toward the throne. The Sardaukar guards stood wary, as if afraid the Mentat might lunge toward the Emperor. Fenring turned the slender man to face the throne and shook him by the shoulders. He said apologetically to the Emperor, "He is deep in his projections and analyses, Sire."

The failed Mentat reached into a fold in his tunic and withdrew a vial of sapho juice, which he gulped. A drop of the blood-red liquid ran from the corner of his mouth.

Count Fenring snapped, "Tell His Majesty what you said about Imperial spice shortages."

"Spice, spice, spice . . ." Dardik stared at the floor, not meeting the Emperor's gaze. Suddenly, his expression brightened, and he grinned up at the throne with stained lips. "Ah, you want to know where all the missing spice is! How it is being sold through illicit channels!"

Emperor Shaddam took an exasperated breath. "My Mentat accountants have already identified a suspected problem. What else can you add? How are the smugglers selling spice that my observers cannot see?"

Dardik let out an odd chuckle. "Smugglers are not your problem. The smugglers are, dare I say, quite honest."

"Honest smugglers?" The Emperor glared at Fenring. "That is his conclusion?"

The failed Mentat's head bobbed. "Many things pass through my mind, Your Greatness. In my detailed projections, yes, these smugglers are more honest than many. They operate in the shadows, but in full view of Count Fenring. He sees. He knows."

"Then how does so much spice slip away without being accounted for?" Shaddam asked. "And without paying my surtax? Baron Harkonnen is under the most intense scrutiny. There must be a secondary channel."

"I project . . . another spice operation behind the scenes. A new operation." The eccentric Mentat began to hum in an odd, irritating imitation of Fenring's mannerisms. "Completely different."

"Details, man, details! What are the details?"

Dardik looked up suddenly. "Details?"

"How did you arrive at that conclusion?"

With an arrogant stare, he replied, "Sire, a Mentat cannot unpack his mind to a non-Mentat."

Shaddam looked up at the ornate, painted ceiling, counted slowly to himself in an effort to remain calm. "Where is this behind-the-scenes spice operation you refer to? Who is running it?"

"I don't know where, and I don't know who."

Frustration flared in Shaddam, but Mohiam moved quickly to his side, whispering, "He does not lie to you, Sire. He makes his projections, but is not capable of explaining how he arrived at his conclusion."

The Emperor looked at the old Truthsayer in her black robes, then turned to Fenring, considering the new information. He sighed. "Hasimir, you are my Imperial Spice Observer. Find the answers. Go back to Arrakis and dig deeper." He softened his voice. "That is an area in which you excel, old friend."

AFTER THE COUNT had withdrawn with his eccentric Mentat, Shaddam sat through another meeting, a request to mediate the dispute between two feuding noblemen. Both were allies he needed, but the Emperor was too preoccupied, and he dismissed them without even hearing their arguments. He stalked out of the audience chamber and went back to his contemplation chamber.

Mohiam remained in the empty throne room, pondering, assessing. In a sense, she felt like the peculiar Mentat, contemplating an array of incomprehensible facts.

For now, though, she found it refreshing to deal with "normal" treachery again, the familiar workings of Imperial politics. Mother Superior Harishka had given her a specific task. Here, back at court, she would begin new overtures to the recalcitrant young Viscount Giandro Tull, hoping to restore at least a thread of Bene Gesserit influence on the important noble house.

But the bulk of her thoughts remained on Wallach IX. Mother Superior Harishka had dispatched a summons to Caladan, demanding the presence of Jessica at the Mother School, so she could face Lethea.

What was the murderous, unstable woman's interest in Mohiam's secret daughter?

After Jaxson Aru vanished from the crowded area around the lighthouse statues, Thufir Hawat and Atreides security forces scoured the promontory and the park, searched around the immense monolithic statues, and ordered a full sweep of Cala City. The Atreides Mentat looked deeply troubled by the lapse in security, even embarrassed when he reported to the Duke that afternoon.

He held a fat metal cylinder in his hands. "You asked me to search, my Lord. We found some surprises Jaxson left for you, but it . . . wasn't what we expected."

Leto felt prickles of sweat on the back of his neck. He couldn't take his eyes from the thick metal cylinder. "Is that one of the bombs?"

"In a sense." Hawat extended the cylinder and released a small access flap in the metal.

Leto stiffened. "Has it been deactivated?"

The security chief explained, without making excuses, "We did not initially detect these, Sire, because they contain no explosives. They pose no physical threat to our people." Hawat reached inside and removed a strip of paper. "We found seven of them. Each one contains the same message."

Leto took the paper and read the words written by the terrorist. "'I would never harm your people, Duke Leto. I would never commit such a reprehensible act against true innocents. I am sincere in my efforts to make you sympathetic to the Noble Commonwealth cause. I merely wanted to talk, to try to sway you. Please consider what I said, and remember that the Corrinos are the true villains here. Caladan has its honorable Duke, and that is all the planet needs, not an Imperial despot. I wish only prosperity for you, your world, and your people.'"

Leto crumpled the paper and set it aside. "It was still a threat. Jaxson Aru showed us that he could harm us anytime he likes, if I do not cooperate."

"And will you cooperate, Sire?" The Mentat raised his bushy eyebrows.

"Silence will be my only response—the safest response."

LATE THAT AFTERNOON, four sleek Atreides attack flyers rested on the military field above Cala City. They were loaded with incendiaries and ready to depart for a swift and devastating firebombing run of the drug fields. Their hulls were heavily armored, and an Atreides hawk, a fierce bird of prey, stood out prominently on the fuselage. After they burned the barra fern field to ashes, the next phase would send additional ground troops to locate other camouflaged fields. The Duke was confident he would eradicate any cultivated areas with the potent drug ferns.

With the cool sea breeze in his face, Leto admired the aircraft. With their articulated wings, the shielded flyers could soar swiftly overland, and their jet boosters could provide a burst of speed for faster aerial maneuvers. Paul stood next to him, as did Thufir Hawat and Gurney Halleck.

"We will wipe them out, my Lord," said Reeson, an officer in an impeccable flight suit, his rank insignia gleaming from its place on his chest. Captain Reeson had reddish hair that contrasted with his dark olive complexion. His lips were thin, highlighted by a neatly trimmed mustache. Three fellow pilots stood beside Reeson with matching military bearing.

"Obliterate the fields and cut off the source of ailar," Leto said. "I want to destroy the black market for this *Caladan* drug."

Hawat regarded the lined-up attack craft and spoke in a clipped voice to the four pilots. "You have the coordinates for the known field, but it is safe to assume there are other barra growths in the vicinity. The operations we uncovered at the moonfish processing plant suggest a substantial cultivated acreage. The amount of drug being harvested and distributed is far more than that lone caretaker could have managed."

"Ground troops will come mop them up, and they can hunt down and apprehend Chaen Marek," Leto said. "But this is a first strike."

"We know what to look for, Sire," said Reeson, and his fellow pilots nodded. "Sensor nets are tricky things, but a little operation out in the middle of nowhere can't be too sophisticated."

"It certainly *can* be." Hawat sounded skeptical. "We do not know how long these drug operations have been going on."

"No matter how long it's been, the drug scourge ends today," Leto said, his words laced with carefully modulated anger. "Caladan will not be the source of a deadly substance that harms my people and spreads throughout the Imperium."

Duncan Idaho looked cocky as he regarded the four attack ships about to depart. "Are you certain you do not want me to pilot, my Lord? The operation might require some fancy flying."

Paul stood beside him, bright-eyed and intense. "I can go with him. Duncan's been training me."

"Sometimes I worry about what Duncan's been teaching you," Leto said with a hint of teasing. "I may need to hire a different pilot just to teach you proper safety precautions."

Duncan took mock offense. "I am preparing your son to deal with complex situations, my Lord. Real-life experiences." He did not look the least bit guilty. "I would be willing to take him as my copilot. He and I can be part of the attack wing."

As Captain Reeson and the other pilots awaited the order to depart, Paul grew more formal with his father. "I really would like to go along, sir. I was there when we found the barra field. I should be there when we firebomb it."

Leto considered. "What do you think, Captain?"

The officer seemed uneasy. "This is our mission, Sire. It could be dangerous. We don't want to put the young Master at risk."

Leto chuckled. "Paul, we have to let our troops do at least some of the work defending House Atreides." He lowered his voice. "I heard about what happened when you and Duncan flew out into the elecran storm."

Paul flushed with embarrassment, which was quickly replaced with pride. The four pilots laughed softly, a much-needed release from the tension. Leto said, "You can be at my side, watching from the command post. You can help with the duties of a Duke."

Hawat spoke in a cautionary tone. "When they drop their incendiaries, Sire, bear in mind that there may well be casualties and collateral damage, a few farmworkers perhaps. I trust you are prepared for that?"

Leto's expression hardened. "If those people harvest the deadly ferns, they are responsible for addicting and killing many people." He drew in a cold breath. "I do not consider them innocent by any measure."

The pilots each climbed into their attack craft. Reeson reached his arm out of the cockpit, slapped his palm against the Atreides hawk on the hull, then sealed himself inside.

Leto and his companions stepped back as the engines fired up with a roar, heating the brisk wind around them. The suspensor engines glowed. The wings unfolded as if stretching, then began to operate in a blur as the craft lifted from the ground. Flying in close formation, the four fighters moved off like angry birds of prey. Leto shaded his eyes and watched them.

"We can better observe the operation from the post headquarters, my Lord," Hawat said. "All four attack craft are fitted with augmented imagers."

"Good." Leto was anxious to see flames eradicating the enhanced ferns from his planet.

The headquarters building at the edge of the military field was a half-domed hut, crowded with administrative desks and operational files. Inside, Atreides officers moved about studying topographical maps on the wall, images taken from significant altitude, high-resolution scans of the wilderness areas that Leto and his companions had explored on their recent outing. Highlighted in red was the zone around the barra field they had found.

Leto was anxious to see the strike completed. Sooner or later, Chaen Marek would realize that his hidden operation had been exposed, and the Duke wanted everything destroyed before the drug lord could respond.

Leto looked to Thufir Hawat but spoke also to his military commanders. "Even after this operation is finished, I want multiple teams combing that landscape. I don't want a single barra fern to remain."

"It will be done, my Duke," Hawat said.

One large screen displayed images transmitted from the foremost attack fighter. The beautiful rolling wilds of northern Caladan streaked below in a dizzying blur—trees, rivers, irrigated rice fields, rugged mountain crags.

Leto pondered all that pristine emptiness, so many resources, so much beauty. He considered himself a steward of Caladan and realized that was how the Muadh people had thought of him.

Reeson transmitted his report. "My squad is approaching the coordinates. Shields are up for the initial flyby, then we'll circle around to drop the firebombs."

"Scout carefully," Leto said. "If Marek found his dead worker, he may have brought in reinforcements."

"He will not expect an attack like this," Duncan said.

"Decreasing altitude. Heading in," Reeson transmitted.

Paul stepped closer to his father, both of them looking at the screen. They studied the towering firs and meadows filled with pale grasses and flowers. Streams ran like silver ribbons down mountain slopes. In a rush, the attack flyers swept in, following the river canyon, passing in minutes what Leto and his companions had taken days to traverse on foot.

The four aircraft topped a rise and came upon the small growing field, which was little more than a blur of indistinct greenery thanks to the sensor web. Flying in formation, the armored vessels zoomed along. "Ready with incendiaries."

Suddenly, several figures ran out of the shelter of towering fern trees below. They carried projectile weapons, cylindrical launchers. "They were expecting us!" Duncan said. Others in the headquarters building muttered uneasily.

On the ground, the attackers fired projectiles, and the pilots took evasive action. Although some of the explosives struck the flyers' shields, they caused no damage.

"Taking fire," Reeson transmitted. "Coming back around."

The four flyers soared past the cultivated area, then arced and accelerated toward the camouflaged field. "Target confirmed, my Lord Duke. Ready to begin our attack run." He hesitated. "Is there a change of plan now that civilians are below?"

"Not civilians—enemies," Leto said, cold as he spoke the words. *The first responsibility of a Duke . . .* "Those are not peasants or pundi rice farmers. Destroy the field, as planned."

The audio on the transmission grew to a roar, a background thrum as jet boosters drove the craft down toward the barra ferns. Captain Reeson modulated the shields and dropped a line of firebombs, with the other three aircraft right behind him.

Rows of red-orange fire ripped like waves across the drug field. Leto did not tear his gaze away as the flames washed over and incinerated the workers along with the ferns.

Paul stared, said nothing.

"There won't be a frond left, my Lord," Reeson promised.

"Exactly as I wanted," Leto said. "Now circle out and expand your operations. Given those armed workers we just saw, there may well be other fields nearby. Find them and burn them, too."

The four attack craft streaked away from the rising curtain of smoke, then banked and flew at lower altitude for a more intensive search. Their scan penetrators dissected the landscape below, peeled apart the thick fir forests. "I see several likely patches on the next ridge," Reeson said.

Two other pilots transmitted, their voices partially overlapping as they identified more terrain as being camouflaged. "Significant areas of cultivation." A pause and then, "Shall we investigate further or destroy, Sire?"

Leto saw the mottled green and gray of blurred foliage on the screen and knew what it was. "Destroy. That is your mission."

The attack ships flew in close formation, readying their incendiary loads.

Then, ahead of them, six small black ships rose like flies startled from a bloated corpse—unmarked, armored 'thopters. Leto hadn't even seen the clearing on the scans.

"They've got their own aircraft," Hawat said. "Expensive ones."

"Military-grade 'thopters, my Lord," Duncan said with an edge of alarm in his voice. "That's nothing they picked up from a salvage yard."

Leto transmitted to the squadron. "Be careful. They are likely armed and shielded."

The Atreides flyers dropped their shields for a fraction of a second, just long enough to launch their own artillery, but the projectiles deflected harmlessly off the shielded enemy craft. The dark 'thopters drove in on a collision course, trying to intimidate the Atreides vessels. Captain Reeson entered a tight roll, but the enemy ship struck the top of his shield a glancing blow, deflecting both craft.

The other Atreides pilots also attempted to evade, struggling to gain control. The attack flyers realigned themselves, soared side by side, and launched a more significant defense, hitting the dark 'thopters with another round of high-powered projectiles.

"Our armaments will burn out their shield generators, given enough time," Reeson said. Then he spoke to the other pilots in his squadron, sending two of them against the black craft while he and the last fighter continued to drop fire-bombs on the fern-growing area below.

Under another spray of fiery explosives, the sensor web shorted out. With the camouflage gone, extensive acres of ferns were revealed, wave after wave of cultivated ground.

In the headquarters building, the observers let out a collective gasp to see the magnitude of the drug operations, dozens of huts and camouflaged processing areas. The fields' edges were on fire, but now there was so much more acreage to be destroyed.

Captain Reeson and his companion came back for yet another run.

The enemy 'thopters continued to pummel the shielded Atreides fighters in an aerial battle. One of the enemy craft drove in, buffeting Reeson's vessel, then the attacker dropped his shields, and new gunports lit up.

"I can destroy them now, Sire," Reeson said. "Targeting—"

Paul's eyes flicked back and forth. "Those are lasguns! And we've got shields. They wouldn't—"

Realizing the danger, Leto shouted, "Get out of—"

The screen flared with a white-hot surge, blinding them. Leto flinched, covered his eyes as the transmission went to static.

Even Hawat was astounded. "They knew our ships were shielded. He intentionally used lasguns—against shields!"

Duncan coughed as if he were about to be sick. "By the gods, pseudo-atomic explosions!"

The Mentat ran an analysis before Leto could form words to express what he had just seen. "They knew they would all die," Hawat announced. "They violated every standard of the Great Convention, sacrificed themselves in order to hurt us."

"Not only that," Duncan said. "They meant to send us a message as well. They are fanatics."

Thoughts spun in Leto's mind as he thought of the suicidal caretaker in the first barra field, and he remembered the fear expressed by the ailar sellers and users at the moonfish operations. What could drive such fanatical, inflamed devotion to a cause? To mere drug operations?

Then a second thought sent a wave of ice down his spine. He had almost— almost!—agreed to let Paul and Duncan fly along with the attack wing. No matter their piloting skills, they would both have been vaporized in the blast. Paul . . .

Leto said in a choked voice, "Chaen Marek thinks he can scare us. But he cannot." He clenched his fist, looked down at the ducal signet ring. "I want full ground operations ready to launch as soon as possible. We are now at war."

Expect to hear this from me again: Observe the plans within plans within plans.

—BARON VLADIMIR HARKONNEN to his nephew Feyd-Rautha

A s her husband pored over filmbooks, production manifests, and shipping records, Margot Fenring entered his study in the Arrakeen Residency. Silently, she watched him for a long moment, heard him humming to himself. He remained unaware of her presence, although he was a man of keen observation, but she knew how to move without a sound. It could have made her an assassin as skilled as he was, if she had chosen a different profession.

When she made an intentional rustling noise, he spun like a viper, ready to strike. As he recognized her, though, no smile crossed his face. His steel-gray eyes looked tired. Without preamble, he asked, "Do you think Shaddam's Mentats are right? That we have an unseen hemorrhage somewhere, that melange is being whisked away from Arrakis without anyone knowing? Not Baron Harkonnen, not the smugglers . . . not *me*? The Emperor blames the smugglers, but he merely wants an easy answer." He looked down at the records again. "And if it is not Esmar Tuek's doing, then how is the melange being smuggled off-planet? And who is the purchaser?"

Margot stepped up behind him, began kneading his tense shoulders; it required some of her best skills to make him relax. "Your failed Mentat seems to agree with the Emperor's Mentat accountants, but has Dardik ever been wrong? Have the other Mentats been wrong? Or is something genuinely amiss?"

"Hmmm-ah, with Grix it is difficult to tell given such eccentric behavior." He hummed again. "But the Emperor's Mentat accountants noticed a subtle discrepancy. Melange is very carefully inventoried, all sales accounted for down to the gram." He shook his head. "Whoever is doing this is, hmmmm, masterful."

She kissed the top of his head. Count Hasimir Fenring was not a handsome man, far from it, with close-set eyes and pointed features, but he was the most intelligent, dashing man she'd ever met. He was involved in the Emperor's darkest schemes, but he cared deeply for her, and Margot felt the same about him.

"Perhaps you need to look more carefully at the smugglers, my husband," she said. "If nothing else, a visible crackdown from you would reassure Shaddam, who sees traitors everywhere. Even if Tuek is not guilty, he and his people have much at stake here. Could they be selling spice to—I don't know—the Spacing Guild, because of the quantities needed for their Navigators? With so much usage, an external source of melange could save money and offer additional stability. Of course, the quality of any such illicit spice would be critical."

He stroked his chin and finally smiled at her. "Ahhhhh, we think alike, my dear. The Guild seems like a possible culprit. And you have made a projection without being a Mentat." She continued to work his shoulders, and his sigh was genuine, not the vocal mannerism he so often adopted to make others think him a dithering fool.

She heard a rapping on the half-open study door, saw the strange half Mentat lurking outside in the corridor. Dardik shuffled his feet. "You sent for me, Count Fenring?"

Fenring's shoulders slumped, and he turned away from his reports, looking up at the most-peculiar Mentat. "So? Have you found anything more? What is the source of this additional spice infiltrating the black market? How are they getting it off-planet, and who is selling it? Where is our leak?"

Grix Dardik stood there rocking like a pendulum. "I know only that it is happening, but not how. The plot is very clever and devious."

"Hmmm-ah, could the Spacing Guild be involved? My wife points out that they need a lot of spice."

"I have run that possibility, with no suitable answer. The same for large mercantile Houses involved in the spice trade. The same for conglomerates. Even CHOAM could be involved. The Combine Honnete Ober Advancer Mercantiles is complex, and their records are obtuse, secure from any prying eyes. The same can be said for the Spacing Guild. The Guild not only runs Heighliner ships; they are also bankers. If they could save many solaris in melange purchases, that would put more solaris in their coffers."

"As far as we know, both the Guild and CHOAM only work through primary channels," Fenring said. "They pay the surtax."

Dardik nodded, as if his neck had become too loose. "Yes, yes, they do. Of course they do. But they are clever, and secretive."

Fenring pursed his lips, and deep furrows appeared on his brow. "But if the Spacing Guild or the CHOAM Company have found a way to circumvent Imperial channels and bypass standard fees and tariffs, including the surtax, that would be troubling." He smiled. "And if such activities were discovered, and proved . . . the consequences would be, hmmm, catastrophic to them."

Margot added, "As for CHOAM, the Ur-Director has been closely watched ever since her terrorist son attacked Otorio. Malina Aru publicly renounced him. She is known to have a close relationship with Empress Aricatha. She would never take such a terrible risk." She paused to reconsider. "Or is that part of the deception as well?"

Fenring said, "Hmmmm, the plot would be too big, too intricate, and I would need much more time to investigate and unravel." His eyes flashed at his wife. "I will investigate, but in the meantime, I need to convince the Emperor that I have the situation under control. He is outraged and volatile, and under such circumstances, he tends to overreact. I have seen it many times before. I have to distract him, perhaps find a scapegoat to buy myself some time." He chewed at his lower lip.

Dardik took a jittering step backward. "I am not a good candidate for that." The failed Mentat scuttled out of the office.

Fenring nodded, lost in thought. "I am the Imperial Observer here. We will find someone appropriate."

When Leto returned to Castle Caladan from the military base, he was
sickened, reeling. Four good pilots had been vaporized in the senseless
pseudo-atomic explosion.

He had underestimated the size and power of Chaen Marek's ailar production and smuggling operations—twice now, in fact—but far worse, he
had not conceived the fanatical recklessness Marek's people would exhibit.
To any civilized mindset, it was inconceivable that a person, no matter how
desperate, would initiate an appalling lasgun-shield interaction on purpose.
The rules of the Great Convention were so ingrained in every person in the
Imperium. . . .

Who was this drug lord, and how was he funded? Leto would not underestimate Chaen Marek again, and he vowed to strike back against the man's illegal operations with the complete military of House Atreides. Swiftly, his forces
would overwhelm any defenses the barra fern growers could mount.

As soon as he was back in the castle, he summoned Thufir Hawat, Gurney
Halleck, Duncan Idaho, and several other advisers for an immediate war council. The Atreides troops would move out as soon as the fighters were armed, the
equipment gathered, the ships fueled, the plans operational.

Before the meeting, Leto stalked back to his private office and increased the
glowglobe lights because the afternoon skies had become overcast and gray. The
decorative fountain in the corner trickled a diamond-like stream of water with
a pleasant soothing noise, but very little could soothe him now. Four men were
dead! Now he took some time alone to think. His throat went dry. If he had
allowed Paul to go along with the pilots. . . .

Unexpectedly, he found a message cylinder resting in the center of his desk,
delivered by a recent courier. Lady Jessica had placed it there for him to read. He
saw that the seal had not been broken, knew Jessica would never breach his trust
by reading a private message without his permission.

He turned the cylinder in his hands, noted the leaping stag and recognized the symbol of House Verdun. He sat back, his interest piqued, realizing that this must finally be a response from Duke Fausto Verdun about his daughter's betrothal to Paul.

Sensing someone, he saw Jessica standing at the doorway in a blue gown, her long, bronze hair bound up in pins and carved seashell combs. He realized this was the same dress she had worn when recording the hologram image he'd taken with him to Otorio. That seemed so long ago, but it was only two months. Her green eyes were bright, her expression full of anticipation.

Leto held up the message cylinder. "You know what this is, of course."

"I suspect it pertains to me, as well as you, and our son, but I didn't open it."

Leto softened his tone. "I have often shared the Duke's business with my Lady." His thumbprint unlocked the seal, and he opened it to remove a single sheet of instroy paper marked with the leaping stag. Leto prepared to read aloud to Jessica, but halted as he skimmed the words. His fingers clenched the paper, which wrinkled and then instantly smoothed itself when he shifted his grip. "That . . . pompous . . . weasel!"

Jessica was instantly at his shoulder. She read as he continued to absorb the words:

"Duke Atreides, I received your message with surprise. So, my lovely daughter has caught the attention of your son as a possible marriage prospect. She has caught the eyes of many a desirable young man, all of whom are, unfortunately, beneath her station.

"House Verdun is a prominent member of the Landsraad, a powerful House Major with an influential CHOAM Directorship. Since I am a Duke, like yourself, I must make my political decisions with great forethought. The Verdun name is clearly on the rise as our wealth expands. We anticipate that the Padishah Emperor will present us with expanded holdings, now that so many Landsraad seats are empty. I will meet personally with Shaddam IV in the very near future."

Leto frowned. The man did go on at great length.

"House Atreides, however, oversees only one world, and while I am assured that Caladan is a pleasant place, it is no adequate home for my daughter. In recent memory, House Atreides had greater wealth and clout, but after you voluntarily surrendered the assets of House Kolona, you diminished the weight and worth of your name. To me, this does not demonstrate wise leadership, and I do not share such a vision for my own House."

The words took on a sickening weight as Verdun continued.

"I applaud your ambition in trying to join our Houses, but I cannot accept the idea of my daughter's betrothal to your bastard son, who is not even a true heir. We believe that dear Junu will find a more acceptable suitor in the near future. Your interest is noted and appreciated—Fausto Verdun, Duke of Dross."

He had appended one last barb beneath his signature. "Lord Atikk is my friend, and I know what your Caladan drug did to his son."

Leto let the instroy paper fall, feeling a different kind of rage and dismay from what he had just experienced after the loss of his four fighter craft. Duke Verdun's message was another kind of sneak attack, one that insulted his honor and his son. Leto pounded a fist on the desk. "He says Paul isn't worthy!"

Jessica snatched up the sheet, also taking offense. "But in the Landsraad, you hold the very same rank as Duke Verdun." She reread the note, then reassessed. "This is not a setback. We will make a different choice, one that is a far better match for Paul."

He said, "It is clear that Junu Verdun was by no means acceptable. Her family is not worthy of sharing the Atreides name." He knew it wasn't the girl's fault. He had no idea of the young woman's character, in fact, but Duke Verdun had responded in such an insulting way, it defied all expectations of honorable behavior. "He insults my son!" He took the instroy paper from her and crumpled it, but maddeningly it unfurled itself. Instead, he plunged it into the fountain basin. "And therefore he insults me as well, and all of House Atreides." He lowered his voice. "He also clearly blames me for the ailar drug, but I am taking care of that."

Jessica kept her voice calm, and he briefly wondered if she was trying to manipulate him using Bene Gesserit techniques. Right now, he didn't want to be calm, but he appreciated what she was doing. Just by being there, facing this insult together, he felt closer to her.

She said, "His behavior should have been expected. Fausto Verdun has demonstrated his ambitions, striving to climb much higher than his current station. We knew this from the recent Landsraad reports and announcements from Kaitain. How did he get such an impressive CHOAM Directorship in the first place? Now he has leaped into the gap after Otorio, jockeying to be granted some of the leaderless holdings, the most valuable ones."

"While I did not," Leto said, feeling the bitterness rise. "Does that make me someone with low ambitions? Is that how I am perceived in the Landsraad? Because I won't rummage in the pockets of a corpse? Because I wasn't aggressive enough to grab the scraps after Otorio?"

Her voice was soothing. "It makes you look devoted to Caladan, exactly as you have always been."

"But now that singular focus is apparently hurting Paul's future! Have I damaged my birthright because I did not care about petty politics? Even my father knew how to play Imperial games."

"As do you, Leto," Jessica said. "When you set your mind to it. That has never been your focus."

"The first duty of a noble is to the Landsraad and to the Imperium, that's what the code says. Is Caladan enough for House Atreides? I thought it was. I thought Paul would be satisfied, but if his marriage prospects are now ruined—"

Jessica laid a hand on his. "This is only one response, our first exploration, and this other noble family is clearly not a fit for House Atreides. It is a blessing in disguise. Do not dwell on it. Paul doesn't even know the girl. He says he dreams about someone else."

Leto would not be so easily calmed. "The man called him a bastard." Verdun's malicious words struck deeply. The idea sent him reeling. Had he made a mistake by not pouncing on the opportunities left open after the Otorio disaster? Had he made many mistakes, by focusing on his people rather than wealth and power? Should he had been more focused on tallying up his influence and holdings? With more wealth and power, he could do more for the people of Caladan.

Some things had to be done, regardless. Leto remembered going to the Imperial Court after discovering how Emperor Elrood had blackmailed Duke Paulus into the overthrow of House Kolona, so long ago. Leto had shored himself up with honor and rectified the situation. Now Verdun complained about that?

But the Landsraad was different now. He had not wanted to take advantage of bloodshed and tragedy, but so many planets were indeed leaderless, their noble leaders wiped out. If not House Atreides, then some other family would rule those worlds. So why should it not be him? Why not build a larger foundation for Paul to inherit, and to rule with Atreides justice?

But Caladan had problems of its own, including Chaen Marek and the illegal and deadly drug operations. Was that not his priority? The first duty of a Duke. . . .

"There are many other choices, Leto. There is nothing remarkable about House Verdun. Better that we have nothing more to do with them. We will pick a better potential wife for Paul."

"I can erase her name from my list," Leto agreed, "but this offense will remain." He felt hot, and the blow stung twice as hard coming right on the heels of the tragedy of his obliterated flyers. "I will have Hawat submit a new summary to me. I want to see all the names and make my own choice."

Jessica's eyes took on a sudden gleam, and she flashed a glance to one side. "I would be happy to assist, my Lord. In fact, while you are preparing your attack against the drug lord, perhaps you should use Thufir Hawat's expertise in the military operation instead. Let me be the one to submit the list of candidates."

"Hawat already knows," Leto said. "I want him to do it." He softened his voice and his expression, realizing he had lashed out inappropriately at her. "In the meantime, I'll need your help so we can decide how to tell Paul."

Jessica smiled at him and rested a hand on his shoulder. "I always look for ways to ease your burdens, Leto. I will take care of it." She went to the door.

"You've already fought enough battles today, and you must prepare for a bigger one as soon as you can."

FROM THE DOORWAY of his room, Jessica watched her son. He was fourteen, but small for his age, and Paul still looked like a boy in her eyes, though she knew better. In the Sisterhood school, she had been raised to assess details objectively, to detach personal feelings and find the best answer. Now, though, the answer was difficult.

Bene Gesserit training cautioned against the weakness of love. Some Sisters took that to mean they should never open their hearts, should remain cold, aloof, and shallow. Other Sisters, though, argued that experiencing love was a critical part of human experience, so long as they did not succumb to it, did not let love become a weakness. It was a fine line.

The Bene Gesserit had sent her a list of names, bloodlines they wished to cut off, and a command to eliminate those names from consideration, by any means necessary. Some of the blacklisted young women had indeed appeared in Thufir Hawat's analysis and selection process. With so many possibilities on hand, she'd had little difficulty diverting the decision to someone else—Junu Verdun—and she had been glad to accomplish her mission so easily.

But now the question had come up again, because of political drama she had not anticipated. She would surreptitiously guide the choices again.

But first, she had to tell Paul.

After she explained about the rude rejection letter from Duke Verdun, she watched the flicker of emotions play across his face, cycling through various responses: insulted, confused, but also relieved. She knew how her son's mind worked, because she had trained him in great depth.

He folded his hands together on his desk and looked up at her. "Please sit, Mother. We have to discuss this."

"I know it is a blow, Paul . . ."

"A blow to my father," he answered. "For his sake, I find it offensive and disappointing, but I never met the girl. I do not have a schoolboy crush on Junu Verdun, and I am not swayed by those romantic songs Gurney always sings. That's not what this is about."

"No, it isn't," Jessica admitted, sitting next to him. "It is about House Atreides, our rank, our wealth, our prestige."

Paul shook his head. "No, Mother, it is about House Verdun and a petty nobleman with poor self-esteem, a man who convinced himself he can catch larger fish with a newfound net. Duke Verdun could have declined our offer in a respectful way, yet he intentionally chose to belittle our House. It says much about his own character. He must be a weak man, frightened and small, and this response makes him feel less small."

Jessica raised her eyebrows. "An astute analysis."

"You taught me how to do it. Whether or not my father marries you, I can see you are the correct partner for him."

She felt a warmth spread through her chest. "The Bene Gesserit unknowingly outdid themselves when they assigned me as his concubine. They thought it a mere business transaction." Her wry smile was faint. "Sometimes the Sisterhood is even more skilled than they themselves realize."

I resent being coerced or lobbied into taking actions that I would not otherwise have considered. When I am approached in this manner, even by my closest advisers and friends, I may feign interest, but whatever I do will be my own idea, for my own reasons.

—PADISHAH EMPEROR SHADDAM CORRINO IV

Attired in his finest robes, the Emperor glided through the Imperial Court, but his most beautiful accompaniment was Empress Aricatha. She looked as lovely and regal as he'd ever seen her, in an ermine-white robe and a tiara studded with Hagal crystals and soostones. For his own adornment, Shaddam wore commemorative medals for military campaigns he'd overseen from the throne, all of which had been declared victories. The medals made him feel proud of how he had advanced House Corrino, enlarging his power base and his personal fortune.

Other less successful military ventures were never mentioned.

Recently, with his secret investigators and private spies, along with work by his Sardaukar, he had pushed harder to root out Noble Commonwealth sympathizers. He was alarmed to discover that the whispered uprising was known far more widely than he thought, and now the Emperor had to work harder to eradicate the traitors. Whenever his investigative forces uncovered evidence of a potentially disloyal noble, Shaddam added the name to his list. He would soon direct his Sardaukar to take care of those traitors definitively. No more subtleties.

Aricatha saw the mysterious smile on his face. "You are lost in your thoughts. I hope I occupy at least some of them?"

"Of course," he said, and she obviously knew he was lying.

When he and the Empress walked through the court, they were like a singular parade. The throng of gaudy sycophants, dandies, and foreign dignitaries faded to a blur as they spoke niceties to him. He was adept at blocking out the bland noise while mouthing the proper responses, making the briefest eye contact. Since Aricatha was skilled in remembering names, he allowed her to add further pleasantries before the two of them strolled on.

Now he and the Empress stood together on one side of the portrait gallery, where images of past rulers hung on the walls, extending into the distance like an optical illusion. So many Corrino Emperors in ten thousand years. . . .

Silent and unobtrusive in her distinctive black robe, Mohiam stood nearby, where she could hear everything that was said. He relied on his Truthsayer to know whom he could trust. The Noble Commonwealth had already opened up too many cracks in the foundation of the Imperium.

Court guards kept a safe perimeter around the Imperial couple, allowing dignitaries or members of various Houses to approach one at a time. Because he now needed to select names to fill the vacant Landsraad seats, Shaddam forced himself to focus more on what was actually being said to him. He considered each comment, noted the mood and mannerisms. It was an art to keep all these candidates soothed and feeling important, while never committing to anything. The Emperor made no promises, but he did make silent judgments.

He spoke to the obsequious lords of House Bonner and Suruda, and the reticent Lord Onivondi, none of whom made much of an impression on him, and they were ushered away. Next came a tall and dashing man with a pointed Vandyke beard and colorful clothing, who was introduced as Duke Fausto Verdun of Dross. He made a sweeping bow, as if to demonstrate his limberness.

"Sire, I am honored that you invited me to call upon you at court, and I am pleased to be considered for an expanded holding in the Landsraad." His voice had an erudite accent that struck Shaddam as an affectation.

Empress Aricatha smiled and filled in the conversation, "We invited you, Duke Verdun, as well as many others, as a courtesy. We consider all members of the Landsraad to be equally important."

Verdun laughed and said with forced wit, "Certainly, some nobles are more equal than others. For instance, I hold an important upper-echelon CHOAM Directorship, even though my planet's exports are comparable to other worlds'. Thus, I demonstrate my skill in leadership as well as commerce. I could do the same on other planets that now need new administration." He stroked his pointed mustache. "All in the name of my Emperor. The first responsibility of a Duke is to the Imperium."

Shaddam had mixed feelings about this ambitious nobleman. He remembered the briefing compiled by the young aide Aina Tere about potential candidates. For the most part, according to Tere's analysis, Verdun showed loyalty to the throne, but he had been frustratingly neutral or absent a number of times, enough to make the Imperial investigators study him more closely. Verdun had close familial relationships with two other Major Houses that had expressed criticism of House Corrino.

And he had conveniently not been in attendance at Otorio.

The Emperor noted Mohiam standing silently to the side, listening carefully to every word Verdun said.

The lord went on without a pause. "I've written a proposal on how I might expand my ventures beyond Dross, with Imperial cooperation, to our mutual benefit. I will have my ambassador submit the document to your court chamberlain. I hope you have a chance to review it, Sire."

"It will be given the attention it deserves," Shaddam said coolly.

Verdun was cocksure about himself. He wore silks and jewels, as if trying to outshine the Emperor's raiment. Something in his tone of voice, his demeanor, made Shaddam wary.

Barely taking a breath, Verdun continued, "Sire, as a voting member of the Landsraad, let me express my earnest desire to increase my value to the Imperium, to make more substantial contributions for the benefit of our citizens. I hope that now, in the wake of the tragedy, I might have a fresh opportunity to serve." He listed humanitarian causes that he and his wife had sponsored.

Noting the hungry sparkle in Duke Verdun's eyes, Shaddam said, "This is not really the place for such a discussion, is it?"

Of course, that was exactly the reason for this reception, so Shaddam could review the names the exploratory committees had given him. Positions needed to be filled, and he had already dismissed many suggested candidates. He needed only loyalists.

"Apologies, Your Eminence, but if I am allowed just a few moments to make my case, I believe you will be quite satisfied."

Shaddam looked at him dispassionately, but let the man keep talking. He wanted Mohiam to absorb more information. "Duke Verdun, I am eager to hear more, but perhaps first you can explain why you did not attend the grand opening of my Corrino museum on Otorio? How did you manage to stay safe, when so many thousands died?"

Verdun paled. "I-I intended to be there, Sire, but my life was in danger, too. My palais on Dross was encircled and attacked by a rebel force, and all my resources and attention were required to quash the unrest. It is a local matter, but the rebels are also implicated in a wider plot against the Imperial throne. I dealt with them, and now my prisons are filled to bursting, nearly five hundred agitators. A full report is being prepared at this moment. I can show you how the throne benefited from my actions."

"My, you have been busy." Shaddam's voice oozed skepticism.

The Duke of Dross—a ridiculous name, he thought—was preoccupied enough with the Emperor's attention that he had forgotten completely about the Truthsayer standing nearby. Excellent. Mohiam had a talent for sliding into shadows, so people often forgot she was there.

Shaddam decided to cut off further discussion. "I suggest you apply your energies to finishing that most vital report. I am still assembling applicants for the open holdings in the Landsraad. You will be notified of my decision."

After Duke Verdun retreated, clearly dissatisfied, the Emperor motioned for the guards to block further supplicants so he could consult with Mohiam. He could tell by the sour expression on her face that she had something to say.

"Verdun is the most blatant of liars," she said, in a low tone. Aricatha leaned closer to listen, and Shaddam allowed it. "He is fabricating that story about rebels and the attack on his palais. I suspect his report is 'delayed' because he is fabricating evidence and falsifying witness accounts."

The extent of the ruse surprised Shaddam. "He did not expect me to ask about it. Now he is caught."

"There is more," Mohiam said, glancing around to make sure they were not overheard. "Fausto Verdun, Landsraad member and proud descendant of Imperial heroes for centuries, holds clear sympathies to this alleged plot against the Imperial throne. I heard the intonation in his words. Any 'rebel' prisoners he holds must be for show, perhaps even reserve troops of his own."

The Emperor felt a deep chill. "He endorses the Noble Commonwealth? Do you think he supported Jaxson Aru's attack? He was conspicuously absent from Otorio when the impacts occurred."

The Reverend Mother bowed. "That is beyond what even my abilities can determine, Sire, but the implication is clear."

Flushed and wanting to go, the Emperor extricated his arm so he could leave Aricatha behind. "I was expected to welcome the visitors, my dear. You go ahead and deliver the speech for me. Just say nice things and then host the banquet. Keep them calm and happy."

She smiled and accepted her new task. Sensing his urgency, the Imperial guards swept the other nobles and dignitaries clear so Shaddam could depart without delay.

ALONE IN HIS private offices, Shaddam summoned his Sardaukar commanders in order to seize this opportunity. They marched in with a crisp, alert demeanor, and he felt energized. He finally had the excuse he had been waiting for. He would at last make a very clear statement.

Colonel Bashar Kolona stood in front of the ornate desk, holding his officer's cap. Two officers of equal rank joined him.

Shaddam sat in his plush chair, faced them. "I have identified a member of the insurrection, Duke Fausto Verdun. My Truthsayer confirms this."

He had expected some flicker of surprise or dispute on their faces, but the Sardaukar remained implacable, waiting.

"Prepare a strike force. Wait for Duke Verdun to return to his homeworld, then lead a punitive raid. Wipe out that treacherous man and his entire family. It will be a message the Noble Commonwealth cannot fail to comprehend."

Two of the officers straightened and acknowledged the orders. Only Kolona showed some hesitation. "Sire, all of the family? Some of Verdun's children and relatives are young. They could not have done anything against the Imperium. Is it necessary to punish the entire family?"

"No survivors! I want the Verdun bloodline terminated, every last one of them erased from Imperial records." He rested his elbows on the desktop. "This will be a warning for all to know."

Nodding, Kolona took a half step back. "Yes, my Emperor."

Shaddam thought of the "rebels" that Verdun had mentioned, the captives supposedly held in the prisons. They were likely part of the overall plot as well. "And bomb every prison, too. Kill all of them."

Kolona was the first with a brisk salute. Shaddam liked him, this good man. All three officers left.

The Emperor looked down at the paperwork on his desk, saw files of candidates proposed by Aina Tere, possibilities of nobles to be elevated.

After the strike on Fausto Verdun, there would be yet another vacant holding in the Landsraad.

Historically, great progress comes about through bold visions. Only weak leaders make decisions based upon the phrase "Thus it has always been done."

—JAXSON ARU, *Justifications for the Noble Commonwealth*,
widely distributed leaflet

Tucked inside her CHOAM craft aboard the Guild Heighliner, Malina Aru pondered and worked, confident no one had any inkling she was aboard the great ship. The Guild always supported her privacy.

Malina's mind was her office, and she continued her work wherever she was. Now on her way back to Tupile, she was almost home, and she longed to be there. Her planet was not on any marked route, but the Guild representative had quietly acknowledged her presence when the private ship docked. All transport records would be disguised and filed away. Security and secrecy were paramount to her.

It was a weakness to be homesick, but she did miss the bubble of safety that Tupile offered, both physically and psychologically. She longed to sit on her veranda and gaze toward the smoky-purple horizon, where other worries droned into background noise.

She also missed her two adoring spinehounds. Har and Kar were the only soft spot she allowed herself.

In her private stateroom, Malina studied documents, looked at the subtle connections and threads of commerce, reviewed hints and fine shadings that resulted in millions of solaris, profit or loss. She was intrigued to see that, due to the increased cost of melange, many minor nobles had turned away from the consumption of spice to alternative, lesser drugs. In particular, something called ailar, or the Caladan drug, was on the upswing, even though she couldn't see how it was moved through normal CHOAM channels. Interesting.

Once she committed the financial analysis to memory, she tapped a glyph on the upper-right-hand corner of the document, which activated the acid in the ink and destroyed the papers in front of her.

Even though the Noble Commonwealth had been shocked to its core by Jaxson's violence, supporters of the rebellion continued to sow the seeds of doubt among ruling families. The brash attack on Otorio had rattled the staid, contented nobles who had spoken, theoretically, about independence for generations, but perhaps the people needed a shock to the system. Other potential supporters had actually been inspired by the enthusiasm (fanaticism?) that Jaxson's act had demonstrated.

As a mother, she loved him, but she did not approve of such wanton bloodshed, which served no purpose other than to underscore his impatience. She could not justify what he had done, although now she began to see some of the effects. Positive effects. New recruits had appeared unexpectedly, and maybe the movement was growing again. Perhaps her son could be an unwitting catalyst. Disavowing him and declaring him an outlaw before the Landsraad had only been part of what she had in mind. Ur-Director Malina Aru never did anything for simplistic reasons.

Though Jaxson should not have gone off on his own, perhaps he was right, at least in some sense. A strong hand was necessary to force the eventual breakup of the Imperium, a cudgel instead of a scalpel. His resounding strike had caused titanic shock waves across the galaxy, revealing just what the Noble Commonwealth could accomplish if they were inflamed.

Now Shaddam's reactionary spice surtax served Malina's purpose further, by driving countless wedges and angering noble houses that would not have previously considered leaving the Imperium. On the other hand, with so many slots open in the Landsraad, Shaddam IV would install only loyalists and lapdogs, and that would make the Noble Commonwealth's work more difficult. . . .

While the Heighliner was in transit on its roundabout route home, Malina received a transmission on her private comm from the Guild contact, and it surprised her. "Urdir, we have arrived over planet Borhees for a scheduled stopover. We will experience two days of loading and off-loading. In the interim, we request a private meeting with you. An escort will come and provide access to the Steersmen's piloting deck."

The voice cut off before she could respond. She suddenly wondered if the Spacing Guild had uncovered her agreement with Baron Harkonnen to provide off-books melange. Though that spice was still prohibitively expensive, it remained out of Shaddam's clutches. Since her actions were technically against Guild policy as well, she had hoped to keep the matter secret, but she was not so naïve as to think that the Guild did not also have discreet side channels for spice.

Malina couldn't decide if this summons was some sort of provocation or power play. The Spacing Guild was as important a pillar to the Imperium's stability as CHOAM, separate but intertwined, associates of equal rank. No Guild representative could command the Urdir, yet neither could the Ur-Director ignore such a meeting. Malina rose from her desk and brushed away the fine powder of ashes from the destroyed document. She hoped this was an opportunity rather than an obligation.

Less than ten minutes after receiving the message, as she finished preparing herself for the mysterious meeting, her security captain announced, "Urdir, a Guild escort has appeared at the hatch claiming you have an appointment. I was not aware of this." He looked concerned. "Shall I arrange a team of guards for your safety?"

"No, my safety is ensured," she said. Whatever this was about, it would be no amateurish assassination attempt. "You are not aware of this meeting. You were never aware. You do not know it is happening."

He bowed and stepped back. "I do not know it is happening."

Like all the other craft hauled aboard the Heighliner, her ship was attached to the inner hull of the enormous hollow ship, each vessel locked into a docking cradle and linked with various umbilicals. Now a connecting tube sealed against her ship's external hatch to let her enter the gigantic Heighliner proper.

After she traversed the connector tube, Malina met a bland-faced, bald man in a gray shipsuit that bore the Guild's infinity symbol. He stood with arms straight at his sides, face forward, shoulders square. "Ur-Director, I am here to escort you to the piloting deck. We will use back passages, out of respect for your privacy."

Expecting her to follow, he walked at a methodical pace along a bright, featureless corridor. After traversing several sections, the gray-clad man turned abruptly and walked face-first into a smooth wall. He didn't hesitate, didn't blink, simply stepped directly through the bulkhead. As he vanished inside, Malina realized it was a hidden door covered by a camouflage hologram. She followed him through the illusion and found herself in a dim passageway that led to a private lift. The Guildsman motioned for her to enter, then stepped back. He did not speak another word.

The door slid shut, and the lift capsule circled around the curved hull of the enormous Heighliner. It shifted course to travel along the axis, then locked in place with an abrupt stop. She emerged onto the secure piloting deck as if she were attending an ordinary business conference.

The woman waiting for her was as tall as an Amazon warrior and muscular enough to fill out her Guild shipsuit. Malina could not identify the numerous rank insignia, but this was obviously a person of some note, dominating the chamber.

The piloting deck was encircled by wide plaz windows. The view was filled with the stars of empty space in one direction and the half-lit sphere of the planet below. As the Heighliner orbited Borhees, homeworld of House Kolona, bright sparks of ships disembarked from the hold, but Malina's attention was drawn to the large tank inside the chamber. Sealed within, a soup of orange spice vapor curled around the distorted silhouette of a Guild Navigator.

Malina narrowed her eyes. This would be a most interesting conversation.

She said, "I am here. You wished to meet?" She glanced at the towering Guild woman, then faced the mutated shape inside the swirling gases of the tank. She knew the power nexus in this conversation.

Navigators were advanced, evolved human subjects whose superior minds were so saturated with spice that they dwelled in a universe of mathematics, physics, and prescience. Only under the rarest of circumstances did they deign to speak with normal humans. Even important Guild officials such as this towering woman could barely relate to the creatures.

"Ur-Director." The Navigator's voice wobbled from a speakerpatch in his tank. "You are CHOAM. I am the Spacing Guild. We are the warp and weft of the tapestry that is the Imperium."

Malina took a step closer to the tank. The Amazon woman stood silently, watching her.

"Spice is the thread," Malina said. She smelled lingering cinnamon undertones, hints of melange gas that had escaped from exhaust vents.

The Navigator bobbed, the silhouette swelling larger so that she caught a clear glimpse of his bloated head and eyes, the shriveled body floating in dense gases. "We must speak of spice and the tapestry . . . whether it can be unraveled, and rewoven. You, Ur-Director, are a tangle of these threads."

Malina frowned. "I was not aware that Guild Navigators were so skilled with metaphors."

"Atasia will explain," the distorted figure said. With a trickle of static from the speakerpatch, his voice fell silent. The shape retreated into thicker vapors.

The Guild woman, Atasia, took charge. "Our Navigators see safe paths through the galaxy, while our engines fold space and carry us from place to place. Without spice, Navigators could not see. The Spacing Guild is dependent on spice."

Malina was impatient. "I know all this. Every child in an Imperial school knows this."

"Spice is necessary." Atasia followed the comment with a surprising statement. "But the Imperium is not the only possible construct for human governance. The Imperium was sewn together as a convenient framework after the Butlerian Jihad. House Corrino became predominant among the League of Nobles, and the basic ruling structure has remained unchanged for millennia."

The Urdir faced the woman who stood a head taller than she, though she did not think Atasia was trying to intimidate her. Malina said guardedly, "CHOAM has long been part of that framework. The stability of the Imperium is better for commerce than the chaos of civil war."

"Independence and free trade are also good for commerce, as you know well, Urdir." The Guild woman's voice was cold and flat. "We know what the Noble Commonwealth aims to achieve. We saw what your son did at Otorio, and we do not approve of such action."

A chill went down her back, and Malina responded sharply. "Nor do I approve of it! I already denounced Jaxson on Kaitain. I am not associated with his terrorist acts. I have had no contact with him."

"You are not entirely disassociated," said Atasia. "We know of CHOAM's long-standing and secret advocacy of the Noble Commonwealth."

"That has never been proven," Malina said, realizing it was not a denial.

"Political projections and models of government suggest that a myriad of independent planets may be beneficial to the expansion of civilization. The structure of the Imperium, and specifically the rulership of House Corrino, may not be the best format for the Spacing Guild or CHOAM to thrive. Given the constraints of distance, the lack of instantaneous communication, and the sheer magnitude of worlds and populations, a central autocratic ruler may not be wise for our future. It is a limiting factor."

"Why are you saying all this to me?" Malina asked, feeling unbalanced. "The disruption of a civil war would be bad for business."

"But history shows that war is often good for business," Atasia pointed out.

Malina could not deny the assertion. "What do you want me to say?" She didn't understand what the Guild hoped to accomplish with this unfocused conversation.

"We mean for you to listen. That is why we brought you here."

Atasia turned back to the spice-filled tank and waited in tense silence. Finally, the speakerpatch activated again, though the Navigator was now concealed in the orange mist.

"We see safe paths through space," said the surreal inhuman voice, "as well as safe paths into the future . . . And this is very dangerous terrain."

Risks are managed through careful training and observation. And yet the trickster universe presents us with an unavoidable fact—life itself poses a risk that will one day become fatal. For everyone. No one survives forever.
—SWORDMASTER RIVVY DINARI of the Ginaz School

On the night after the four flyers were destroyed, Paul again dreamed of the red-haired girl with the elfin face and large eyes. Some of his dreams were blurred with mystery and uncertainty, but other dreams stayed in his mind with crystal clarity when he awoke, as if a holo-image floated before his eyes.

This was one of those definitive dreams. He had a clear image of the girl who would be important to him one day.

All this talk of arranging a political marriage—and the rude, personal rebuff from Duke Verdun—made Paul consider his future wife, whomever she might be. As the son of a Duke, he had the best trainers in the Imperium, as well as the sterling example set by his father, but he was only fourteen, and all his training could not erase the fact that he was a young man with uncertainties and doubts.

Was the girl in his dreams the one he would eventually marry, or was she someone else?

He needed to find out who she was. He was convinced he had caught a glimpse of her in Cala City when he was with Thufir. Though it had been but a flash, her features, hair, and eyes were so similar to what he remembered from his dreams. Was that girl on the streets the one he had envisioned? Maybe it was wishful thinking, but he had to find her.

Duke Leto was in the final preparations for his major offensive against Chaen Marek's drug operations. Leto, Thufir, and Gurney were embroiled in strategic planning over which weaponry to use, now that they did not dare risk shields, but his father insisted that they mobilize all the Atreides forces and launch their retaliation within another day. It was an enormous operation.

Paul felt left out in the frantic, but efficient preparations. After awakening from the vivid dream again, and remembering it all morning, Paul could not sit still. He couldn't get her image out of his thoughts, and that at least was a problem he could solve. Duncan Idaho remained at his side, ever-present friend and bodyguard, and Paul said, "Come with me into the city, Duncan. I need to . . . look for someone."

The Swordmaster was surprised. "As you command, young Master."

Paul hesitated, but he could never keep secrets from Duncan. The two had shared too much together. "I am looking for a girl. I spotted her not long ago on the streets, but lost her. I need to track her down."

Duncan grinned. "Ah, so now I understand! That foppish Duke Verdun says his daughter is too good for you, and you need to be reminded of how many pretty young women are on Caladan."

Paul forced a smile. "They are the most beautiful women, if you believe Gurney's songs."

"Gurney sings whatever words he can rhyme," Duncan said. "But you will see for yourself. You're at an age when the fires start to burn in your veins. Come, we'll stay out of the way of the military preparations."

Paul donned a merh-silk tunic with the Atreides hawk on the breast, gathered his shield belt and personal weapons. He would look the part of a Duke's son, the heir to the noble family that had ruled this planet for so many generations.

Duncan would walk at his side, an impressive figure of contained violence. "You can do better than Junu Verdun, lad," he muttered. "Someone like that would only make you miserable."

That was not what worried Paul. "I had no idea what she was like. My father consulted with Thufir and my mother to develop a list of viable marriage prospects, and they will pick another one soon enough." Distracted, he shook his head. "But there is someone who . . . haunts me, and I need to understand why she is in my dreams."

Duncan clapped him on the shoulder as they set out for town. "Politics be damned. Let your father worry about appropriate alliances. No need to concern yourself with marriage today. You still have much to learn about flirtation and simple conversation with a girl your age." His grin widened. "Once again, I can be your reliable tutor. Come with me. We'll walk among the restaurants and taverns where you will see plenty of beautiful prospects."

"I am looking for one person in particular. I thought I made that clear."

"They are all *particular* young women. Do not limit the possibilities, especially at your tender age."

As they worked their way down to Cala City, gulls wheeled overhead, soaring high above the great stone towers. The sky cracked with a thrumming roar as six Atreides strike craft performed maneuvers in the sky. Paul paused to look up, and Duncan followed his gaze. "We will fly together again soon, young Master, but not today. Your father finds himself in a private war on Caladan."

"*Our* private war," Paul said. "The assault launches tomorrow."

"And we each do our part. For now, it is my mission to help you find this *particular* girl."

In Cala City, the people went about their daily activities. Restaurants opened, fish markets set out the morning's catch, weavers displayed hypnotic tapestries that were unworthy imitations of those woven by the Sisters in Isolation on the Eastern Continent. A baliset maker trained on Chusuk demonstrated his wares by pulling melodies from the air.

Increased numbers of Atreides city guard patrolled the streets, and Duke Leto had drawn together all his remaining forces for the assault against Chaen Marek. All leave was suspended, and perimeter missions and policing actions had been recalled for a singular focus on the illicit drug operations.

Duncan strode beside his young ward. Paul barely came up to the Swordmaster's shoulders. The two passed taverns and cafés, including the same establishment where he and Thufir had sat during their "impossible choice" exercise only a few days ago. From there, Paul was able to locate the street and corner where he had spotted the girl.

Alas, he had no reason to suspect she would be in the same place, but Paul had nowhere else to begin his search. "Let's go over here."

A young woman was scrubbing tables and gathering tankards in an outdoor tavern. Seeing her, Duncan nudged Paul. "Look, that one's pretty enough. I like her braids and smile."

The tavern worker knew they were talking about her and glanced up. Recognizing the Duke's son, she flushed and offered a shy smile.

Paul lowered his voice. "I'm certain she is sweet, but she is not my 'particular' one."

Duncan grunted. "I think *you* are too particular, lad."

As they walked past the outdoor tavern, the serving maiden went back to her work, straightening tables and chairs, and found a package left in a corner. The parcel was wrapped in a strange folded covering, adorned with metallic ribbons. She looked around, but saw no one taking ownership of it.

Something caught Paul's eye. He paused in his step, suddenly alert. An ominous crackle of dread flared up inside him. He turned.

The tavern maiden picked up the box, bent closer to it.

A rush of foreboding shot down Paul's back, demanding action. His hand moved in a blur, and he slapped his shield belt, activating the shimmering field though he didn't know who or where the enemy was. "Wait!"

He lurched in front of Duncan just at the moment the box erupted in a firestorm. The front of the tavern blasted inward with a deafening report. Windows shattered, and the façade caught fire. The explosion ripped the innocent tavern maiden to pieces.

Paul's shield deflected the hammer blow even as the shock wave hurled him back into Duncan. Shards of shrapnel, flaming wood, and razor-edged glass flew in all directions, but the shield dampened the blast and diverted the deadly debris from harming them.

Stunned, Paul staggered backward. Duncan recovered first and grabbed Paul, dragging him toward any nearby shelter.

Screams echoed up and down the street, growing louder. Pedestrians in front of the businesses fell bleeding and burning. Paul glimpsed several bodies thrown to the ground, some twitching, some motionless. Surging fire devoured the tavern.

As dust and smoke roiled out from the blast, a blizzard of leaflets drifted to the ground.

Before Paul could grab one of the drifting pieces of instroy paper, though, a second explosion rocked the opposite side of the street, where the baliset maker had been playing a love song. In slow-motion increments of time, Paul watched a gout of fire rip open the front of the shop, splintering and scattering the baliset maker's wares while the shock wave flattened even more pedestrians, including a hapless family that had paused to look at a glassblower's display.

Moments later, a block away, a third bomb blast roared out.

Duncan reached through the shield to seize Paul by the shoulders. "Come, young Master. It is my duty to keep you safe." He added in a ragged voice, "And thank you for saving me. If you hadn't activated your shield in front of me . . ."

"You saved me enough times, Duncan. But all those people, all the injured . . . We have to help." Paul snatched one of the drifting sheets of paper. The durable material had survived the explosion. On the leaflet, he saw a crude drawing of a curled barra fern.

Duke Leto Atreides: You threaten my operations, attack my business. The barra ferns are mine. The ailar is mine. More will die if you keep interfering.

The note was signed by Chaen Marek.

Paul felt sick. He pulled away from Duncan, who kept trying to drag him away. "No, we do not run! We stay and help these people. We can't abandon them."

Duncan was a coil of spring-wound muscles, casting his alertness about like a sensor net. Before the Swordmaster could object, Paul insisted, "An Atreides does not run and think of his own safety first!"

"Spoken like your good father," Duncan replied, resigned. "But I must keep *you* safe. Nevertheless, let us save whomever we can." He glared at the leaflet. "Although right now, I can think of at least one person who needs to die."

In its most logical form, all life can be viewed as a decision chart of positive and negative influences, as we attempt to reach an optimal determination. But not all decisions are logical, and it is on that path that trouble often lies.

—COUNT HASIMIR FENRING

On the outskirts of Arrakeen, Count Fenring waited at the designated meeting place, in the murky shade of an industrial building. Esmar Tuek and his smugglers were growing more and more mistrustful of him. That was understandable, considering the Harkonnen crackdowns under way, which had put normal Arrakis operations on edge.

For this encounter, Fenring wore a stained desert cloak and a stillsuit that had been provided by his contacts. The suit seemed a little loose on his slender frame, but it functioned well enough. For now, he left the nose plugs loose. He preferred to breathe without them. Following the surreptitious instructions, he'd smeared his face with streaks of dirt. Previous assignments had taught him how to disguise himself.

The Emperor demanded answers about the mysterious slippage of spice that bypassed his Imperial taxes and restrictions. Knowing his volatile life-long friend, Fenring knew Shaddam would soon lose his temper and overreact, which Fenring had to stop at all costs. For now, he realized he didn't need *correct* answers, as much as something that would satisfy the Emperor.

Grix Dardik was adamant that such a secret conduit existed, and Fenring believed these new pirates must be independent from his smugglers—Esmar Tuek would never be so foolish. Even so, the failed Mentat had not been able to track down the mysterious other operators. Where was the illicit spice coming from?

Someone would have to pay, publicly, for the offense, and the Emperor wasn't particular, so long as he could declare that Imperial justice had been served. He had placed that burden on Count Fenring's shoulders.

Thus, he had to dig deeper, root around the underbelly of society. He would have liked to bring Dardik along for this secret meeting with the smugglers, but too much was at stake, and the eccentric failed Mentat was unstable. Thus, Fenring would see Esmar Tuek alone.

The smugglers had moved to a secondary base after Baron Harkonnen had stepped up ruthless efforts to cut down on the illegal operations. Apparently, he also wanted to demonstrate his indignation about the missing spice, and so he went after any obvious target. It was futile, blunt-force meddling, and the harassment had driven Tuek's smugglers deeper into hiding.

Fenring, though, would get to the heart of the matter. Through his Arrakeen contacts, he transmitted a message to Tuek, demanding a meeting. The smuggler leader feared a trap, with good reason, but the Count had agreed to security measures and given his own reassurances.

In the dusty side alley, now he could feel eyes watching him, making certain he had brought no guards or assassins. Fenring was amused by this, because he could personally deflect any efforts the smugglers might make against him. He kept both hands inside his dirty cloak, gripping stilettos in hidden sheaths.

Several large ornithopters flew overhead, buzzing toward the main landing field, and he heard the engines and rhythmic wings of a smaller 'thopter at lower altitude. Looking back over the rooftop, he saw an unmarked private aircraft approaching from the other side of the city. The 'thopter circled over the hardpan that separated Arrakeen from the basin protected by the Shield Wall. The smaller aircraft landed in a vacant lot not far away, exactly as he had expected. Fenring emerged from the shadows to meet the occupants.

As the articulated wings continued to beat slowly, two bearded men in cloaks swung down from the cockpit and bounded toward him. "It is time." One seized him by the elbow and pulled him toward the craft. Fenring ducked under a moving wing as he clambered aboard. He was instructed to sit on the floor, while one man pressed a blindfold over his eyes.

Annoyed, the Count pushed the cloth away. "I refuse to permit this. I am the Imperial Observer on Arrakis."

"Is that any reason to trust you?" The man dangled the blindfold. "Wear this, or Esmar will not see you."

These men were Fremen, and he could tell they would not budge. Despite his resentment and suspicion, he allowed them to tie the blindfold in place.

He turned to his other senses and felt the 'thopter lift off with a vibrating thrum of wings. Having kept his nose plugs loose, he smelled dust and the ever-present bite of melange. The aircraft flew away from Arrakeen, banking multiple times to throw off his sense of direction, followed by periods of silent gliding. The two Fremen did not speak.

Fenring had a good internal sense of time, which he could use to gauge distance. He estimated that they flew for an hour in a principal direction, before the 'thopter landed.

As the engines shut down, one of the men pulled off the blindfold, letting him blink and adjust, trying to see. The 'thopter's instrument lights and external lamps lit a hollow grotto in a massive rock outcropping with high walls all around. Hovering glowglobes added more light. Far above, through a narrow crack, he could see filtered sky, dimmed by electronic veiling.

Climbing out, he stretched his cramped muscles and limbered his joints, ready for business.

The scarred smuggler leader strode up to greet him. "Welcome to our new base, Count Fenring. As you can understand, we have had to increase our security measures. The Harkonnens are causing us many problems."

Fenring responded with a sour expression. "Hmmmm-ah, I did not appreciate being blindfolded." He brushed off his dusty cloak. "Have we not always had an understanding? I thought we could trust each other."

"Trust? If I didn't consider you trustworthy, you would not be here at all. You are my ally, Count Fenring, a respected partner, perhaps even a friend. But still, in these times . . ."

Fenring had few enough friends, but his long-term dealings with Esmar Tuek and the smugglers did make him feel a certain sense of camaraderie. But the demand he was about to make did not fall under any definition of friendship. Circumstances shifted like desert sands, and life required constant situational awareness.

Tuek's rugged face twisted in a scowl. "Nevertheless, the Harkonnens destroyed our former base, and some of us did not get out alive. They knew exactly where we were and made a concerted strike in the middle of the night. I lost seven good men, and my wife and son barely made it out."

They walked into the new cave complex. Fenring remarked, "Yes, we must always have a way out." He looked at the gray rock walls streaked with mineral veins. More 'thopters rested inside the grotto, along with cargo haulers and camouflaged equipment.

The new base of smuggling operations looked much like the previous one, a round cavern office with a metal desk and simple chairs. Fenring took a seat, while the smuggler leader leaned against the wall.

"And how did the Harkonnens find you?" Fenring asked. "I know you take significant security precautions."

The smuggler leader wrestled with the answer. "Rulla thinks the Harkonnens tracked you to our base the last time we met."

Fenring snorted. "I took appropriate measures, and I know how to avoid being followed." Tuek's aloof young wife had always set him on edge. "Just as likely, she or someone else in your crew revealed the location. By clumsiness . . . or on purpose."

Tuek did not react defensively, as Fenring expected. Instead, the scarred smuggler's expression darkened. "That is also a possibility." He reached for a tarnished tea service waiting on the desk. "Something to drink?"

On any other world, it would have been a meaningless social nicety; here on Arrakis, it was a significant gesture. Fenring graciously accepted.

"Since we are . . . friends, as you say, I must bring you a problem. It is a closely guarded Imperial secret, and Emperor Shaddam demands that I do something about it."

Tuek's interest was piqued. "What problem?"

"Income from the new spice surtax falls short of expectations. One particularly troubling factor was uncovered through intense Mentat analysis. It seems that a small but significant channel of spice is being smuggled off Arrakis." He hardened his voice. "Either you are not forthright about your profits, deliveries, and bribes . . . or, mmmm, someone else has a side operation, and the Emperor has noticed."

Now Tuek appeared indignant. "My people know full well that we operate under your sufferance, Count Fenring. You made clear what we are expected to deliver, in terms of money and information. Do I look like such a fool that I would flaunt that? Years ago, my own father paid a terrible price when he sold out the location of Dominic Vernius and his renegade smuggling operations." He paled at the memory. "And I barely escaped from the Harkonnen raid a week ago. We could never survive an assault of Sardaukar if the Emperor turned his wrath on us. I hide nothing from you, Count Fenring."

Fenring stroked his chin. "And yet, someone is taking melange from Arrakis, unreported and untaxed."

"So we have competition."

"Hmmm, yes, and Shaddam demands that I give him some kind of answer."

Tuek poured himself a cup of steaming tea, a distracting gesture. "We are just now learning of this. It will take time to uncover what is going on."

"Alas, you know that Emperor Shaddam is not a patient man. He tends to act, ahhhhh, *decisively*, even when subtlety is called for. Now he demands that I find a way to stop it. Immediately. I need to give him something." The Count took a sip. "The solution will be painful for you, I'm afraid."

Looking troubled, Tuek glanced up quickly. "My people have nothing to do with these other pirates. Why would you punish me?"

"You are known smugglers with black-market connections. I need a way to divert the Emperor's attention and maintain my own position here while I conduct a more thorough investigation. That could take time, and time is a luxury we do not have." He leaned forward, his gaze boring into the smuggler leader. "I require a victory now, someone's head to give Shaddam, even if it is only a diversion." He drew a breath of the warm, painfully dry air. "Consider it, mmmm, another tax. One time only."

Sickened, Tuek rose to his feet and stood behind his desk as if it were a fortress. Fenring had no doubt the man possessed weapons he could bring to bear in an instant. He slipped his hands into his cloak, touched his stilettos.

Tuek growled, "And you want my head?"

Fenring chuckled. "Ahhh, I would rather not, Esmar . . . friend. That would cause too much disruption in our delicate fabric of alliances here. Bad for business. I expect your own connections and contacts might help me find evidence of these other pirates, eventually. I'll need you."

The smuggler leader remained tense. "Then what do you mean?"

Fenring said, "I must prove that I've cracked down, made progress on this matter. I require some obvious sacrifice, or Shaddam will indeed send in his Sardaukar to 'take care of the problem.' We do not want that to happen."

"No. We do not."

"Name a high-level person in your organization. We will claim they betrayed you, circumvented your secret channels, and set up their own operation without your knowledge or authorization. Once the Emperor has seen the payment of blood, he will turn his attention elsewhere, at least for a while. He has the Noble Commonwealth to worry about. I can keep him occupied." He kept his hands and his knives hidden under the cloak. "And, I am sorry, but it must be a sacrifice that *hurts*."

"Such a request!"

"It is to assure your own survival. Barring that, ahhhhh, as the Emperor's emissary on Arrakis, I can always give him your name."

Esmar Tuek stewed for a long time, then glared at him in a dangerous way. "I have a name," he said at last. "Rulla."

Even Fenring was astonished. "Your wife?"

"Yes . . . my wife. She is second in command here. My son, Staban, will take her place."

Fenring remembered the last time he had seen the woman. "But she is pregnant!"

Tuek's expression darkened, and he looked away. His answer explained many things. "Yes . . . with another man's child."

Fenring considered the response for only a moment. "She will do nicely. The Emperor will indeed be impressed."

As planetary leader, I make difficult decisions and take harsh actions, whether for the good of my people, my family, or myself. Every such decision is personal.

—DUKE LETO ATREIDES

Leto did not respond well to threats—especially where his son was concerned.

The explosions that rocked Cala City killed nineteen bystanders and injured many more. The Duke and his advisers rushed away from the military preparations to join the rescue response, pitching in to put out the fires and give any necessary aid to the injured. Dr. Yueh grabbed his medkit and joined the first-aid workers already there.

When Leto arrived with the response group, he found his son helping move debris and calling out orders as if he were the Duke himself. Duncan Idaho and the young man worked together in the thick of the response.

After barking orders to his crew, Leto rushed forward and swept Paul into an embrace. "Thank the gods you're alive!" He shot a questioning glance at Duncan. "What happened here?"

The Swordmaster squared his shoulders. "The young Master saved my life, Sire. He activated his body shield in time, managed to deflect the blast. He put himself in front of me. Without that, I would not be alive."

Leto took just a moment to feel relieved, then steeled himself and dove into helping, side by side with Paul and Duncan. Soon, his hands were dirty and covered in blood. *The first responsibility of a Duke is the safety of his people.*

Within two hours, the wounded were tended and moved to medical facilities, the fires in town put out, and the bodies recovered. Leto finally picked up one of the leaflets, clenched his jaw, and tossed the instroy paper aside.

The drug lord was sowing a path of reckless bloodshed and destruction. Because Paul and Duncan had gone to the city without announcing their destination, they could not have been explicitly targeted by Chaen Marek's bombs. Even so, Paul had been directly in harm's way, and all those killed and injured victims had been innocent in the war against the ailar operations.

The drug lord had escalated the conflict, and Leto vowed to put an immediate end to it.

Halleck, Hawat, and Duncan Idaho all stood next to their Duke. Leto kept his voice to a low, dark growl. "That vile man thinks to intimidate me, but he has only goaded me into action. Our attack forces are ready enough! We have our weapons and ships loaded. We launch our retaliation tomorrow at dawn. Time to get rid of this Caladan drug and everyone associated with it. All-out war, against a true enemy of Caladan."

Gurney agreed. "Aye. The longer we wait, the more chance Marek has to build his plans against us."

He and his advisers returned to the war room in the castle. Leto had studied images of the northern wilderness until his eyes ached, and he promised himself that once this military operation was over, he would commission detailed surveys of his ancestral planet, just as Yueh had suggested. The Duke of Caladan needed to know every square meter of his holding, just as he needed to know his people.

In the war room, Paul surveyed the terrain charts with his father. Overlays showed sky mappings from decades ago, long before any barra growing fields had been established. By comparing the two images, they could identify areas of blurred green, subtle changes that implied sensor camouflage nets.

Leto said, "We do not know where Chaen Marek has his base for processing ailar, but we will strike any possibilities and follow up with significant ground troops. We will find them."

Gurney's grin made his inkvine scar squirm. "Aye, we will cause some mayhem of our own."

This would not be a small operation, like Captain Reeson's quick and overconfident strike that had ended in disaster. This full-scale Atreides assault would have air support, along with a thousand ground troops in personnel carriers. The Duke's forces would sweep across the northern terrain, discover any drug fields, and destroy them.

Afterward, thorough search-and-seizure operations would unravel whatever black-market network was in place to distribute the dried ferns across Caladan and offworld to other users.

Thufir Hawat recited the number of soldiers who had been trained and cleared for the next day's assault, the weapons available, the troop carriers and assault craft that could be dispatched, the battle groups that would fly air cover. Leto would use his armored processional frigate as his flagship.

Duncan was hesitant about the operation. "My Lord, are we still convinced that we must not use shields in the fight? We would be sending our men into such an engagement without body protection. Shields are part of every man's defensive repertoire.

"Perhaps we should go in naked!" Gurney scoffed.

"And yet . . ." Leto looked at a terrifying image from swift overflights near where Reeson's squadron had been obliterated. The lasgun-shield explosion had flattened all the trees in the vicinity, obliterated the terrain for hundreds of meters. A swath of ground had even been turned to glass. "If the fanatics are willing to do that, if they are prepared to sacrifice themselves in a way that rivals the use of forbidden atomics . . ."

Paul finished Duncan's thought. "If our forces go in wearing body shields, a single enemy firing a lasbeam could annihilate them all."

Hawat nodded solemnly. "The lad is right."

Gurney said. "My Lord, I can handle a sword perfectly well, with or without a shield. So can your fighters. Best not to take the risk."

"Duncan says I am already very talented with many kinds of blades," Paul interjected. "I can fight them also, sir."

Leto looked at his son, coming to a quick, firm conclusion. "As my heir, you will likely be a specific target for Chaen Marek. You will stay here. Safe." Before Paul could protest, Leto insisted, "You just survived a bomb blast. I want—no, I *need* you safe."

The young man's eyes flared, and he grew obstinate. Paul became stiff and formal. "I respectfully disagree, sir. I am a part of this fight. I want to be at your side."

Leto smiled and felt compassion rise within him. "Remember how you yourself felt after I came back from Otorio? How angry you were that I'd almost been killed? Do not make me feel the same about you. This is an unnecessary and unacceptable risk. There will be other times when you can fight at my side, but tomorrow, I need you to stay here at Castle Caladan."

Paul looked at Gurney and Duncan for support, found none, then looked back at his father.

Leto said, "That is my command as Duke. You will obey."

Paul lowered his gaze and sat down. "Yes, sir." After a moment of concentration, he shifted his mind to the battle preparations. "Then I will help as much as I can before you depart."

Leto laid out the list of his squad commanders, consulted with Gurney on the distribution of troop carriers. He felt more confident now that plans were moving forward. They selected numerous possible strike zones from the topographical maps, potential fern-growing areas and ailar processing camps, but it was all uncertain. He narrowed his gaze, as if his vision were a sophisticated scanner. "We are handicapped because we can't be sure. I cannot afford to waste manpower on simple geographical anomalies."

Hawat scrutinized the charts. "I can give only my best approximation of where we should strike."

Leto had immediately increased city guard patrols throughout Cala City after the bombings, and now his Mentat suggested an even greater lockdown of the city until after the assault had launched. "My Lord, we must see that no word gets out. I suggest we blockade the city overnight, shut down transport, close the roads. Nothing until our troops set out at dawn tomorrow."

"Gods below," Gurney muttered. "Chaen Marek could have spies here in the city. No doubt they have already reported the damage his bombs caused."

"We have to keep our plans confidential," Leto said. "The soldiers will learn of the departure time only when we call them to the troop carriers." He studied the charts again, shaking his head. So many potential target zones. "If only we had more specific information . . ."

A distinguished old man from the castle staff rapped on the door of the war room. "You have a visitor, my Lord. He insists on seeing you."

"We cannot be disturbed right now," Leto said.

The old servant was respectful, but also familiar with his Duke, whom he had served for years. "It may benefit you to listen, sir. It is Archvicar Torono, and I believe his urgency is genuine."

"That man may be a spy," Gurney complained. "After what his followers have done . . ."

"Maybe, and maybe not." Leto still felt some remorse after his stern clash with the Muadh followers and his hard punishment, assuming they were entirely guilty. The pundi rice farmers had access to barra ferns for their mysterious ritual, so they had an obvious connection to the drug operations. The basic evidence seemed clear, yet the details did not add up. "I will grant him the courtesy of hearing what he has to say. In these times, I will not go out of my way to find other unwanted enemies."

The stately Archvicar entered the war room, eyes downcast. He wore his sharp-angled cap with its embroidered fern frond. His brown robes flowed with importance, but his demeanor was contrite. He pressed his palms together and pulled them apart, widening his fingers as if pulling unseen elastic strands from the air.

"Duke Leto, my Duke, circumstances and honor require that I come here." He bowed. Leto searched Torono's face, saw only sincerity. The Archvicar continued, "Atreides honor is famed across Caladan, but so is Muadh honor. I bring you information about the barra ferns, where they grow and . . . and how the drug has been subverted."

Leto stepped back, guardedly hopeful. "If you have valuable intelligence, I would very much like to hear it."

"My people were dismayed by your unfounded accusations, my Duke. We did not understand why you would believe such terrible things about us. Pundi farmers are your peaceful and loyal subjects, but when you appeared before our temple and forbade our use of the sacred ferns, we . . ."

Leto thought of the appalling obliteration of his four military flyers and the hidden bombs in Cala City that nearly killed Paul. Leto couldn't believe the pundi rice farmers were the same as the vicious fanatics who followed Chaen Marek. *The first responsibility of a Duke. . . .*

The Archvicar continued, not making excuses. "We Muadh devote ourselves to contemplation and centering. That is what the purification ritual is about. So

I called my followers together, and we asked ourselves questions. We realized that we had to help our Duke. We have found answers for you."

He touched his fingertips together and pulled them apart as if playing an imaginary game of cat's cradle. "My people have heard whispers. Across the land, in other villages, some farmers have vanished from our fields. They stopped tending the terraces their families had worked for generations, and just . . . disappeared.

"I learned that a few of my people were indeed involved in growing barra ferns, in shipping and selling ailar . . . including the new, potent strain that has killed so many." His brows knitted together, and his bearded face became angry. "We found the individuals who sold ailar to your Lieutenant Nupree." His face filled with sorrow. "They . . . have been dealt with."

"How did you deal with them?" Thufir Hawat asked. "Justice rests with the Duke."

"We dealt with them in the Muadh way. It was sufficient." The Archvicar gave no further details. "The barra ferns these evil people are using . . . they are not the same ferns we use for our ritual. Our special plants are more delicate, less mottled, and the ailar they produce is a gentler alternative. It is what benefits us." Now his fingers clenched as if he meant to strangle the invisible lines in the air. "These other ferns have been genetically altered to produce a dangerous form of ailar. We have determined that a man named Chaen Marek is growing them by the ton. His hidden operations in the wilderness are significant." Torono's expression became stormy and paternal. "He has corrupted something we consider sacred. It is our desire that these people be stopped. We must end this shame, Duke Leto, my Duke."

"The Caladan drug." Leto felt an ache in his muscles and in his heart. "That is precisely my intent, Archvicar."

"Good. Then perhaps I can help."

Leto solemnly accepted the religious leader's assistance. "If you intend to give us a blessing, we will accept it."

"I will give you a blessing, and much more than that." The Archvicar reached into his robes and withdrew sheets of folded brown paper. "I can identify the sites of the largest barra fields and give coordinates of where their main operations are. Your forces will know exactly where to strike."

Leto's heart leaped. Hawat lurched forward to pick up the papers, and Gurney let out a burst of laughter. "That is precisely what we need!"

"Thank you, Archvicar," Leto said. "That is good news indeed."

When the Archvicar smiled, his rough beard poked out in wild directions. He looked relieved, as if basking in forgiveness from his Duke. He touched his fingertips together again and bowed. "Now I will give you the promised blessing."

The Sisterhood views the future of humanity by considering an infinite number of possibilities. We can step back and consider which threads are best for the species as a whole. That is the difference between the Bene Gesserit and an individual, whether noble-born or street urchin. We do not think, "What about me? What is my future?"

—Bene Gesserit Perspective on History, "Executive Summary"

Golden morning light swept like a scimitar across the high stone edifice of Castle Caladan. At the bustling military field on the headlands, dozens of troop carriers loaded up. Incendiary-filled attack flyers were piloted by grim officers, every one of them ready to go despite knowing the fate of the previous squadron. The fast ships would provide air support and bombing runs once "the fields were exposed, but the main attack would be a direct ground assault. Large carriers would bring an overwhelming force of well-armed and vengeful Atreides soldiers to the drug harvesting and processing camps, which Archvicar Torono had identified.

Duke Leto ordered a scorched-earth response. No mercy for the drug lord who had exploded bombs in Cala City, harmed his subjects, and threatened Paul.

Thufir Hawat wore a long cloak with military insignia over his uniform. He surveyed the distribution of troops and the loading of soldiers and weapons, assessing it all in Mentat silence. Duncan Idaho stood proud with a fine sword in its scabbard. Gurney Halleck barked orders as he herded fighting squads into their assigned troop carriers. He had already promised to write a song about this day.

Paul stood at his mother's side as they watched the large military force prepare to depart. He faced the cold breezes, and felt a chill of concern for his father's life—again. In the few hours of sleep he'd managed before dawn, he had experienced no predictive dream, but knew the dangers the Atreides military would face.

"Come home safe to me, Leto," Jessica said with a softness she rarely showed in front of others.

"I will, my love," he said quietly, then became more formal in front of his troops. "I will come home victorious."

After satisfying himself that the ships, troops, and weapons were readied according to his exacting standards, Hawat joined Leto to report. The warrior Mentat would accompany the Duke in the ornate noble frigate, which would be protected by outflyers and heavy gunships. This time, the armored Atreides craft would serve as a mobile command center, Leto's base of operations, rather than a mere processional barge.

Hawat wiped his stained lips, and his eyes were intense, as if seeing every detail in the entire assault with a single glance. He nodded formally to Jessica and Paul, then cleared his throat. "Tying up loose ends, Sire. In the middle of the night, I delivered my revised list of betrothal candidates to your office in the castle. I believe there are many acceptable options for the young Master." He glanced at Paul and grew more somber. "I did not want to leave any unfinished business, in case . . . events do not go as planned today."

Leto turned to the Mentat. "I will deal with such matters later, after I destroy all remnants of the Caladan drug." He placed a hand on the older man's shoulder. "After *we* return victorious."

Gurney came up, his face flushed and his blond hair windblown, his inkvine scar prominent. "Our ground forces can't wait to fight the scum face-to-face, my Lord. They want to look those bastards in the eyes as they cut them down, with or without shields." He lifted his head and recited from the Orange Catholic Bible, "The hand of God goes with the hand of justice. And we are justice incarnate." He cracked a smile. "I will use that as part of our victory song after today. This fighting is going to be personal."

"Oh, it is personal." Leto looked pointedly at Paul. "Chaen Marek almost killed my son."

Paul knew he wasn't the only one who had been at risk. So many others had already died, not just from the drug lord's direct violence but also victims, like Lieutenant Nupree, Minister Wellan, or Lord Atikk's son . . . so many others killed by the use of tainted ailar. Leto refused to let it continue. Not from *his* Caladan.

"It is personal," the Duke repeated. This was his reputation and his people.

When all the soldiers were loaded aboard their respective ships, Leto walked up the ramp to the flagship frigate, which sported a fierce Atreides hawk. His gray eyes met Paul's in a long, meaningful gaze, before he ducked inside. The hatch sealed shut, and the engines roared to life.

Paul and Jessica stood together on the edge of the field as the entire strike force lifted into the air, a silver squadron, birds of prey. The sky filled with the sounds of the aircraft and their barely contained energy. They swept north, wave after wave, heading across the cloudless multi-hued sunrise. Paul watched them go, and his heart went with them.

NOW THAT ARCHVICAR Torono had provided accurate coordinates, the Atreides battle group covered the northern terrain at top speed, squadrons of outriders, swift scouts, attack craft, and heavily loaded troop transports. Chaen Marek would have no warning other than the roar of the engines.

The wind of the passage thrummed against the hull of the flagship frigate, and Leto hunched beside his warrior Mentat, counting down the hours in flight, knowing all the aircraft were soaring at top speed into the thick wilderness. He received regular reports.

The vanguard scouts transmitted reconnaissance for the troop carriers. "Not much detail below. We're scanning the terrain, but it's like viewing through a fog, Sire. Obviously, a sensor web. Covers a large expanse."

"But we do know where to find the hidden operations, thanks to the Arch-vicar," Leto responded over the comm. He raised his voice over the background noise inside the flagship. "Drop the first firebombs. That should flush them out. Hit the perimeter and knock out the sensor web. Then our troops will come in and finish the fight—we're on our way, right behind you."

"We will hit them like a spring flood, my Lord."

As the troop carriers roared in behind the front attack craft, Leto and Hawat watched a rain of incendiaries fall from the bellies of the warcraft, spraying lines of fire across the cultivated terrain. Inside the transport, the anxious Atreides soldiers cheered, ready for their turn.

Following the first wave of eruptions, the camouflage over the wooded land-scape shifted, section by section, to reveal expansive cleared fields with a cordu-roy of green fern plantings surrounded by tall, mature barra trees. As another section of the sensor web faded, Leto saw several buildings arranged in clusters at the boundaries of the growth area.

"That will be their outpost, my Lord," Hawat said.

"We will take what prisoners we can, interrogate them, scour the area for records," Leto said. "And destroy everything else."

With stomach-lurching deceleration, the troop carriers descended to the newly exposed fields, their suspensor engines flattening any foliage in their way. From the flagship frigate, Leto watched with hard satisfaction as his entire army swarmed over the ground. The fires from the incendiary bombs rose high along with greasy curls of smoke.

Marek's people scrambled to respond. As the assault began, the compound looked like a nest of riled-up cliff beetles. Astonished workers in drab jumpsuits ran from camouflaged huts. Others raced to grab weapons. The building clusters consisted of long barracks, processing structures, small huts, and a cleared land-ing field with several ready unmarked aircraft.

Once solidly landed, his flagship shut down its engines, gull-wing doors opened, and his personal guard troops boiled out. The Duke himself emerged with a hand on the hilt of his favorite sword. Dour Thufir Hawat stood beside him, surveying the operations with Mentat intensity. Nearby, the last of the troop carriers set down heavily across the fern plantings, the roaring engines overwhelming the shouts of both Atreides fighters and compound workers.

Squads of troops quickly formed fighting ranks. With blades drawn, though without shields, they moved like predators in a pack. Emerging from separate transports, Gurney Halleck led one large group of fighters and Duncan Idaho another. With green-and-black colors prominent, the soldiers jogged into the exposed compound, howling their own battle cries.

Leto and the old veteran stood outside the flagship frigate as the last soldiers charged in to overwhelm the drug operations. Leto felt immense pride in his Caladan troops.

Hawat observed with sharp eyes. "The size of this complex is far more significant than I anticipated, my Lord."

Leto could see lines of small barra ferns poking out of the ground like scorpion tails, thousands and thousands of them waiting to be harvested. The air had a sharp resinous scent, a dangerous undertone he recalled from the dried ferns in the Muadh village, but now there was also fear, smoke, and blood.

Soldiers hurried forward, wearing full protective gear and masks. They extended flame-nozzle weapons, squirting and igniting gel fuel so that the stockpile of dried ferns became an inferno, gushing noxious smoke. More suited fire warriors made their way methodically through the cleared fields, and the long rows of growing ferns went up in smoke. The smoke in the air made Leto's eyes burn, and he fitted his own mask in place. Hawat did the same.

Angry shouts filled the air, mixed with the crackle of flames. Workers in roughspun clothes bolted into the fields and the thick sheltering forest, trying to hide. Others, though, stood their ground with weapons raised and turned to fight. They had an intense gleam in their eyes and a fanatical set to their expressions. From the way the determined opponents moved to defend themselves, Leto recognized hardened mercenary fighters. But they had to be more than just paid fighters—these people had a *cause*. The drug lord's security men were not merely frightened peasants out of their depth. They were trained and deadly, and would clearly fight to the death.

"Round up prisoners if we can," Leto said. "Some of those out in the fields are truly just uneducated workers. The rest will face the Duke's punishment in my own time."

Duncan and Gurney led their squads deeper into the ailar processing camp. An explosion erupted near one of the outbuildings, and Leto saw a front line of Atreides attackers flattened by a hurled explosive, while mercenary fighters had been protected from the brunt of the blast by body shields.

With a whistling shriek of engines, the Atreides attack craft circled overhead. Leto glanced up. "Our air support needs to have the other sensor nets down."

Hawat shouted orders into the comm. "Priority, find the sensor webs so we can expose this entire area."

The first sorties cut down the tall fern trees, and as the stalks tumbled, the sensor webs snapped with a twang. The shimmering field overhead disappeared. The Atreides forces pushed forward.

Leto and the warrior Mentat strode away from the flagship frigate, while Atreides combatants swept forward to clash with Marek's fighters.

At the edge of the hidden landing field, two insect-like vehicles began to move, armored black aircraft that had been covered with protective nets, now exposed. Their engines were powering up.

Leto shouted a warning, "They have combat 'thopters!"

The illicit aircraft lifted into the air, pumping their jointed wings either to escape or to attack. Nearby, Duncan Idaho led his squad of fighters toward the landing field. As the 'thopter rose above the tall fern trees, Duncan hurled a compact explosive that detonated just shy of the lower hull. The second 'thopter powered up its shields swiftly enough to thwart another thrown explosive.

The damaged craft's wings flailed and snapped, and it tumbled to the ground, plowing a long furrow as it skidded into one of the outbuildings. It fishtailed and caught on fire. Three men inside boiled out, racing for the trees.

Two more unmarked aircraft from the far side of the outpost took off, reached altitude, and streaked away. They were pursued by Atreides attack craft, which activated their jet-pod boosters and raced beyond the forested horizon. Leto lost sight of them.

"Where did Chaen Marek get such significant weapons and equipment?" Leto demanded under his breath. "Mercenary troops and military aircraft do not simply come through the Cala City Spaceport!"

"I will interrogate any prisoners we capture, my Lord. But first, there's a battle to be won." Hawat drew his sword and looked at his Duke. "I am not so old that I cannot throw myself into personal combat." He turned toward the clash of forces, the clamor of blades, the shouts of fighting.

Leto pulled out his own sword. "Neither am I." With weapons drawn, they ran into the battle.

Love is a dance between trust and secrets.
—LADY JESSICA, letter to the Duke

After the Atreides military had departed for the north, Castle Caladan felt empty and cold, rather than safe. Paul's frustration at being left behind was difficult to tamp down. Though he could not countermand his father's orders, he tried to make peace with the Duke's decision. He was not a spoiled child.

In his room, Paul assessed his instinctive response and compared it with his analytical one. He was not excited for war, not giddy for reckless adventure. Oh, he had read stories and history, and Gurney Halleck sang many songs about the glory of victory; Duncan Idaho talked about his training as a Swordmaster, the fiery conflict that had brought about the downfall of the Ginaz School, and his battles against the Tleilaxu on Ix.

Although such stories captured his imagination, Paul was not a starry-eyed fool. He knew full well the hardships and dangers of a military operation, and he was the son of the Duke, trained to be a leader. Nevertheless, he had been impacted by the illicit ailar business and its ruthless mastermind. He should have been included in this retaliation!

He had been cut out of other things as well.

Though the castle rang with silence, he knew that by now Atreides forces would have reached the target zones identified by the Archvicar. Paul knew the Atreides troops would be successful. Illicit drug producers could never match a fully trained army, especially an Atreides army under the Duke's direct command.

Still, the reality of the situation weighed on him. Who knew what weapons Chaen Marek's operatives would turn against the attackers? They had already demonstrated uncanny fanaticism. His father might be facing a life-or-death battle.

Restless now, he wandered the castle halls. The household staff went about their duties cleaning, arranging things, hanging holiday colors, adding fresh-cut flowers where appropriate. In the dining room, the kitchen staff polished the dark wood table with a citrus-scented wax, then arranged a damask runner down the length. As he entered the hall, the workers were startled. Before he could tell them to stay, they withdrew like nervous pigeons, giving him his privacy and leaving him in the suddenly oppressive hall.

Paul's gaze was again drawn to the painting of his grandfather in his dashing matador outfit. Trapped in the persona he had created for himself, the flamboyant Old Duke had been obliged to demonstrate his fearlessness again and again, until Death finally defeated him.

Was this operation against Chaen Marek now Duke Leto's version of the reckless bullfight? A spectacle that his father felt honor-bound to participate in, whether or not there was a true military necessity for the Duke to go personally? Leto could have directed the operations from the safety of the headquarters building, just as he had watched Captain Reeson's squadron fly off to their deaths. Thufir, Duncan, and Gurney were capable of commanding the operation on the ground.

The barra fern growers had already shown disregard for their own lives, as demonstrated by the blasted crater left by the pseudo-atomic explosion. If their entire drug operations were about to be overrun by Atreides forces, would the defeated criminals be willing to do the same again? Vaporize everyone and everything, especially if it meant they could kill the Duke as well? What would make them so fanatical?

Paul turned to regard the ugly bull's head mounted on the wall. Even though the beast now hung as a trophy, first it had killed the Old Duke. . . .

Paul was the presumed heir of House Atreides, but everything in the Landsraad had changed after Otorio, Houses thrown into turmoil, succession lines forever changed. That constant question mark was like a barbed hook in his gut. Paul had dealt with the thread of uncertainty all his life, even though he loved, trusted, and revered his father. And now he himself was being offered up in marriage.

And rejected.

Jessica had taught him how to clear his thoughts and see a situation logically rather than through the fog of emotions. Paul had not objected to the young woman whom his father and Thufir Hawat had decided was the best political match for him.

Now that Duke Verdun had terminated the betrothal possibility, however, Leto would consider other candidates. Thufir had already delivered a new list, as he had reported before the Atreides troops launched that morning. Soon, it would begin all over again. Leto would study the names, weigh their family advantages and disadvantages.

Paul was committed to doing whatever House Atreides needed. He understood his duty as the Duke's son, and if necessary, he would find a way to be a good husband to his noble wife. Still, he wanted to have some input in the matter. This would be his life, his future.

Frustrated, he left the dining hall, knowing everything could change in an instant. Questions and uncertainties burned like coals in his stomach. Could he not even look at the names suggested, see some background on the women, one of whom was destined to be his duchess?

On impulse, he went to his father's study. No guards or household staff were in the area when he entered the private office. Inside, bound books were interspersed with curios on the shelves: a polished coral cluster presented to Leto by a fisherman, various rare and colorful shells, an ancient scrap of parchment sandwiched between two layers of plaz from the Muadh Archvicar. A cabinet contained categorized records of ongoing matters, trade contracts, reserve estimates, and reports from his ministers.

On the Duke's polished desk was a file marked with Thufir Hawat's personal sign, containing the dossier of marriage prospects that the Atreides Mentat had compiled.

Paul hesitated. These were the names. Thufir had made no secret about it when he reported to the Duke on the military landing field. Didn't Paul have the right to read about these young women?

His mother had always advocated for him. His father might just inform Paul of his decision, but the young man hoped he would consult with him first. . . .

Being here now would be considered a breach of trust . . . but Paul needed to know. He *deserved* to know. Didn't he?

He opened the folder and skimmed down the names and summaries, knowing that any one of them would change his life dramatically. The women ranged from a girl of eleven to a widow more than twice Paul's age. Sheet after sheet delineated names, physical descriptions, traits, family summaries, and a crossconnected web of advantages and disadvantages for House Atreides.

It was the Duke's final decision to make, to do what was best for House Atreides. Paul kept reminding himself of that. But still, he wanted to look, hoping he might find the dream girl in there. . . .

Paul studied each listing, portraits and holo-images, realizing that appearances were a small factor in the discussion and determination of the best political alliance. But what about *him*? Paul wanted to know the character of these candidates, their personalities, temperaments, interests, habits. Were these potential wives studious or vapid, good-humored or moody? And what would they think of him? Would he and his betrothed have anything in common at all?

Paul turned the pages, one after another, trying to be objective. One of these names would bind House Atreides in an alliance and shift their fortunes and political clout. Which young woman would be the best suited to him?

"Many of those remaining names would be acceptable choices, Paul," said his mother, startling him. Though his senses were always alert, thanks to Thufir's careful training, he had not heard her stealthy approach. She stepped inside the study, smiling at him. "I did not expect to find you here."

Embarrassed, he tried to cover the papers, but she had already seen and drawn her own conclusions. He saw that she held a folder as well—one that looked identical to the file on Leto's desk. He noted a flush in her cheeks, a tiny hesitancy. Apparently, she hadn't expected to find anyone here.

"What is that report?" he asked.

She responded with only the slightest pause, a hint of boldness designed to disarm him. "Oh, I reviewed Thufir's dossier and made some slight modifications to the initial sorting." She stepped forward, set the new folder on the desk, and took the old file from Paul's hand. "Come with me." She turned, expecting him to follow.

Paul sensed something unusual and followed his instincts. Opening the new folder, he reviewed the pages, all of which appeared to be in Thufir Hawat's handwriting. But there were fewer pages, and entire sections were missing. He also saw minor variations, details in a loop of a letter, a flourish of punctuation.

Jessica had imitated the Mentat's writing—masterfully—but Paul saw the differences.

"Why do you deliver this now, when my father is away, rather than giving it to him directly?" Paul studied her and instantly understood the answer. "You made changes that you don't want him to know about. Why?"

As a concubine offered to Leto by the Bene Gesserit Sisterhood, Jessica was in a situation similar to Paul's. She was his father's true partner, and yet the security of her position was entirely based on faith, not Imperial law.

Jessica was the Duke's lady, as well as her own woman. She had taken it upon herself to give Paul deep training in Bene Gesserit skills to enhance his abilities, perhaps more than his father was aware of.

"I had to make some . . . adjustments," his mother continued. "It is a matter between your father and myself, and it concerns the welfare of House Atreides." Her smile was disarming. "I know you, my son, and I want you to be happy. And if there's to be an argument over this, I will stand up for you."

Paul could see he had put her off balance, and concluded that her reasons might very well involve the Bene Gesserit.

Frowning, he followed Jessica out of the study. He had learned enough from the dossier to determine at least one important thing: None of the candidates were the young woman he kept dreaming about.

His future was being decided by Thufir's suggestions, his mother's intervention, and his father's ultimate intentions. He wished someone would ask for his own opinion on the matter.

There is law and there is vengeance. I embody both.
  —DUKE LETO ATREIDES, address to
    Caladan War Council

As the men in his squad ran with swords raised, Gurney's lips drew back in a predatory grimace as he remembered how much he enjoyed this. He was in his element. A good day of mayhem made his blood sing. His life under the Harkonnens and years of serving Duke Leto Atreides had prepared him for moments like this.

Although he felt naked without his body shield, the kindjal in one hand and rapier in the other gave him all the protection he would likely need. And if those weapons failed him, he always had his bare hands.

He raised his voice to his squad. "You were all getting tired of practice, weren't you, lads?" The din of landing ships, burning fields, and clashing blades was deafening, but his voice rolled above it all. "Gods below, nothing smells as good as an enemy's blood."

He and his fighters ignored the drab workers who scurried to escape through the flaming barra fields. Those weren't his real adversaries. Atreides troops had found stockpiles of packaged ailar and burned them all. With a loud *whump*, a windowless storehouse erupted in flames. Gurney kept pushing forward, with more soldiers spreading out behind him. The Duke's army would overwhelm the entire complex in no time.

Near the tents and low dwellings, behind long processing barracks protected by shimmering shields, Gurney spotted a generator hut. "There! Let's take out their power and cut some of their defenses and camouflage."

A hard grin was a slash on the face of the man beside him. He was young and impatient. "I want to poke my sword tip into a few soft bodies, not wreck some old machinery!"

"Go ahead, lad. There are plenty of mercenaries to kill. I'll join you once I take care of this business." He grinned. "An explosion can be as enjoyable as a sword thrust, if you do it right."

His fighters bounded ahead, weapons raised, eager to face Marek's mercenaries, but no one stood against Gurney as he loped ahead to the generator shack.

Standing by the thrumming machinery, he removed a small explosive and attached it to the metal housing. He, too, was eager to get to more personal fighting. He bounded away, drawing his blades, one in each hand. Gurney counted out the seconds, then braced himself.

The eruption blew shrapnel in all directions, destroying the generators. The camp's entire sensor net went down, exposing even more of the fern-growing operations to Atreides air support. A column of smoke and fire swirled up from the ruined machinery.

Gurney paused to admire his work, looked up to the sky. Within minutes, he heard the boom and roar of Atreides warcraft coming back around. They dropped firebombs on the far side of the fields, spreading a carpet of fire on the perimeter of the complex.

He ran, catching up with his fighters as they collided with Marek's armed forces. The enemy mercenaries fought viciously, professionally, and they stood their ground as if the thought of retreat had never occurred to them. From the range of facial features and skin tones, Gurney realized these recruits were drawn from across the Imperium, attracted by whatever pay Chaen Marek offered. But there had to be more than simply money involved to buy such fanatical loyalty.

These enemy fighters were obviously willing to die, and Gurney was willing to let them have their wish. "For Atreides!" he roared.

His fighters responded. "For Atreides!" The words gave their hearts a surge of energy.

The enemy defenders wore shields, but all of the Duke's soldiers knew how to fight shielded opponents, slowing each blade enough to slip through the Holtzman field. It was second nature to them. They clashed and danced, defended themselves against enemy swords, pressing close enough to deliver a death blow, even through the thrumming barrier.

As his squad kept fighting, hand to hand, blade to blade, Gurney leaped in to engage a scar-faced mercenary. He thrust in slowly from the side, penetrating the shield and then, in a quick motion, stabbing the kindjal into the man's kidney. It was a natural movement for him, and he had defeated more opponents than he could remember, shield or no shield.

Another group of mercenaries flooded onto the battlefield from a side cluster of buildings. More than a hundred new fighters. This entire installation—generators, processing barracks, 'thopters, sensor webs, enemy fighters, equipment—everything spoke of a major, well-funded operation.

But Gurney knew the Atreides forces would uproot this compound like a weed and stomp it. The fighters would not let their Duke down.

Gurney spun to face a dark-skinned man with jade eyes. He had a blank expression as if he were drugged, but his reflexes were not sluggish at all. Gurney defended himself with both rapier and kindjal, searching for an opening. They fought, evenly matched. Gurney pushed hard, straining to get his weapon through the shield, and the mercenary shoved back. The thin rapier vibrated under a blow from the enemy's thicker sword, but Gurney drove the opponent's weapon aside, running the rapier's edge along the other blade, then pulling back.

Panting, just out of the opponent's reach, Gurney held up both of his blades. "Which would you choose for your mortal blow? Kindjal or rapier?" He slashed at the air, driving the enemy one step back. "I'd be happy to kill you with either."

The man didn't answer. Gurney threw himself against the shimmering shield, while the mercenary thrust and slashed. Ironically, the other man wasn't accustomed to battling an opponent *without* a shield, so Gurney pressed his unexpected advantage. He was more nimble, felt the sting of a gash across his shoulder, and spun, ducked. He parried the other blade, then ducked again. He fought, easily feeling out the man's defenses and his patterns, until he killed the man with a clean thrust with the rapier. As the victim fell, Gurney followed through with the kindjal. "I made the choice for you."

With both of his blades slick with blood, Gurney easily found another target. He was just getting limbered up.

As they continued to battle their way forward, his squad left a trail of bodies behind them. Gurney glanced sideways, intrigued by a fortified hut protected by a full shield. Details and anomalies clicked together in his mind, and he realized that this must be more than a mere supply storehouse. Gurney made the unusual structure his priority, leaving the hand-to-hand combat to his squad. They could handle it.

Reaching the perimeter shield, he tested the barrier, then pushed his way slowly through it.

Once he entered the structure, he saw it was a records complex filled with papers and spools of shigawire, shipment manifests, contact names, routes—a treasure trove of information. Given this data, Thufir Hawat might be able to unravel the web of ailar operations, find out who on Caladan helped distribute the drug, where the funding came from, and where the offworld customers were concentrated.

Delighted, Gurney laughed out loud. "The rewards of God shall belong to the righteous!" He broke the seal of a storage cabinet and began ransacking the documents. He lifted the lid of a box—and heard a thin fiber snap. He instantly knew something was wrong. A puff of searing flame gushed into the enclosed records and incinerated them. He stumbled back and raised his blistered hands.

With another small *whump*, flames engulfed a second box of records, and then a third, as a protective self-destruct sequence obliterated the information.

"By the seven hells!" He shoved his hands into the container and yanked out a jumble of papers and two shigawire spools, whatever he could grab before the fire shot too high. He stumbled back, and within moments, the entire records cabinet went up in flames. More fires sparked from adjacent containers, and the blaze spread, hot and white.

Cursing, Gurney saw he would be trapped as the inferno rushed higher. He threw himself out the door as the flames rose and the smoke thickened inside the shielded hut.

Clutching the few scraps he had rescued, he blinked his burning eyes and hurried away from the fire. He stashed the spools and papers where he could retrieve them later, then flexed his reddened fingers. He took up his weapons again and strode toward the melee.

Hand-to-hand combat . . . he decided to stick to what he was best qualified to do.

The most successful empires grow out of the seeds of concisely targeted destruction. From the Imperial throne, I nurture this garden.

—EMPEROR ELROOD CORRINO IX

The transport hold of the Spacing Guild ship, which had been commandeered by the Imperial military for this mission, was filled with hundreds of Sardaukar warships, battle equipment, and soldiers. This was the biggest attack force Colonel Bashar Jopati Kolona had ever supervised.

After years of ruthless Sardaukar training on Salusa Secundus, he had led smaller attacks on his own and had served as second in command of large battle groups. In each instance, Kolona had excelled, just as he would today.

Emperor Shaddam IV meant to send an unmistakable message to any secret traitors in the Landsraad and the Noble Commonwealth movement at large. The Verdun holdings on Dross would be left in cinders.

Wearing full combat uniform, Kolona stood in the forward command module of his flagship. Issuing orders to the pilot, he led the vanguard that poured out of the Heighliner's belly and sped toward the planet below. They approached on the night side of Dross. Duke Fausto Verdun and his family would be asleep at this hour, but they would soon awaken.

On a tactical screen, the colonel bashar watched his ships flaring pale blue sparks with intermittent orange bursts as they cut through the thickening atmosphere. The punitive operation looked smooth, even beautiful to the eye.

Kolona was not the sort of commander who would send his troops into harm's way and remain in the background, observing and receiving reports. If his soldiers were in danger, he would put himself in danger. If they died, he would die with them. The Sardaukar were his family, and he loved them all. He had no other family anymore, and he felt a strong sense of camaraderie with his fellow soldiers. He could think of no greater honor than to perish among his military brothers and sisters.

Now as Kolona looked down at the darkened skies of the Verdun homeworld, he spoke into a comm, transmitting to the entire fleet. "We have caught them sleeping, but activate battle shields and remain on full alert." As planned.

The warships shimmered with blurred fields protecting them. This first major command was a great opportunity for Kolona. Emperor Shaddam considered him worthy of the role, and Kolona would not let him down. He would carry out the orders.

Even so, he could not entirely dispel his uneasiness. With mixed feelings, Kolona considered the sparkling jewels of the planet's major cities and the Verdun central holding. People down there were going to die, and most of them were innocent, even if Shaddam's suspicions were correct about Fausto Verdun's complicity with the Noble Commonwealth.

It reminded him of the similar assault on his own planet of Borhees, the unexpected nighttime raid led by Paulus Atreides—coerced into it by Elrood, Kolona now knew. Duke Paulus had succeeded with the help of Sardaukar soldiers wearing Atreides uniforms. After hunting down the last survivors of the ousted noble family, a Sardaukar commander had captured young Jopati in the hills. Instead of killing him, the Sardaukar had committed him into rigorous training on the prison planet of Salusa Secundus. He had been fourteen at the time.

Jopati had lived through it, had even excelled.

Yet as he led this assault, it felt that history was repeating itself, and he was causing it. With this sneak attack on House Verdun, would he be creating a new set of aggrieved survivors from a disgraced noble family? Was someone down there just like he had been, a teenage boy watching his whole world uprooted? What if this ruthless action effectively inspired more people to sympathize with the Noble Commonwealth movement?

Nevertheless, Colonel Bashar Jopati Kolona would do his duty, and do it well.

The battle group soared in over the darkened skies, weapons hot. Per Imperial order, Kolona issued no warning, no statement, no explanation; he gave no opportunity for anyone to evacuate.

The Sardaukar simply attacked.

His gunships unleashed explosives, destroyed buildings, drew down a curtain of fire. Troop carriers landed armed, merciless soldiers—not worried about wearing Imperial Sardaukar uniforms now—and suicide drones filled with explosives that flew into targets.

Streaking gunfire filled the sky of Dross, and the Verdun palais was in flames. Kolona directed the pilot of his flagship to swoop over the engulfed mansion, and he scanned downward, absorbing detailed images.

As walls collapsed and roaring fires swooped up the towers, he saw a beautiful teenage girl on a high rampart, dressed in a filmy nightgown. From his mission briefing on the Verdun family, Kolona identified her as Junu Verdun, daughter of the ambitious Duke. Palais guards ran toward her, but they were too slow, and she fell to her death as the floor and walls collapsed in flames.

Murdering the girl and her family like this did not give Kolona pleasure. It was another black mark on history.

Despite his inner reluctance, Colonel Bashar Kolona led a flawless mission. The Sardaukar attack was quick, efficient, and overwhelming. Verdun military aircraft scrambled to take off and flew in disorganized patterns before being shot down, one ball of flame after another. Soon enough, it was completely over.

If Duke Verdun was truly involved in the sedition to break apart the Imperium, then Noble Commonwealth spies and messengers would spread the word swiftly. Shaddam himself would not wait long to make his announcement either, proclaiming that Duke Fausto Verdun had deserved his fate. The Emperor's word was not to be disputed.

This was a brutal message, and Jopati Kolona doubted it would be the last.

In the equation of survival, one must calculate what there is to gain, and what is left to lose.

—*The Mentat Handbook*

Leading his group of well-trained fighters, Duncan Idaho pushed past the line of outbuildings and shielded huts. Behind them in the tall fern forest, he spotted a low structure that was clearly different from the other industrial, flimsy prefab units. This one looked sturdier, more lived in—a dwelling? And it was surrounded by at least fifty mercenary guards.

A group of bodyguards whisked a lone man out the back of the structure and headed into the dense foliage, away from the fighting.

Duncan yelled to his fighters, "Follow me!"

The front line of mercenaries formed a cordon to block Atreides pursuit while the man escaped. Duncan and his companions crashed into them in a flurry of swords. The fighting deflected the Atreides momentum, but Duncan killed the first man he encountered, then engaged a second. Around him, his companions were making short work of the cordon, breaking through. But the real target was fleeing into the thick stands of fern trees.

He guessed who the heavily guarded person must be. Chaen Marek.

Duncan collided with an opponent, but his blade was deflected by the enemy's body shield. He paused, redirected, and thrust through the shimmering field into the man's heart. "They are stalling us. That man is our target!" He pointed his sword and ran even as the body fell to the ground.

Atreides fighters fought the fanatical guards, killed several more, and broke through their line. Rather than finishing off the opponents behind them, Duncan led the pursuit of the man being rushed away. "He's escaping!"

Duncan still had fifteen soldiers with him. That should be enough.

They tore through the underbrush, knocking weeds and branches out of the way. Duncan felt a stinging twig snap against his left cheek, knocked it away, and continued running. His comrades kept up.

Five more bodyguards turned, prepared to sacrifice their own lives in order to grant their master just a few more minutes. Duncan and his companions struck them in a flurry of long blades. Though the Atreides wore no shields of their own, they fought with surety, penetrating the enemy body shields. Duncan already knew that the mercenaries were competent fighters, but the Atreides had more finesse. These men beside him were the best in House Atreides.

Even so, three of his companions fell in the fighting, but they made the enemy pay dearly. Now only a handful of bodyguards surrounded the fleeing drug lord as they bolted with him into the tall barra trees, ducking through the maze of fronds and making a beeline into the wilderness. Duncan put on more speed. Perhaps Marek had a hidden escape 'thopter?

Duncan vowed the drug lord would not get away.

The spiky mature ferns towered around them with fronds splayed out like sharp fans. Duncan slashed through a wide frond, burst into a small clearing, and could see his target at last. He paused in surprise.

Chaen Marek was a small man in gray robes, and he scuttled along, dodging the fern-tree trunks. In a flash of panic, the drug lord glanced over his shoulder, and Duncan saw pointed features and a clear grayish cast to the skin. His heart lurched.

A Tleilaxu!

Chaen Marek was a member of the Bene Tleilax, reviled experimenters, genetic manipulators, torturers. Duncan had seen them before, fought them, and reviled them. What were the Tleilaxu doing on Caladan?

"I know who you are, Chaen Marek!"

Duncan sprang forward, and swiftly killed one more of the bodyguards who turned to stall the pursuit. The rest of the Atreides fighters were right behind him, more than evenly matched with the few remaining mercenaries. The drug lord could not get away.

While two of Duncan's companions engaged Marek's man, the Tleilaxu halted for a last stand. Only three of his protectors remained. They stood in a tight circle, weapons raised, shields shimmering, ready to sacrifice their lives.

If necessary, Duncan would take them all. Chaen Marek had no place to go.

Cornered, the Tleilaxu man glowered at him. "Are you the Duke's man?" Surrender was not even a flicker in his hard eyes.

"I am Swordmaster Duncan Idaho. The last time I fought Tleilaxu was in the caverns of Ix. We restored House Vernius after your takeover." He grinned. "I killed many of you then, and now I plan to add one more to the tally."

Anger darkened Marek's pinched, gray face as he looked out between his clustered bodyguards. "You do not know the enemy you are fighting, Duncan Idaho. You cannot imagine the repercussions of your actions."

"I know we are eradicating your ailar operations here. Is Caladan a Tleilaxu test operation? We will stop the drug shipments, and that will prevent more deaths." Duncan strode closer. "Duke Leto has decreed it."

Marek's mouth twisted into a sneer. "Duke Leto is not a man who sees opportunities." The drug lord seemed to believe he had all the power in this situation, though he had clearly lost this battle.

The Tleilaxu reached into his gray robes and removed a small handheld lasgun. His expression became wily. "Consider my situation, Duncan Idaho. If I let you capture me, your Duke will execute me anyway. You know it. Even more so, I know the Atreides Mentat will interrogate me. I cannot allow that. There is too much at stake." His thin lips formed a smile. "Instead, I think you will let me go."

Holding his sword, Duncan tensed like a laza tiger ready to pounce. "We can kill your bodyguards and bring you to justice." His own soldiers had their weapons out; some even carried projectile weapons, which would not work against the shielded bodyguards.

"No, I think you will let me go," Marek repeated. "You should have learned your lesson when we vaporized your four attack craft. I had to show you how serious we are, how devoted our followers are. We have a cause you cannot understand. I was stung by the loss of one of my fields, but House Atreides was stung worse. You know what I am willing to do." He raised the lasgun. "Now you *will* let me go. Back away."

Duncan scoffed. "I am a Swordmaster of Ginaz, and I intend to take you prisoner." Even against the lasgun, he and his fighters could press forward and take the drug lord before they all fell.

"I see your men do not wear personal shields even in this battle. A wise precaution." Marek activated the power button of the pistol. "But my men *do* have shields." He swung the weapon toward one of his own bodyguards. "Lasguns and shields. You know exactly what will happen—and it does not have to be an enemy shield. These men will do. They are willing to die anyway."

The fierce-looking bodyguards did not flinch.

Duncan froze. He knew this man could do exactly as he threatened.

Marek mused, "We live with the rules of kanly, the binding laws of the Great Convention, rigid strictures for a War of Assassins." He laughed. "Who could even conceive that a person would fire a lasgun into a shield on purpose, knowing the pseudo-atomic explosion that would result? What act of desperation would provoke such forbidden behavior?"

"No one would . . . ," Duncan said, but he felt a rush of cold. These people, bound by some kind of fanaticism, had already proved what they were willing to do.

Then he realized an even greater consequence. A lasgun-shield detonation would not only kill Duncan and Marek but all the Atreides soldiers, vaporize the entire site. And Duke Leto.

The Tleilaxu laughed at his expression. "You said that you consider my race dishonorable. I know that you despise us for our very existence. You honestly think I would not consider it a worthy end, a flash of glory? If I touch this firing button, the lasbeam strikes my guard's shield. Then you, I, and everything for a kilometer around vanishes in a flash of white heat. *Everything.*"

He paused, his eyebrows arched. "Ah! Is your Duke here with his army as well? Of course he is! Duke Leto Atreides would not sit at home while he sends others into battle. One touch of the firing button, and I will be forever known as the man who obliterated the Duke of Caladan and the House Atreides troops. A far better legacy than being interrogated and tortured to death, don't you think?" Marek let out a louder chuckle. "As I said, you will let me go or you, your soldiers, and your Duke will all die."

Duncan strained against the manacles of fury, trying to find a way out. The Tleilaxu was right; Duke Leto was within blast range. Even with the speed of a Swordmaster, he could never move faster than a lasbeam could strike the nearby shield. It was a set of impossible choices.

Two Atreides soldiers moved up on either side of Duncan Idaho. He growled in frustration.

Marek didn't wait for Duncan to answer. Knowing he had the upper hand, he bolted away, taking a pair of mercenary guards with him, while one remained to give his life and delay pursuit. Duncan hesitated at the prospect of the lasgun-shield explosion, but then he threw caution to the wind. He bounded after the Tleilaxu.

Marek would not obliterate them all in a pseudo-atomic flash, so long as he felt he had a chance of escaping. Duncan killed the lone remaining bodyguard, then surged after the drug lord who was already dodging through the enormous full-grown ferns, weaving between slatted shadows and straight, spiny trunks.

Then in a tangle of vines and thickening underbrush, he was gone. Duncan couldn't find the grayish man. Both the drug lord and his bodyguards had disappeared.

Duncan shouted out Marek's name, but received no answer. The eerie fern forest thrummed around him, as if taunting. He could still hear the sounds of battle back at the main compound and see veils of smoke rising into the sky from the burning fields.

"Marek!" he yelled again. The survivors of his squad came up, breathing hard, and spread out to find the Tleilaxu man. "It was a trick to buy time, but he had a plan all along."

After a thorough search, half an hour later, he and his companions finally found a hatch cleverly disguised on the trunk of one of the thickest barra fern trees. It opened to a narrow shaft hollowed from the bole of the trunk just wide enough for a person. It plunged down into a complex of tunnels, an interconnected maze.

Chaen Marek could be anywhere by now.

Duncan stood adjusting his eyes and knew that the Tleilaxu had escaped.

On the grand scale of the Imperium and the future of humankind, nothing can match the danger of emotional attachment.

—Bene Gesserit admonition

It was early evening when Count Fenring, blindfolded again, was escorted off the 'thopter by a smuggler. He removed the eye covering as soon as they arrived at Tuek's new base. Brushing himself off, Fenring stood on the rocky floor of the hidden grotto under the illumination of bobbing glowglobe lights.

Today, for appearances' sake, he would perform his duty as the Imperial Observer. Shaddam would watch the recordings later, and then he would be satisfied, at least for a while.

In the sheltered grotto, Tuek's smugglers used pumping mechanisms to load spice into shipping containers, then sealed and loaded them onto a waiting cargo 'thopter. Even with suspensor assists, each container required two workers to maneuver it on board.

The air was redolent with cinnamon, strong enough to make his eyes burn. "Hmmmm, richer smell than I remember," he said, taking a long sniff.

"We found a pure unweathered patch this afternoon, right on top of a fresh spice blow," his escort said. "We filled a harvester bay and escaped with the cargo. A Harkonnen patrol swept in and attacked us even before we spotted wormsign. Had to leave a lot of our equipment behind." The smuggler was angry, keeping his voice low. "This harassment is causing a great deal of harm. Esmar says we're supposed to have an understanding with the Emperor."

"We do," Fenring said, knowing he needed to have sharp words with Baron Harkonnen. "After today, that understanding will be even more clear."

When he entered Tuek's new office chamber, he saw more metal furnishings than before, four desks, records cabinets, additional workstations. Before Fenring had a chance to sit, the scarred smuggler strode in, weary and obviously upset. He chased away the workers at the desks, then sealed the office door so he could have privacy with Fenring. "Your timing is perfect, Count. In a matter of minutes, we will bring in Rulla and her secret lover." He ground his teeth together. "This will be unpleasant, but beneficial to you, and to me." He looked sickened and disturbed, but a hard expression came over his face. "I trust the sacrifice I offer up will be of sufficient magnitude for your purposes."

"Hmmm-ahh, we shall see."

They heard a commotion down a side tunnel, gruff voices shouting. A woman cried out, "Don't hurt him!" Moments later, Rulla was pushed roughly into the office chamber, thrashing like a trapped predator. She sneered at Esmar, "Your men are hurting him!"

"Then he should not be resisting." Tuek looked expectantly toward the tunnel. "He knows what he has done, and knows his life hangs in the balance, along with yours. You have both betrayed me."

More dusty smugglers entered the chamber, wrestling a man forward. When they hauled their captive into the stone-walled office and released him, Fenring was astonished to see that it was Staban Tuek, the son by Esmar's first wife. The young man had deep scratches on his face, and blood trickled from his mouth.

The smugglers brought Esmar's son to him and released their grip. Staban simmered, tried to recover some of his dignity. Esmar stepped forward and struck him hard on the face with a closed fist.

The younger man flinched and reeled, but did not raise his hands in defense. Esmar hit him again, even harder this time, causing Staban to fall and then struggle back to his feet. "Why don't you fight back?" He struck his son a third time, a hard slap.

Staban said, "Because I would never strike my father. I cannot—"

Esmar raged, "You will not hit me, but you take my wife?"

Rulla watched, seething but held back by other smugglers. Fenring was pleased to see how utterly loyal the crew was to Esmar Tuek. She shrieked, "He ravished me! I never gave my consent—"

Esmar silenced her with a vicious glare. "My son has betrayed me, but he is not a rapist." He shoved Staban back into the arms of the men who had brought him. The young man looked down at the rock floor.

"But you, Rulla . . . I also know what you are." His tone was low, menacing. When he turned to face Count Fenring, his demeanor changed as he concocted his story, the tale they would report back to Kaitain. He spoke while looking at her, but it was for the benefit of Fenring and the other men present. "Rulla, I also know about the rogue smuggling operation you ran, that you hired a band of pirates, stole melange, and sold it off of Arrakis without any of us knowing." He glared at her. "If you would deceive me in love, you would also deceive me in business."

Fenring smiled, nodding in satisfaction. "Yes, hmmm, I have seen the evidence of your involvement, and it is quite convincing. That will do, indeed."

Rulla stopped thrashing long enough to look entirely baffled. Confusion took the place of her fury. "I do not know what you're talking about. I have done no such thing!" She looked at the other smugglers, saw only stony faces. "I'm not involved in any pirate operations."

"The Emperor is not happy about the black-market spice being diverted from his oversight," Fenring said. "He will be most pleased when I report to him that we have found the perpetrator."

Rulla continued staring. "This is nonsense!"

The smuggler leader lowered his head somberly. "My only question is whether my son was also involved . . . or if he can be salvaged." He looked at the young man.

Staban stood straight and faced his father, unafraid of being beaten again. "I know nothing of Rulla's other activities." He made no additional excuses.

Esmar stared at him for a long moment, and Fenring could feel the tension rising to a boil. Finally, the smuggler leader turned away. "I believe you."

"Lies!" Rulla cried to her husband. "Lies! How could you betray me like this?"

"Look in your own mirror for the true traitor." Esmar stepped closer. "Count Fenring, the Imperial Spice Observer, will witness how we mete out justice in the desert. In this case, it is also the Emperor's justice."

Staban looked broken, but he shored himself up. "And me, Father?"

The smuggler leader remained silent, then said, "I still hold out a faint hope that you might be worth keeping alive."

Rulla writhed, arched her back as if to intentionally emphasize her swollen belly. "No! I am carrying a child!" She flashed a glance at the stoic Staban, then said to Esmar, "Your . . . your grandson!"

"The product of your seduction, and your schemes." Tuek turned away, gestured for his crew to drag her away.

"But the child is innocent!" Rulla wailed.

"Many innocents die in the desert," Esmar said. "But you are not innocent."

Fenring was impressed by the surprise. He had told Tuek to produce a scapegoat, a sacrifice of sufficient magnitude to convince Shaddam that the gesture was painful and real. His seductress wife *and* his unborn grandchild? The Emperor would be more impressed than he ever expected. He would have no doubts at all.

Fenring extended the cloth band that had been his blindfold while he was brought out to the hidden base. "If I might suggest . . . this can also be used as a gag?"

AT NIGHT, FROM a ridge high enough to provide a superb view, Count Fenring and Esmar Tuek each watched through oil-lens viewers as Rulla was brought onto the open sand. An imaging unit also captured high-resolution video of the event, because Shaddam would want to see every detail. He would know Fenring was doing a good job.

The dunes were illuminated by pale light from both small moons. Fenring adjusted the lenses to see a contingent of Tuek's smugglers pulling the pregnant woman's arms and legs, extending them so that she was spread-eagled on the sand.

"A shame we cannot hear her last words, hmmm?" the Count said.

Tuek snorted. "She has already said enough. And done enough. She should have known better than to betray her husband."

The men thrust a Fremen thumper into the sand not far from the woman, activated the syncopated device, and rushed away to a small escape 'thopter. With a flurry of articulated wings, the craft took off, flitting away.

Through the viewer, Fenring zoomed in. The imaging panel followed his view. "This should not take long."

Esmar Tuek seemed to be carved from sandstone. "No, it will not."

His son, Staban, stood next to him, unbound, but he looked as if he had been wrapped in strangling shigawire. His skin was as pale as bleached sand. Esmar turned to him, his voice filled with so much anger it was like an accelerant waiting for a spark. "But for my mercy, and my faith that you are not permanently corrupted, you could be out there beside her."

Staban's response was so quiet it seemed little more than a breath. "This is worse."

The scarred smuggler looked at him with hardened blue-within-blue eyes. "As I intended it to be."

Esmar Tuek had also offered two other smugglers to be surrendered as co-conspirators, men he had wanted to get rid of, regardless. While they, like his wife, were not involved in the still-mysterious piracy efforts, Tuek had caught them stealing and used the opportunity to clean house. It would reinforce the story Fenring needed to weave for Shaddam. These other victims would meet a different end, though. Tuek had plans for them.

Though he heard no sound due to the distance, Fenring watched Rulla thrash and try to break free of her bonds. Staban stared, swallowed visibly, but made no sound.

The nearby thumper sent out the rhythmic percussion that would call a worm. *Thump, thump, thump!* When Fenring concentrated, he could hear the faint sound and felt the anticipation build. Few non-Fremen ever actually saw the enormous, territorial sandworms of the deep desert.

Esmar Tuek just stared ahead into the night. He had lowered his oil lenses. "Can you hear it?"

"The thumper? Yes, it is quite distinctive, even at such a distance—"

"Not that. Listen."

When he concentrated, Fenring heard a distant rumbling noise, a hissing vibration like a rolling wave. With stark shadow edges from the moonlight, he could see the advancing front, a mound in the sand that traveled forward with amazing speed.

A huge, long shape moved toward the staked woman with the inevitability of a planetary collision. Screaming, Rulla managed to pull one arm free and rip the stake out of the sand. She spun, curled, and lashed with her free hand, trying to yank the other stake loose. Liberating both arms, she worked at her feet. She was amazingly nimble, considering her late pregnancy.

"She is a strong Fremen woman," Esmar said in a dead voice. "She may even get the knots loose."

Fenring wondered, "If she gets herself free, can she run far enough away?"

"No."

Staban whispered, "She is also carrying your grandson."

The older man's face pinched. "She died for me at the moment of her betrayal with you. I have no grandson."

Fenring could feel the tension crackling between the two men. Life, and decisions, were hard in the desert. He had left his nose plugs loose, and he drew in a deep breath of the arid air. He smelled dust and melange. He had never been this close to a sandworm before and found it exhilarating. Somewhere deep inside, he felt an uncharacteristic tinge of fear.

Rulla was still struggling to get free when the sands shifted and engulfed her. The monster went deep beneath the dunes and then erupted upward, devouring her and the thumper in a massive blast of sand.

Fenring stared in awe at the primal power of the scene, then lowered his oil-lens binoculars. No sign remained of her.

The imagers recorded everything for Emperor Shaddam. Fenring decided he would keep a copy for himself.

The smuggler leader stared for a long moment in silence. "I will make Staban watch her execution over and over again." He heaved a hitching breath. "To reinforce the lesson I want to teach him."

Trust, love, and honor are intertwined, yet too often they remain three separate strands.

—DUKE LETO ATREIDES, private journals
(thought to be destroyed)

The smoke of burning barra fields smeared the sky like a stain on Leto's reputation, yet the destruction all around felt gratifying—a cleansing of the insidious Caladan drug.

This scorched-earth attack was necessary, like a surgeon excising gangrenous flesh. No mercy for the murderous Chaen Marek. These ailar drug operations had harmed his people and had blackened his honor. As the Duke of Caladan, he considered himself inherently responsible for letting the deadly drug spread across the worlds of humanity.

He took no comfort in the knowledge that there were far worse drugs than ailar, many more euphoric chemicals and more destructive practices. Humans had a penchant for finding addictive and deadly vices. The use of such recreational substances had grown more widespread in response to the dramatically increased costs of melange, thanks to the Emperor's spice surtax.

But this problem had struck *here*, in *his* home, not on some distant desert planet or in the jungles of Ecaz. Barra ferns grew only on Caladan. Chaen Marek had cultivated and processed the ailar right here, and that practice shamed House Atreides.

Recently, the grieving Lord Atikk had filed a formal complaint in the Landsraad, although the nobles were far too preoccupied with filling countless empty seats to give priority to a petty inter-House squabble.

Leto meant to eradicate every channel. Half measures would not be sufficient. His beloved Caladan would no longer be the source, and that was all he could do. His response would be swift and sure, and plain for the whole Imperium to see.

After gathering reports from his network of sources, Thufir Hawat had already unraveled the surprising spread of ailar usage across the Imperium, with Caladan at the nexus. And the Mentat had only just begun to turn over rocks to see what data he could find. Many more dark and hidden facts were sure to come scuttling into the light.

Leto stood with a hand on his bloody sword, turning to watch as mercenary prisoners were taken and workers rounded up. The Atreides fire crews torched the remaining fields, cutting down mature fern trees that loomed over the compound.

Duncan Idaho looked sullen after reporting the escape of Chaen Marek. Atreides searchers had scoured the newly exposed tunnels beneath the forest and found a secret exit hatch and the burn marks of jet-pod exhaust where a small escape craft had taken off.

Though deeply disappointed, Leto still felt victorious. "Marek may have slipped away, but we castrated his operations. His ailar production has been ruined, and we will dismantle the entire distribution network, destroy his black market. The man has nothing left but to lick his wounds."

Leto was shocked to learn that a *Tleilaxu* had set up his operations here on Caladan. He already had many good reasons to despise the Bene Tleilax for what they'd done to his ally House Vernius, as part of Shaddam's secret scheme to create a synthetic spice. Now a Tleilaxu had come here, genetically modified a native Caladan plant, and turned it into something more addictive, more deadly.

After seeing the scope of the barra fields, the equipment, mercenaries, and weaponry, Leto was convinced this was no simple one-man operation. Tleilaxu genetic manipulation was a complex process, not performed on a whim.

Who was financing Chaen Marek? Shaddam Corrino had commissioned the earlier Tleilaxu work on Ix, but that entire plan had disastrously failed. Was the new Tleilaxu drug lord an independent operator, or was there some larger scheme? What if the Emperor himself was involved as he had been on Ix?

"Most of the records are destroyed, my Lord," Gurney Halleck confessed, his face flushed. With burn-reddened hands, he carried a small set of scorched documents and two shigawire spools. "It was my own damned clumsiness, a self-destruct setup. I should have noticed the trigger. This was all I could salvage. I hope Thufir can get something worthwhile from it."

"Thufir will find anything there is to be found," Leto said, accepting the illicit records. "We are not finished here, but we did the right thing."

It put into perspective how little he needed to care about the insulting rejection from Duke Verdun. Hawat had already compiled a list of new candidates for Paul, and the names were waiting for him on his desk back at the castle. Leto would review them as soon as he returned, even consult with his son this time. He didn't have to rush to marry off Paul; he just needed to dangle the possibility, play the game. Yes, he would select one of the names and send another carefully worded letter.

Without question, allying his House with House Verdun would have been a terrible mistake. Even so, the obnoxious nobleman's implication that House Atreides was too lackluster bothered him, that Paul was not worthy. How many other Houses Major secretly thought the same? Would his son and heir be turned down again?

Previously, he had convinced himself that ruling only Caladan—his home, his world, his entire universe—was sufficient. But if Fausto Verdun and other Landsraad nobles considered Paul and House Atreides beneath their notice, was that partly Leto's own fault? Perhaps he should work harder to play the political game, especially now with so many opportunities on the table.

Caladan was close to his heart, but in the reality of Imperial power and influence, perhaps one small planet wasn't enough. An Atreides Duke had ruled here for twenty-six generations . . . did that make House Atreides appear to be stagnant? His father had once told him that contentment is the first step toward downfall.

Perhaps Leto should have demanded more, been more ambitious, grabbed possibilities for wealth and power. Hawat had advised him, and even Jessica had understood the need to look for opportunities. After Otorio, there were plenty of holdings available. . . .

He watched his troops finish their mopping-up operations. A lieutenant jogged up to deliver a casualty report, and Leto was sad to learn that he had lost nearly a hundred fighters, although Marek's mercenaries had suffered far greater casualties. Still, that was more blood on the drug lord's hands.

His thoughts kept circling back to the same question. Perhaps House Atreides did need more power, more political influence, more clout.

Leto said he was willing to do anything for Paul and the future of his House. Then he corrected his thought. *Anything honorable.*

BACK IN THE castle behind closed doors, with glowglobes dimmed to a warm orange light, Leto allowed himself to be a man and a lover. He let down his personal walls and opened his heart to rest in Jessica's arms. Now that he was home safe, she made love to him with a desperation that revealed just how worried she had been.

As they lay in the spacious bed, they fit together in perfect harmony, warm skin softly touching. In the afterglow, they faced each other, Leto's gray eyes looking into her green gems. They spoke in whispers because they did not need to be louder. He stroked a strand of bronze hair that had drifted down her cheek.

Even here, he was still the Duke, and they did not speak of trivialities. Jessica was his most important adviser, his quiet and steady confidante. He spoke to her about what he had been thinking, how he needed to seize the opportunities. "Jessica, I am . . . reconsidering my priorities."

"How so?"

"I should strive to get more for House Atreides, for Paul. There are great power tides in the Imperium, and I should not feel I am above them. My heart will always remain centered on Caladan, but we can have more for ourselves and our legacy. I have been too aloof. I've decided to go to Kaitain and petition the Emperor for governorship over one or more of the holdings left leaderless after Otorio. I am his loyal Duke. Why should I not be the one to rule those worlds?" He lay back on the soft pillow and sighed.

He thought of Fausto Verdun, like a carrion bird swooping down over fresh carcasses, and the image made him uneasy. Leto was not such a man. But whatever strengthened House Atreides would benefit Paul.

Jessica said, "Everyone knows you are the one who raised the alarm and saved those people on Otorio. The Emperor, his wife, Count Fenring, and many others are only alive because of what you saw and reported. Make sure they don't forget that fact."

"Shaddam does not like to be reminded of his obligations," Leto warned. "If I press that advantage too hard, he may resent me." He thought about their son, and hardened his resolve. "Then again, Shaddam will resent me or not as he sees fit. He makes up the reasons he needs." He sat up in the bed. "Other pandering nobles have been pressing him. So many worlds left without noble rulers. . . . I consider myself a decent man and a good leader. Would those planets not all be better off with an Atreides as their ruler? Think about the poor populations suffering under Baron Harkonnen."

He made an angry sound deep in his throat. "House Harkonnen holds Giedi Prime as well as Lankiveil, and for eighty years, they have controlled the spice operations on Arrakis. Does a House like that deserve more holdings than House Atreides? I can get more for my family and for future generations. There may come a time in the future when our livelihood depends on it."

"I cannot dispute what you say, my Lord." She paused. "My love."

"It is decided, then. I will go to Kaitain and speak privately, or publicly, with the Emperor. It is time House Atreides receives the holdings and respect we are entitled to." He pulled Jessica close, feeling her against him. She hooked a smooth leg over his, and they lay without moving for a long moment. They drank in each other's presence like a rare and expensive wine.

"I go to Kaitain as the Duke of Caladan, and maybe I will become much more than that."

Lines of worry furrowed her brow. "Beware of the corruption of the Imperium, though—especially now. The nobles are displaying their raw ambition, squabbling like dogs over bones. They are not your friends."

He gave her a long, warm kiss. "I know whom to trust. And whom to love."

AS HE THOUGHT of more ways to build a secure future for Paul, Leto returned to his private study and found the dossier Hawat had left for him. He began to peruse the candidates laid out, and he was sure someone else would be appropriate. No, more than appropriate . . . *perfect* for Paul. He studied the pages, remembering his long discussions with the Mentat and further conversations with Jessica, the negotiating, the consideration, the many Landsraad daughters who were available.

He picked up page after page, reviewing names, reports of marriage prospects, advantages and disadvantages of their families, read the marginal notes in Hawat's shaky handwriting. This wasn't all politics. Leto was determined to find a better marriage for his son. Fausto Verdun's callous rebuff had, in fact, averted what would surely have been misery for Paul.

Leto pondered when everything had changed so dramatically. Had it truly only been a few months since he'd gone to Otorio? He remembered the glittering reception, the well-dressed nobles, all the historical artifacts displayed in the Imperial Monolith. Through the shock and turmoil, he hadn't thought much about the chitchat, but now he did remember the hushed conversation, the mutterings about the Noble Commonwealth movement. He had been with Armand Ecaz and Lord Attik. He wondered if any of them had been coconspirators, although the grumbled words had likely been typical complaints about governments and bureaucracy.

As he studied Hawat's list of potential marriage candidates, he recalled one of the nobles in that airy conversation, Count Dinovo, who had mentioned his own daughter of marriageable age when Leto broached the subject of Paul. Ah, yes, Dinovo had indeed escaped, one of the few nobles rushed away in time with Armand Ecaz.

Dinovo's daughter had also come up during the earlier discussion down in his father's fishing shack. What was the girl's name? Something from ancient history, the Time of Titans. Hecate! Yes, that was it. Hecate Dinovo.

Count Dinovo had seemed pleasant enough, not arrogant like Fausto Verdun. Leto wanted to look at his daughter as a possibility, but as he flipped through the pages, he did not see an entry for Hecate Dinovo. He double-checked and wondered why Hawat would have removed her.

In the previous discussion, a couple of other names had been considered seriously, and they came to mind as well: Noria Bonner, Maya Ginia, or Greta Naribo. He searched for their listings, since they had been close runners-up in the previous round, and found Naribo but not the other two. His brow furrowed.

He had expected to make his own decision, but it seemed the Atreides Mentat was already eliminating good candidates without discussion. Wanting to hear more, Leto sent for Thufir Hawat, and within moments, the old veteran arrived.

"When I send my next letter of invitation, I want to make a better choice for Paul," Leto said, tapping the report.

"Considering Duke Verdun's rude response, that would not be difficult, my Lord."

Leto held up the dossier. "I wanted to look further at Hecate Dinovo, but I see you have removed her name. What made her unacceptable after all?"

Hawat's heavy brows drew together. "Hecate Dinovo? She was indeed a strong possibility, Sire. I did not remove her."

"She is not listed here," Leto said. "And what about Noria Bonner or Maya Ginia? They were also under serious consideration before."

The old Mentat shook his head. "No, Sire. I assure you I included them with my recommendations." He took the report and paged through it, then paused and turned back, scrutinizing the details. "My Lord, this has been altered. Some of these other marginal notes are not my handwriting. A clever forgery."

Leto felt a sudden chill. Someone had tampered with the report? Right here in his office? It had to be a person from the household. Was there a spy in their midst, manipulating the choice of who would marry the Duke's heir?

He turned as Jessica appeared at the doorway, smiling. Her hair hung loose around her shoulders, and she wore an Atreides-green house gown with a softly glowing soostone brooch on her left shoulder. "Time to choose another candidate for Paul? Together we can find the best one. I have some suggestions."

Hawat kept paging through the dossier, clearly astonished.

Leto looked up, feeling incredulous and angry. "Someone altered the report my Mentat delivered! It must have been done while I led our assault on the drug fields to the north." His nostrils flared as he drew in a quick breath. "Here in my own house!"

Jessica paled, and Leto immediately sensed something odd as her expression became wary. She calmed herself and seemed to come to a conclusion. In a quiet voice, she said, "I . . . revised the list myself, my Lord. There were candidates I considered unacceptable, as we previously discussed. I wanted to save argument, especially after your recent trying times."

Leto's breathing quickened and his stomach lurched as this unexpected trap-door opened beneath him. "Without consulting me?"

Jessica did not look away. "I had no reason to believe you would not take my advice. I was thinking of Paul's best interests, as we discussed." Leto could see she was intentionally being quiet, calm. Now she averted her green eyes. "My apologies, my Lord. I overstepped my bounds. You know I would do nothing to harm you or House Atreides."

For a moment, Leto could not find words to respond. He wrestled with his storm of emotions, feeling as if some predator had dropped down out of a tree and attacked him.

The old Mentat quietly listened to every word and observed every detail. Leto would ask Hawat for his analysis later, but now he wrestled with his own feelings, his own surprise. He had never distrusted Jessica, never even imagined such a thing.

She remained silent, poised and beautiful with her chin lifted just slightly, exposing her graceful neck. A subliminal gesture of submission?

Leto barked, "Hawat, leave us!"

The Master of Assassins briskly departed without a word.

Leto rose and approached Jessica, who stood where she was, looking down. "Hawat says you forged his handwriting in the additional notes." She didn't respond. "Nothing? I suppose silence is better than a lie. Tell me what was so unacceptable about Hecate Dinovo? Or Noria Bonner? Maya Ginia? You could have talked with me about it." Before she could answer him, he added, "I'll have my Mentat verify whatever you say, and I will also have him re-create his original list, so I can verify every name that was removed."

She was pale, but her voice remained calm and soft. "I have reasons that I considered sufficient. I am sorry that I am unable to justify them for you."

He was dismayed to realize that she had no better answer for him. Even if she made excuses, he wasn't sure he would want to hear them. He could not comprehend what her reasons might have been.

Then further suspicion tingled at the back of his mind, scraped along his nerve endings, and brought a heated flush to his skin. She had done this so easily, seemingly without a second thought. How many other times had Jessica taken similar actions, making decisions in his name without being caught? Without him realizing?

She knew him so well. . . .

Was he truly so naïve that he hadn't seen it earlier?

That was when he suspected that her manipulation was likely part of some insidious Sisterhood scheme, which made him even more upset. It reminded him that the Bene Gesserit dispatched their concubines with instructions to pull strings as if they were puppeteers in order to achieve the Sisterhood's goals. Another thing and another thing.

He should have kept in mind that her beauty and shrewd intelligence came with a price: conflicted loyalties. The very people who raised and trained Jessica also had a claim on her allegiance.

"You learned too damned much in that Bene Gesserit school," he muttered, taking her off guard. "But I have learned, too."

Jessica's expression fell, and she looked lost and devastated, completely convincing. Leto didn't think it was an act, but he did not know what to believe right now. "Leto, I—"

"You should leave. I do not trust myself right now. Go, and close the door before I make a decision that I cannot retract."

The person who appears to be stark raving mad, especially a Reverend Mother with an ocean of Other Memories churning inside her head, might be much more than what she seems. Rather, she could have a sharper grasp on sanity, because she sees things no one else can see.

— LARIBA PYLE, embattled Mother Superior in the
Dark Ages after the Butlerian Jihad

L ethea had begun her precipitous decline only a few days earlier, but the crone's violent instability made the time seem much longer to Harishka. The Mother Superior hated going to the guarded medical room, where danger simmered in the air. Instead, she viewed the patient remotely, from her own office.

Before departing for Kaitain, Reverend Mother Mohiam had helped Harishka craft an appropriate letter to Lady Jessica on Caladan. A firm, undeniable letter laying out the other woman's obligations. Considering Lethea's rasping demands, and dire warnings, Jessica might be the only person who could unlock the mind of the failing old Kwisatz Mother. She needed her to come here immediately. *Take her away from the boy! Disaster to the Sisterhood!*

If Lethea lived long enough . . .

They had no choice but to pull Jessica from Caladan. Perhaps permanently.

The Mother Superior stood at a wallscreen observing the seemingly harmless old woman on her bed. As anxious medical Sisters tended the ancient patient, Lethea squirmed and struggled to get out of bed. She showed surprising strength and resistance when four Acolytes and a Reverend Mother named Venedicto tried to get her under control.

An Acolyte approached with an injector, but Venedicto expressed reservations about the harsh tranquilizers and antipsychotics. "Not yet. It could harm her prescience, and we need to know what she will say."

"If she says anything worthwhile," Harishka muttered to herself as she watched the images. "We have always needed to know, but that woman withholds it from us."

In a croaking voice, Lethea began to rant. "It is not right! I see it in my mind, and *it is not right!* Jessica . . . I must see Jessica of Caladan. *Now!* She and the boy. The patterns are not correct!"

The medical Sisters managed to wrestle Lethea back into bed. Reverend Mother Venedicto leaned close and spoke soothingly, her words clearly picked up by the wallscreen in Harishka's room. "Lethea, listen to me. Jessica has been summoned. The message was already sent."

Harishka whispered, "She will be here soon. She must obey."

Venedicto made another soothing sound, leaning close to the old woman. "Please calm your thoughts, so they do not overwhelm you. Use prana-bindu breathing exercises and find your inner calmness. When you reach that serene place inside, all will be better."

Lethea lunged at her, trying to claw out Venedicto's eyes, and the Acolytes barely grabbed her in time. "My *inner* calmness? Do I appear *calm*? There is no reason for calm." Faint, rippling waves appeared in the air around Lethea's head, and her brittle white hair crawled and whipped around from the psychic energy stirred up by her powerful mind.

Venedicto tried to control the writhing crone while the medical Sisters retreated, terrified. "Be still. You must not fear! Fear is the mind-killer. Fear is—"

Lethea fought back with surprising strength. "You do not understand! Patterns are out of alignment! One failed Kwisatz Haderach after another, dead-end breeding lines, birth mothers unwilling to follow commands, not considering the consequences of their actions. Jessica must not remain on Caladan! It may already be too late!"

Her voice rattled, and she wheezed exhausted breaths. "Some Sisters allow themselves to fall in love! What can we do about that? Put them all to death?" She let out a staccato, acid laugh. The psychic waves rippled around her head, reflecting her internal turmoil. "It is breeding chaos, completely out of control!"

Harishka continued to observe, growing tense but listening carefully as Venedicto asked the necessary questions. "What patterns are out of alignment? Kwisatz Mother, tell us what you mean!"

The old woman slumped back on her bed and began to cackle. Before long, her laughter turned into a moan. "You could never begin to understand what I am saying, what I am *seeing*, images folding off into the past and the future." She tried to throw herself out of bed again. "Let me out of here. I will go to Jessica myself."

The strange energy continued to swirl, pounding ripples that seemed to emanate from within her anguished, dangerous mind. Lethea's crackling hair gave her a feral, crazed look. Such a dramatic manifestation of her mental abilities alarmed Harishka. She recalled the terrible, long-vanished Sorceresses of Rossak back in the time of the Butlerian Jihad. There might still be genetic markers of Sorceress bloodlines in the human race. Perhaps Lethea had them.

The crone's powerful mind shifted like a burning beacon in the cosmos, searching for one thing, and one thing only.

Making up her mind, Harishka activated a speaker in the room. "Lethea, I will be there right away. I need to talk with you."

The fragile patient looked around the medical room, desperate and confused, as if she did not know who was speaking to her.

Leaving her office, the Mother Superior began to run. She reached the medical chamber in minutes. Venedicto met her at the door, hurrying her inside. "Your voice triggered something. She is much worse." On the bed, all four Acolytes used their strength to hold Lethea down.

Instead of ranting, though, Lethea had lapsed into senseless muttering. Her hair still crackled with energy, and translucent ripples swirled over her bed.

"You have given her no drugs?" Harishka asked. "Nothing to alter her mind?"

"Nothing, Mother Superior. Her mind is . . . twisting on its own. She needs deep psychological treatment, not drugs."

"I do not need a psychologist!" Lethea shrieked. "I need Jessica. Bring her to me from Caladan! There are things I must say to her, things she must realize! We have little time to control her! Take her away!"

Harishka went to the bed and placed a reassuring hand on Lethea's forearm. "She will be coming. Our summons will arrive very soon."

The ancient Kwisatz Mother was drenched in sweat from the effort she expended, but Harishka's words finally calmed her. She relaxed her shoulders and looked up with filmy, bloodshot eyes. "Is that true? She will be here?"

"I sent the command myself. She must obey."

Lethea shuddered and sighed. "Then the patterns may be back in alignment. Take her away from Caladan. You would not understand. Only a Kwisatz Mother can comprehend this." She closed her eyes and appeared to fall into a deep sleep. The roiling energy faded, and her waving hair settled.

Filled with questions, Harishka stared down at her. For decades, the Sisterhood's breeding program had been Lethea's sole domain, and this woman grasped threads and tangles that no one else could, and straightened them out. Lethea saw the countless necessary paths that would someday lead to the ultimate Bene Gesserit goal: creating the Kwisatz Haderach, the male superhuman who could bridge space and time.

Jessica, daughter of Mohiam and concubine of Duke Leto Atreides, somehow played a key role here. But when she finally received her summons and traveled to Wallach IX, Mother Superior Harishka would have to protect her. Lethea had already proved deadly.

Some part of human instinct allows people to sense things about others. It is an innate survival skill to intuit that another person is dangerous. This also applies on a larger societal scale, when a leader feels he may need to kill millions of people.

—Bene Gesserit teaching

Twenty spindly date palms stood in front of the Arrakeen Residency. On many worlds, such trees would have been unremarkable, but here on Arrakis, they stood like victory banners. The palms had been planted as a defiant affirmation that humans could conquer such an inhospitable place, that by brute force and the extravagant use of resources, those in power could make even *trees* grow here.

Today, Count Fenring watered them with blood.

Dressed in light, cool clothes, he and Lady Margot observed the activity, satisfied but appropriately stern. Margot looked up at the palms, admired the broad fronds and noted tiny clusters of dates, none of which were ripe.

Sullen workers came forward with bowed heads, and opened sealed containers. Bending before the base of the palms, they poured the thick red liquid into the sand, where it could seep down and water the roots. A gathered, uneasy crowd watched, but no one commented.

Humming to himself, Fenring looked up at Baron Harkonnen, who also observed the spectacle. The enormous man was dressed in grand finery, heavy garments lined with whale fur, utterly inappropriate for the desert heat. He sweated, and his fat face held a look of confusion. The Baron did not know why he had been called here.

When Fenring sniffed, the dry air burned his nostrils. "Ahhh, Baron, it is said that out in the desert, wild Fremen distill the blood of their victims and drink the resulting water." He watched as workers moved from one palm to the next, pouring measured amounts of red liquid onto the ground around the trees. "In this instance, I thought we would simply use the pure blood and save a step of distilling, hmmm?"

"I am sure human blood has certain essential nutrients to help the palms thrive," the Baron said. He thrust out a thick lip, clearly wondering whether or not he was in trouble. "But I am less interested in horticulture than in knowing whose blood that was."

Fenring reassured him, or at least distracted him. "No need to fear, Baron, hmmm . . . although the matter does concern you. You are fully aware that my own private Mentat, Grix Dardik—"

"*Failed* Mentat," the Baron interrupted. When Fenring flashed him a deadly glare, the fat man quickly added, "Very well, I will not question his competence. Go on."

"Dardik, along with the Emperor's Mentat accountants, discovered subtle anomalies in melange production, shipment, and reported income. Collectively, we have analyzed all available CHOAM records of sales, taxes, and fees paid, as well as the solaris allocated to the new spice surtax."

"I am fully aware of the damnable spice surtax." The Baron bit off his words like a man chewing on a particularly tough piece of meat.

"I also conducted a thorough analysis from the Arrakis end. I found the exercise, ahhhhh, highly informative."

Margot slipped her arm through his. "My husband is the Imperial Spice Observer, Baron. He watches very closely."

Fenring continued, "I assigned my spies and observers to the task, particularly my contacts within the smuggler network. I was determined to find out what is really happening here, and then inform the Emperor."

Now the Baron looked alarmed. Fenring could read subtle changes in his expression and demeanor, although the other man covered it with swift and forced indignation. "If you are concerned about illicit spice operations, Count Fenring, you should arrest all the smugglers. I have done my part by unleashing Rabban, letting him hunt them down so we can eliminate their illegal activities."

"Yes, ahh, that will no longer be necessary. I have taken care of the core problem." He smiled at the blood being poured around the palm trees.

The Baron narrowed his close-set eyes. "You executed them all?"

"I found certain pirates who refused to operate within the rules, but the others have my tacit acceptance. Emperor Shaddam has long been aware of the smugglers here on Arrakis, and some of them provide worthy services. You will henceforth leave them alone."

"You want me to just . . . just ignore smugglers?"

"Those smugglers are *my* smugglers, and they provide services and pay appropriate fees. The Emperor is satisfied with them." Fenring paused and then spoke in a hard voice that slashed like a sharp, curved knife. "He is not pleased with those who bypassed our known network."

The workers poured more blood around the trees, moving down the line of palms, emptying two of their containers. The crowd remained silent, cowed.

"I was able to expose a separate band of pirates working the sands," Count Fenring said. "Parallel smuggling operations that steal spice from the desert and sell it directly to offworld customers. Their activities were isolated from our ability to monitor or document. A large amount of melange was sold on the black market, circumventing the Emperor's spice surtax and all of the normal fees, hmmmmm, or the appropriate bribes."

The Baron quivered, held upright by his suspensor belt. "Indeed!" He seemed shocked.

"We apprehended the ring leader of these pirates. Rulla Tuek, the wife of the primary smuggler chief. She was running a side game, cheating the Emperor and her own husband." He paused to sniff the dry air again. "She has been dealt with."

Fenring saw the confusion change to genuine glee on the Baron's face. Interesting. This was not what he had expected.

BARON HARKONNEN TRIED to control himself as he heard this revelation. From his own spies, he knew that somehow the Emperor and his maddeningly clever Mentat accountants had found questionable results. They suspected the existence of an independent flow of spice from Arrakis, which meant that the Baron needed to cover up his secret business dealings with CHOAM and Malina Aru more carefully. If Shaddam was suspicious, then Fenring was damnably more dangerous.

But his own Harkonnen pirates continued their operations, undetected and working through their established back channel. In fact, they had just delivered another large shipment from the Orgiz refinery complex, and that spice had quietly been sent to CHOAM—for a substantial fee.

And yet Fenring said he had caught the head of the illicit smugglers? The detestable Count thought he had cracked down on the operation and executed the leader. He had already reported the victory to Shaddam.

But he had the wrong person!

Delighted, the Baron looked down at the blood the workers emptied from the containers, trying to shake out every last drop. "And that is the blood of Rulla Tuek? The guilty party?"

"Ahhhh, hmmm, that is the blood of two of her compatriots," Fenring said. "I oversaw the execution and drained their bodies for this rather poignant gesture."

"Then what happened to the woman? Rulla, you say?"

Fenring reached into his pocket and removed a small shigawire spool. "This contains a recording of her being staked out in the desert and devoured by a sandworm. All of the evidence is here. My lovely wife and I"—he reached over to take Margot's hand, and she responded with an adoring smile—"will travel back to the Imperial Court. I wish to present this personally to my friend the Emperor. He will be most relieved."

Did Fenring have to make that point, that he and the Emperor were personal friends? Was he emphasizing his power and clout in front of the Baron? Of course he was!

The Baron accepted the shigawire spool, as Fenring continued, "This is a copy for you. I thought you might like to enjoy it in private, at your leisure."

"I will indeed, Count." He could barely contain his joy. Fenring had found the wrong culprit! The Baron's own operations were now safe, provided he could keep a low enough profile.

Upon discovering hints of the piracy operation, Shaddam had sent letters of demand, raging for answers from the governor of Arrakis. The Baron feared he would himself face punitive actions. In the worst case, House Harkonnen might even be removed from its role here on Arrakis.

Now Fenring's faux "pirates" had already met the Emperor's justice. Shaddam had his scapegoat, and his fury would be deflected. The Baron and his clandestine plans were safe.

"I shall indeed review it most carefully." The Baron pocketed the shigawire spool. "I am sure my nephew will enjoy it as well."

"One more thing, Baron. I must emphasize that Esmar Tuek and his son, Staban, are under my protection. Their operations are carefully monitored and supervised. You are not to interfere, and you will have Rabban stop harassing them. You have your own work to do as siridar-governor."

At the moment, the Baron was happy to concede whatever the Count wanted. "Indeed I do."

They watched the workers take away the empty containers, letting the bloodstained palms bake in the sun. The Baron thought it was a nice gesture, an ominous and memorable showpiece for the people of Arrakeen to see.

In his own residence in Carthag, he had caught a housekeeper stealing trinkets and selling purloined water in the back alleys. His guards had apprehended the woman, and she would soon be executed. Now he had an idea. He decided to drain her completely of blood and send several more containers back here to Arrakeen, as a gift to Count Fenring.

After all, the palms would always need more water.

This sort of damage, once done, cannot be undone. I can only hope for forgiveness.

—LADY JESSICA, dispatch to Reverend Mother
Gaius Helen Mohiam

Like all Sisterhood trainees on Wallach IX, Jessica was brought up to believe that emotion—especially romantic love—was a vulnerability, and therefore to be guarded against. Despite all warnings about such weakness, Jessica had slipped because her feelings for Duke Leto went far beyond what her teachers would approve of.

Earlier, Mother Superior Harishka had instructed her to eliminate certain candidates as potential wives for Paul. Of course, the Bene Gesserit did not see "wives," but only pawns in their breeding program, chess pieces to be moved into position, as the Sisterhood planned countless moves ahead.

Jessica had been obligated to follow the Mother Superior's commandment. She did not know what flaws or vulnerabilities those particular young women possessed, because she was not privy to the details of their breeding program. She had reluctantly completed the task, however, diverting the discussion away from the indicated names in the first round. Junu Verdun was an acceptable choice.

The second time, though, Jessica had been forced to take swifter action, and she had been caught. Even Paul knew what she had done, but Leto's discovery was far worse. She had no answers to offer her Duke, no excuses.

She hated the fact that the Bene Gesserit had forced her to deceive him. Even now, after she had lived here so many years, they could still yank her strings, like an abused pet on a leash.

Jessica drew on her training to build a thick wall and activate a metaphorical shield around her heart, but she still felt vulnerable.

Given the closeness of their relationship, she hoped Leto would eventually forgive her. She had indeed hurt him, overstepped her role, but from his point of view, she had become yet another surprising betrayal in his life, thus increasing his distrust of the Sisterhood and their techniques. It was no small thing, and she feared that something between them had broken. He remained walled off to her, and she wanted to repair their bond, no matter how much time it might require.

Deep inside, she was still that young girl who had never known her parents, raised from infancy among the Bene Gesserit. Their goals were her goals, and their training had made her a well-placed concubine for Leto. The Sisterhood planted many women among the noble houses, wealthy CHOAM Directors, and other influential politicians and business leaders. Except for what might have been an administrative whim, the Bene Gesserit could have assigned her to some other House, offered her to any of a number of Landsraad nobles.

Jessica had always considered her role special. She genuinely loved Leto, and her heart was heavy with the rift between them. He had been icy to her for days. Jessica tried to speak with him, but he refused.

She would have to let the fires of his anger subside and hope they could eventually come to a resolution.

Perhaps to distract himself, Leto had embraced his new decision with Atreides tenacity, and he was more determined than ever to expand the holdings and respectability of his House. He made prompt arrangements to travel to Kaitain, anxious to leave Caladan—and her. A Guild Heighliner was due to arrive the following day. He would go to the Imperial capital alone, and perhaps that was the distance he needed from her right now. As the Duke of Caladan, he would use the weight of his noble blood, as the cousin of the Emperor himself, to present his case and negotiate more political power and holdings. When he returned, Jessica hoped they could repair their relationship, for Paul's sake if nothing else.

That was when a new message cylinder arrived from Wallach IX, covertly delivered and sealed to Jessica's thumbprint only. Apprehension settled deep within her as she opened the metal cylinder, unfurled the note, and read words that terrified her.

She sat heavily in her high-backed chair in her private withdrawing room. She set the cylinder aside and read the message again, as if she could somehow change the words.

"Sister Jessica, come immediately to Wallach IX. The Mother School has urgent need of your presence. This is not a request. Do your duty. Your Mother Superior commands it." Harishka had signed her name.

The words, the seal, and the signature triggered a response within her. Her life, her mind, and her heart had been indoctrinated by the Bene Gesserit, and every cell in her body was wired to respond as components of that intricate machine. She was a part of it, and it was a part of her. Throughout the Imperium, the Sisterhood's net was invisible, but as strong as shigawire. If she struggled against it, those wires would tighten and strangle her.

Worse, there was a second message.

Hidden, encoded, from her teacher and taskmaster, the woman who knew her better than anyone, in some ways even better than Leto did. The words sent a river of ice down her spine. Fighting a building sense of dread, Jessica ran her fingers over the raised dots of code and began to read.

"You belong to the Bene Gesserit, Jessica. We assigned you to the Duke of Caladan and can change your assignment if we so choose. You may believe yourself free, but you are ours to command. Come to Wallach IX now, or you may have nothing on Caladan to return to.

"I know your obstinate nature all too well. If you defy us, we will destroy not only you but Leto and everyone around him. As the Emperor's Truthsayer, I can see to it that the Duke and all of House Atreides are disgraced and ruined. And in the end, you will still be ours. Come at once!"

Breathing hard, Jessica sat back, thinking through the implications. Black specks danced around her vision, and the room spun. She used her Bene Gesserit techniques to bring herself back under control.

Leto would never understand, but she could not refuse the summons. Even though she was the Duke's bound concubine, the Sisterhood still owned her soul.

But this was the worst possible time! She could not leave now. Everyone in Castle Caladan could sense the icy barrier between them. Leto was departing for Kaitain, and if she also went her separate way . . .

Why did the Mother Superior want her? How long would she be gone? Jessica was forced to make an impossible choice and could not appeal the order. The Bene Gesserit would show her no compassion.

As she went to tell Leto about the message, at least to tell him she had to go, she murmured the Litany Against Fear. *I must not fear. Fear is the mind-killer. Fear is the little-death that brings total obliteration. I will face my fear. I will permit it to pass over me and through me. And when it has gone past I will turn the inner eye to see its path. Where the fear has gone there will be nothing. Only I will remain.* It did little to comfort her.

She stood at the doorway of Leto's study until he looked up from his desk. Today, his expression was especially unreadable, even to her. He could be brusque when he was preoccupied, but it felt different now, as if she had become an outsider, suddenly excluded from his inner circle where she had been for so long.

He looked back down at his papers. "I asked not to be disturbed."

She controlled her breathing, her pulse. "Apologies, my Lord, but I have received a summons. The Bene Gesserit Sisterhood has recalled me to Wallach IX." She swallowed hard. "I must go immediately."

He looked up at her, and his gray eyes probed deep into her expression with a gaze as sharp as a scalpel. "No. I cannot let you leave now. I am about to depart for Kaitain, and you must remain here to manage Castle Caladan and watch Paul. No matter what issues stand between us, you are still the Lady here, and I depend on you. We cannot both be gone at the same time." He looked back down, as if that put an end to the matter.

"The command comes from Mother Superior Harishka herself," Jessica said. "I have no choice."

Leto flushed. "The person who claims to have no choice has no imagination. Find a way around it."

"I cannot, Leto. I belong to the Sisterhood. They raised me and trained me. They dispatched me here."

"And you accepted the terms. You are also my *bound* concubine, the mother of my son. I don't care what those manipulative witches want from you. Your obligation is here on Caladan. To me."

Jessica hung her head. She could not reveal the threat Mohiam had made, because that would merely make matters worse. "If only I could refuse. This is not unlike when I was pregnant with Paul and Lady Anirul summoned me to Kaitain so the Bene Gesserit could monitor the birth."

Leto was not convinced. "I know all about your Sisterhood training. I've always known, and I accepted it. Yet I opened my heart to you. All these years, I believed you were ultimately on my side, my true partner, but of late, I have seen evidence to the contrary."

The words cut her like a dagger. "I am true to you, Leto. How could you ever doubt that?"

"I never thought I would, but I now realize that many things were happening right before me that I was too foolish to notice. I will go to Kaitain. You will remain here."

"But I have no discretion in the matter. You must understand, this is not my choice."

She could see him visibly wrestling with his anger. "Then you are choosing the Sisterhood over your own family. You make it plain that the schemes of the Bene Gesserit are more important to you than I am. If that is true, then go. You are a liability to House Atreides. It shames me that I was manipulated yet again—and for so many years."

Jessica's hand shook involuntarily, and she forced calm upon herself. "Leto, you misunderstand. My loyalty to you is unchanged. I love you and Paul dearly. I do *not* love the Sisterhood, but I have sworn obligations to them. Of all people, you should understand duty." She drew a hitching breath. "Out of a sense of honor, I have to obey the Mother Superior's orders."

Leto's face was unreadable, and he walled his anger inside himself, which she found all the more frightening. He said, "Do you remember the day when Reverend Mother Mohiam first presented you to me? I was suspicious of you even then."

Jessica swallowed hard. "You put a knife to my throat."

"I did. I was sure it was Bene Gesserit treachery. You were forced upon me when I was already involved with Kailea, when I already had a son with her." He placed his hands on the table. "Because of you, my relationship with her fell apart, and her poisonous jealousy led to what happened to Victor. Was that intentional? Part of your instructions from the damned Sisterhood?"

She gasped. "No, Leto! It just . . . happened."

"Truly? With all of your years of training and your polished Bene Gesserit skills, you worked your way into my household, destroyed my relationship, and it 'just happened'? After Victor died and Kailea threw herself from the tower, it took me years to learn to trust and love you." He looked away, shaking his head. "You know honor and loyalty are the core of House Atreides. Now I see that your true loyalty lies elsewhere." His voice cracked, just a little. "Was it all just some Sisterhood scheme? Everything?"

"No." She wanted to scream her answer, to beg him to believe her, but she also knew Leto well enough to understand that no answer would be sufficient.

Desperate, she dredged deep and found a fact that he did not know, something she had never told him. Something he could never know. She might use that now as evidence of her love, an ultimate gambit. The Sisterhood had commanded her to bear only Atreides daughters, to dance to the strings of their breeding program. But after Victor's death, she had seen how devastated Leto was, how deeply he needed healing, and she had given him another son instead. Paul. That had been her first defiance, and the Bene Gesserit would never forget it.

Nothing short of complete obedience would be acceptable now. The Sisterhood would get what they demanded, or they would destroy her beloved Leto and his entire noble house.

Jessica realized he was still waiting for an answer.

She could not tell him.

His face was carved in stone. "I see you are still keeping secrets from me. Maybe that's all you are at your core—secrets. We see things very differently, you and I." He turned back to his work, ignoring her.

Jessica retreated, using Bene Gesserit techniques to shore up her dignity, to control her emotions. But inside, her heart had shattered into a million pieces.

For a strong person, defeat is merely a matter of perspective. What some would consider a setback, others view as inspiration. Thus, I have been "inspired" many times.

—JAXSON ARU, *A New Dawn for the Noble Commonwealth*

From a small camouflaged craft in high orbit, Jaxson Aru looked down at the blue-green expanse of oceans and untouched wilderness of Caladan. As he waited impatiently for the delayed cargo shuttle, he thought again that this planet should be free and independent. All worlds in the Imperium must be allowed to determine their own political futures, control their own economies and commercial alliances, without being entangled in a suffocating Imperial net.

Duke Leto Atreides did not recognize or appreciate the potential he controlled as ruler of a world with so many resources. Jaxson had held such high hopes for the man and saw a kindred spirit. He *liked* Leto. The Duke did not seem to be a political patsy, but apparently, he was not a visionary either. Disappointing.

Leto defended Caladan like a loyal guard dog, but he did not see the larger perspective. Jaxson fumed at how the man had rebuffed his offer, at least for the time being, but that might change. He would give it time. In certain things, the rebel leader could be patient.

Could Leto Atreides really be so weak and afraid? Or would he see the great things he could accomplish if he made the right decision, one that would go down in galactic history and help change the course of civilization?

Pacing the open deck in his frigate, Jaxson glanced at the Ixian chronometer and frowned once more. His ship was a private customized vessel, obtained through CHOAM channels, with an inert exterior hull that turned the ship into a mere scan shadow, a ghostlike image that could easily go unnoticed. He had used his mother's techniques to book secret passage from the Spacing Guild by leveraging his CHOAM connections.

Although Malina Aru had disowned him in the Landsraad Hall, and his brother and sister were publicly outraged by his troublesome violence, Jaxson knew they understood the worth of what he was doing, even though they couldn't admit it. He did not believe his mother had entirely ostracized him. Since he was an outlaw, though, he stayed away from her.

For now.

Below, Caladan seemed such a perfect world, so different from seismically active Tupile. He had smelled the fresh ocean air down there, heard the rush of waves, the cries of seabirds. He'd stood in the majestic primeval wilderness absorbing the power of nature and burgeoning life. Caladan had enormous prospects, just like so many planets that were oppressed by the Corrinos. Under a new Noble Commonwealth, they would be a million independent economies, a million trading partners rather than consolidated under one autocratic and bloated despot, strangled by tariffs and surtaxes.

He looked through the plaz viewing window, and his impatience began to transition to anger. Where was that damned cargo shuttle?

Jaxson wished he could have spent more days on Caladan strolling through the rustic capital city, or exploring the seas and forests. This planet reminded him of pleasant times on Otorio with his father, before Shaddam had violated the place, destroying the sacred Aru olive grove and paving over it. . . .

Eventually, Jaxson would meet with Leto Atreides again and make his case one more time, now that the Duke had been able to ponder the possibilities. Jaxson had seen something in Leto's eyes, sensed that there was still a chance to make the man see reason and opportunity. Perhaps his non-reply could be turned into a positive response. Why would Duke Leto not plan for a better future than the stagnation of the Imperium? Jaxson would not give up hope.

Finally, he saw an orange streak of afterburners like a fingernail scratch against the edge of the atmosphere. The engines of the cargo shuttle had been invisible in the cloudy skies, but now Jaxson knew where to look.

Up front, his pilot's voice was gruff. "Target ship scheduled to dock within fifteen minutes, sir. They report a diminished crew and request our assistance in moving the cargo."

"Whatever is necessary to achieve the final result," Jaxson said. Four loyal converts were with him on board, security guards who were also hatchet men, fixers, observers. They were perfectly capable of lifting heavy packages. "We do what we must," he muttered.

After the other ship matched orbital velocity with Jaxson's frigate, the hulls maneuvered together. The second craft had similar camouflage coating, which had also been provided by his own connections. The work of the Noble Commonwealth was intertwined—even his mother knew that. She would approve of what he was doing here on Caladan, as would his father, if he were still alive.

The hatches locked together, and the seals engaged. Jaxson folded his arms over his roughspun blue shirt, which he had bought on Caladan during his last trip. He looked like a local.

His companions joined him at the hatch, ready to begin transferring the cargo into his private hold. The bulkhead door opened, and Jaxson faced the small-statured Tleilaxu man in gray robes. Chaen Marek looked disheveled and bruised, his expression erratic.

Jaxson could not contain his surprise. "Marek! You never come personally to make a mere delivery. Is it safe to leave your operations on Caladan?"

"My compound was just wiped out," the Tleilaxu said as he boarded the stealth frigate. "Duke Leto's strike on our barra fields was swifter and more destructive than I anticipated. I gave him severe warnings to leave my business alone, and I thought he would heed the threat. You said you considered him a reasonable man!" Marek's thin voice dripped with accusation.

Jaxson didn't like the other man's tone. He had already received some reports, but he assumed they were exaggerated. Now he shook his head. "I listened to his speech to the public. You provoked him by planting real bombs that killed innocent townspeople and nearly injured his son. Your people were willing to create a lasgun-shield explosion. That goes against all civilized rules. How did you expect him to react?"

"Imperial rules," the Tleilaxu muttered bitterly. "As you yourself would point out."

"*Human* rules," Jaxson said. "It was uncalled for." He lowered his voice. "At least I only used inactive bombs as a threat against Leto."

The Tleilaxu snapped his head back in disbelief. "'Against all civilized rules'? After you obliterated the entire museum city on Otorio?"

"I made my point, and I did not break any rules of the Great Convention." Jaxson raised his eyebrows, looking at the little Tleilaxu man. "You are a mess."

In a huff, Marek said, "I barely made it out alive. Luckily, we had prepared for takeoff, and had a full cargo of ailar, but our main operations are destroyed, all the barra fields ruined. It is a great setback." His black, close-set eyes flickered back and forth. "Why are you not more upset?"

Although Jaxson was discouraged by the defeat, he looked at the larger picture. "Because if we let Duke Leto have free rein like a wild horse, he will be ours in the long run."

"In the long run, we will not survive if we have no supplies, equipment, or product. How will you fund our rebellion without ailar? We greatly expanded our market for the Caladan drug, and the Emperor's spice surtax inadvertently drove more customers to us. But if we have no more ferns . . ."

"The Noble Commonwealth has other financial resources," Jaxson said. "And the cargo you brought will tide us over. I have a tight-knit network of addicted users. I will inform them of our losses and increase the price accordingly, but not so much that they go back to using melange." His brow furrowed. "But I am displeased with the number of deaths reported among users. Far more than you estimated. What was your mistake with the new strain? Our customers are afraid to use the stuff."

"You instructed me to use Tleilaxu methods to alter the barra ferns and thus increase the potency of the ailar. It succeeded admirably well, far beyond expectations."

"And many people died because the drug was *too* powerful."

The Tleilaxu scoffed. "They were poorly informed, and we were unable to institute a thorough enough analysis. The drug concentration in the new ferns is potent, but varies greatly. Despite all the resources you gave me, sophisticated equipment was difficult to come by in the deep wilderness. Caladan is not Tleilax, nor Ix."

Jaxson remained dubious. "Once word gets around, users will be afraid of ailar."

Marek shook his head. "But the euphoria is so much more intense, they will risk it. The new barra ferns obviously still need genetic adjustment to modulate the potency. Too many shipments went out with extraordinary potency, which we discovered only after the string of fatalities. We can fix that." He smiled. "And the extremely powerful strain is an advantage, since we can generate far more ailar with the same amount of ferns, if we process it properly!"

The two men stepped aside as workers moved cartons of sealed ailar onto the frigate. Jaxson intercepted one of the boxes, opening the lid to find tightly packed brown curls of product. A rich smell wafted up, loamy with an undertone of peat and smoke. He had never tried ailar himself—the thought nauseated him—but he did not need to understand the vices of human beings in order to profit from them.

And Jaxson used that profit to partially fund his operations in a widespread and ever more powerful rebellion against the Corrino Imperium. He smirked. "That is why I sent out specific feelers to recruit discontented Tleilaxu. I knew we were natural allies."

The gray-faced man scowled. "If only more of my people understood the opportunity offered by the Noble Commonwealth. Right now, in the corrupt Imperium, we are reviled, not given the same rights and privileges as noble houses. Your cause may be more vital to my people than to any other planet in the Imperium, and our indoctrinated followers support us with their lives. No member of the Bene Tleilax has a seat in the Landsraad, nor do we have a Directorship in CHOAM. You promised that would change."

"It will change, as soon as our movement is victorious. And I promise you will not have to wait another century or two, as my mother would prefer." Jaxson looked down at the lush globe of Caladan. They had orbited over the wide seas and now came upon another landmass. "We need a continued supply of ailar. You need to reestablish your operations from scratch, but Duke Leto will be much more wary now. Lay down subsidiary barra fields on the Eastern and Southern Continents. Triple your production."

"We will face more primitive conditions over there," Marek said. "That makes it more difficult to get reliable workers and ship the product once it's packaged."

"I prefer to see the advantages," Jaxson said, his tone cocky. "Under more primitive conditions, you will have an easier time covering your operations. You can increase production, but keep a lower profile. Your mistake was that you let too much of the drug trickle into Caladan society. Duke Leto Atreides is very protective of his people. He would turn a blind eye to a thousand wealthy nobles addicted on countless planets in the Imperium, but if one of his peasants dies by accident, then you spark his vengeful anger. Be more careful next time."

Marek thrust gray fingers into the organic mass inside the open box, stirring the dried plant matter. "The original Caladan barra fern was an extraordinary specimen, but my alterations have made it vastly more suited to our uses. Unfortunately, we still have not been able to make the species thrive off of Caladan."

"Then you can make do here, on this planet." Jaxson looked at all the boxes being loaded into his customized frigate. "After you expand your growth operations on the other continents, our movement will once again be flush with solaris. The Noble Commonwealth will continue its work."

"And all will benefit," said the Tleilaxu man. "Our worlds will eventually be independent. The Bene Tleilax can make their own choices, perform their own work, and make their own *profits*." He hissed. "We will no longer be downtrodden scapegoats treated with disrespect at every turn!"

"Wealth is something you must earn, Chaen Marek," warned Jaxson. "And so is respect."

When the workers finished transferring the packaged ailar, Jaxson realized it would be the last full load for some time. He had already stashed substantial funds in a secret war-chest account in the Guild Bank, but his allies would have to be more frugal.

Nevertheless, because they spoke the truth and told the downtrodden planets what they needed to hear, the rebellion would continue to resonate.

In the worst-case scenario, Jaxson could always go back to his mother. Despite her words of public condemnation, he was confident Malina would come around and give him the financial resources to assure the victory of their shared cause, even if they differed in approach. He could make her see.

Chaen Marek looked as if he wanted to stay with Jaxson Aru, perhaps to fly off to the luxury and security of the Silver Needle on Kaitain or some other CHOAM complex, but Jaxson was firm. "Go back down to Caladan. You have work to do."

Petulant, Marek slipped back through the connected hulls to his camouflaged cargo ship, and Jaxson returned to his stateroom. The frigate would ride in a secret berth aboard the Guild Heighliner to his next destination, his sister Jalma's private holding on Pliesse. She was still consolidating her rule there since quietly disposing of her decrepit husband.

Jaxson smiled. He would convert his sister as well.

Yes, they all had work to do.

Supreme, death-defying challenges are never merely physical. They are mental as well, and the more severe the challenge, the more thought processes are required to overcome the obstacle and survive.

—DUKE LETO ATREIDES

The crashing seas seemed peaceful compared to the tension that filled Castle Caladan, the coldness between his mother and father. Paul didn't understand it, but something felt truly broken there.

In the morning air, the young man scrambled over rocks at the base of the cliff beneath the main lookout, then cut his way through a protective wire barricade meant to keep daredevils out. Squeezing through the opening, he picked a route over the treacherous, mossy rocks. He needed to focus his impatient energy on a challenge he could defeat.

This climbing obstacle was not as imposing as the Arondi Cliffs in the north, but the precipice beneath Castle Caladan was not for the weak of heart. The physical exertion would help Paul work out his helpless frustration and clear his head.

He'd climbed these sea cliffs before, starting from the base during low tide, but he had never approached via this route, which was steeper and more treacherous. High above, he could see the girded underside of the cantilevered lookout structure and the Atreides colors flying from a pole. He clenched his fingers, flexed his hands, and prepared for the ordeal.

Before the wire barricade had been installed, some offworld thrill-seeker had gotten halfway up the rocks before falling to his death. Paul remembered that day. Hearing the man's faint scream, he had dashed to his balcony to see the broken body in the rocky tide pools far below. Not long afterward, two Cala City fishermen had drunk too much kelp wine and dared each other to climb the cliff, also with fatal results. Afterward, Duke Leto had blocked access for public safety reasons.

Though his thoughts were in turmoil, Paul was serious, fully alert, and determined to accomplish this. An intentional risk, controlled and managed, would focus his thoughts as tightly as a lasbeam.

His father and mother both disapproved of him taking chances, but Paul knew that Duke Leto often took risks of his own, and each of those harrowing experiences had shaped and honed him into a better leader and a better man. Right now, his parents were taking great risks with their relationship, and Paul could sense the rift. He needed to burn off the edge of his uneasiness.

Paul clutched a handhold, looked up at the sheer cliff and found the line of his intended route—cracks, outcroppings, accessible ledges. He hauled himself up, wedged his boot into a cranny, and used upper-body strength to lift himself to the next spot. He was on his way, one hand and foothold at a time.

A life spent taking no chances was not a life. Paul wanted experiences, to know the joy and the danger. He didn't want to sit back and listen to others describe exhilarating experiences and not seek them out himself. If Paul received warnings about dangers, he could avoid them, or he could find a better way to deal with them, growing mentally and physically stronger in the process.

He felt a cool, moist breeze on his face. Looking up the cliff, he could see the sheer stone bulwark of the castle rising even higher. Up on the sheer wall, he spotted the small balcony of his own bedroom, a comparatively safe place. Much safer than this thing he was doing.

If anyone found out about this, they would all reprimand him for such reckless behavior.

Grasping another rock, shifting his fingers to avoid slippery moss, Paul pulled himself up to the next foothold. He knew—yes, *knew*—that he needed to put himself at risk in order to advance. Just as he had to climb higher and trust in his abilities, mental and physical.

Duncan taught him swordsmanship and shield combat, fighting to the brink of death or serious injury, and accepting no less than excellence. Perhaps better than all of his other instructors, Duncan understood the necessity to push himself, but this steep, slippery cliff was not a controlled training environment. This was something else.

And Duncan wouldn't understand Paul's inner turmoil over his parents' relationship. Duncan barely remembered his own parents, who were murdered by the awful Rabban when he'd just been a boy. Paul's emotional turmoil was an entirely different kind of wound, but he did not minimize the pain a strained relationship would cause.

After spending his life focused on Caladan and its people, Leto was heading off for Kaitain, trying to play Imperial politics for the advancement of House Atreides. The Duke insisted that he was doing it for his son's sake, but he had never asked what Paul wanted.

At the same time, Paul's mother was departing for Wallach IX, summoned back to the Bene Gesserit. Would she ever come back? Paul didn't understand exactly what had caused the rift between his parents, but he knew the distance between them was a sudden, wide chasm.

And Paul was out here alone, on a cliff face. He continued to climb, focused on each handhold, each placement of his feet.

As if from a great distance, cutting through the rumbling rush of the ocean waves, he heard a voice overhead. "Paul!" He turned and saw Duncan on the lookout platform at the top of the cliff. He tossed a long, knotted rope over the edge, swinging it so that it dangled near the young man. "Grab the rope!"

Paul let the lifeline move past him and continued to climb the steep face, hand over hand, seeking narrow footholds and handholds.

A black rock wobbled in his hand and pulled loose like a rotten tooth. He had put too much of his weight on a single handhold. Scrambling for balance, he slipped a few inches down the rough wall, but caught his feet on a hard ledge, panting.

Above him, Duncan shouted in alarm, but Paul could not spare a speck of concentration for any distraction. He moved laterally away from the rope, inching along the ledge, testing each handhold, pressing down with each toe to make certain his foot was secure. Climbing a little higher, he stretched sideways across a gap, found a small ledge, and pulled himself up.

Duncan moved the rope closer. "Paul, grab the line! Don't be foolhardy!"

The young man caught his breath and shouted back, "It's just another lesson. You say we can't control risk in real life, but I am choosing this risk. This is my own decision. I'm testing myself."

He continued climbing, slowly and carefully. Moments later, a second rope dangled down beside him, but Duncan did not urge him to grasp it. Instead, the Swordmaster painstakingly climbed down to his level. "Your father would have my head if he knew what you are doing."

"My father is leaving for Kaitain, and my mother will go to Wallach IX. I am left here with a challenge I know I can surmount. On my own."

Duncan tried to sound understanding. "I know about their quarrel."

"I think it's more than a quarrel. I'm not sure it's something they can recover from. What if this rift is permanent?" He grunted with the effort as he hauled himself up again. By now, he could feel his arms and legs trembling. His fingers ached and bled. He drove the thoughts from his mind. "Climbing allows me singular focus. There is no room for worries about the future—only the here and now."

"I understand your need to take a risk and press your abilities, but at least use a safety rope. It is unwise to make the risk greater than necessary."

Paul stubbornly shook his head as Duncan rested on a ledge just beside him. "What would I learn if I knew I was still safe?"

The Swordmaster's voice grew sterner. "Three have died on this cliff in the past year." He balanced on a thin outcropping and let go of his own rope, edging closer to Paul. "If you fall, young Master, then I might as well leap after you. My life and my honor would be forfeit if I let you die, especially in such a foolish way. I'll have failed my most important duty."

"I can take care of myself."

"That is not how your father would see it. You know that full well."

Stabilizing himself, Paul stared at his friend as the wind rippled around them and the void below taunted him. "So I hold your life in my hands as well as my own?"

"That's the fact of it, boy." He reached back to grab the first dangling rope, extended it to Paul. "You will be Duke someday, and your father has done his best to prepare you. What was his most important lesson? What did Duke Leto the Just say is his primary responsibility?"

Paul paused, recalled the words with sharp clarity. "The first responsibility of a Duke is the safety of his people."

"And you know that I must come down here to protect you, no matter how dangerous these cliffs are or how foolish this climb is." Duncan continued to hold the rope out to him. "I have no choice in this. My life is in your hands."

Paul realized what the Swordmaster was implying. "I'm putting your life at unnecessary risk."

"It's not as if I like dangling on a rough cliff. I can think of other things I'd prefer to do." He dug his boot heel into a crack, pressing hard to stabilize himself. "Preparing yourself to face risk is one thing, young Master. Recklessness is a different matter entirely. With the politics and intrigue in the Imperium, you need not seek out danger. It will find you of its own accord."

Anchored to the narrow ledge, Paul contemplated. He had climbed out here to work out his own frustrations, his emotional turmoil, but he had not given thought to how his actions would send ripples throughout his friends, his family, his trainers. If he slipped and fell, just like those other intrepid climbers who no doubt considered themselves equally talented, then his death would cause irreparable damage to Duke Leto . . . just as the death of young Victor had. Duncan would be broken and disgraced forever for failing to protect his ward. And if Paul fell and injured himself, Duncan would risk his own life to retrieve him.

The first responsibility of a Duke is the safety of his people.

Duncan was one of his people. Paul had to think like the next Duke of Caladan.

He recalled the most recent thought experiment Thufir Hawat had given him, the set of impossible choices that left Paul with so many lives and deaths on his conscience. "I will not let you down, Duncan."

He reached out to grab the safety line. The Swordmaster looked greatly relieved. Duncan cinched a rope around his waist and followed Paul, climbing alongside and finding his own handholds. Together, they chose a route along stable rock, heading toward the top of the headland cliff above.

Nearby, Paul heard piercing bird calls, a whistle and a chirp, and suddenly, a large white bird took wing from a ledge directly above him, flapped away from the cliff, and wheeled back to swoop close. It shrieked and scolded in an attempt to drive them away. One of its wings brushed him, but he flattened his chest against the cliff, holding on. Paul identified it as one of the male spreybirds that nested in the cliffs.

The bird flew away from the cliff, then circled back, shrieking. It came at Paul like a missile, and he braced himself.

Duncan somehow kept his balance, tossed a rock, and the bird careened away, squawking, then flew above them to disappear into a sheltered overhang.

Panting, Paul tried to see where the bird had gone. "My mother says there's a nest up there."

After making sure his position was stable, Paul strained to look around the rock. He saw two birds poke their large heads out, one white and the other gray. Yes, a nest. Though he changed the line of his climb to avoid the nesting area, the spreybirds continued to watch the intruders warily, ready to attack.

Glancing at him, Duncan said, "Remember when we talked about the Imperium, the Landsraad, and politics? You said you were overwhelmed by it all. It is not unlike climbing. One handhold after another. Find stable points. Maintain your balance." He paused. "And keep climbing."

Paul found a wide enough ledge to catch his breath, and Duncan joined him. The Swordmaster seemed to have no more words for this situation, but Paul did. "There are times when the most important focus in the entire universe is what is right in front of you." He reached down and gave his friend a hand, helping Duncan join him. "What we have at our fingertips."

They were not far from the top now, but Paul decided just to rest there for a while, where the risk was under more control, and by extension, his life. He was glad to have Duncan's company. Each of them had proven themselves today.

The best leaders assemble information and take actions that lead to political stability. The worst leaders dissemble information and generate chaos.
—A lesson from Imperial history

With Lady Margot settling into her usual lavish guest quarters in the Imperial Palace, Count Hasimir Fenring donned a fur-lined cape appropriate to his office and strode off to see the Padishah Emperor. He was ready to announce his success against the pirates on Arrakis. Shaddam would rejoice, and Fenring could continue the deeper investigation.

Margot had already gone to see Reverend Mother Mohiam and other important Bene Gesserit Sisters at court, which served Fenring's purposes as well. His wife had her own set of schemes, as the Count had his, and none of their machinations worked against each other. The two had worked out the diversion to keep the Emperor's Truthsayer away when Fenring delivered his report, falsely naming the culprit as Rulla Tuek.

He had dispatched messages ahead to inform Shaddam of the importance of the information he carried, and his friend would see him without any prior appointment. Fenring had conducted Imperial business and made unannounced visits for years.

An aide showed him to a tastefully appointed waiting chamber, and he saw that he wasn't alone. The Sardaukar colonel bashar, Jopati Kolona, sat rigidly on a chair, military cap in his hands and a sheaf of papers and a thin shigawire spool at his side. The officer rose and greeted Fenring with a formal half handshake. He was taken aback to see the Sardaukar officer there ahead of him.

Kolona responded to his curious expression. "It seems we both have business with the Emperor, sir."

"So it seems, hmmmm." Fenring sat in the other ornately padded seat, glanced at the report and spool the colonel bashar held. Even if it were classified, Shaddam would eventually show the information to him. He placed his own small parcel on a side table, unconcerned if the trusted Sardaukar saw the information. The awkward silence stretched out.

An attractive female retainer came in and offered tea to Fenring. Kolona already had a cup at his side, but declined to drink from it. The Count accepted the tea, but also left the cup untouched. Though the officer was accustomed to maintaining a blank face, he seemed troubled, and did not try to make polite conversation. Kolona did not look happy.

"Hmmmm." Fenring made the sound under his voice, and caught himself.

Presently, Chamberlain Ridondo entered. He looked paler than usual, and his high forehead glistened with perspiration. From this, Fenring inferred that the Emperor was not in the best of moods.

Though his own report about Rulla Tuek was a clever red herring, which would keep Shaddam from interfering with the real investigation on Arrakis, Fenring knew the news would cheer and excite his friend. He wondered what the Sardaukar officer's mission had been.

The chamberlain looked at Fenring, surprised to see him. "Apologies, Count Fenring. The Emperor asked me to summon Colonel Bashar Kolona. I don't believe he was expecting you? I will inform him that you are here."

"And that I am waiting," Fenring said.

"And waiting. Yes."

The Sardaukar rose to his feet, unfolding himself like a weapon about to be launched, and tucked the report against his side and clutched the spool in one hand. Before Kolona could follow the tall, dour chamberlain, though, brisk footsteps came down the hall.

Emperor Shaddam strode into the waiting chamber. "I want the report of my Sardaukar strike on the planet Dross. Colonel Bashar Kolona?"

Fenring sprang to his feet. Without missing a beat, the Sardaukar officer saluted crisply.

The Emperor noticed Fenring. "Oh, Hasimir!" His voice hardened. "Are you here to deliver good news about the pirate operations on Arrakis?"

Fenring grinned. "Ahhhh, yes, I am, Sire. You will be pleased."

Chamberlain Ridondo dithered in the waiting chamber. "It was a matter of protocol, Sire, as to which man would speak to you first."

Shaddam paid no attention to him. He turned expectantly to the Sardaukar officer. "And your report? Is it good news you bring me about the operation? Is House Verdun eradicated, as ordered?"

Fenring was surprised and listened closely.

"Yes, Sire. I bear the news you want to hear." Kolona relaxed his salute. "A complete success. The family eradicated . . . just like other noble houses in the past."

Fenring observed the officer's mannerisms, and the man did not act victorious. The Emperor seemed not to notice.

"Then it is a day filled with good news! I shall see both of you at the same time." Shaddam turned. "Follow me. Chamberlain, send refreshments to my private contemplation chamber. Tea, and those local pastries I like. And Tikal champagne, so that we may celebrate." He paused. "Bring the tray yourself. Don't entrust it to a servant. This is a highly confidential meeting."

The chamberlain hurried off, and the other two men accompanied Shaddam into his private chamber. Taking the proffered seats, Fenring and the colonel bashar each removed items from their packages. Kolona took out printed documents and image sets; the Count produced a shigawire spool. It felt as if they were in competition.

While Shaddam waited, the two men cleared the area to display their information. The Emperor folded his arms over the thick brocade on his formal tunic. "Shall we choose randomly which report comes first? Or should I have you fight for it?"

Fenring looked at the Sardaukar, assessing. Kolona was taller and more muscular. They regarded each other quizzically, then moved a little apart. Fenring didn't believe the Emperor's taunt, but Shaddam could be capricious. Nevertheless, he did not want to waste time or attention.

Fenring glanced at the unsettled Sardaukar and activated his own holo projector. After a moment's hesitation, Kolona brought out his images and projected them as well, so that the reports were side by side. In tandem, the Emperor's chamber was filled with video displays of explosions, fire, a massive air and ground assault from uniformed Sardaukar, a young woman falling to her death from a rampart. Fenring's images showed a woman staked on the sand, struggling as a giant sandworm surged in to swallow her in a magnificent display of primal power.

Emperor Shaddam seemed equally satisfied with what he saw. Apparently, he already knew some details of the colonel bashar's mission, but he turned to the Count. "And who is this woman in the desert? I hope she was guilty of something."

"A criminal being executed, Sire. You tasked me to track down the source of the missing spice from Arrakis, the pirates who somehow managed to slip melange past our observers. This doomed woman, Rulla Tuek, was behind those operations. She hid that secret operation even from her husband, who represents our . . . ahhhh, sanctioned group of smugglers with whom I work."

The Sardaukar officer studied the desert images, but avoided looking at the violence and destruction still playing in his own report. Fenring observed him, wondered why he seemed so unsettled by his own successful mission.

Shaddam leaned closer, watched a replay of the sandworm images. "And how do I know this poor woman is not just a sacrificial lamb? Someone given up so that we would stop searching for the real culprit?" He rubbed his fingertips on the bridge of his nose. "Oh! Is she pregnant?"

"Yes, Sire. She is the wife of Esmar Tuek, an influential smuggler leader, and she is indeed pregnant." He drew a deep breath, making certain he could present the information in the most convincing manner possible. He was glad the

Truthsayer Mohiam had not joined them. "Tuek gave up his own wife in order to prove his compliance with our instructions. And the child." Fenring didn't add any other details. "She is not a mere throwaway sacrifice to distract us, Sire. Tuek is obviously sincere in his contrition, and I require this man for my own work on Arrakis, hmmm? The fact that he was willing to make such a painful decision, to relinquish someone so dear to him, proves it is not a sham."

When Shaddam's penetrating gaze continued, Fenring added, "I, ahhhhhh, witnessed the execution myself. Tuek was profoundly shaken by it. From now on, he will be firmly under our thumb."

Fenring still did not know the real connection between spice smugglers on Arrakis and a possible secondary group of pirates and other black markets. Given time, perhaps Grix Dardik would figure it out . . . once Fenring got back to Arrakis and without the Emperor so frantic for an answer.

Shaddam watched in silence for a long moment, viewing alternately the sandworm attack and the Sardaukar assault on Duke Verdun's city. His face brightened with good cheer. "We shall have breakfast together tomorrow, Hasimir, to discuss this further. Bring your lovely wife."

"I will join you as well." Empress Aricatha entered the office, glided up to Shaddam's side, and turned to look at the horrific images. The Emperor did not stop her, and together, they watched the loops again. Aricatha seemed disturbed at first, but her eyes glittered with fascination.

The Emperor rose. "Count Fenring and Colonel Bashar Kolona, you have both done superb work. I expected no less."

Both men bowed slightly, in unison. Then, looking at the Sardaukar officer, the Emperor frowned. "You do not seem pleased, Colonel Bashar."

Kolona remained rigid for a moment, then confessed, "To be perfectly honest, I . . . questioned certain aspects of the mission, Sire. But I completed the objective, as ordered."

Shaddam stared at him long and hard, as if searching for some sign of disloyalty, some measure of opposition to his orders.

For his own sake, Kolona added, "I understand it was necessary. May I be dismissed, Sire?"

"Yes, Colonel Bashar. Take a day of furlough." He seemed happy and magnanimous.

Fenring promised himself he would reward Margot later for getting the damned Truthsayer out of the way.

Shaddam said, "We will continue to investigate this Noble Commonwealth conspiracy. Soon, I expect to have more work for you and all your troops. There will be even more Landsraad seats to fill after I have cleaned house."

There are casualties beyond number on the battlefields of the human heart.

—The Songs of Gurney Halleck

Before leaving for Kaitain, focused on his ambitious new purpose, Duke Leto Atreides met with his most important advisers. He'd already had his servants pack a variety of fine clothing for his trip to the Imperial capital: jeweled belts, formal capes, tunics, trousers, and boots, all in green and black, all bearing the Atreides hawk crest.

His purpose now was different from when he had gone to Otorio. His primary focus was to draw attention to himself in the Landsraad, like the other nobles always did, and finally claim the political power that was his right. By necessity, he would show himself as a different Leto from this day forward, although his heart and honor would remain the same.

Did anyone in the Imperial Court care whether the people of Caladan loved their Duke? No. Would he earn any respect among the backstabbing nobles because his subjects called him Leto the Just? Highly unlikely. They saw only wealth and holdings.

No, he had to do more. To *be* more.

Though it did not fit with his nature, Leto intended to play politics by their rules. *The first responsibility of a noble is to the Landsraad and to the Imperium.* His entire perspective had changed. He recognized how many opportunities he had ignored, and now he would make up for it. Paul and future Atreides generations would benefit.

He had not spoken a word to Jessica since their last conversation, when she announced she had been summoned to Wallach IX, implicitly confirming that she was more loyal to the Bene Gesserit than to him. She had left a black scar on his heart, and in defense, he had built a wall around his emotions. He didn't know if she would actually go. If so, did she intend to arrange her own transit to the Guild Heighliner when it arrived? She would not be aboard the Atreides frigate.

Years ago, he had developed a hardened heart as a protective measure, first as a defense against Kailea's coldness when she turned against him, and then as the only way to endure the grief of Victor's death. Now he was as much stone as the gigantic colossus of his father that stood as the lighthouse at the edge of Caladan Harbor.

Hawat, Idaho, and Halleck met him in the dining hall rather than his private study. Cutting an impressive figure in a merh-silk cape and an embroidered vest over a flowing green shirt, Leto stood beneath the painting of the Old Duke, looking equally resplendent. Paul, silent, formal, and obviously uneasy, took a seat beside his father.

The three retainers stood at attention on the other side of the dining table, as if they knew this was not a casual conversation among friends. Thus far, Leto had provided no explanations of his intent, but they were aware of the serious undercurrent in the castle for the past week. They all knew the Duke was departing for Kaitain, and they waited to receive their orders for the time when he was away.

"I charge you three with a most important mission. While I am at the Imperial Court, you must not—" His voice cracked. He had meant to be firm and unwavering, but suddenly, emotions clawed at his throat. "You must not let anything happen to my son. Promise me that." He glanced at Paul.

The loyal Atreides men overlapped their voices and reassurances. Gurney Halleck said it best. "You should not even need to ask that, my Lord!"

Paul looked up at his father. "I am your presumed heir, sir, and while I remain here on Caladan, I will represent House Atreides with honor and diligence. You can count on me to do that."

"Yes, Paul—yes, I can. I'll depart knowing my world is in good hands." He squeezed the young man's shoulder. "You know that I am doing this to make a better future for you and our family holdings."

"I know you are, but . . ." Paul looked away, his body tense. "Why is my mother not going with you?"

Leto felt ice surround his heart like a kind of body shield. "Your mother has made her choices."

He had spent the past several nights in his own chamber. For the most part, Jessica had left him alone, giving him space to reflect, but they both knew the distance between them was widening by the moment. With both of them departing, there would be no way to resolve the matter quickly, and the emotional wound would only fester.

Yet maybe, given time . . .

The night before, Jessica had encountered him in a corridor of Castle Caladan—not by accident, he was sure. She looked at him, her clear green eyes revealing love and an unexpected hint of desperation. "Leto, please, I . . . This could be the last time I see you! There's something you don't know."

She had kept far too many secrets from him already, though. He had continued walking past. Jessica had gone back to her own rooms, where he assumed she packed for her separate departure.

Now Leto turned to Paul and said in a cold voice, "Your mother is leaving us, too."

THE SISTERHOOD HAD placed Lady Jessica in an untenable situation, posing a conundrum for which none of the outcomes were acceptable. She had been assigned to Caladan since she was a young woman, fresh-faced, bright-eyed, glad to be offered to a handsome and ultimately kind man like Leto.

But the Sisterhood was in her core. It was not merely a choice on her part. She could defy them, yes, but the Bene Gesserit had ways of ensuring compliance that Leto could never guess. She knew what they could do, how vindictive they could be.

If she did not go to Wallach IX, they would disgrace and ruin Leto, out of spite. For a man with such a solid code of honor, destroying his good name and reputation would be far more painful than killing him.

She had to go.

Jessica packed, stuffing her garments resolutely into a travel case. She had made arrangements to ride in a common passenger shuttle in plain attire. She would make her own way back to the Mother School, a place that resounded with her earliest childhood memories. She'd been born and raised there, living in a crèche with other parentless girls, none of whom knew their heritage.

If you defy us, we will destroy not only you but Leto and everyone around him.

Jessica felt caged, unable to escape the Sisterhood. She had been born into the order and would die a member of it.

THE HULL OF the Atreides frigate had been painted in dazzling colors. Leto had arranged for cheering crowds, waving green-and-black banners in a grand send-off. It was like part of a new costume he had to wear. Even Archvicar Torono made his appearance.

Leto did not smile as he marched across the armor-paved surface of the Cala City Spaceport with a much larger entourage than he had ever taken with him before. Much more than his smiling pilot Arko and the wide-eyed retinue he had taken with him to Otorio. . . .

As they all marched aboard the frigate, he put those thoughts behind him. Leto sealed himself into his private stateroom without a word. He could not wait to be on his way.

For appearances, he could have brought his Mentat along as a mark of status, but Leto had left Hawat behind to protect Paul and to monitor Caladan security, and to continue his investigations into any remnants of the ailar distribution network. That was what mattered most to Leto.

His decision was made, although he took no joy in it. The Duke would go to the Imperial Court and go through whatever formalities were necessary to raise the status of House Atreides.

Unseen in space high overhead, an enormous Heighliner orbited Caladan. And around him, the bustling labor of loading and unloading cargo vessels, dump boxes, and passenger craft continued as the Atreides frigate made final preparations for takeoff.

Looking out the plaz window of his vessel across the spaceport, Leto saw a passenger shuttle ready to depart. His eyes stung when he realized it was likely Jessica's. He had not even said goodbye. Once the ships were inside the cargo hold of the Heighliner, he would remain in the Atreides frigate, and she would stay in the shuttle cabin with other passengers bound for various routing points. Eventually, she would make her way to the Mother School on Wallach IX.

A universe would soon separate him from her.

One of his chosen household retainers arrived at the door of his stateroom. The young man was dressed in a formal Atreides uniform, as Leto had instructed all of his staff to wear. The man looked as awkward in his finery as Leto felt in his new role.

"Excuse me, m'Lord. This message was just transmitted from the Heighliner. It is designated high priority."

Leto accepted the document sealed in its privacy sheath. Though preoccupied, he remembered to thank the retainer, who seemed embarrassed by his Duke's graciousness. Leto waited for him to depart, closed the door, and slid the opaque covering into place over the windowport before considering the message.

The document was marked with the sigil of the Bene Gesserit order, which immediately put him on his guard. The message was abrupt and unambiguous.

"Duke Leto Atreides, the Bene Gesserit Sisterhood hereby rescinds its assignment of Jessica as concubine of House Atreides, and recalls her permanently to Wallach IX. Should you desire another concubine, submit a formal request, and arrangements can be made."

The emptiness already inside him swelled a thousandfold. He set the message aside, slumped onto the bed in his stateroom, and withdrew into his own sheltered world. Before long, he felt the suspensor engines power up as the Atreides frigate lifted off.

Leto closed his eyes. Out there, Jessica was flying as well.

The Duke and his former concubine left their safe, beloved Caladan and went their separate ways, leaving more than memories behind.

ACKNOWLEDGMENTS

We are grateful to the following people for contributing to the complex route of getting this novel into print: John Silbersack and Robert Gottlieb, our literary agents; Tom Doherty and Christopher Morgan at Tor Books; Jan Herbert and Rebecca Moesta, our wives who provide comprehensive guidance; Diane Jones for test reading and providing comments; Kim Herbert and Byron Merritt at Herbert Properties LLC, who are dedicated to maintaining the Frank Herbert legacy. And, of course, it's important to acknowledge Frank Herbert and his wife, Beverly Herbert, whose contributions as far back as the 1950s led, ultimately, to this new novel in the magnificent Dune series.

ACKNOWLEDGMENTS

We are grateful to the following people for contributing to the complex route of getting this novel into print: John Silbersack and Robert Gottlieb, our literary agents; Tom Doherty and Christopher Morgan at Tor Books; Jan Herbert and Rebecca Moesta, our wives who provide comprehensive guidance; Diane Jones for test reading and providing comments; Kim Herbert and Byron Merritt at Herbert Properties LLC, who are dedicated to maintaining the Frank Herbert legacy. And, of course, it's important to acknowledge Frank Herbert and his wife, Beverly Herbert, whose contributions as far back as the 1950s led, ultimately, to this new novel in the magnificent Dune series.